Highland Fling

Katie Fforde lives in Gloucestershire with her husband and some of her three children. Her hobbies are ironing and housework but, unfortunately, she has almost no time for them as she feels it her duty to keep a close eye on the afternoon chat shows.

She is the author of fourteen novels: *Living Dangerously, The Rose Revived, Wild Designs, Stately Pursuits, Life Skills, Thyme Out, Artistic Licence, Highland Fling, Paradise Fields, Restoring Grace, Flora's Lot, Practically Perfect, Going Dutch* and *Wedding Season.*

Praise for *Katie Fforde*

'Warm, witty and entertaining . . . as satisfying as a cup of hot cocoa on a chilly night' *Woman and Home*

'Old-fashioned romance of the best sort . . . funny, comforting' *Elle*

'Katie Fforde produces gentle cheering comedies that feature heroines whose waistlines are not what they were and who are gifted with humorous self-deprecation'

D1438138

Further praise for *Katie Fforde*

'Joanna Trollope crossed with Tom Sharpe' *Mail on Sunday*

'The innocent charm of Katie Fforde . . . belies a perceptive wit' *Sunday Express*

'Fforde is blessed with a lightness of touch, careful observation and a sure sense of the funny side of life' *Ideal Home*

'Gaily paced and told with trade-mark chattiness and smooth dialogue' *Herald*

'Katie Fforde has built up an enthusiastic readership that is thoroughly well-deserved' *Good Book Guide*

'Can be scoffed at one sitting . . . Tasty' *Cosmopolitan*

'Katie Fforde writes entertainingly about country life – and love' *Woman's Journal*

'Acute and funny observations of the social scene' *The Times*

'Katie Fforde hits the mark honestly and entertainingly' Hilary Norman

'Lively and engaging' *Woman's Weekly*

'Entertainingly written – a fine romance indeed' *The Lady*

'Perfect holiday reading. Pack it with the swimsuit and suntan lotion' *Irish Independent*

'Top drawer romantic escapism' *You Magazine*

'Delicious – gorgeous humour and the lightest of touches' *Sunday Times*

KATIE FFORDE

Highland Fling

arrow books

Published in the United Kingdom in 2003 by Arrow Books

13 15 17 19 20 18 16 14

Copyright © Katie Fforde 2002

Katie Fforde has asserted her right under the Copyright, Designs and
Patents Act, 1988 to be identified as the author of this work

This novel is a work of fiction. Names and characters are the product
of the author's imagination and any resemblance to actual persons,
living or dead, is entirely coincidental

This book is sold subject to the condition that it shall not,
by way of trade or otherwise, be lent, resold, hired out, or otherwise
circulated without the publisher's prior consent
in any form of binding or cover other than that in which
it is published and without a similar condition including this
condition being imposed on the subsequent purchaser

First published in the United Kingdom in 2002 by Century

Arrow Books
The Random House Group Limited
20 Vauxhall Bridge Road, London SW1V 2SA

www.randomhouse.co.uk

Addresses for companies with The Random House Group Limited
can be found at: www.randomhouse.co.uk/offices.htm

The Random House Group Limited Reg. No. 954009

A CIP catalogue record for this book
is available from the British Library

ISBN 9780099415558

The Random House Group Limited supports The Forest Stewardship Council
(FSC®), the leading international forest certification organisation. Our books
carrying the FSC label are printed on FSC® certified paper. FSC is the only forest
certification scheme endorsed by the leading environmental organisations,
including Greenpeace. Our paper procurement policy can be found at
www.randomhouse.co.uk/environment

Typeset by SX Composing DTP, Rayleigh, Essex
Printed and bound by CPI Group (UK) Ltd, Croydon, CR0 4YY

Acknowledgements

I would very much like to thank the following people for their help with this book. All technical errors are my own.

To Paul Baxter, who told me about snow-holes. To Paul and Judy Rose of Roseland Llamas who had me to stay, told me all about unusual fibres, and let me stroke their beautiful llamas. Bridget Postlethwaite for not only telling me all about Virtual Assistants, but becoming my own, excellent, V.A. and helping me with my research. Andrew Rough for showing me round Cam Mill. Steve and Sally Marshfield for lending me books about mills. To Harriet Longman who told me her story, which was difficult for her. To the Cairngorm Mountain Rescue Team. To Miranda Kirkby, she knows why. To Jane and Ian Peters and the Edge Reelers, who gave me a crash course in Highland dancing, and didn't grumble when I couldn't do it. To Polly Stirling for inventing nuno felt and allowing me to use it in my book and to Jane Ford for her invaluable advice about textiles.

As always to my tolerant family, my wonderful agent Sarah Molloy, everyone at Random House who do such a good job for me, in every way, and to others who can't be mentioned, probably because I have forgotten their names.

Chapter One

'I gave you a home, for goodness' sake!' said Henry.

Jenny put her suitcase in the boot and slammed it shut. 'I think if you cast your mind back, Henry, you asked me to move in with you several months before I actually did. And then I found out that what you really wanted was a housekeeper!'

'You were homeless at the time, though.'

'I had had to sell my flat. It's hardly the same as living on the streets.' She frowned. She didn't want to argue with Henry just as she was going away. 'Let's go and have a cup of coffee. I don't need to set off just yet.'

Henry followed her inside, and watched as she ground beans and set up the machine. Jenny would have preferred a quick cup of instant, but real coffee was one of Henry's things, and now wasn't the time to try to convert him to the other kind.

'I just think,' he said, as she set down the large, thick dark green and gold cup and saucer before him and added a homemade biscuit to the saucer, 'that you should put family commitments before your – your . . .'

Jenny's good intentions about not having a row were stretched. She sipped her own coffee, thinking it tasted bitter. 'It's a business, Henry. Not very large, but important to me. And it's your family who've got cousins coming over from America, not mine.'

'Practically the same thing,' he muttered into his shortbread.

Jenny was tempted to waggle the large ring-shaped space on her bare left hand to point out that they were neither married nor engaged, but she didn't, because she suspected he wanted them to be more than she did. His family did consider her part of theirs, but she didn't make the same assumptions. There had been many reasons why she had gone to live with Henry, including her feelings for Henry at the time, but since then she had begun to wonder if the deep fondness she felt for him and his domestic dependence on her were really enough to sustain a relationship.

'Why do you have to go this weekend? Wouldn't next week do?'

'I told you. My client wants me up there now. I've already delayed going because of your parents' anniversary party last weekend. I can't afford to lose him, Henry; I haven't got that many clients.'

'You could go out and get a job, like normal women do.'

Jenny was tempted to ask why, if he wanted the sort of woman he considered normal, he was living with her? But instead she said, 'I could, but I don't want to. I want to work for myself and control my own destiny. I'm not going to be at the whim of some bloody management consultant or accountant ever again, thank you. Besides, it's convenient for me to work at home. It means I can do the cooking and collect your suits from the cleaners.'

He totally missed the sarcasm. 'It seems only fair – after all, if you're at home all day . . .'

'Make up your mind, Henry. Either you like me

2

working from home, or you want me to get a proper job. Like "normal women" do.' To Henry, a normal woman had streaky blonde hair, was a size ten and dressed precisely as the fashion magazines dictated. What he'd ever seen in her slightly below average height, dark hair and less than cutting-edge dress sense, she had never quite worked out. Cynically she decided it was probably something to do with her breasts, which were more ample than being a size ten would allow.

'What I don't like is you shooting off to Scotland on the whim of a man you haven't even met! It's ridiculous! Why can't he do his own dirty work? It's nearly winter, for God's sake!'

'Because he's abroad! Which is why he uses my services. He hasn't got a base here and needs an assistant. And it's only October.'

'End of, and it'll feel like winter in Scotland, believe me. And "assistant" is only a fancy word for "secretary" you know. You may like to call yourself a "virtual assistant" but no one's ever heard of them. You won't be able to stick it. You'll be back here within the week. You're far too soft to sort out a business in trouble. You'd want to keep on all the workers as pets.'

Jenny ignored this last bit to avoid losing her temper. 'Luckily people who need them have heard of virtual assistants. And if a lot of my work is secretarial, at least it's honest labour and doesn't put anyone else out of a job. Anyway, this won't be just secretarial work, will it? He's trusting me to go and look at a failing business and report back. You could view it as a promotion.'

'He's using you, Jenny.'

'Yes, and he pays handsomely for the privilege! You

should be pleased for me, Henry, not carping! It's loads more money and I've got a chance to really build up some capital.' Now wasn't the moment to mention that she wanted the capital as a deposit so she could move into a place of her own.

'You're just being suckered, Jen. He's getting a management consultant on the cheap.'

Jenny scowled at him. He knew the words 'management consultant' would get her going. 'I am not being suckered. I am my own boss. I can stop working for him at the press of a button.'

'You're soft-hearted and impulsive. Look at the way you gave that beggar all your loose change on the way back from the paper shop this morning! You might as well throw your money away as give it to someone who'll just go and buy drugs with it!'

'I don't call that being impulsive; I call it being compassionate! Just because you would die rather than buy a copy of the *Big Issue* doesn't mean we all have to be the same! Now I really think I should be off. I want to get at least halfway today. It's a long drive.'

'A drive you don't have to be doing. Don't worry about washing the cups; I'll do them.'

Jenny stared at Henry, wondering how or why she had ever got involved with him. Then he smiled, and his hair flopped forward and she remembered, he reminded her irresistibly of Hugh Grant.

She went over to him where he stood pouring coffee grounds down the sink. 'Let's not quarrel when I'm going away.' She kissed his cheek.

He pulled away from her. 'Goodbye, Jenny. But I really wish you'd reconsider.'

Jenny sighed. Hugh Grant would have thought of

something witty and affectionate to say, something that might make her stay. 'I'm sure your mother will be able to entertain the American cousins perfectly well without me. I've given her my apple pie recipe.'

He didn't answer her, so she took a last trip to the loo, put on her coat, and then checked that she'd got everything.

By the time she'd reached the motorway, she'd stopped feeling guilty and sad for leaving Henry, and just let herself enjoy the sense of adventure. She was escaping from her solitary life for a little and was going to be doing some hands-on work. It was a challenge and she relished it.

It was the following afternoon, and seven hundred miles later, when Jenny, near her final destination, stopped at a tartan-painted mobile refreshment van, endearingly called 'The Homely Haggis', and asked for a cup of hot chocolate. Still annoyed with Henry, she had vowed never to drink coffee again.

The pretty, enormously pregnant young woman pushed the polystyrene cup across the counter. 'There you are. And there's your change. Ow,' she added, as Jenny took it, and put her hand to the small of her back.

Jenny hastily put the hot chocolate back onto the counter and stared anxiously at the woman. 'You're not going to have your baby now, are you?'

The woman laughed. 'Oh, no. I shouldn't think so. I'm not due for another fortnight. That was just a twinge.'

Her Scottish accent seemed to add to the air of cheerful optimism that surrounded her. She had a lot of chestnut hair swirling round her head and a wide,

5

smiling mouth, and now she picked up a cloth and wiped the counter. 'They say first babies are always late.'

'Do they? I don't know anything about childbirth except what I've seen on television.' Jenny bit her lip. 'Which means babies only come when there's not an ambulance or a doctor within a hundred miles, and have to be delivered by someone who has no idea what to do. Like now, really.'

The woman laughed again, unconcerned that they were in a lay-by in, what seemed to Jenny, a very remote corner of Scotland. 'And have you noticed? They never take their knickers off? Seriously, though, I know we're isolated up here, but there is a GP in the next village.'

'Which is only about fifteen miles away. I came through it. Hardly any distance at all,' Jenny smiled sipping her hot chocolate.

'In these parts fifteen miles is practically next door, so no need to worry.' The woman, bored with her condition, turned her bright eyes on Jenny. 'So what are you doing in this neck of the woods, apart from having a warming drink? I know the heather's still out, and the midges are more or less over, but unless you're a walker or a mountaineer, we're a bit off the tourist route. There isn't a shop selling models of Nessie for miles.'

Jenny hesitated. There would be no point keeping anything secret, not in an area so far away from the rest of civilisation that a new face would always be cause for speculation. She'd have to say something. She adopted an open expression. 'I'm visiting Dalmain House for a while.'

The young woman became even more interested. 'Oh? Friend of the family?'

This was tricky. Jenny didn't want to admit she'd been sent to investigate the Dalmains' knitwear business by a client. On the other hand, she didn't want to claim friendship with people she'd never met, particularly when they were almost bound to hate her. She'd been more or less told by Philip Dalmain in his letter to pretend to his mother she was installing a new computer system, implying, by what he didn't say, that if she let on there was anything wrong with the mill his mother would either have hysterics and die of apoplexy, or throw Jenny out of the house. 'Not really.'

The young woman sighed. 'I may as well introduce myself. I'm Meggie Dalmain. I'm married to the younger son.'

This was a bit of a surprise. Jenny had been led to expect that the Dalmains were a fairly old, aristocratic, and, she suspected, snobbish family. She wasn't expecting to meet a member of it serving in a mobile burger bar. It was a cheering discovery. She held out her hand. 'Genevieve Porter, known as Jenny.'

'You're right,' went on Meggie, having shaken the hand and read her thoughts. 'They disapprove of me terribly. Iain and I hardly ever go up there – only if we're summoned by the Matriarch, and only then because I don't see why Iain shouldn't see his family, just because of that old cow.'

This didn't exactly promise weeks of happy harmony and co-operation for Jenny, but she couldn't just turn tail when Henry had been so sure that was exactly what she'd do. 'The Matriarch?'

'The old lady. Fancies herself as the chatelaine of the

castle, or she would if it was a castle, and not just a gloomy old house. She conveniently forgets that her own father wasn't exactly out of the top drawer.'

By training, Jenny was discreet, but Meggie Dalmain obviously had a lot on her chest, and any little scraps of information she let fall could be very useful. She gave an interrogative 'Oh?' It wasn't exactly prodding, but it gave the young woman an opportunity to unload if she wanted.

Meggie did want. 'Look, why don't you come this side of the counter? There's a couple of seats here. We can have a proper chat. It's not fair to send you up to the big house without giving you a bit of briefing. You've got time?'

Jenny nodded. 'I'm a bit early, actually, which was why I stopped for a drink. I didn't want to turn up before I was expected.'

Meggie nodded. 'Very wise. They wouldn't like it if you arrived before they were ready. They're difficult at the best of times, which, as I'm sure you know, these aren't.'

Jenny squeezed herself in through the door at the side. When she first agreed to do some on-the-spot investigation for her biggest client, she had cherished a little hope that a few weeks in the Highlands would be almost like a working holiday. And if it wasn't, at least it would prove to Henry that she was more than just a glorified secretary. Since the initial request she had done a little investigation, and the working holiday myth had dispersed, but pride would prevent her from leaving a second before her job was done.

Sadly, Henry had been right about it being cold in Scotland. The trouser suit she was wearing, which in

the Home Counties had seemed appropriately practical, had become less and less suitable the further
north she drove, and her naturally curly hair was
curling furiously in the damp. She felt crumpled and
chilly, far from the efficient businesswoman image
she'd tried to create. It had been early autumn yesterday, when she left England – now it was early winter;
she'd have to buy some extra sweaters at the first
opportunity.

'Have a seat,' said Meggie, squashing herself down
onto the folding chair. 'If I get any bigger, I'm going to
have to stand up all day.'

'I don't know how you manage. This sort of work is
terribly tiring. I remember from my student days.'

'Well, I won't be able to for much longer – oh damn,
actually, I really need to wee. Would you mind looking
after things here while I go? The nearest tree is over
there, which seems miles away when you're heavily
pregnant. The baby is in an awkward place and
whenever I sit down it squashes my bladder. Do you
mind?'

'Of course not. It's not as if there are any customers.'

'Oh, er – I think you might find that Land Rover
that's just pulled up has a customer in it, which means
I'll have to walk even further, to where there are two
trees. Damn.' Meggie squeezed herself out of the door
and disappeared into the heather.

Jenny hardly had time to murmur 'Oh my God!'
under her breath before a man walked purposefully up
to the counter.

'A bacon butty and a cup of tea, please.'

Jenny tried an endearing smile. Or at least, she
hoped it was endearing. Without being able to check,

she couldn't be sure it wasn't just making her look simple. 'I don't suppose you'd care to wait a minute? I'm not really in charge here, and –'

'I only want a bacon roll and a cup of tea. But I am in a bit of a hurry.' He spoke with the authority of someone who was more accustomed to demanding wine lists and tossing credit cards onto plates than ordering fry-ups at his local greasy spoon. Although he was dressed as a walker, with well-worn outdoor clothing and a tanned complexion, he sounded to Jenny more like a business executive, a breed with which she was tiresomely familiar.

She decided to give it a go. How hard could it be to cook a bit of bacon and butter a roll? Even Henry admitted she could cook. And it would be easier for Meggie if the kettle was on and the bacon frying when she came back from behind her trees.

It took Jenny a while to track down the bacon and still longer to work the cooker. What was Meggie doing? Please don't let her have started having her baby, squatting over the sphagnum moss like a Native American. Jenny's customer was regarding her with doubt and suspicion – possibly because a navy-blue trouser suit and silk blouse weren't *de rigueur* for short-order chefs. Well, it was his fault. He had insisted on placing his order. He wouldn't let her explain she was only a customer herself.

'Where on earth is the kettle?' muttered Jenny, louder than she had intended.

'What the hell is going on?' Her customer leant over the counter, peering at Jenny with disapproval. 'You may be new to the job, but surely you can make a cup of tea?'

'I'm sure I can, but as I'm only a passing customer, much the same as you are, I'm having to feel my way.'

'What do you mean? If you don't work here, what are you doing behind the counter?'

Jenny, who had at last located the kettle, and was grateful to discover that it had enough water in it for a cup of tea, shrugged and hunted around for matches.

'I was having a chat with the proprietor. She's gone off to go to the loo. I said I'd take care of things. She's being an awfully long time. I hope she's all right.'

'What could have happened to her?'

'Nothing, I hope, but she's extremely pregnant. You're not a doctor, by any chance, are you?'

'No.'

'Or, better still, a midwife? Even a student nurse would be better than nothing.' She felt the need to get back at him for mocking her attempts at tea-making. She'd put up with too much mockery lately.

'I'm a businessman, and I'm on holiday. And if you're not any of those things, and you can't make a mug of tea without help, what are you doing here?'

Jenny could easily have told him to keep his nose out of what didn't concern him, but it would be unprofessional of her to insult Meggie's customer. Something about him made her think longingly of Henry's sophisticated elegance. Henry would never do anything unexpected or untoward. This man had an energy about him, an untamed quality that was unsettling, and his voice had a timbre that was a hundred miles away from Henry's mellow tones.

'As I said,' she explained firmly, 'I was having a hot chocolate –'

'But why were you having it here? *You* don't look as

11

if you're on holiday.' He gave her a quick glance up and down as if to check on this. 'Designer trouser suits aren't exactly leisure wear in the Highlands.'

Jenny resisted the urge to check that she didn't have too many buttons undone. 'Marks and Spencer's, actually, but thanks for the compliment. Would you like onions with your bacon, by the way?' She'd just spotted a string of them and wanted to distract him from asking too many pertinent questions. Her mascara was probably all under her eyes by now and her lipstick wouldn't have survived more than an hour.

'Yes, please. And you haven't answered my question.'

She could have gone on refusing to do so, but decided that mystery would only increase his curiosity.

'I've got a job in the area. Only for a short time, but I might buy a tweed skirt or a kilt, if navy worsted makes me look out of place.'

'So, where are you working?'

Now she was really tempted to tell him to mind his own business. It wasn't fair on the Dalmains for her to tell a complete stranger that she'd been sent from afar to pry into their business. 'It's confidential and it's not local. What about a tomato?'

'I see. Well, you don't have to tell me if you don't want to.'

'I know. So what about the tomato?'

'Yes, please. If you can manage that, of course.'

His curiosity and remarks about her appearance had been understandable if not acceptable, but this was a definite dig. 'I'm sure I can. How long would you like it boiled for?'

He frowned, took a breath, let it out again and shook his head. 'We seem to have got off on the wrong foot . . .'

'Well, you have. I'm dealing with you with the tact and patience that are my trademark.'

Reluctantly, he laughed. 'I realise that I should be grateful to you for even attempting to serve me –'

'But you're not,' she helped him out. 'You're too accustomed to giving orders and getting your own way without having to say thank you to anyone.'

He raised an eyebrow. 'Well, thanks for the character analysis.'

'A pleasure. And, unlike the bacon butty, it's free.'

'Well, I did at least get the character analysis. The bacon butty still eludes me.'

Jenny took a breath. It was annoying to be unable to deliver something so simple, but further protest would just make her look more incompetent. She was about to demand that the man go away and come back in half an hour when Meggie appeared.

'Ah, here's the proprietor,' Jenny said with relief. Very tempted to leap into her car and drive away in a shower of gravel, she felt obliged to check that Meggie was all right. 'Everything OK?'

'Absolutely. How are you getting on?'

'Well, I hope you're not planning to give her a permanent job,' said Jenny's customer. 'She seems totally unsuited to the work.'

Jenny frowned at him. He was being very unfair and now she couldn't leave without it looking like an escape.

'Really?' said Meggie, bright but dismissive. 'Why

don't you go and sit down at one of the tables, and we'll bring it over to you?'

'Now why didn't I think of that?' said Jenny, as soon as he was out of earshot. 'He's been hanging around watching me and asking awkward questions and I haven't a clue where anything is.'

Meggie had taken out the bacon and added the onions. 'Oh, I don't know. You seem to have been doing a grand job.'

'I haven't done anything like this since I was a student. Several lifetimes ago.'

'Not that long, surely? How old are you?'

'Twenty-seven. How old are you, yourself?'

Meggie laughed. 'Twenty-five, and I'm sorry for being so nosy. I'm always getting into trouble for being outspoken. Rude, my husband calls it.'

Jenny laughed back. 'I wouldn't call it rude, exactly.'

Meggie sighed. 'Iain says I can be as rude as I like when the business closes. Then it'll just be to him.'

'The business closes? That seems a shame!' The merry little tartan van suddenly seemed a haven in the gathering bleakness of the afternoon.

'Well, only for the season, in theory. The trouble is, if I close early, and I may have to because of this little bundle,' she patted her stomach, 'I may not get this spot next year. There's someone else after it, and it wouldn't be worth my doing The Homely Haggis if I had to travel any further to get to it.' Meggie sighed again.

'How much longer has the season got to run?' It already seemed quite late in the year for tourist-based businesses.

'Only a few weeks. Come December I'll close completely.'

'Isn't there someone who could do those for you? It seems a shame to risk losing the business because you're pregnant.'

'It does, doesn't it?' Meggie was pleased that someone understood her feelings. 'But I've tried everyone local and they none of them can.'

'I almost feel like doing it myself, except that I've just failed to make a bacon butty and a cup of tea and would obviously drive the customers away in droves.'

'You wouldn't, would you?' Jenny bit her lip. Meggie was looking at her as if she had seen her saviour in her tea leaves, and Jenny hadn't seriously been offering, more just making sympathetic noises.

'Well –'

'It would be so brilliant if you could. But would you be able to? It's only weekends and the odd fine evening, but you will have your other work.'

This was the moment to say, no, she wasn't offering, but she didn't. Henry's jibes about her being impulsive, and her own assertion that it was compassion came back to her. Why shouldn't she be impulsive and compassionate if she wanted? It was her life, and it might need a little light relief in it.

'I'm sort of tempted, partly to help you out and partly because it seems – fun.'

'Oh, it is! It's great! And it would only be for a short time. I reckon I could manage next summer, even with a baby, and Iain and I need the extra cash.'

Meggie was looking at her in a very persuasive way.

'And you really can't find anyone else to keep it open for you?'

'I haven't been able to so far. Until you came along.'

'Meggie!'

'Perhaps you'd better tell me why you're going to Dalmain House. And how long you're likely to be visiting. But before you do, just take this over to your favourite customer. Tell him it's on the house as he's been kept waiting so long.'

'Not that long! I was doing my best.'

'Just take it over. Then come back and get the tea. Please!'

With more than a little reluctance, Jenny crossed the shingle parking area. The heels of her boots, fine in Surrey, were too high for the Scottish Highlands.

'Here you are,' she said churlishly, putting down the plate. 'Meggie says it's on the house.'

He narrowed his eyes in a way that was both sinister and attractive at the same time. 'Would that be Dalmain House?'

Jenny suddenly felt her mouth go dry. 'What do you mean?'

He hesitated, just for a second, as if he was about to say something, but then thought better of it. 'Nothing. I just thought that's where you might be working, Dalmain House.'

'What on earth gave you that idea?'

'Well, aren't you?'

'It's none of your business where I'm working!'

She wobbled furiously back to the van. 'Bloody man! He's just tried to make me tell him I'm working at Dalmain House, and it's supposed to be a secret!'

'Oh, why? Does he take sugar?'

'Well, he's certainly not "sweet enough already".'

Meggie put a couple of sachets of sugar and a stirrer

16

into Jenny's hand. 'I'd take it myself, only it'll make me want to wee again. But we need a talk.'

Grim-faced, Jenny marched back to the table, holding the mug of tea. 'There you are!' She put it and the sugar down on the table, noting with satisfaction that the sugar had gone on a puddle caused by a dip in the plastic.

'Thank you. Oh and, miss?'

'What?' 'Miss' seemed like the ultimate insult.

'You've got grease on your blouse. That won't make a good impression at the big house.'

Jenny nearly twisted her ankle as she whisked back across the car park. 'Oh piss off!' she muttered under her breath.

'It's no good asking me to run this place for you!' she told Meggie. 'I'd swear at the customers.'

Meggie shook her head. 'No you wouldn't. Most of them are sweeties. And they're so grateful! I really like this job. It's so easy to make people happy!'

Jenny sighed. She certainly couldn't say that about her job – at least, not the aspect of it that was occupying her now.

'I'll make you another hot chocolate and then tell you who's who up at the House of Usher. If you tell me what you're doing there, of course. Has Philip been fiddling the books?'

'I shouldn't think so, but that's not why I'm here.'

Meggie raised a sceptical eyebrow and Jenny felt she might as well be as frank as she could be. 'I've been sent by my client to see what's going on in the business. I won't make any decisions, I'll just report back. But there's been no suggestion that there's been any fiddling.'

17

Meggie sighed. 'Pity. Philip's so much his mother's blue-eyed boy, it would have been nice if, just for once, he'd done something really wicked. But I expect he's just been his usual charming self.'

'Don't you like him?' If Meggie was willing to give her information, she might as well get as much as possible.

'You can't really dislike Philip. He's "awfully nice".' She put on an exaggeratedly posh English accent. 'But he's so lacking in initiative. He'd have made a perfect younger son. And my Iain, well, he'd have loved to get his hands on the family business.' Meggie sighed. 'So, do you work for the man the estate owes all that money to?'

Jenny licked her lips, slightly horrified that so much of Dalmain's business seemed common knowledge. 'It's not quite as straightforward as that. It's a syndicate which has invested in the business. I work for one of the members. Or I should say, one of the members is one of my clients.'

Meggie ignored this finer detail. 'But if the syndicate has invested money, it will have to be paid back?'

And at a crippling rate of interest, added Jenny silently. 'Eventually, yes. Not necessarily all at once.'

Meggie shrugged. 'They never tell Iain and me anything anyway. We just put two and two together and make a bit of gossip. So, what do you do, exactly?'

'I'm what's called a virtual assistant. It's like being a secretary only I never get to meet my boss, and I have several of them. People I work for, that is.'

'Sounds complicated.'

'It's not really. With the Internet it's so easy to communicate. I usually work from home but when my client' – no need to mention his name – 'asked me to come up here and look into things myself, I was tempted by the thought of being more hands-on. It needn't affect my other clients at all, and you can get lonely working from home all the time.' As well as being expected to do all the domestic chores, she added silently.

'I'm not sure Dalmain House will be able to offer much in the way of sparkling company, but there's always me.' Meggie laughed. 'While I'm here. What did you say your name was, again?'

'Genevieve Porter. Jenny for short.'

'I expect the Matriarch will insist on calling you Genevieve, if she doesn't just stick to Miss Porter.'

'I quite like Genevieve, actually. It's just a bit of a mouthful.'

'Well then, Jenny, or Genevieve, how about standing in for me here, while I'm out of action? For just as long as you're here.' Meggie's brown eyes were very appealing.

'Really, I'd love it in theory, but I'd be useless! Look what happened just now, with that man.'

'He was unusually difficult. And you wouldn't be useless if you had a little training. And you'll need somewhere to escape to. Dalmain House is like a cross between a museum and a funeral parlour, only not so cheerful.'

Oh God, don't say Henry was going to be right about this, as well as everything else. 'Really? Perhaps I should cut my losses and just go home . . .'

'No, don't do that!' Meggie backtracked furiously. 'It'll be fine, I'm sure. And I will enjoy having you

19

around. A little female company of my own age will be wonderful. You said you got lonely.'

Jenny laughed. 'Did I? But this place isn't exactly jumping at the moment, now is it?'

Meggie shrugged. 'Well, I know. And I've got a dreadful cheek to even suggest it. But you did sort of offer and you said you'd worked in a café.'

'Well yes.'

'The nicest thing about it,' went on Meggie, sensing that Jenny was tempted, 'is that people are always so pleased to see you. They've often come off the mountain,' – she gestured to the heather-covered hill that swept on up towards the sky – 'walked for miles in the pouring rain. A hot cup of something is just what they're wanting and you provide it.'

'I can see that would be satisfying.'

'And there's no worrying about it when you go home. You've either sold lots of hot drinks and bacon butties or you haven't. You can just lock up and forget about it.'

Jenny sighed. She often found herself working very late, her brain still chewing things over. 'That does sound attractive, I must say.'

'And the mountains are famous. There are always walkers and hikers and things in these parts. Most of them are lovely.'

'That one wasn't.'

'The exception, I promise. And he was quite attractive. All the local men are spoken for and you'll need someone to have a joke with.'

Jenny laughed. 'So you think I should take over The Homely Haggis to pick up men, do you?' How would Henry feel about that?

'There are worse ways. Unless you're taken yourself?'

'I am, in a manner of speaking, but even if I wasn't, I wouldn't want to mix business with pleasure. There's no point in meeting a bonnie Scot I'd have to leave behind.'

Meggie shrugged. 'I thought you could do your job anywhere.'

'I can, but there's the rest of my life! I mean, no offence, but I'm from the Home Counties, and this is rather a long way away from Bond Street, isn't it?'

Meggie chuckled. 'Here, I'll give you my address and telephone number. If you're going to be around long enough and want to help me, you can give me a ring. Or if you don't, you can just come for a chat and a dram. I won't put any pressure on you.'

Jenny wondered about that. Meggie was obviously very determined. On the other hand, Jenny was genuinely tempted by the cosiness of the van. 'I'll let you know one way or another as soon as possible.' She paused. 'I would like to do it, in a way. Just to prove I can.' And not only to herself. Part of her, deep down and barely acknowledged, wanted to prove to that man that a bacon butty and a cup of tea were not beyond her, though why she should care what he thought, God alone knew.

'Good. Well, I can't ask for more than that.'

Jenny looked at her watch. 'I suppose I'd better be on my way. Do you think I should ring and say exactly when I'll be arriving?'

'How would you do that? Mobile phones are no use out here.'

Jenny made a face. 'God! How *uncivilised*!'

21

'Away with you! Do you need any directions?'

Jenny fished a crumpled bit of paper from her jacket pocket. 'There's a little road about a mile from here, and then up a long track to the left?'

Meggie nodded. 'That'll get you there. Good luck.'

Chapter Two

It was one of those doorbells that didn't make any sound when you rang it. Jenny stood on the doorstep, shivering, wondering if the bell, which she had pulled with difficulty out of the doorjamb, was actually connected, or if it was just there for show. Or maybe it jangled in some far-off servants' quarters, possibly unheard.

She had already used the time to unload her luggage from the car, and now it was heaped about her, pinning her there. She didn't want to try the bell again and risk annoying whoever might be coming to answer it, going as fast as they could. But supposing there wasn't anyone? She couldn't be left standing on the doorstep for ever.

She looked about her, forcing herself to be optimistic, only to find her surroundings even less promising than Meggie had suggested. The house was constructed out of large blocks of very grey granite, a colour that might have been beautiful if the lavish, if not excessive, woodwork hadn't been picked out in dark red. There was a plethora of rustic posts apparently supporting the second storey, with cut-off branches still protruding, looking like bloody spikes. Bargeboards ran underneath the overhanging windows, and outlined the little turrets and window embrasures. In fact, Jenny thought grimly, the whole place looked like an extra-large gingerbread house, whose inhabitants, instead of disguising their evil intent by decorating their home with sweeties, had decided instead to advertise their gruesomeness with blood-coloured banners.

Thinking longingly about her warm little car and the beautiful, though long, road back to civilisation, she was about to try the bell again when she heard someone approach.

The sound of footsteps was followed by someone talking crossly to a dog. The door took a long time to unlock.

'Hello – you must be –' The woman was in her forties, and would have been pretty had it not been for her agitated expression. She had a lot of dark-blonde hair which she wore piled up on top of her head and a very beautiful pair of gold dangly earrings.

'Genevieve Porter, Jenny for short.'

'I'm Felicity Dalmain.' The woman put a cold hand into Jenny's.

'You knew I was coming?' asked Jenny, when she'd shaken it.

'Oh yes. My mother is expecting you. We're all expecting you. Come in.' The woman picked up a couple of document cases. 'Don't mind the dogs. Once they've smelt you, they'll be fine. Just don't touch them straight away.'

With one bag tucked underneath her arm, and both hands full, this was not a temptation, but even if she had been free to do so, she probably wouldn't have. Jenny liked dogs in theory, but the thought of a pack of them, sniffing her over, did make her sweat slightly.

24

And dogs could smell fear. She should have run away while she still had the chance, before the door was opened, and definitely before she weighed herself down with luggage.

There seemed to be about five dogs. Large and grey or small and brown, they applied their noses to her clothes with interest. They'd probably never smelt Marks and Spencer's navy worsted before, she thought. Possibly expressing their opinion of it, without even brushing against her they instantly covered her in hairs.

'Leave your bags there,' said Felicity Dalmain, dumping the ones she was carrying. 'You seem to have rather a lot of luggage. We'll take it up later. Come into the kitchen. Would you like a drink?'

Jenny was desperate for a cup of tea, only she had a more pressing need. Unlike Meggie, she hadn't taken advantage of the distant tree and the heather earlier.

'Please could I find a loo first?'

'Oh yes. There's one through that door – no, the next one. I'll be in the kitchen.'

Jenny found the cloakroom – a lavatory and a wash basin tucked in the corner of a large room full of old riding macs, coats, fishing paraphernalia and probably spiders, but with no lock on the door. It wasn't cosy, but, she supposed, it was an improvement on the heather and the biting wind. She washed her hands and even after running the water sometime, it remained stone cold. Perhaps the kitchen will be really warm, she thought; the heart of the house, full of hot soup, freshly baked bread and comfort.

Assuming she could ever find the kitchen, of course. Given that they were at the back of the house, and it wasn't Chatsworth, she was amazed at the choice of doors before her. The first two revealed larders, with granite slabs, cruel-looking hooks and torn zinc fly screens, the third was full of bottles and jars, a fourth was full of dog beds, bones and torn blankets, and the fifth was the kitchen.

It was a little warmer than the rest of the house, but it wasn't the haven of warmth she'd been longing for. Jenny glanced across it, hoping to see a range of some sort, something that promised hot water, or at least somewhere warm to lean. But, judging by the number of cats on top of it, the heat source was an ancient boiler and the cats didn't look any too cosy.

The woman who had opened the door – Felicity, Jenny reminded herself – came towards her. She was holding a glass. A wisp of hair had escaped from her bun. 'Would you like a whisky? I know it's early, but I'm in a bit of a state. A friend – well, an old boyfriend actually – is coming to dinner.'

As Felicity was already pouring the whisky, Jenny didn't feel she could now ask for a cup of tea, as to do so would both point up her hostess's bad habits and add to her agitation. 'How terrifying. No wonder you need a drink, but please make mine a small one. I'm working, after all.' She gave a slightly nervous laugh. Either Felicity's anxiety was catching, or Jenny felt she'd made a very grave mistake, driving seven-hundred-odd miles, committing herself to spending anything up to a couple of months in this freezing mausoleum, mostly just to prove a point. 'Is he an old flame?'

'Not exactly, more a spark that was never allowed to develop into anything else.' Felicity paused. 'I haven't told my mother that he's coming.'

'Oh. And will she have to stretch the lamb chops to feed an extra person? Might she be annoyed?'

'She'll definitely be annoyed, but not because she does the cooking. It's just that she didn't approve of him twenty-odd years ago, and she's not likely to now.'

'Oh.'

Felicity tucked the wisp back out of the way. 'I'm sorry. I shouldn't be telling you all this. We've only just met.'

'It's sometimes easier to tell strangers things than people who are connected to you.' People found Jenny easy to confide in – she must look as though she was a good listener, and not easily shocked.

'Yes,' said Felicity tentatively, not yet ready to unburden completely, but reserving the right to in the future.

Jenny took a sip of her drink. 'Should I meet Lady Dalmain first? Or get my stuff upstairs?' Jenny was aware that she was there slightly on sufferance, and felt that Lady Dalmain would not be pleased to find her hall full of cases.

'I suppose I should show you to your room. My mother's in her study. She's writing a book.'

'Oh? A novel?'

Felicity shook her head. 'She despises novels, or at least, all novels published after 1900. No, she's writing a history book. She doesn't like to be disturbed. Her work is very important to her.'

'Will you tell her about your friend coming?'

'Oh yes. I'll have to. I'm just putting it off. Cheers.' Felicity took a gulp of whisky that should have felled a horse.

Jenny tried to match it and nearly choked. 'Your mother does know that I'm coming?' Jenny's own anxiety was feeding on Felicity's, and she was beginning to think this hands-on work was very overrated. Give her a nice, safe computer, where she could just do everything in her own home, by email. People made things so complicated.

'Oh yes. We've all known for weeks.'

Jenny took another sip. 'Miss Dalmain, I don't suppose you could fill me in about the family, before I have to meet them all? It would help stop me making any dreadful blunders about who's who.'

This made Felicity smile, and Jenny saw what a very pretty woman she had once been, and could be again if she wasn't so jumpy. 'Well, there's me. Do call me Felicity. I'm the eldest; should have been a boy. It was my father who named me Felicity; my mother wasn't at all happy about my arrival. I adored him.' She sighed. 'Then there's Philip, he's the elder boy. My mother thinks the sun shines out of him, and he is really sweet, but I do get fed up with him being able to do no wrong, and me being unable to do anything right. Then there's Iain. Iain is the youngest and doesn't live here. He managed to get out. He's married to Meggie who is . . .' Felicity inspected Jenny to see if references to class would be acceptable. Deciding they wouldn't be, she said, 'well, not like us. She can be rather blunt. My mother doesn't approve of her because she talks with a Scots accent. Scotch, my mother calls it.'

'Oh, I thought that was terribly politically incorrect to call things or people Scotch, unless it's whisky?'

Felicity laughed, more enthusiastically than Jenny

felt her remark warranted. 'Sorry, it's just the thought of Mama being politically correct, ever. You'll understand when you meet her.'

'Oh.' Felicity had managed to make the Matriarch seem even more daunting than Meggie had. 'Actually, I've met Meggie. I stopped for a drink on my way here, at The Homely Haggis, her café.'

Felicity stiffened slightly. 'Oh?'

'She asked me where I was going and, when I told her, she introduced herself.'

'Yes, well, Meggie always has been a little too ready to press herself on people.'

Jenny sensed that snobbishness might be a family characteristic, and not just Lady Dalmain's weakness. 'Oh she didn't press herself on me,' she said. 'She just asked me where I was going and then told me she was part of the family.'

Felicity's glance was more than slightly disbelieving. 'And she didn't say we were a rum lot?'

Jenny looked into her glass, which still contained enough alcohol to allow painless limb amputation. 'Sort of. So tell me quickly about the old flame, before he gets here.' Such an intimate question was rather a risk, but Jenny wanted to change the subject and most women like to talk about their men.

'As I said, he never got a chance to be a flame. Mama told me that he was common and I wasn't to have anything to do with him. In my early twenties, I didn't have much choice. She's a crashing snob, I'm afraid.'

Ignoring this statement of the obvious, Jenny asked, 'So how did you get in touch with him again?'

'A friend of mine has alpacas over the valley. Lachlan is a sort of peripatetic alpaca clipper. She mentioned his name to me and I thought it must the same Lachlan that I'd known, all those years ago. I finally plucked up the courage to get in touch, and said that, when he was next in the area, he must come over.' Felicity drained her glass. 'I've no idea why he agreed to come. I'm sure he must be married, or have a girl-friend or something. Either that or he'll think I'm a complete tart for inviting him.'

'I'm sure he won't.'

'Because actually, whatever my mother says, I'm not a complete tart. I'm just very lonely. And if I don't make some effort to change my life soon, I'm going to be stuck here looking after Mama for the rest of her life – and mine, possibly – she's as strong as an ox.'

'I see,' Jenny said rather uncomfortably. 'Well, well done for taking action.'

Felicity sighed. 'Come on. I'll take you to your room. You can get unpacked and stuff, and then come down to the drawing room at about seven for a pre-dinner drink. Lachlan's coming at about seven thirty. It'll be better if you're here when he arrives. Then Mama won't be able to make too much fuss.'

Jenny's room was large, in one of the turrets, which meant it had plenty of windows, with panoramic views and draughts that would clean corn, as her mother would say. As requested, there was a table suitable to use as a desk, a high, old-fashioned bed, a chest of drawers and a wardrobe.

'I've emptied one of the drawers and there's a bit of space in the wardrobe,' said Felicity. 'We had the separate telephone line put in, as requested.' This was said with a visible wince. 'Mama was livid! We're supposed to be saving –'

'But the firm paid?' Jenny interrupted.

'Oh yes, but she hates spending money, even if it's not hers, unless it's something she approves of, like books, or antiques. Nothing remotely electronic. Still, I hope this is all right. The bathroom's just down the hall. My mother has her own bathroom, and the rest of us share this one.'

'Just show me where it is. This house is so big, I'm sure to get lost.'

'Oh, OK.' Felicity led the way down the passage. 'It's in here. Don't use the shower; it doesn't work. And the bath is always cold because there's never enough hot water to heat it through. I usually fill a bucket with hot water, wash with it standing in the bath, and then sluice myself off with the plastic jug. My mother's bathroom has its own immersion heater.'

'Oh. Right, fine,' said Jenny, vowing to get her work done as quickly as possible. While everyone, Henry in particular, had warned her that Scotland was a lot colder than England, no one had mentioned this applied to the water as well.

'So I'll see you downstairs in the drawing room at seven, then?'

'If I manage to find it, yes.'

Jenny went back downstairs to bring up the rest of her bags and her laptop. It wasn't that she necessarily expected anyone else to carry them, but it would have been friendly for Felicity to have taken something, if only the carrier bag containing chocolates and a plant, gifts for her hostess.

Once in her bedroom, she plugged in her laptop. She

was reluctant to unpack. It was as if she thought the clothes in her suitcase would take on the cold of the room the moment she took them out. Besides, she couldn't think of anything she'd packed that would be warmer than her trouser suit. However, Felicity hadn't mentioned changing for dinner, but Lady Dalmain sounded like the sort of woman who would, and as Jenny had been wearing the same clothes for a long time, she did want to put on something else.

Reluctant to get out of her clothes until she'd sorted out a substitute, Jenny logged on to her email. She didn't read any of the ones awaiting her attention – from other, less demanding clients than the one who had sent her here – she just dashed off a quick one to her mother.

Dearest Mum, well, I've arrived, and as you predicted, it's freezing here. You were right about the thermals, I definitely need them. And to save me spending hours on the Internet ordering some, could you be a darling and send me some? Vests, petticoats, nighties, in fact, to save time, you could just get the whole contents of the Damart catalogue sent to me. Don't, for God's sake, tell Henry, he'll laugh. Oh, and an electric blanket. With luck, I might be able to scrounge a hot water bottle until then. The scenery's pretty, though. But the family seem to be mad as cats. Haven't met the mother yet. She sounds the worst of the lot. Why did I agree to come here? No need to answer that! Your loving daughter, Jenny.

While she was logged on she thought she might as well confirm her arrival to her client. She typed,

> Uneventful journey, arrived safely. Haven't met the family yet. Will report again shortly. Yours, G. Porter.

She didn't email Henry. She wanted to wait until she had some positive news. Anything she said now would just make him say something scathing, disguised as sympathy – 'A bit out of your depth, sweetie? I did warn you . . .' She was going to show Henry a thing or two.

At seven she made her way down the stairs. In winter it's perfectly acceptable to look as if you've wrapped up warm. In October, it somehow appears rude to be wearing every stitch you've brought with you. On the other hand, so was letting your teeth chatter while you tried to make small talk with your hostess. Besides, Jenny hadn't brought any winter clothes as such and had had to improvise.

She had on two pairs of tights, a slip, the skirt that went with the jacket of her trouser suit, and a clean cotton shirt over the silk one that had got spattered with grease. On top of this she put her only cardigan, a fine lambswool one, and then her jacket. She did feel a little like a sausage in a skin, but it was preferable to openly shivering. She had resolved that at the first opportunity she would hightail it to the nearest woollens shop having an end-of-season sale and buy up their entire stock. She could always turn a tartan rug into a skirt, at a pinch, particularly without Henry there to comment.

She was a little nervous as she approached the room from whence came low, muttering voices, of the kind that were guaranteed to stop the moment a stranger entered – thus informing the stranger that she was the topic of conversation, but she took a breath and went in.

'Ah, hello,' said Felicity, jumping up. 'Let me introduce you to my mother. Mama, this is Genevieve Porter. Jenny, this is my mother, Lady Dalmain.'

It was with a flutter of anticipation in her stomach that Jenny turned to the Matriarch.

Chapter Three

The woman who rose was dressed in a tweed suit and a silk blouse. She must once have been handsome, but bitterness and discontent had pulled in her lips and narrowed her eyes. She wore her greying hair in a bun at the nape of her neck. A thick rope of gold sat uneasily with the crêpe de Chine but went well with her heavy gold earrings – this was a family that went in for jewellery, thought Jenny. Lady Dalmain, who held herself very erect, extended a regal hand. It was covered in rings and was designed to keep whoever dared to take it strictly at arm's length.

Perhaps it was the whisky she'd drunk earlier or perhaps it was the sheer theatricality of the situation, but Jenny was beginning to enjoy the hideousness of it all.

A huge stag, whose head emerged from the wall behind Lady Dalmain, squinted slightly, and other badly stuffed beasts stared glassily at nothing. Faded tapestries, depicting tartan-clad warriors and fainting maidens hung disconsolately from the oak panelling. Complicated wooden lamps hung with cut-glass pendants fought for space on the occasional tables with Staffordshire models of Flora Macdonald and Highland gentlemen with lions at their feet. Different generations of The Family, immortalised in sepia, stared grimly from richly decorated photograph frames. There were enough silver stags at bay, deerhounds and Highland cattle to populate a small zoo, and these were flanked by an equal quantity of drinking vessels and dishes. She even spotted an elephant-foot wastepaper basket. Felicity was neurotic and her mother was apparently a monster, but there was a funny side to this situation. Her mother, Henry and his friends, would love hearing a detailed description. Henry's mother would have been hugely impressed.

Then Jenny caught sight of Felicity trying not to bite her nails, and suddenly felt guilty for her amusement. It was all right for her, Jenny, to be entertained by how awful it was, she could just go home to Henry, and his nice maisonette, when her job was done. For her, it would definitely be over by Christmas. Felicity had to live here.

Jenny took her hostess's outstretched hand carefully, unwilling to spear herself on antique diamonds.

'How do you do, Miss Porter?' said Lady Dalmain, in a deep, surprisingly melodious voice. 'Would you be connected to the Wilmsbury Porters, by any chance? A very old family.'

'No, I think we're connected to the Billingsgate Porters.' Then she bit her lip; this was no place for flippancy. She imagined Henry frowning at her; she sometimes didn't take his mother quite seriously enough for him, either.

But Lady Dalmain nodded sagely, and for a moment Jenny wondered if there really was a family of Billingsgate Porters.

'You've met my daughter,' Lady Dalmain went on,

'but sadly, my elder son, Philip, has been held up. He'll join us later.'

There was a sound from Felicity that indicated the 'hold-up' might have been tactical, but she didn't actually say anything.

'Would you like a drink?' Lady Dalmain went on, either ignoring or not noticing her daughter's interjection. 'Felicity, give Miss Porter a glass of sherry.'

'Oh please call me Jenny.'

'Or she might prefer a whisky,' said Felicity.

'We don't say "a whisky", Felicity. If Miss Porter prefers whisky she can say so.'

'Miss Porter' yearned for the courage to say that what she really wanted was a boiling hot toddy, but didn't dare. She was still shivering, although neither of the other two seemed to feel cold. 'Whatever is easiest,' she said, wanting whisky for its more warming characteristics, but feeling sherry was probably safer.

'It's no trouble for Felicity to give you whisky if that is what you prefer.'

Rashly, she said, 'Yes, please,' glad that Henry wasn't there to disapprove. He didn't like her to drink spirits. She tried to picture her own mother being like Lady Dalmain, having her own hot-water supply, ordering her daughter about as if she were a servant, or a delinquent teenager, driving the daughter to drink. She couldn't make the necessary leap of imagination – it was too far from reality. Her own mother was a sweetie and Jenny found herself suddenly wondering guiltily if she took advantage of her.

While Jenny was sipping her whisky, she heard a bell jangling deep towards the back of the house.

Neither Lady Dalmain nor the dogs appeared to have heard it, but Felicity jumped.

'That'll be Lachlan,' Felicity said, relatively calmly but with a slight edge of hysteria in her voice. 'He's coming to supper. I hope you don't mind, Mama. There's plenty. It's only stew.'

Lady Dalmain's expression froze. It was as if she didn't know which of her daughter's *faux pas* she should pounce on first: the unexpected guest, the mention of food in that vulgar way, or the use of the word 'stew'. Jenny bit her lip, her sense of the ridiculous heightened by alcohol.

'And who, if I may ask who is to be dining at my table, is *Lachlan*?'

'Lachlan McGregor. You remember. I knew him years and years ago. I got in touch with him at Elaine's and he's coming to dinner. I'll just go and let him in.'

Jenny would have liked very much to be able to offer to do this for her, but that really would be presuming on her position as very new guest. She had to stick it out, alone with Lady Dalmain, who was smouldering far more effectively than the logs in the grate, which issued forth smoke, but no heat.

There was an uncomfortable silence. Jenny tucked her hands up her sleeves in an attempt to warm them, but found it only made her colder. The largest of the dogs got up and shook itself, obviously keen to match Jenny's skirt with her jacket and her trousers with an application of dog hairs.

'Actually,' said Jenny, 'I brought you a little present. Shall I run and fetch it?'

Lady Dalmain inclined her head, which Jenny took to mean yes, and escaped, aware as she passed through the hall that Felicity and Lachlan had disappeared. Possibly Felicity had taken him into the kitchen for a pre-pre-dinner drink, or a health warning about Lady Dalmain. Glad that Lachlan was at least Scottish, and therefore less sensitive to the cold and more impervious to strong drink, Jenny scanned her clothes to see what else she could put on. She found a silk scarf that more or less matched the rest of what she was wearing, and she tucked it round her neck. With luck no one would notice she hadn't always been wearing it. She found the carrier bag with the presents, feeling mean for giving them to Lady Dalmain, and not Felicity. She'd have to get Felicity something else, when she had the opportunity. The worst part was that she knew she was only giving presents to Lady Dalmain because she had already picked up Felicity's anxious-for-approval-daughter habits. She was even worrying in case the Belgian chocolates and African violet screamed 'bought from a service station'.

You don't need to panic, she told herself. Lady Dalmain has probably never darkened the doors of a service station in her life.

She ran downstairs and back into the drawing room. She presented the carrier bag.

Lady Dalmain accepted it graciously. 'Thank you. It was kind of you to be so thoughtful. I realise that your position here is not really that of guest in the conventional sense, so I appreciate the gesture.' She inclined her head. 'I gather you have something to do with computers, and are going to do something which will help Philip?'

'That's right.' It was also almost true. 'It's very kind of you to let me stay while I do the work.'

39

'It will be pleasant for Felicity to have some young company. Besides, there are no hotels in the vicinity. We rather treasure our remoteness.'

Jenny smiled, unable to think of anything to say.

They sat in silence for a few moments, listening to the fire spit and hiss and the dogs grunt and trying not to listen to the distant murmur of voices that was growing no nearer. Obviously the kitchen was more attractive than the drawing room.

Covering the obvious absence of her daughter and her guest, Lady Dalmain drew breath. 'Felicity's rather a vulnerable girl, you know. She lets herself be put upon by people. I expect this Lachlan is after her money. I must make it clear to him that she hasn't got any.' Lady Dalmain squeezed her eyes in an imitation of a smile. 'Tell me about your family.'

Jenny limped through a description of her parents, how her father was dead and how her mother occupied her days. Lady Dalmain nodded, satisfied that Jenny's family were humble, yet respectable. Then she said something which made Jenny nervous.

'Explain to me about this computer business. Philip says you work for a man you haven't met. Forgive me if I appear to be stupid, but how can this be?'

Jenny took a breath, fervently wishing she had spoken to Philip directly, so she knew what story he'd fed his mother. 'It is a bit strange when you're not used to the idea, but it's quite simple. I communicate with him through my computer, or the telephone, or fax. We don't actually have to meet at all. I work for a couple of other people as well, though, as it happens, I have met them. Mr Grant-Dempsey was out of the country when I was recommended to him. Still is, as far as I know.'

Lady Dalmain was regarding Jenny as if she'd just announced she was from another planet, when Felicity and Lachlan entered the room.

Lachlan was tall and thin with pale hair and freckles. He didn't look like the sort of man to set a girl's soul on fire, but he didn't look like a fortune-hunter either. Felicity, by his side, looked flushed and extremely pretty. The session in the kitchen must have gone well.

'Mama,' said Felicity, drawing her friend into the room, 'I'd like you to meet Lachlan McGregor. Lachlan, my mother, Lady Dalmain.'

'I think we've met already, many years ago,' said Lady Dalmain, nearly smiling and looking almost benign. 'You must forgive my daughter for forgetting that. Her memory's not what it was.'

'Her memory's just fine, Lady Dalmain. She remembered my name when we hadn't met for years and she didn't have the benefit of being reminded of me.'

Lady Dalmain accepted this rebuke with a modicum of respect. She obviously enjoyed male company far more than female. 'I think that might say more about you than about my daughter.'

'Have a drink, Lachlan.' Felicity tipped the end of a bottle of whisky into a glass. 'Do you want water with that?' She waved a crystal jug over the glass in an enquiring way. 'No?'

'Felicity, I hope you've left enough whisky for Philip when he comes in.'

'Oh yes. I've got another bottle here. Jenny, how about another one?'

Jenny shook her head. She had to get through dinner

without passing out, forgetting why Lady Dalmain thought she was here, or making some dreadful social blunder.

'I would like some more,' said Lady Dalmain, holding out her glass.

'Oh, sorry, Mama.'

'Mama', Jenny noted, accepted the same half tumblerful that Felicity had given everyone else.

The dogs, who had paid no attention to Lachlan's arrival, suddenly leapt to their feet and charged out of the door, scraping the tartan carpet into a heap as they did so.

'That'll be Philip,' said Lady Dalmain, a flash of real pleasure lightening her features. 'They always know their master.'

'Yes,' muttered Felicity, out of her mother's earshot, flattening the rug with her foot. 'But they don't care a damn about their mistress, who feeds them and takes them for walks.'

'How maddening,' muttered Jenny back.

Woofing and barking and 'Get down you ridiculous brutes' noises came from the hall. After a few moments, the door opened and Philip came in.

He was tall and extremely good-looking, his mother's severe features better suiting a man. He smiled broadly at his mother, strode across the room and gave her a huge hug. Then he turned to the others.

'Fliss – how are you? Haven't seen you since yesterday! You weren't up when I left. And you must be Miss Porter, the terrifying lady sent to sort us all out. With her computers,' he added, too late for Jenny's comfort. He took her hand and shook it hard. 'How nice to meet you. I think we were expecting high

42

heels, a sharp suit, a French pleat and glasses and we've got a very friendly looking you instead. And who's this?'

'Lachlan McGregor,' said Lachlan.

'He's a friend of mine,' said Felicity.

'Then welcome!' said Philip.

Jenny could see why he was his mother's favourite, and why he was hard for his older sister to compete with. He reminded her of Henry and she warmed to this familiarity.

Philip got himself a drink and went to sit down next to his mother. 'How's the writing gone today, Mama? Did you manage to translate that bit of Latin?'

'I think I've made a bit of progress. It's so nice that some of my family take an interest.'

Felicity visibly squirmed under the implied criticism. 'I'll just go and check on supper.'

Jenny got to her feet, planning to join her. 'Do you want a hand?' But she was not allowed to escape.

'I'm sure Felicity can manage,' said Lady Dalmain firmly. 'Or she wouldn't have invited guests.'

'I just meant with setting the table and stuff.'

'I'm sure Felicity has arranged all that already, and we don't expect guests to help.'

Jenny decided it was time she stood up for herself. 'But I wasn't exactly invited. If you all have to put up with me being here, I think I should pull my weight, domestically.'

'Why are you here?' asked Lachlan, bravely getting his word in before Lady Dalmain could take another pop at Jenny.

She glanced at Philip, hoping he would answer for

her with whatever story he'd told his mother. 'It's a bit complicated,' began Jenny.

'Jenny's come to install a new computer system,' said Philip. 'Designed by her client.'

Although he smiled – charm being so much part of him he couldn't help it – Jenny saw anxiety and resentment in the back of his eyes. She was suddenly aware how much harder it would be delving into a failing company and relaying the failings to her client now she knew the family. Balance statements and figures were all very well, but dealing with human beings was different. Having been treated as a mere component part relatively recently, she knew she would find it hard to be so detached. On the other hand, she was not going to prove Henry right and run away from the challenge.

Now, far away from Henry and his views of her character, she took a breath and smiled. 'I think the new system will be very useful.' She put on a cheerful, positive expression, knowing in her heart that her client was halfway to pulling the plug anyway. She sensed he wanted Dalmain Mills to fail, so he could do something else with either the plant, or the money, or both. Something told her that there was more involved in this particular business than just profit.

Lady Dalmain, who had not been the centre of attention for some moments, reclaimed it. 'Philip, darling, do you think you could go and see what is taking Felicity so long in the kitchen? And tell her to make sure the vegetables are properly cooked. The other night the carrots were almost raw.' She turned her critical gaze on Lachlan. 'So, Mr McGregor, what do you do?'

Lachlan took a breath. Jenny felt a sense of kinship with him. They were alone with the gorgon and either of them might be turned to stone at any moment.

'I'm a peripatetic camelid clipper.'

Jenny took too large a gulp of whisky and coughed, and then turned her attention to an arrangement of dead birds that stared beadily at her from inside a glass coffin.

'I beg your pardon?' demanded Lady Dalmain, no beg about it.

'I travel the country, though I'm in the North and Scotland mostly, clipping llamas, alpacas, and similar animals.'

Lady Dalmain considered, stiffened and became unbearably regal. 'You mean, you're a sheepshearer?' She couldn't have made it sound a less desirable profession if she'd said 'whoremonger'.

'No,' said Lachlan calmly. 'I shear other animals, not sheep.' He held Lady Dalmain's gaze and Jenny noted with relief that she appeared to respect him for it; he may be a manual worker, and therefore quite beyond the pale, but he wasn't a coward.

Jenny found she'd drained her glass and realised that since she'd arrived she'd consumed more neat whisky than in the whole of the previous year. Henry would be horrified. If she were being driven to drink before she'd even spent a night in the place, in what condition would she be by the time the job was finished? She resolved to become teetotal before her liver forced her into it.

'So, Lady Dalmain, do tell me, what is your book about?' Jenny felt it was her turn to break the deadly silence.

'It's really quite involved, Miss Porter, I doubt if you're really interested.'

'I did read history at university, so I might be able to grasp it,' she replied evenly.

'And was it a proper university? Or one of these jumped-up polytechnics?'

'A proper university.' She longed to say Oxford or Cambridge, but was afraid to be caught out in the lie. 'So, please do tell me about your book? I'd be *fascinated* to hear about it.' Oh God, the whisky was affecting her already.

But before she could be fascinated, Felicity and Philip came in. 'It's ready,' said Felicity. She looked hot, her hair was coming down in swathes, and her nose was shiny. She glanced anxiously at Lachlan, checking to see if he'd been turned into a pig, or bore any other physical scars of her mother's rancour. Lachlan, Jenny was touched to observe, smiled reassuringly back.

Philip went to help his mother, although Jenny thought she looked perfectly spry. Felicity went to Lachlan and peeped up at him, suddenly girlish.

Everyone got to their feet and Lady Dalmain said, 'Philip, dear, you lead the way with Miss Porter.' Somehow, she managed to manipulate everyone so that Felicity was last in the queue to leave the room. 'Just see to the fire, dear, will you?' Satisfied that her daughter was in her rightful place in the pecking order, she processed on.

In the way of dining rooms, it was even colder than the rest of the house. A beautiful long mahogany table was set with what must have been Dalmain's best. Jenny saw the Georgian silver cutlery, small and showing centuries of use, the dinner service that could have been Sèvres, and the heavy lead-crystal glasses. There were lace mats under every glass and plate. It was all charming – faded, gracious, an antique collector's dream (she made a note to tell Henry about it) and yet it seemed to Jenny to have poignancy: all this beauty and apparently no happiness.

Lady Dalmain took the head of the table. 'Mr McGregor, if you go on my right, Philip on my left.' She hesitated. Jenny realised she was trying to work out a *placement* that would prevent Felicity sitting next to Lachlan. Lady Dalmain's lips tightened further with the effort. Eventually she gave in. 'Miss Porter, you'd better sit next to my son. Felicity can go next to Mr McGregor.'

We're in for a cheery evening, thought Jenny and smiled desperately around the table. She exchanged glances with Lachlan, whose expression was unrevealing. Felicity came in with a tray and set it on the table.

'Do be careful of my china, Felicity; you know how clumsy you can be, and it's quite irreplaceable.'

Jenny saw Felicity flinch, and wondered how her mother could possibly be so vile to her in public. 'I have lived with it all my life,' said Felicity. 'I know exactly how precious it is.'

'This looks jolly good!' broke in Philip before his mother could reply. 'Well done, Fliss.'

Jenny, seeing the pale, mouse-coloured cubes emerging from the beautiful tureen, couldn't agree with him, but resolved to eat every scrap even if it tasted like pigswill.

Eventually, everyone was served. The plates were

glacial, so by the time it was handed round, the food was too. Had it been hotter, it might have been more appetising; cold, it was like chewing lumps of cloth. The vegetables were cooked to a vitamin-free state and huddled limply round the meat, as if for warmth. The sauce shrouded everything in greyness like a November fog.

Philip stood up and began to pour wine. Jenny decided to become teetotal when she had better control over her personal thermostat. The wine, at least, was delicious.

'I see you've got out the *good* wine,' said Lady Dalmain, having taken a sip.

'Yes, Mama,' said Philip. 'I thought as we had guests we should take a couple of bottles from the cellar.'

'There'll be no more of that when it's gone. Your father expected it to last me out.' Lady Dalmain put down her glass.

'I'm sure it will, Mama,' said Philip, not cast down by his mother like his sister was. 'There's dozens of bottles left. Well, here's to Jenny's safe arrival, and to Lachlan coming back into our lives after all these years.'

Lady Dalmain did not join in the toast.

'So, Felicity, what have you done today?' asked Lady Dalmain.

'This and that. I got Jenny's room ready, cooked supper.'

'That couldn't possibly have taken up your whole day. Mrs Sandison came, didn't she?'

'Yes,' said Felicity. 'But you know she only cleans the reception rooms and yours. She doesn't do the rest of the upstairs.'

'Preparing for visitors always takes me ages,' put in Jenny, quickly. 'All those sheets. And so does cooking.'

Lady Dalmain gave Jenny a quelling look. She turned her Medusa's stare on Lachlan. 'Tell me, Mr McGregor, are you from these parts?'

'No. I hail from nearer Glasgow, Lady Dalmain.'

'Glasgow.' Lady Dalmain gave the city some consideration. 'And what school did you go to?'

'Just the local academy,' said Lachlan.

Lady Dalmain pursed her lips. 'The trouble is, these days, parents just aren't prepared to make the sacrifices so that their children can be decently educated. So that they can enter a profession.'

'Oh come on, Mama. Not everyone can afford private education, however much they might like to,' said Philip, jollying the party along as best he could.

'Yes, and my parents were Socialists,' said Lachlan. 'They wouldn't have educated me privately, even if they could have afforded to.'

Felicity gave a little squeak of distress, obviously wishing she had warned Lachlan not to say things like that.

'And where were you educated, Miss Porter?'

'The local comp – comprehensive school,' said Jenny. 'It had a very good reputation and we prided ourselves on the amount of Oxbridge entrants we had.'

'But you didn't go to Oxford or Cambridge yourself?'

'No.' Jenny wished she hadn't fallen into the trap of trying to please Lady Dalmain. She was a crashing snob and shouldn't be pandered to. If I wasn't so cold, and so far from home, she thought, I wouldn't have succumbed. She longed for Henry: from a good family, educated at all the right places, an expert at saying the right thing. He would be just up Lady Dalmain's street.

Eventually, everyone stopped eating. Although the portions had not been large, eating them seemed to take a long time. No one was tempted to scrape their plates, and no one would have dared to if they had wanted. Jenny wondered if Felicity had been conditioned to make food that people would just pick at and thus not scratch the china. And she wouldn't have been allowed to heat the plates either. Nor would less precious plates, which could have been warmed a little, be permitted. Lady Dalmain probably considered an enthusiasm for food vulgar.

'I'll just go and get the pudding,' said Felicity, having accepted the plates that Jenny handed her and making a pile.

'Felicity, how many times do I have to tell you? Take the plates out one by one. Please don't behave as if we're in some dreadful canteen.'

'It'll take ages like that, Mama,' said Philip, stacking merrily. 'I'll give Fliss a hand.'

Brother and sister bore away the antique china watched anxiously by their mother. Jenny wondered if it all had to be washed in cold spring water and dried, piece by piece, with silk squares, or possibly the hair of a virgin.

Anything would have been preferable to being left in the room with Lady Dalmain. Jenny and Lachlan both tried to speak at the same time.

'Sorry,' said Lachlan, 'you go first.'

'It's all right. I was just going to say how lovely the

scenery was on the drive up,' said Jenny, seeking approval again.

'Yes, we are fortunate to live in a beautiful place.' Lady Dalmain bowed graciously, then added in a chilly voice, 'It's only to be hoped that we will be able to continue to live in it.'

Chapter Four

Jenny swallowed. Lady Dalmain was not supposed to know there was anything wrong with the mill. Now what was she supposed to do? And where was Philip when she needed him?

'Why wouldn't you be able to?' Innocently, Lachlan sprung the trap set for Jenny.

'Because, although dear Philip has tried to protect me from the knowledge, I'm not entirely stupid, and realise that our business is suffering a little difficulty. It happened once before, in Philip's father's time. He mortgaged the house in order to raise money.' She glowered at Jenny, expecting an explanation.

'I don't really know . . .' she began, hearing herself sounding horribly like a schoolgirl in front of the head mistress.

'Oh, I realise that it is not your responsibility, Miss Porter. You obviously work for someone with designs on my house.'

'I'm sure – I'm sure he's got nothing like that in mind,' Jenny said, moderately confident that this was the truth. Her client had given her no indication that he'd gone stark staring mad since she first worked for him. He could not possibly wish to live in this shrine to Caledonian excess. 'I'm just here for the computers.' She copped out, remembering the old saying about living to fight another day. 'I haven't heard anything about the house being involved.'

'All I know,' went on Lady Dalmain, refusing to be pacified, 'is that the home that my dear husband brought me to, as a bride, is at risk. I am sure you'll understand if I am a little defensive.'

'Of course.' Jenny decided to keep her mouth shut. While she *hadn't* heard about the house being involved, it was useful to have the hint that it might be.

Felicity came in with another loaded tray. 'Apple snow,' she announced.

Jenny shivered merely at the name, and waited for Lady Dalmain to declare that her heart was already packed with snow, or something equally poetic and melodramatic. It was a little disappointing that she didn't.

'Have you travelled far today, Jenny?' asked Lachlan, when the apple snow, looking disturbingly like cuckoo spit, had been distributed on tiny, bird-painted saucers.

'Only a couple of hundred miles. I came up the rest of the way yesterday.'

'You must be shattered,' said Felicity. 'All that driving.'

'I'm sure Miss Porter is a perfectly fit young woman,' said Lady Dalmain. 'Not everyone gets tired all the time.'

'Actually, I am quite tired,' said Jenny, who suddenly felt exhausted and saw an opportunity for escape. 'I wonder if you would excuse me? I have to send an email before I go to bed.' She felt a traitor to Felicity, but the thought of leaving that poisonous atmosphere, even if only to retreat to the ice box that was her bedroom, was heavenly.

'Don't you want a cup of coffee?' asked Felicity.

Jenny shook her head. 'It stops me sleeping.'

'Camomile tea?' suggested Philip.

Unable to say she thought it tasted of cat's pee, Jenny shook her head again. 'No, really. I must just email my mother. She'll be worried, it being such a long way from home.'

'And where is home?' enquired Lady Dalmain.

'Guildford,' said Jenny, not bothering to explain that she didn't live there herself. She got to her feet, fatigue, tension and depression weighing her down. 'I am sorry not to help with the washing up or anything, but I will tomorrow, I promise.'

'Until I know you better, Miss Porter, I'd prefer you not to help,' said Lady Dalmain. 'All my china is antique and has to be handled very carefully.'

Not half as carefully as its owner, who'd give a sensitive porcupine a run for its money, thought Jenny, wishing she could say something very rude. She said her good nights, genuinely hoped she'd see Lachlan again, and made her way up to bed.

Upstairs, she brushed her teeth, creamed her face and got into bed, wearing all her clothes, to warm up her bed before facing it in her pyjamas. She pulled the laptop on to her knee and signed on. She was still cross with Henry and certainly wasn't going to tell him how awful it all was, and her mother would be surprised to hear from her again so soon. Never mind.

It's so cold I think I might get hypothermia in the night. Could you please send a hot-water bottle as

54

well as an electric blanket? I don't think they've heard of them here, and there may not be a plug I can use. Lots of love, J.

This done, Jenny got out of bed and undressed quickly, putting her cardigan back on the moment she could. She then found a pair of socks and looked around the room for more bedding. There was a moth-eaten tartan rug on the back of the chair, and although it smelt musty, she added it to the bedclothes. She couldn't be sure, but she had a strong suspicion that the bed was damp.

She lay down and shut her eyes. She was bone-tired but couldn't sleep; she was too cold and tense. What she wanted was a mug of hot chocolate, a hot-water bottle and a good novel. What she had was a damp bed and something off the Booker shortlist that wasn't worth turning the light back on for.

She heard Lachlan leave, and the rest of the family come up to bed. She listened to the trooping along the corridor to the bathroom and thought bitterly about Lady Dalmain's private hot-water supply.

Eventually, when all was quiet, she switched on her bedside light and got up, wondering if she went to the bathroom it would help her settle. She didn't dare go downstairs to the kitchen to find a hot drink in case the dogs woke up and ate her.

She met Felicity coming out of the bathroom.

'Hi,' she said. 'Have you got everything you need? Mama said to put flowers in your room and I forgot.'

'I don't mind not having flowers, but I could really do with something to read. You haven't got anything, have you?'

Felicity chuckled. 'Come with me.'

Felicity's bedroom was full of furniture and books. There were bookcases along every wall, and the shelves were double-stacked. 'It's how I get through,' she said. 'Now, what do you fancy? Light romance, thrillers, fantasy, crime? I've got them all.'

'My goodness, it's like a library.'

'I've got a tame bookshop which posts them to me. Books are my one extravagance, and at least it's one Mama vaguely approves of. Not that she knows what I read. She thinks I just reread the Brontës, Jane Austen and George Eliot. Even Dickens is a bit too much of an easy read for her.'

'You're very patient with her.'

Felicity sighed. 'She can be very difficult if crossed.'

Jenny refrained from further comment and moved to a bookcase. 'Georgette Heyer?'

'I've got them all. Which one do you fancy?'

'I haven't read any for ages.'

'Take a pile. Here.'

Jenny went back to her room. Maybe she would survive this house after all.

In the morning, having put on as many layers as she could, she found her way downstairs. She'd heard the dogs being let out earlier, and hoped they would remember her from last night, and not attack her. She badly needed something hot to drink.

Felicity was in the kitchen, in her dressing gown, with her hair hanging down her back. Her features were smudged from sleep and she did not look happy.

'Good morning,' said Jenny, gently.

'Good morning. Did you sleep all right? I'm just

making Mama's tea. Could you keep an eye on that toast under the grill while I get the milk?'

Jenny thought of all the times her mother had brought her tea in bed when she was waking her up for school. She resolved that she would make her mother tea every day she spent at home.

'Would you like an egg for breakfast?' went on Felicity, setting a tray. 'I'll do you one when I've taken this up.'

Butter, honey and marmalade were put in little cut glass dishes. A small silver teapot was filled with hot water and milk put into a matching jug.

'It's very kind of you to do that for your mother each day. Or is today a special treat or something?'

'No, it's every day. And it's easier to do what Mama wants than to argue. Also, it's nice to have one meal in peace.'

As she watched Felicity take out the tray, Jenny wondered why on earth she was still living at home when she was obviously so unhappy. She noticed that the kitchen table was set for three and assumed that Philip would be along soon.

This was good. She needed to talk to Philip, and wanted to go with him into the mill as soon as she could. She couldn't make any assessments until she'd seen the books. Also, she needed to find out exactly what his mother knew about the situation, so that she could avoid putting her foot in it.

Philip appeared in a smart suit with his skin shiny. He looked as if he might have had a cold shower and enjoyed it.

'Morning, Jenny, morning, Fliss. Good night everyone? The house ghost didn't bother you, Jenny?'

'Don't be silly, Phil; there isn't a house ghost, and don't be so hearty. I can't stand it and I don't suppose Jenny can either. I'm just not a morning person.'

'I'm a morning person after I've had a cup of tea,' said Jenny.

'Here, let me pour it for you,' said Felicity, and handed her a huge breakfast cup and saucer.

'So, are you going to come with me today?' asked Philip, 'or do you want a day to settle in?'

Jenny shuddered and took a sip of tea, hoping it just looked as if she was cold. She *was* cold, but the thought of spending a whole day in that house, with Lady Dalmain constantly sniping at Felicity, was enough to give her violent cabin fever.

'I think I should get down to work straight away.'

'You don't need time to recover from your journey?'

Felicity's question made Jenny feel guilty. She could escape so easily and Felicity seemed stuck here.

'Oh no, I'm fine,' said Jenny. 'Do you find driving tiring?'

'I'm a bit agoraphobic, so I only ever go to Inverness, because I know the way really well. But that's over three hours away, so if I do go, I usually stay over with a friend. Then I don't have to do the journey both ways in one day. I only manage that about three times a year. It's hard for me to get away with so much needing looking after here.'

A banging at the back door reminded Felicity of some of her responsibilities and she went to let the dogs in.

Only halfway down her breakfast cup of tea, Jenny pondered. Was Felicity really so housebound? Could she really not escape her mother's influence and break out on her own?

'Sit down, Jenny, do,' said Felicity, when she had come back in and the dogs had given Jenny a cursory sniff and a more thorough layer of hairs, and settled themselves in a selection of baskets. 'I'll get the eggs on. How many would you like? Two?'

'One and some toast, please. But there's no need for you to wait on me. I could easily do it myself.'

'I'm cooking them for Philip and me anyway, so I might as well.'

Jenny sat down at the table. Philip was already halfway through a piece of toast.

'How is Mama today?'

'She asked me if I was looking after Jenny properly, and didn't I think I should have got dressed before coming down as dressing gowns look so slutty.' Felicity pulled out a chair and sighed. 'Does anyone mind if I smoke? I don't do it when Mama is up, but she never comes down before eleven, and then not in here.'

'Why does Felicity go on living here?' demanded Jenny, when she and Philip were driving away in his low-slung convertible, which at least had a blissfully efficient heater.

'I know my mother seems hard on her,' said Philip, 'but Fliss likes living there really. She could escape if she really wanted to. But a little flat in Glasgow wouldn't suit her. She doesn't have a lot of stamina. I don't think she could manage an ordinary job. And Mama does need someone to look after her.'

'What exactly have you told your mother, Philip? I

thought she wasn't supposed to know there was trouble at t'mill.'

Philip acknowledged this feeble joke with a raised eyebrow. 'She obviously knows more than I've let on. I've tried to keep things from her so she won't worry, but of course Papa ran the mill for years, and he wasn't that good at it, either.'

'Well, I'll try not to tell her anything bad – if there is anything bad, of course.' Jenny smiled. 'It's very kind of her to have me to stay, in the circumstances. I could easily have stayed in a B&B near the mill.'

Philip shook his head. 'My mother likes having people to stay, believe it or not. And it gives both Felicity and her someone new to talk to. Besides,' he shot her a glance, 'if she suspects there are problems, she wouldn't want people to gossip. If you stay with us, there's less chance of people finding out there's anything wrong.'

'I see.' Jenny wondered if she offered to take a vow of silence she would be allowed to stay somewhere warmer, but decided probably not. She changed the subject. 'And what about you? Does living at home cramp your style?'

'Not really. I have a bit more freedom than Fliss has, of course, but no, I like the old place.'

Jenny sat back and looked at the mountains, layer upon layer of them, rising up to the sky. Now, the lower slopes were bright with heather, but in winter, when the heather was over, would they loom gloomily, or inspire the lifting of one's eyes? She sighed. Perhaps she was tired, but this job was already depressing her.

'Oh! Would you mind stopping? There's something

in that shop I need.' They were passing a filling station that had a shop selling woollens and souvenirs attached to it. It was having an end-of-season sale. 'If you could just park somewhere, I'll be in and out in a brace of shakes.'

It wasn't quite a brace of shakes, but when she did emerge, she felt a lot happier. She was wearing a pair of tartan trews and an Aran sweater. Under it she had on a silk polo-necked top. She was carrying a bag containing several lambswool jumpers, a cardigan and a couple of tartan skirts.

'My credit card will need a while to recover from that, but now I think I've got the right clothes.'

Philip looked into the plastic carriers. 'Mmm. All made by the competition, I'm afraid. We just can't compete on price.'

Jenny's brief uplift in spirits faded, but at least she was warm.

'That's so beautiful!' declared Jenny. They came round the corner and there it was, Tombuie, nestling at the base of the hills where two rivers met. 'I had no idea Tombuie was so pretty! And is that the mill?'

She pointed to a group of long, grey buildings, about four storeys high, with regular rows of windows and slate roofs. There was a huge mill wheel at the side of the biggest building. A second glance showed her this was no longer functional, but the whole was extremely picturesque.

'The buildings look fascinating, and I wasn't expecting anything half so attractive. With the mountains going up behind like that, it's delightful!'

'It's all pretty enough, I suppose.' Philip seemed

unmoved by the sight of his heritage but Jenny looked in delight at the millrace, the wide flower borders, stone troughs planted with flowers, and hanging baskets. It was a pretty site for a factory, and someone obviously cared enough about their surroundings to make it even prettier.

Philip ignored the signs to the car park and pulled up outside the entrance to the building. 'Do you mind if I leave you to look at the books this morning?' He got out and came round and opened Jenny's door. 'I've got some things to do.'

Jenny heaved herself up out of the car. 'Well, don't you want to be there with me?' She didn't stand on her dignity, but her visit was important to the company. He should have been taking it all a little more seriously.

He held the swing door open and let her pass. 'To be honest, I know you're going to find things in a bad way, and I know some of it is my fault. But have a good look at the books and you'll be able to tell which is my fault and which is market forces.'

'Market forces' sounded like a good, fat, coverall excuse and Jenny was surprised he'd chosen to use it. Personally she would have liked to make quite sure that anyone scrutinising the figures was absolutely clear on what was what.

Philip signed her in and got her a security badge.

'You don't mind, do you?' he asked as he clipped it on. 'You're not offended?'

She hesitated, wondering if she should tell him the bad impression his attitude had given her. She decided there was no point. She shook her head. 'No. You just show me to the office and introduce me to the staff; I'll have my guided tour later.'

'Oh, you don't want a guided tour, do you? It's only some machines, and not really relevant. It's the books you want to see.'

She didn't point out to him that the figures could have been got to her without her actually driving seven hundred miles to see them. She had been sent so she could get the feel of the place, meet the workforce and recommend decisions based on facts, not on balance sheets.

'Yes, but I'd like to get an idea of the whole business, so that the paperwork relates to something.'

He shrugged. 'Jenny, my whole humble factory is yours to inspect whenever you want but, I'm afraid, today I can't be your guide.'

'Well, whenever. I'll stick with the accounts for now.'

His lack of interest bothered her. It wasn't only his livelihood that was at stake, and that of his mother and sister, but also that of the entire workforce. If Dalmain's went into liquidation, dozens of families would be affected. But maybe Philip felt that somehow he personally would be all right, and so wasn't worrying about anybody else.

As they walked through the building together it occurred to Jenny that her client hadn't expressed a lot of interest in the workers, either. Grant-Dempsey's last email had just asked her to look at profits and losses. He specialised in really short emails, but this one had been even curter than usual. 'Give me the bottom line.' It had annoyed Jenny at the time. Now she was here, and was beginning to see the human side of the business, it seemed even more heartless. Perhaps she shouldn't work for such a blatant capitalist. The trouble was, he was a blatant capitalist who gave her a lot of work and paid her well and promptly, which couldn't be said about all her clients. Henry might tell her that her Mr Grant-Dempsey was using her, but she'd be mad to give him up – he was her route to a bit of independence from Henry, something Jenny wanted badly.

'Come and meet Miss McIntyre, my right-hand woman,' said Philip, opening the door to an office without knocking. 'Kirsty's worked here all her life.'

Late middle-aged, and smartly dressed, from her iron-grey hair to her sensible, leather-shod feet, Philip's 'right-hand woman' was hostile. She was wearing the kind of well-cut tweed that was both warm and smart, if formal. She made Jenny terribly aware of her Aran sweater, her tartan trews and her loafers. If it hadn't already been too late, Jenny felt she would have suffered frostbite rather than have appeared before this woman so eccentrically dressed.

Completely unaware of any tension, Philip breezed on. 'Kirsty, this is Jenny Porter, who's here to sort us all out.'

'Good morning, Miss Porter,' said Kirsty, making her position on the use of Christian names on brief acquaintance quite clear. She had the kind of Scottish accent that made Miss Jean Brodie seem lacking in refinement.

'Good morning, Miss McIntyre,' said Jenny, taking the hint.

Philip turned to Jenny. 'Anything you want, just ask Kirsty. She'll make sure you have everything you need. Now, I'll be off. I've got a lot on.'

Without Philip, Jenny felt the chill of Miss McIntyre's dislike. She looked as if she would make sure Jenny had everything she needed only if it included strychnine.

Jenny swallowed. 'I hope you won't find my visit too much of an intrusion.' It was a hope doomed to die before it had been uttered. Seeing the other woman raise a disapproving eyebrow at her clothes, Jenny felt obliged to explain. 'I brought all the wrong things for Scotland. I had to buy some others. It was either trews or a kilt, and I didn't know which tartan I should have.' Jenny smiled, although she knew she would get no woman-to-woman understanding about sartorial cock-ups from Kirsty McIntyre.

There was not even a twitch. 'Mr Dalmain said you must be allowed to see everything you ask for.' Her scepticism was blatant.

'Yes.' Jenny was emphatic. 'I'm here to help, but I can't unless I know everything.'

'Are you here to help? I had the impression that you were here to prove the company was unviable, and to close us down as soon as possible.'

Jenny suddenly felt too hot in her Aran sweater. It could have been the central heating, but she knew that, really, it was the rush of guilt, because what Miss McIntyre said was probably true.

'I'm to find out what is going wrong with the company. If there's something that can be done to make it go better, well, that is what I'll tell my client and he will act accordingly.'

'Your client?'

'Yes. I'm what is known as a virtual assistant. I work for several clients. Mr Grant-Dempsey and his syndicate are just one of them. We communicate mostly by email.'

Miss McIntyre nodded so slightly it was hardly noticeable. This tiny movement conveyed every negative emotion from disbelief to disgust, barely stopping short of hatred.

Jenny's smile felt artificial, even to her. Fleetingly she wondered if her client stayed in California to avoid actually meeting the people he put out of work, but she rejected the idea. He probably wouldn't be bothered at all. After this job was over, Jenny resolved to dump him, whether she needed his business or not. Without him, she would have to work harder to build up her client base, but there was more to life than money. (She waved her thoughts of a place of her own a reluctant goodbye.)

'What would you like to see?' asked Miss McIntyre, possibly wondering why Jenny had gone silent.

'All the books, and the spreadsheets. And' – for a moment she considered admitting to her need for caffeine, but lost her nerve – 'please could you show me where I could get a cup of coffee, later?'

Chapter Five

It did not take Jenny's postgraduate course in basic accounting to see that the company was not making a profit, nor was it difficult to see why. They were spending far too much on materials and selling finished items far too cheaply. They had financed this expense with a massive loan from M. R. Grant-Dempsey and his syndicate. With this they rented machinery, the payments for which were more than what was coming in most months.

Jenny felt a little warmer towards her capitalist client. He didn't need to have sent her to know what the problem was, and he could have just forced Dalmain's into liquidation without the courtesy of a personal visit from her. Perhaps he did want her to find a way forward for the company, although, if so, why didn't he say?

A little late in the day, she started to wonder about her client. In the eighteen months she had worked for him, he hadn't done any obvious (to her, anyway) asset stripping. But she knew he had an office somewhere in Europe, and kept her for his UK business. It was possible that the European office dealt with his really shady deals.

She chewed her pen, then realised it wasn't hers and put it down quickly. If M. R. Grant-Dempsey had an office already, why did he use her? The whole point of virtual assistants from the client's point of view was that you could have the services of an office and secretary, but not the overheads. Of course, it might have been difficult to send someone from Central Europe to do what she was doing, and if he was abroad he couldn't do it himself. She just had a nagging suspicion that she might have been there as a gesture to correct behaviour when, really, he meant to asset-strip all along. Otherwise, why had he invested in a company that was going nowhere good?

Jenny had been scrutinising the computer screen all morning, trying to find something positive and she had a headache. She was rubbing her forehead with her palms when Miss McIntyre came in. Jenny looked up and saw that although she was holding a cup of coffee, it was not a peace offering.

She put it down firmly. 'Well, Miss Porter, have you managed to pin the blame on anyone?'

Jenny found Miss McIntyre's hostility intensely irritating and unhelpful. Making allowances for the older woman's position, she dredged up her last drop of human kindness and forced a smile. 'Please call me Jenny, or Genevieve, if you prefer. If we are going to work together it would help if . . .' She'd been about to add 'if you weren't so openly unfriendly,' but realised that, of course, she couldn't.

Miss McIntyre wasn't so squeamish. 'I prefer to keep a proper distance between us. I'm sorry, but I'm quite incapable of trying to ingratiate myself with someone who is jeopardising not only my job, but the jobs of many others, people with families to support.'

Jenny took a breath, too angry to count to ten, but

trying for some control. 'Miss McIntyre, I am not asking you to be my friend, I am only asking for a little co-operation. I'm not entirely stupid. I know perfectly well how communities are affected when the main employer goes. But it would be a lot easier for me to find something constructive to say about this company if I had someone to answer a few questions! For example – why do you appear to have a shed full of wool when it says here that only a few bales a week are being used?'

Miss McIntyre clenched her teeth. 'It was a management decision taken at the time for which I was in no way responsible.'

'I'm not holding you responsible! I only want to know why!' Then, feeling she'd been a little too outspoken she sighed, and started again. 'I'm not Sir John Harvey-Jones; I can only report back what I find, but I would like to report something good about this company, even if it makes no difference, even if it's just to stop me having to say that this is a tin-pot little mill that makes cheap jumpers for the tourist trade and can't sell them at a profit! And that didn't come out right. I'm sorry.'

The two women faced each other, both on the defensive. Jenny wished fervently that she'd just said, 'Thank you for the coffee.' There was enough hostility in the world without her antagonising Philip's 'right-hand woman' even further.

Miss McIntyre pursed her lips, as if she was contemplating making some concession, but was not quite ready to back down. 'I'm sorry if I appear unco-operative,' she began. 'It's just that there's no other employment hereabouts. A lot of people depend on this mill, and have done for a long time. It employs at least one parent of almost all the children in the school. If the mill closes, people will move away and the school will close. Even those who have jobs in tourism or agriculture will move if they can. The whole community will die.'

'I know,' said Jenny, touched how talking about her beloved mill made this buttoned-up woman suddenly passionate. She was not the only one who cared about their workplace. The flower-filled troughs and hanging baskets were evidence of that. 'And I promise you,' she went on, 'if there's anything I can do to prevent the mill closing, I will do it.'

The second the words had left her mouth she wondered how she'd let them escape when she had no way of following them up. She must have been mad! Henry would say it was because she was impulsive, sentimental and foolishly optimistic. It was a shame you couldn't unsay words in the way you could 'unsend' emails. Already a little colour had crept into Miss McIntyre's cheeks. She didn't exactly smile but she did relax her hold on her lips a little.

'The wool is there because a manager we had years and years ago was once held up by a dock strike. Couldn't get wool for weeks. Since then, it's been company policy to maintain large supplies.'

'I see.' Jenny didn't comment on the folly of tying up thousands of pounds in stock that probably wouldn't realise its value in finished products.

'So,' went on Miss McIntyre, 'what can you possibly do?'

Jenny bit her lip and shook her head. 'I don't know. Possibly nothing. But I don't have to report back immediately. I can take my time, look at all the options, and then try and make a case for keeping Dalmain's open. I will need a little help, though. I know nothing about textiles, I only understand figures, and it's not rocket science to see that if you pay too much for your raw materials and then turn out a low-cost final product, with the help of expensive machinery, you're not going to be financially viable.'

Miss McIntyre regarded Jenny. 'I've worked for this company all my life, my father before that, and it has not always produced "a low-cost final product".' Her disdain dripped from the words. 'There was a time when Dalmain's had a name for quality!'

Jenny said nothing for a few moments. Her brain was in a whirl – thoughts about wool, machinery, the beauty of the surroundings, bumping randomly into each other, making no sense. She wasn't worried, it happened sometimes. Eventually, the thoughts would settle down into something that might be quite logical. She once tried to explain this process to Henry but he had only laughed.

'When you've had your coffee,' said Miss McIntyre, 'shall I show you round? It might be useful for you to meet some of the workers.'

Jenny forced a smile. 'I'd like that,' she lied, knowing perfectly well she should have refused. Once she'd actually spoken to the workers, the thought of putting them out of work would be even more horrendous. She'd been in that situation herself – being treated like some surplus machinery. It was only when you'd experienced it that you understood why redundant workers referred to themselves as being 'on the scrap heap'.

And while she'd made a wild promise that she would do what she could to save their jobs, she probably couldn't do anything. Money would have the loudest voice here – a few jobs more or less would mean little or nothing to M. R. Grant-Dempsey and his syndicate.

But she couldn't tell Miss McIntyre that she had been wrong, there was no point in meeting the people, that the whole mill was doomed, not after she'd promised to do what she could.

She gave a deep, shuddering sigh. Her first loyalty was to her client, but he was just an email address. He paid her handsomely and regularly, for the work she did, but she didn't know him. They hadn't even spoken on the phone. How could she feel more loyalty to him than to people who planted hanging baskets and had children? Especially now, when she had started to wonder about his motives.

Miss McIntyre took her into a huge building, about half the size of an aircraft hangar. It was incredibly noisy and had wooden floors that were tacky underfoot. Miss McIntyre reached into a box and produced two bright yellow pieces of foam. 'Put them in your ears. It's a Health and Safety regulation.'

It would have been hard to hear anyway, because of the noise of the machinery, but with her ears stuffed with polystyrene, Jenny could catch little of what Miss McIntyre said.

'The floor's tacky because of the lanolin,' she eventually comprehended, after several seconds of 'I beg your pardon?', 'what's that?' and 'say again?' 'Off the wool. This is where the process starts. We buy in the wool, mostly . . .'

Jenny gave up trying to hear. She just saw the huge machines, was fascinated by their complexity, smiled at the workers who regarded her with curiosity and, sometimes, hostility. Huge bales of wool, each the size of a car, looms metres long, minded by just one person, a huge machine that fluffed up the wool, turning it into something like candyfloss – the images were confusing, and she knew it would take her a little time before she understood what was going on. But she was fascinated, and knew she couldn't let all this industry, energy and power fall silent if she could possibly prevent it.

At the end of the day, when Philip reappeared to drive her home, Jenny felt tired, deeply depressed and very cross with him. If he hadn't abandoned her to do God knows what, Miss McIntyre wouldn't have got to her. The workers would have remained numbers on the spreadsheet, they would not have become Maisie Nisbet, whose family had worked in the mill for three generations and could rethread a machine in ten seconds, or Donald Mackeen, who'd just got married, whose wife was already expecting and had an invalid mother, or any of the other, real, people she had met. She was a virtual assistant, she shouldn't have to deal with real people. And if she hadn't met them, her job would have been simple. She could have just emailed her client about what she'd discovered and gone home.

It wouldn't have been quite as simple as that, of course; there were a lot more details she had to go into, but another fortnight would have done it. Then she could have upped and offed, left the Hammer House of Horrors, and fled back to Henry, and the South, where winter didn't come until the end of November.

The moment she got through the door of Dalmain House the atmosphere closed round Jenny like a cold blanket. She felt trapped, suffocated by the narrow lives of those who lived here. After the bustle of the mill, the house seemed static and inert.

Felicity was waiting with a tray of drinks. Without asking either of them what, if anything, they wanted, she presented them each with a very large measure of whisky. Although from choice, Jenny would have had a cup of tea, she took the offered glass and only remembered her resolution regarding strong drink when she'd taken a substantial gulp.

'There's a telephone message for you,' said Felicity.

'For me?' Instantly, she tried to remember who knew she was here. Apart from Henry, her client and her mother, there was no one. If it was Henry demanding her return so she could cook for his cousins, he could whistle. If it was her client, that was fine, although uncharacteristic. Her mother would only ring if it was an emergency.

'It's Meggie. She says it's urgent. Can you ring her, or better still pop down.' Felicity regarded Jenny with suspicion. 'I'd forgotten that you knew her.'

'I don't really know her. We just got chatting when I called in at The Homely Haggis.'

Felicity winced at the name, which was fairly wince-worthy. 'Well, if you want to visit, there's plenty of time before supper.' There was an edge of resentment in Felicity's voice, as if Jenny was being in some way disloyal.

'I can't. I've just had a sip of whisky large enough to put me over the limit on its own. I mustn't drive.'

'You can walk to Meggie and Iain's.' said Philip. 'You don't mind a bit of a downhill stroll, do you?'

Actually, some fresh air, positive company, and a little time away from Dalmain House seemed extremely attractive.

'I would quite like a walk, but not if Felicity would like a hand with the supper?'

Felicity shook her head. 'Oh, it's all right. It's all ready. I've nothing else to do all day, after all, and you've been working. You go and visit Meggie.'

Jenny resolved that soon she must learn more about Felicity, but not now. 'Is it easy to find, or will I get lost?'

'I doubt it. You can see the house from the front,' said Philip.

'It's a pity you can't take the dogs, but they'd never go with you,' said Felicity, still ambivalent.

'And Meggie wouldn't thank you for them in her condition,' said Philip. 'She must be very near her time.'

'Huh, women like her have babies like shelling peas,' said Felicity, sounding unnervingly like her mother.

Jenny saw the shadow of loss behind her eyes and wondered if Lady Dalmain had completely stolen Felicity's life, or if Felicity had in part relinquished it.

'I'll lend you a coat,' said Felicity. 'There's a fierce wind and you won't have anything thick enough.'

*

A tall young man, recognisably a Dalmain, opened the door to the little white cottage. 'Hello!' He crushed Jenny's hand. 'You must be Jenny. Meggie's on the sofa, she'll be pleased to see you.'

The front door opened straight into the sitting room. A fire burnt enthusiastically, vying with the curtains and rugs for brightness. In front of it, on a sofa, lay Meggie, looking weary and depressed.

'They say I can't do The Homely Haggis any more. That it's too much for me and I must close up for the rest of the season,' she announced, without preliminaries. 'No one takes my business seriously.'

'Ah . . .' said Jenny.

'Come and sit down, Jenny,' said Iain. 'Can I get you something to drink? Wine? A cup of tea? We can't run to whisky I'm afraid.'

'A cup of tea would be wonderful.'

'Run and get it then, Iain,' said Meggie, waving a hand. 'And let me talk to Jenny.'

'So, what can I do for you?' Jenny knew perfectly well what Meggie was about to say, but wanted to give herself a little time to think about her answer.

'You know, don't you? The Homely Haggis. If you can't keep it going for me, at least occasionally, I might not be able to open again next summer. You did sort of offer . . .'

Jenny sighed. 'I'd really like to help but –'

'Then help! No one understands how important my business is to me! They don't understand that it's my independence and I can't bear the thought of losing it. They all think it's just a "little hobby".'

'That is *so* irritating! I do understand. Because I work

from home, my boyfriend doesn't really believe I work at all. It's one of the reasons I came up to Scotland, to prove to him that I do.'

Iain back in, holding a tea towel. 'I don't think The Homely Haggis is a little hobby,' he said firmly. 'I just think that you have to think of the baby now.'

'I do think of the baby! I just want to keep a little stake in the future which doesn't include the baby! And supposing something happens' – Meggie paused – 'and there isn't a baby?' she added in a very small voice.

Iain took a breath, not wanting to continue with what was obviously a well-worn argument.

Jenny broke in. 'I quite understand how Meggie feels. She knows in her head that life is never going to be the same after the baby is born, but part of her wants to cling onto a bit of her old life.'

Meggie regarded Jenny gratefully. 'That's it! That's exactly how I feel! You are clever!' She paused for hardly a moment. 'So does all that insight mean you'll do The Homely Haggis for me?'

Iain sighed deeply. 'I'll go and make the tea.'

'He seems really nice,' said Jenny.

'He is, and I'm lying here being a cow as well as looking like one. I'm just so fed up.' Meggie suddenly frowned. 'Why are you wearing tartan trousers?'

Jenny looked down at them. 'I didn't bring warm enough clothes. I bought these on the way into the mill. Bright, but cosy. I'm just glad my boyfriend can't see me. He'd die laughing.'

'A man who cares about what you look like? That's nice.'

'Not if it means he makes disparaging comments

every time I wear something he hasn't helped me choose. He's actually a bit of a fashion fascist.'

'Oh. Perhaps I'm better off with Iain who never notices what I've got on.'

Iain appeared with the tea. 'I always notice; I just don't always comment. Now, Jenny, don't let yourself be bullied into doing anything you don't want to do. Meggie can be very persuasive.'

'So go away and let me be persuasive,' said his wife. 'Will you do The Homely Haggis for me?'

'The trouble is, I've no idea how long I'm likely to be here.'

'Why? Is the business going to close down immediately?'

'No! At least I hope not. I haven't had a chance to find out what's what, yet. But what I'm saying is, I don't know how long it's all going to take. I mean, I could say yes, and then be off after a fortnight.'

'You could spin it out then, couldn't you? Make it a bit longer?'

'Technically, as he's my client, not my boss, that would be fraud, as he's paying me a lot extra to be here . . .'

'Oh please! Just say you'll do it for a bit, until I can find someone else.'

Jenny was tired. She'd travelled a long way to get here, her hosts were all damaged in some way, and the business she was investigating was going straight down the tubes. Out of habit, she asked herself what Henry would say. *'For God's sake! You'd never cope. Remember that time you were cooking breakfast for friends after we'd stayed up all night? You couldn't fry more than one egg at a time!'*

Jenny was pleased she'd thought of this – it made the decision so easy.

'I'd love to help, although you'll have to get someone to show me everything, and I might be hopeless. I wasn't that good yesterday.'

Meggie flapped a hand. 'Goodness me! You had no idea what you were doing and he was a difficult customer. I'll come up and show you everything. It'll be a breeze.'

'A howling gale, more like,' said Jenny, 'and I'm not being responsible for anything happening to you or the baby, so you find someone else to show me round.'

'OK. There is a girl who used to help me out before she got a proper job. She can show you the ropes. It's dead simple. You only have to open the odd evening, and at weekends. The weekends are the most important. I'll arrange it.' Satisfied with her evening's work, Meggie settled back into her cushions. 'Are you going into the mill with Philip?'

'I did today, but from now on I'm going to take my own car, and be a bit more independent.' She drained her mug. 'I'd better be getting back. I don't want to be late for supper when Felicity's spent all day cooking it.'

'She won't have spent long cooking it. You'll have noticed that she's not a very good cook.'

'No, but she's doing it, and it can't be easy. You're right about her mother. She's a monster.'

'She is. Like a huge spider, sitting in the middle of the family manipulating them all, pulling them in if they stray too far.'

'Difficult mother-in-law, then?' Jenny laughed.

Meggie pshawed dismissively. 'I don't give two

hoots about her! I just can't bear what she does to the others. Iain has more or less escaped, but Felicity and Philip are completely messed up, both of them.'

'I thought Philip was a bit ineffectual maybe, but not necessarily messed up.'

'Why has he never married, then? He's nearly forty and he's not gay but he's never dared take anyone home to meet his Mama. He's afraid she'd eat them. And not without reason. As for Felicity . . .'

'Poor Felicity.'

'I do feel very sorry for her,' Meggie acknowledged, determined to be fair, 'but why doesn't she get out? It's because she couldn't hack the downgrade. If she left home she'd have to live in some hovel. Somewhere, like this . . .'

'This is hardly a hovel.'

'No, I know it's not, but to Felicity and Lady D. it is. The family name for us is "Love in a Cottage".'

Jenny laughed. 'That's quite sweet.'

'I suppose so. At the moment I've got cabin fever, not being allowed out.'

'It'll be worth it, when the baby's born.'

Meggie made a face. 'How do you know? You haven't children of your own.'

'It's what everyone says; it must be true!' She got up. 'Now I must go. I can't risk offending anyone on practically my first day.'

'I suppose not.'

Jenny glanced round the room, looking at it more carefully than when she'd arrived. The curtains, cushions and throws were all woollen, all full of texture and interest. Scraps of lurex were woven in among the wools, bits of felt and even raffia.

'What did you do before you got married to Iain?' she asked.

'Textiles. I met Iain at college. His family practically disowned him for actually wanting to study what his family made their money from. Why do you ask?'

'No particular reason. Now, I must rush up the hill and eat my dinner. I'll be in touch about The Homely Haggis.'

'Oh, Jenny –'

'Yes?'

'Tartan is such a good look for you . . .'

Jenny stuck her tongue out.

'I'll run you up the hill,' said Iain. 'You must be tired.'

Jenny didn't even make a token protest. She *was* tired; in fact now she felt exhausted. And the prospect of dinner didn't make her feel any less so.

'That would be wonderful. I know it's not far –'

'But it's uphill,' Meggie finished for her. 'I'll put the spuds on,' she added to Iain.

'Now don't –'

'Away with ye, laddie!' she exclaimed, exaggerating her accent to comic proportions. 'I'm not an invalid, you know. I am allowed to totter into the kitchen from time to time.'

'I don't know her well,' said Jenny, when she and Iain were shooting up the hill in his van, 'but I don't imagine she's very good at slowing down.'

'You're right there! She has two paces, fast and stop, and she hasn't located the stop button yet.'

'You must be worried.'

'A bit. She's young and healthy and there's no reason why she shouldn't be fine, it's just . . .'

81

'They wouldn't have suggested she should do less if there wasn't just something?'

'That's it.'

'Well, you can tell her I'll be glad to do The Homely Haggis. The prospect of spending every evening making polite conversation to Lady Dalmain – oh, sorry – I forgot she's your mother.'

'Oh say what you like about her! The old bat! Anyway – here you are – at the Bat Cave.'

Iain pulled on the handbrake and Jenny regarded Dalmain House. 'Not so much a cave as a really great venue for a Halloween Party.'

Iain laughed as she clambered out and then shot away, wasting no time in returning to his own cosy little house.

Chapter Six

꧁꧂

Jenny let herself in and glanced at her watch. It was only ten to seven, but as she was about to go upstairs to change, Felicity came out of the drawing room.

'Oh, there you are. Come and have a drink.'

Jenny really had been hoping for a moment to change out of her tartan trousers and check her emails, but that obviously wasn't an option. Nor was the prospect of more whisky very appealing, though it would look rude to refuse. 'I'd love one, but I must just wash my hands,' she said.

'Don't be too long. Mama is waiting.'

Lady Dalmain seemed in an unusually good mood. She said 'thank you' to Felicity when she was handed her drink, and smiled at Jenny, an experience that was not as pleasant as it might have been, because she had very bad teeth, but Jenny was gratified, all the same.

'And how did you get on at the mill today?' Lady Dalmain asked. To Jenny's relief, she didn't wait to listen to the answer before adding, 'Philip, you must take some time to show Jenny the countryside. It's so beautiful around here.' She bestowed another brown-toothed smile on Jenny and Philip. 'You might even take the day off and take her up to that nice hotel. Do you remember?'

'But, Mama, it's miles!' said Felicity.

'I'm sure they can spare a little time away from the mill. Isn't that right, Philip?'

Jenny became uncomfortably aware that Lady Dalmain was matchmaking. She had decided Jenny was sufficiently genteel and well-behaved, and she was setting her up with Philip.

Philip and Felicity were now arguing gently about how far this particular hotel was, and how long it would take to drive there. Lady Dalmain was contradicting Felicity, although it was clear that she herself hadn't been for many years. Jenny took the time to think about Philip.

He was charming and good-looking in a Henry sort of way, but it wasn't with Henry that Jenny found herself comparing him. It was with the awful customer, who had been so demanding and so unpleasant. Why he should have ingrained himself into her memory was uncertain. She didn't remember him being particularly good-looking, although he was tall and dark. Was it his voice? His energy? Or what? Henry and Philip could both be described as handsome, whereas he never could. But there was something a bit dangerous about him.

She sipped her whisky, aware she was getting to like it. Should she consider swapping Henry and his quite demanding family for Philip, and his mother? She chuckled. Not bleedin' likely, she thought, disguising her smile.

'Well, Jenny?' asked Philip. 'What do you think?'

'It sounds as if the hotel is rather far away,' she said. 'And I will be extremely busy at the mill. On the other hand, it would be lovely to see a bit more of the country. Although I could explore on my own, if you're busy.'

'Not a good idea at this time of the year,' said Lady Dalmain firmly. 'Tourists show no respect for their surroundings. The weather can change very quickly. Far better go with Philip.'

'Or perhaps Felicity would go with me?'

'Felicity suffers from agoraphobia,' said Lady Dalmain. 'It means she can't go out at all. Very tiresome.'

It wasn't clear if Lady Dalmain meant having agoraphobia was tiresome, or Felicity was for having it. Jenny thought probably the latter.

'I'll go and look at what's going on in the kitchen,' said Felicity.

Jenny didn't offer to go with her. She felt too tired to be of much use, and Lady Dalmain probably wouldn't let her help, anyway.

'I had to go to Inverness today,' said Philip, glancing at Jenny, 'and I got this for you, Mama.'

It was wrapped in a paper bag and turned out to be a small, leather-bound book.

'Darling!' Lady Dalmain was ecstatic. 'I've been looking for this for ages, but none of my book services has been able to find it! You are clever!'

He laughed. 'I have my secret suppliers. Toshak and Fiske. Never been known to let me down.'

Jenny regarded Lady Dalmain and Philip enjoying each other's company. Of course she was happy for them, but she couldn't help wondering if perhaps Philip could have got his secret suppliers to post the book to Lady Dalmain. Unless, of course, Philip had other business in Inverness.

He sensed her looking at him and blushed slightly. 'Let's not fall out, Jenny.'

Jenny smiled. 'I hardly ever fall out with people,' she said. 'I think it makes me rather bland.' Then she remembered that man again. She'd had no trouble falling out with him at all.

'Not in the least,' he said gallantly. 'But I wouldn't want you to think badly of me.'

Before she could ask him why on earth she should, Felicity came in to announce that the meal was ready.

Philip produced another couple of bottles of wine from the cellar and poured them lavishly, paying particular attention to his mother's glass. She glowed with pleasure, showing a charming side to herself Jenny hadn't suspected. Even Felicity was included, and Lady Dalmain praised the apple crumble, which in Jenny's opinion was undercooked.

As on the previous evening, Jenny wasn't allowed to help with the washing up. She didn't protest too hard as she was longing for her emails and her bed. Perhaps it was being so far from home, she thought, as she went upstairs, that made one so dependent on communication.

There was nothing from Henry, but she sent him one. Her mother had said,

Don't feel obliged to sort out everyone's problems, darling. You know what you're like.

She replied,

Don't worry, I've only taken on the running of a fast

food outfit and promised to save an entire factory. Nothing drastic.

She knew it would make her mother laugh and shake her head.

Jenny was aware of a lot of commotion downstairs when she woke up. She looked at her clock and saw that it was only seven. She had just decided that whatever it was, it was nothing to do with her, when Felicity stuck her head round the door, her hair about her shoulders, looking as if the entire cast of *The Lord of the Rings* had appeared to her in the night, leaving her frazzled.

'It's awful! Philip's left home!'

Jenny got up.

She threw on as many layers of clothes as she could easily find and went downstairs.

The noise was appalling. Lady Dalmain, her hair in a tidy plait, was standing in the hallway wearing an old tartan dressing gown, probably her late husband's. She was holding a piece of paper. She was obviously in shock. The dogs, disrespectful of the situation, had decided on this moment to quarrel and were desperately trying to out-bark each other. By now, Felicity was holding a bottle of brandy and a glass, wondering whether to give it to her mother, or drink it herself.

When she saw Jenny, she shouted, 'Philip's gone missing!'

'So you said, but he was here last evening,' she shouted back. 'You have to be gone at least a day to go missing. Otherwise it's just "out".'

'You don't understand,' Felicity yelled back. 'He left a note.'

'These bloody dogs!' said Jenny, unable to bear being deafened any longer. She opened the door of the dog room and bellowed, 'Dogs!' at the top of her voice, forgetting that two days ago she'd been scared of them. 'In here! At once!'

Totally surprised at this attack from an unexpected quarter, the dogs stopped fighting and stared at her. Then, recognising a greater authority than their own, they trotted obediently into the dog room and Jenny shut the door. Immediately, they realised they were missing out on the fun and started trying to break back through the door again. Jenny, finding this noise as hard to cope with as the barking, went into the larder and came out with a bag of dog biscuits, then she opened the door, hurled in the biscuits, and waited for quiet.

'They're all on diets, you know,' said Felicity. 'You shouldn't have done that.'

'I don't care. I can't think with all that noise going on. Lady Dalmain, are you all right?'

'Of course I'm not all right, you stupid girl! How could I possibly be all right when my dearest son has run away with – with' – she searched for a word that was both damning and genteel – 'a hussy!'

'I can see that might be difficult,' said Jenny firmly, trying not to see the funny side, 'but standing here wringing your hands isn't going to help. Can I suggest you go into the drawing room and sit down? You need some Rescue Remedy. Perhaps you could put the kettle on, Felicity?'

Lady Dalmain was as unaccustomed as the dogs to

being told what to do by a comparative stranger. Like them, she was surprised into obedience, and allowed Jenny to lead her to a chair by the fireside. Jenny pulled a moth-eaten plaid off the sofa and put it over Lady Dalmain's knees. Then, spotting a small electric heater behind a chair, she got it out and risked her life by plugging it in. She switched it on and was relieved not to find herself flung across the room by faulty electrics.

Lady Dalmain began to make moaning noises, though whether she was grieving for her son or complaining about Jenny's profligate use of electricity was unclear.

'Wait there,' Jenny said firmly, 'I've got something that will make you feel much better. I'll just go and get it.'

She went into the hall where Felicity was still standing, now with two tumblers of brandy in her hands. 'No, thank you; I'd better keep a clear head,' she said, and ran upstairs for her handbag.

She was back with Lady Dalmain in minutes. Producing a small brown bottle, she said, 'Under your tongue, please.' Quickly, she squirted half a pipette of Rescue Remedy into Lady Dalmain's surprised mouth.

'What is that stuff?' she asked, having swallowed it.

'It's Rescue Remedy. It's for when you need to calm down really quickly. Now,' went on Jenny, while Lady Dalmain was still thinking about this, 'what has happened?'

'I don't sleep well, you know,' Lady Dalmain began. She shot Felicity a look. 'Unlike some I don't depend on sleeping pills. I happened to be looking out of the window when I saw Philip leave the house. I knocked on the window, of course. But although he saw me – he definitely saw me – he just waved, in a rather sad way, I fancy, and got into his car. Naturally I woke Felicity.'

'I went downstairs and found a note.'

'Can I read it?' Jenny wanted to make sure it didn't just say, 'Back late for supper' or something.

Lady Dalmain handed it to her.

Dearest Mama, *it read,*

I know you're going to think me an awful coward, but I'm doing what I think is best for the family and the business. I have made an awful mess of things, got the company into debt, with loans it can't service. It's better now if I'm out of the way. I do hope you don't lose Dalmain House, which I know is so important to you. I think there should be enough money left to prevent that, at least.

I'm going to marry Gloria, whom you have never met, and I am afraid do not approve of, but we love each other, and are going to make a new life together.

I have taken Papa's shotguns to sell, for a bit of ready cash. He did leave them to me in his will, so they are mine to take, but I know they really belong to the family. I am sorry about this. I don't see another way to go about things.

The book was by way of a farewell present.

Your loving son, Philip.

Jenny sat on the chair opposite Lady Dalmain and helped herself to a shot of Rescue Remedy. Did Philip realise that by running away he had speeded up the demise of Dalmain Mills by a factor of ten?

'Oh,' she said.

'Have a brandy,' said Felicity, handing her mother a glass. 'I can't believe Philip's really upped and left!'

Possibly the Rescue Remedy had had some effect because Lady Dalmain went from distraught to angry in a very short space of time. 'How could he have done this to me? Those guns were worth ten thousand pounds!'

'Were they?' demanded Felicity.

'Hang on a minute,' said Jenny. 'I thought you were broken-hearted because Philip had run off with an unsuitable woman. Now it seems you're upset because he's stolen some valuable heirlooms. Could you just clarify for me, which is worse?'

Lady Dalmain frowned, aware that she might have appeared mercenary. 'No, no, it's Philip I'm grieving for, but the guns belonged to his father. It's their sentimental value I regret. I always clung on to them, however bad things were, because they were his.' Lady Dalmain closed her eyes and rested the back of her hand against them; she could have been modelling for a painting called *Mother, on Hearing of the Death of her Hero Son*.

Jenny was decidedly sceptical. Guns were hardly the sort of thing you'd want to curl up in bed with.

'Well, you've still got Iain and Felicity.' And probably a lot of other valuable items stashed away somewhere, she added silently.

'Yes,' said Felicity, obviously hurt. 'And I wouldn't run off with the family silver, in case you're wondering.'

'I'll go and see if the kettle's boiling,' said Jenny, not wanting to be alone with two women who seemed to care more about antiques than family members.

'I'll ring Iain and Meggie,' said Felicity.

'It's only half-past seven,' murmured Jenny.

'I'm not having that woman in my house!' said Lady Dalmain.

'Oh Mama, don't be ridiculous!' said Felicity, to Jenny's surprise and admiration. 'Iain was always an early riser. And Meggie's Iain's wife, and she's about to have your first grandchild. Who knows, we may get lucky and it'll be a boy!' She paused and added under her breath, 'I hope it is, for Meggie's sake, because if it isn't, it won't even get a rattle for its christening, let alone the Jacobean quaich picked out for Philip's first child.'

'Felicity!' said Lady Dalmain. 'How dare you speak to me like that? In front of guests, too!'

'Sorry.' Felicity took a large gulp of the brandy she was still holding. 'I just get a little fed up with Philip being the blue-eyed boy.'

'But I have never discriminated between my children! I love you all, equally!'

'Some more equally than others,' muttered Felicity, putting her hand on her mother's shoulder and patting it, awkwardly. Lady Dalmain produced a lace-edged handkerchief from her dressing-gown pocket and considered crying.

'I'll just go and make some tea. Or would anyone prefer coffee? Then I could ring Iain for you. While you look after your mother,' said Jenny, from the doorway.

Felicity stopped patting. 'No! I'll do it. I want the satisfaction of telling them what Philip has done! You stay here. Mama'll be better with you, anyway.'

'I want tea, please,' said Jenny, not convinced she would get any. Lady Dalmain was staring into space, clutching her handkerchief, her jaw slack. Her brandy glass was empty.

'I expect this'll all blow over.' Jenny took the glass before it fell. 'I dare say Philip will lie low for a while and then come back with his bride, and possibly a baby. Wouldn't that be lovely? If Meggie doesn't have a boy, maybe Philip's wife will.'

Lady Dalmain shuddered. 'That woman is past child-bearing age.'

'She may not be,' said Jenny, who had no idea how old the woman was, she could very well be sixty. 'He just ran away to give you time to get used to the idea of him being married. He won't want to lose touch with you. He loves you. He just wants a home life of his own. You mustn't take this personally.'

On reflection, Jenny thought that maybe this had been a platitude too far, as there was no way in the world that Philip's behaviour had not been about Lady Dalmain personally. But as Lady Dalmain seemed not to be listening, she didn't bother to explain further.

'I cannot understand his ingratitude, after all I've done for him! And him, so like his father!'

'I'm sure he'll come back,' Jenny murmured.

'Tell me, dear,' said Lady Dalmain. 'What exactly are you supposed to be doing at the mill? Is it in such trouble that Philip needs to run away from it?'

Trying not to feel personally responsible for the mill's difficulties, Jenny took a breath. 'Things are quite bad, I think. Obviously I haven't had much chance to look. But I'm afraid Philip's disappearance is not going to help.'

'Then you must find him!'

'But I can't! I have no idea where he might have gone

93

to! No, what I should be doing – will be doing – is trying to sort out the mill.'

'It's not the mill that's important!' said Lady Dalmain, suddenly angry. 'It's Dalmain House! This is my home! I can't be turned out of it by a lot of – lot of – businessmen!'

Felicity came in. 'Iain and Meggie are on their way up.'

'I'd better get properly dressed,' said Jenny. 'I must go into the mill as soon as I can and tell Kirsty.'

Lady Dalmain shuddered. 'That woman! Thinks she owns the mill, just because her parents worked there. She's always been after Philip.'

Jenny just managed to get out of the house before Meggie and Iain arrived. It wasn't that she didn't want to see them, but saying hello would take up precious time, and Jenny wanted to get to the mill as soon as possible.

She didn't get there before Kirsty did, and the moment Jenny saw her, she could tell she already knew about Philip.

'He telephoned me,' she said, moderately calm, but extremely worried. 'He shouldn't have done it. He shouldn't have just run away like that, leaving things the way they are. It's dereliction of duty. How can we get the mill back on track again with him gone?'

Jenny inhaled deeply, and then exhaled again, hoping Kirsty wouldn't hear the sigh. 'I really don't know. We'll have to have a look. But now I've got to have a hot drink. Dalmain House could only provide brandy this morning.'

*

Jenny was on her second cup of coffee and was looking through a file that seemed to have nothing in it which was either of use or ornament when Kirsty came in. 'The post's come.'

'Bad news?'

'Probably. His nibs is coming.'

'Who?'

'The man the mill owes all the money to. M. R. Grant-Dempsey.'

There was a long silence. The name hung in the air, neither woman wanting to acknowledge the significance of it.

'Oh hell,' breathed Jenny.

Kirsty nodded. 'Which means we have three weeks to get this mill in some sort of shape, with some sort of future, or he'll just come in and send everyone home.'

Jenny gave herself a mental shake. As a virtual assistant, she wasn't used to being responsible for people's jobs – it wasn't part of her job description. But she wasn't stupid, she had ideas, imagination, and she had Kirsty, who, even on such short acquaintance, seemed to have a lot of other good points.

'Well, it will be tough, and we may not manage it, but I'm sure we can do something in the time. And when M. R. Grant-Dempsey arrives, we'll just have to talk him into giving the mill a stay of execution.'

This wasn't having the bracing effect on Kirsty that it was designed to have. 'There's a problem.'

'A problem! Ha! There are billions of problems, we just have to solve them.'

'But it won't be easy, with half the papers in my office gone. Philip's taken them. I'm not exactly sure what's missing yet, but if he's taken them away, you can be sure they were useful.'

There was a long silence.

'Oh fuck.'

'I don't approve of bad language,' said Kirsty, sounding very like Miss Jean Brodie, 'but "oh fuck" seems entirely appropriate just now.'

Chapter Seven

Being behind the counter of The Homely Haggis gave Jenny a wonderful sense of peace. It was such bliss to be alone. Since Kirsty had announced that Philip had taken half the files in the office, she had been on the go. She and Kirsty had gone through everything, finding what was missing by a process of elimination. All the copies of the deeds to the mill and Dalmain House were gone, also the papers saying what had been put up as security. Further copies of the deeds could be obtained, although Kirsty was reluctant to do anything to draw attention to the situation, but it was still going to be difficult to work out what Philip had pledged.

Fortunately Kirsty had a good memory, but by the time Jenny had gone home, they still didn't know quite where they were financially. And as Jenny had driven the beautiful journey back to Dalmain House, she'd been unable to help wondering if perhaps giving in wasn't the best solution. Perhaps when Mr Grant-Dempsey appeared she should just tell him that Philip had run off and that there seemed no practical way forward for the mill.

But until she and Kirsty had made absolutely sure that this was the case, she was reluctant to do this. She had personally been in the situation when her bosses had just decided that it was easier to give in and dissolve the company, without giving too much thought to the consequences, or the effect on the work-force, and she wasn't going to put other people through the same trauma without at least trying to save their jobs.

The scenery surrounding The Homely Haggis, which had seemed drear and melancholy when she had first arrived barely three days before, now seemed the perfect place to do some hard thinking.

It had been Meggie who had shown her the ropes. Jenny had driven up in her own car and had been waiting for Meggie's stand-in. She hadn't expected the proprietor in person.

'I've snuck out. Iain's off doing something, and if I stay in on my own any longer, I'll start chewing the carpet. Now, are you absolutely sure you want to do this? Things aren't exactly the same as they were when you originally offered.'

Jenny had forgotten for a moment that running The Homely Haggis had indeed been her idea. 'I know. But I think I'll need a place to escape to even more now.' Aware that Meggie was scanning her for more information about Philip's disappearance, she'd said, 'There's nothing new to report. Philip's still missing.'

She hadn't said anything to Meggie about her client's projected visit, as she hadn't to Lady Dalmain and Felicity. They probably wouldn't understand the significance of it, or if they did, it would only add to their anxiety.

'I thought he probably was,' Meggie had said.

'And I thought you were supposed to be resting, Ms. Dalmain.'

Meggie had flapped her hands. 'I promise I won't do anything silly. Now let's have a cuppa while I show you round the place. But do tell me, what did Felicity and the Matriarch say when you told them you were coming up here?'

'To be honest, I didn't tell Lady Dalmain – not that she'd have listened if I'd tried to. She's one of those people who only want to talk. But I told Felicity and she's going to come up later. I explained to her I needed a place to think, and she did understand. Dalmain House isn't exactly a haven of tranquillity at the moment. Lady Dalmain just goes on and on.'

'I bet. It almost makes one sorry for the old bat,' Meggie had paused. 'Not *actually* sorry, you understand, but almost.'

Jenny had laughed. 'You'd better show me how to operate the kettle or this'll be another business in trouble.'

Now, with Meggie gone, Jenny had a foolscap pad and a pen and was trying to brainstorm on her own. Ideas for the mill were as scarce as customers. Jenny sent messages over the ether. 'Come on, Felicity! I need someone to talk to, and I'm starting to get very depressed and very cold.'

To warm herself, she put a light under the kettle. She was just wondering if she should have a hot drink herself when she spotted a vehicle.

Realising it was probably a good thing that Felicity hadn't appeared, so she could face her first customer without an audience, Jenny put her shoulders back and smiled. Only when it was too late to remove the smile did she recognise the man striding over the chippings towards her. Rather than remain grinning like an overkeen stewardess, she let the smile shrink inwards, so that when he arrived it was a barely noticeable smirk.

'Oh my God, it's you,' he said, a few feet from the counter. He paused, frowned and seemed unnecessarily confused. 'And I was hoping for some service,' he added.

Jenny tried not to let her reaction show, or the fact that she was wondering if she could slam down the metal shutter quickly enough to make a statement, or whether it would embarrass her by sticking.

'What can I do for you?' she asked, more abruptly than she'd meant, not daring to risk the shutter. Something about this man made her heart race. It was anger, of course. She was still angry with him because of their first encounter. It was curious. She usually considered herself almost too easy-going. Why was she still holding a grudge, particularly when so much else had happened since they'd met?

His confusion had gone now. 'Very little in the cooking line, I dare say.'

'Cooking and making hot drinks are all I'm offering,' she said, quietly, so he wouldn't hear the tremor in her voice.

'Are you working here, then? I thought you had another job in the area. Dalmain House, wasn't it?'

'And I thought you were on holiday and would have gone home by now, otherwise I would never have agreed to take this place on.' She licked her lips, forcing some moisture into her mouth, which had gone dry. 'Would you like a cup of tea?' Realising she probably sounded as if she was entertaining the vicar, her Home Counties accent emphasised by tension, she added, 'Or something? Bovril, perhaps?'

'Coffee, please, and a bit of flapjack. Did you make it?'

Ordinary good manners somehow seemed beyond her. She found herself snapping back in a most uncharacteristic way. 'Even instant coffee takes a bit longer than that to make.'

His eyes glittered. 'I meant the flapjack.'

'No. But I will be making it in future, so be warned.' There seemed to be some sort of reverse magnetism going on. She wanted to beg him never to come near her again.

Apparently unaware of her difficulties, he went on. 'So where's the owner? Having her baby?'

'No, she's resting, prior to having it. Have you any more questions? If so, perhaps you'd like to prepare a questionnaire and I could complete it at my leisure.' She could hardly believe what was coming out of her mouth. She normally found it hard to be rude to people. And while this man was difficult, he didn't really deserve the sort of antagonism she was throwing at him.

'You really shouldn't be sarcastic to the customers, you know.'

'And you shouldn't be rude to people who are preparing food for you. You never know how they'll get their own back.' She gave him a look that implied she wasn't above spitting in the soup. Keep away from me, she wanted to say, you're dangerous.

'Was I rude? I didn't mean to be.'

'You were very rude, but don't worry, it's probably a habit, and I won't take it personally.'

He frowned. 'No, I don't think I'm usually rude. No one else has complained, anyway.'

'That doesn't mean a thing. It's probably just that other people you are rude to need you in some way. I don't give a toss if you never have another cup of coffee again in your life. And as for the flapjack, you should be eating shortbread anyway, seeing as we're in Scotland.'

He stared at her with bemusement and she couldn't blame him. Her behaviour was appalling. 'You are the most unsuitable person to be in charge of a fast food stall I have ever come across,' he said.

She couldn't snap out of it. 'I bow to your greater experience of fast food outlets, but in my opinion, you're the most unsuitable person to be any type of customer at all, be it of The Homely Haggis or the Ritz. In future, you should make your own coffee and flapjack and carry it about in a little knapsack. And that'll be one pound thirty, please.'

He dug into his pocket for some change. 'I pity your husband.'

'I pity your wife.' She didn't think he had one, actually. The words 'I will' would be too much like giving in, for him.

'I haven't got a wife.'

She shrugged. 'Why aren't I surprised?'

'Have you got a husband?'

She frowned. This was too personal, and yet, strangely, she felt elated by the argument. After two days spent tippy-toeing round people's sensibilities, discarding even the pretence of good manners was extremely liberating. In her working life she had always been polite and charming, anxious that people should like and approve of her. Now, suddenly, it didn't matter what this man thought, she could hurl any old insult at him. She couldn't have cared less for his opinion of her. 'Why would I tell you the time, let alone if I'm married or not?'

'Which means you're not.'

It didn't, quite, but she didn't think Henry fitted into the conversation anywhere, so she carried on, still unaccountably angry. 'And that means there are two people spared from being miserable, doesn't it? I don't know why I don't just throw this coffee at you.'

'And I don't know why, when you are the most disagreeable woman I've ever come across, I ever –' He stopped. 'I do find you extremely attractive,' he went on, almost as an afterthought.

She threw the coffee. At the time it didn't seem as if she had a choice and, joyful though the experience was, she was glad to note, even before the coffee landed, that he was wearing waterproof clothing. She was appalled at herself for acting so out of character, but somehow she felt released.

Her inner tension snapped. He was more surprised than angry and she suddenly found herself laughing. She had aimed low, so it was only a matter of some coffee on his Rohans, and it suddenly seemed extremely funny.

'How dare you laugh! If there wasn't a counter between us, you wouldn't laugh.'

'Maybe not,' she gasped. 'But there is.' She took the precaution of kicking the door to, knowing she could lock it if he looked like coming round the side to do her a mischief.

'I bet you don't dare come out! I could keep you here all night, just by refusing to go!'

'You could.' She was still fairly helpless with mirth. 'But I'm in here with the hot soup and the chocolate and you're out there on the blasted heath.' Trying to get herself under control she bit her lip and tried to think sad thoughts. It didn't help.

'It's not a blasted heath, it's a car park, in October.'

'So they keep trying to tell me. I'm not convinced. I think they have a different calendar up here, and it's actually January. If not February.' She swallowed, shook her head briskly, and managed to get her mirth down to a smile that twitched at the corners. It felt like an achievement.

'That's because you're a nesh Southerner, a Sassenach.'

Now she had laughed a lot of the tension out of her system, she could respond to him more normally. 'I expect you're right. Would you like another cup of coffee? On the house rather than on the trousers?'

He continued to scowl at her for a few moments and then he grinned and something funny happened to Jenny's stomach. It sort of went into spasm, affecting her all the way from under her bra, right down to her knees. It was so powerful she wondered if some previously undiscovered muscles in her inner thighs were actually contracting. She glanced at him to see what it could have been that caused such a strong reaction. He was still grinning and Jenny became short of breath. How could someone so unpleasant, so confrontational and thoroughly bloody-minded suddenly become so – she shrank away from the thought – attractive? He wasn't even good-looking, for goodness' sake!

Jenny's improved mood brought on by release of tension and laughter was evaporating. Aware that she'd just had an extreme physical reaction to someone she ought to dislike was disorientating. Henry had never made her feel her elastic had snapped. 'I'll do you another coffee.'

'Perhaps it would be better if I made it myself?' He seemed aware of her change of mood, which was hardly surprising.

The thought of him coming round to her side of the counter gave her a panic attack. She managed a nearly normal smile. 'It's OK; I won't throw it at you again, providing you're not exceptionally offensive.'

'Like I was before, you mean?'

'Yes.' It was getting easier to cope with. Her usual briskness was returning. 'Would you like another bit of flapjack? The other one must be rather soggy.'

He frowned, or at least his eyebrows drew together into the semblance of a frown, but the twinkle beneath the brows made it unconvincing. 'I don't like it. Something's not right. You're being polite.'

She laughed, a nice, natural-sounding laugh, and it made her feel better, more in control. 'I usually am nice. It's you who are rude and confrontational.'

'And it's obviously infectious since it makes you like that too. You did throw a cup of coffee at me,' he added, as if she might have forgotten.

'It was a plastic cup, which doesn't count, and I didn't throw it at your head, as you deserved, but at your waterproofed middle.' A quick glance down at where the coffee had landed proved to be a mistake. Last week she would never have described outdoor protective clothing as attractive. This week her sense of style – such as it was – seemed to have gone to live with Henry.

'The coffee was still wet, and yes, I would like another piece of flapjack.'

She gave it to him, and then fiddled in the bowl that served as a till. 'Here, take your money back. I'll tell Meggie I spilt coffee on the stock.'

'No. I'll pay for both cups of coffee, and the flapjacks. You're right. I did deserve to get one thrown at me.'

'Well, hallelujah!' Jenny returned his smile as brightly as she could. How could he have gone from unpleasant to so attractive that she couldn't look at him without melting in a matter of seconds? Was it him? Or had something strange happened to her? Perhaps in a few minutes she would find that Philip had not run away with all the important documents. Dalmain House would suddenly have become The House of Fun. Felicity would have turned into Mary Poppins and Lady Dalmain into a sweet little old lady. If only.

'Well, if you really want to pay, it's two pounds sixty.'

He handed over the money and just as he'd counted out the last bit of silver, he said, 'I really want to take you out for a drink.'

The sinking feeling came again. She shook her head. She was practically engaged to Henry. Going out for a drink with a man who did what he did to her libido would be the most ridiculous folly. It was just as well he wouldn't be around for much longer. 'No, sorry. I'm here most evenings. And anyway, shouldn't you be going home? Back to somewhere flatter, and warmer?'

He shook his head. 'I'm not here on holiday.'

'But you said you were! I know you did!' Anger and panic flooded her brain. He had lied to her! Supposing she had gone out with him, thinking he'd be gone in a couple of days? What would have happened?

'I was on holiday when I first met you, but since then things have changed. I've been accepted for training as a member of the local mountain rescue team.' He leant in and took her hand, lying carelessly on the table, and shook it. 'Ross Grant.'

Jenny forced a smile. 'Jenny Porter.'

'Jenny, that's nice,' he said. 'Now what about that drink? We've established we're both single.'

'Have we?' She hadn't wanted to give this impression, and yet somehow, she didn't want to admit to Henry, either. He felt so far away, he somehow wasn't relevant just now.

Ross was looking at her with interest, as if not caring whether she went out with him or not, but being interested in her answer for reasons she couldn't guess.

She realised she had to make a choice. She could either pretend that Henry really didn't exist and go out with this man who did strange things to her sinews, or she could make the sensible decision and just say no.

She shook her head. 'Sorry. As I said, I'm here most evenings, and if I'm not, it's because I have other work to catch up on.'

'About your other work –'

'I'm not saying a word about it. It's confidential.'

'I won't torture you for information about it. You could just go out for a drink with me.'

'No.'

'Well, I might ask again, once or twice.'

'Suit yourself.'

When at last he'd driven away, she allowed herself to sink onto the stool behind the counter. Thank goodness he'd only asked her for a drink. If he'd said, 'Would you like to come to bed with me?' she might not have been able to resist.

Lust did not often affect Jenny. In fact, she had always considered herself rather lacking in that way, but that was one area in her life where Henry was not critical. He wasn't demanding, never asked her to do anything too exotic and always made sure she was all right before he went to sleep. The fact that he didn't notice she was pretending didn't bother her, nor did it bother her that sex was restricted to Saturday nights or Sunday mornings. She just accepted that what the magazines said was overblown hype, and what she and Henry had was perfectly normal.

Before that, it had usually taken her a long time before she wanted anything more than a little gentle kissing, which was one of the reasons she had liked being with Henry; he didn't rush her. So lust, coming as it had, from the other side of a coffee-shop counter, from someone who had proved in every way to be bullying, boorish and rude, was a complete, very unsettling surprise. It meant that her brain and her libido were entirely unconnected, acting totally independently from each other. Jenny liked to feel in control of her life, and this complete disconnection between heart and head meant that anything could happen. She could no longer trust her good sense to keep her safe. She might end up corresponding with a prisoner on death row, and marrying him just before his lethal injection, or something.

Oh God, she thought, wiping up the mess, why has this happened to me? Things like this are not supposed to happen to me! I know Henry thinks I'm daft as a brush, and in some ways maybe I am, but where my love life has been concerned, I've always been a rock-solid, head-in-charge girl, not a hormonally unbalanced firecracker, exploding in all directions at once. Life is difficult enough at the moment, without this!

Fortunately, before she could berate herself too much, Felicity's Volvo appeared. By the time she had got out and arrived at the counter, Jenny at least looked as though she had all her marbles, even if she knew several of them had gone flying.

'Hi, Felicity! How lovely to see a friendly face! What can I get you? A double mocha skinny latte with sprinkles?'

Felicity looked bewildered, and took out a packet of cigarettes.

Jenny realised that Felicity had probably never experienced an American style coffee shop. 'How about a hot chocolate?'

Felicity took a long drag. 'Lovely, and I've brought a little something to put in it.' Holding the cigarette between her lips, Felicity opened a large handbag and brought out half a bottle of whisky.

'Mm, I'd better not join you. One of us had better be fit to drive. Now what do you want to eat? This is on me. You can have a bacon bap, with onions, or a fried egg. Tomato soup? Here, have a look at the menu. I'll open the door so you can come round.'

'This is cosy,' said Felicity a little later, contemplating a bap oozing butter and bacon. 'I wish I could cook like this for Mama. It'd be so much easier. Poor Mama. She's devastated about Philip.'

'You don't have any clue about where he might have gone, do you? It's really important we find him.'

'Mama is certainly desperate to.' Felicity hesitated, as if finding her brother was not absolutely her first concern. 'She can't believe that Philip has chosen to be with – someone not out of the top drawer. I can perfectly understand it myself.'

'So, was that the only reason he left? So he could be with her?' Jenny was trying to ascertain whether Felicity knew of any minor misdemeanour connected with the mill.

Felicity shrugged. 'Mama certainly wouldn't countenance his marrying a woman like her, who's not even young enough to bear children. It was bad enough Iain marrying Meggie, but at least Iain was the younger son, and Meggie was the right age, if not the right class.'

'So what about you and Lachlan? Would you be allowed to marry, if things looked like they were going in that direction?'

Felicity shrugged as if doubtful things would ever go in that direction and lit another cigarette. 'Possibly. I don't suppose she'd notice; she's in too much of a state over precious Philip. Not that we'll probably get that far. He's away so often and I haven't heard from him since the other night. He's probably been frightened off for ever.'

There was something terribly poignant about this woman's faded beauty and her sadness. 'Are you in love with him?'

Felicity didn't hesitate. 'Oh yes. I have been for the past twenty years or so.'

'Goodness, that's faithful! Does he feel the same about you?'

'I shouldn't think so for a minute.' Felicity sighed. 'He never knew how I felt about him. We went out a few times and then Mama put a stop to it.'

'And you just let her?'

Felicity sighed again, even more deeply. 'It may seem ridiculous to you, but I was ill and she managed to stop us communicating. By the time I was better and could have fought back, Lachlan had gone abroad.'

'How tragic. And didn't he leave an address?'

'I don't think Lachlan would have been all that bothered about me.'

'But he remembered you, didn't he?'

'Oh yes. I dare say his memory's OK.'

'But he wouldn't have remembered you if he hadn't cared about you. Honestly, men don't.'

'Are you sure?'

'Perfectly. If you'd just been another girlfriend he possibly wouldn't have remembered at all, and he certainly wouldn't have come to dinner. God! He'd have remembered what your mother was like! Only a brave and keen man would do that twice.'

'You really think so?'

'I certainly do.' And while she was thinking about Lachlan, a thought came into Jenny's mind. 'Next time you speak to him –'

'If there is a next time . . .'

'You must ask him what happens to the clippings. Of the animals he shears.'

'I will if you like, but why?'

111

'It's just an idea I'm tossing round in my head. It probably won't come to anything, but I might as well have a think about it.' Silently she added, I haven't had any sensible ideas, I might as well go with the crazy ones. Aloud, she said, 'Now, a coffee? Or more hot choc?'

Chapter Eight

Kirsty McIntyre was looking gloomy but resigned when Jenny arrived the next morning. It was only nine o'clock, but she had obviously been there a long time.

She led the way to Philip's office. 'I've been trying to sort out what's missing.'

'And?'

'The only important stuff seems to be the copies of the deeds. But I found a sheet of architect's drawings. They were stuck between one file and another. I've never seen them before, which explains why they weren't properly filed. Quite interesting. Coffee?'

'Yes please,' said Jenny. 'But you don't have to make it. I'm perfectly capable –'

'No, you sit there. Here's something to read I found this morning that might amuse you. It's a memory of the time when this mill didn't produce shoddy sweaters for tourists.'

'I didn't say that, did I?' Jenny took the booklet that Kirsty handed to her, abashed.

'You didn't need to. We all know what we produce. Will you have a shortbread biscuit with it? I made it myself. I couldn't sleep last night,' she explained. 'I had to do something.'

Jenny nodded, sympathetic and grateful at the same time. 'I didn't have breakfast. What's this?'

'It's a catalogue. Not one of ours, but it's an indication of the kind of things we used to produce, back then.'

It had 'Ritchie and Ritchie' embossed in gold on the front, and underneath was an address in America, and the date 1932. Jenny turned to the first page. On it was a small, two-inch square of cloth and a description. She ran her finger over the cloth and realised she had never felt anything so soft.

'What's a vicuña?' she asked, when Kirsty came back with the coffee.

'A sort of llama, but you only find them in zoos nowadays. They're so nervous they die if you try to go near them. They produce the hair they used to use for shatooshes but the use of them has been illegal for years now. Except under very special licence, and then only for scarves and things.'

'Oh.' Jenny turned the page. 'Here's another animal I've never heard of. A guanaco?'

'I think they're a sort of alpaca, but to be honest, I've never heard of them either.'

'Alpaca . . .' Jenny went on turning the pages, finding more samples, from more unusual animals. 'You know, I met an alpaca clipper the other day.'

'Did you?' Kirsty picked up a pile of papers and went through it, tossing most of them into an already-full wastepaper bin.

'Do they have fine wool?'

'Yes, but it's not referred to as wool. It's fibre.'

'Right.' Jenny turned more pages. 'You know, this catalogue – you finding it like that – it seems an omen.'

Kirsty peered at Jenny over her spectacles. 'I thought

you were supposed to be a professional, not someone who believes in omens.'

Jenny smiled. 'Look, we have less than three weeks to come up with some sort of future for this mill that we can present to my client. I'd like to help – and if solutions come to me in the entrails of dead animals, I'm not going to knock it.'

'What?'

'Never mind. But this catalogue has given me an idea. If this mill can't produce cheap sweaters at a profit, perhaps they can produce really fine pieces, from unusual animals – fibres, I suppose.'

'What do you mean?'

'Well, you're importing wool at a price which is barely viable. It's processed on machinery that costs an arm and a leg to lease, and, at the end, no one wants the product enough for you to make a profit. We need to look at what's required in, say, Bond Street, and make that, not bother with the bread-and-butter stuff.'

'So you're saying, scrap what we do now, and go up-market?'

Jenny nodded. 'But it might be quite out of the question. I'll need to make some enquiries about the availability of animal fibres. But if Felicity's boyfriend goes round the country clipping alpacas, he must know where they all are. And he might know about some of these other animals too – llamas, for example. What do you think?'

Kirsty raised a fine eyebrow. 'I think you need your bumps felt.'

'You mean, I'm mad? Well, I can't argue with that. But unless we think of something else, it's my mad idea or nothing. Let's do the figures. Let's work out how much we'd save if we sent the machinery back. Then let's work out how we'd manage without machinery . . .' Jenny's enthusiasm evaporated. 'How silly. However skilled the workers are, they're not going back to hand spinning, and it's unlikely I'll convince my client to invest more money to buy specialist machinery.'

'We might not need new machinery. There's a shed full of it. Nothing in a mill ever gets thrown away.'

'But why was it abandoned the first time?'

Kirsty made a dismissive gesture, separating herself from the decision. 'It probably seemed a good idea at the time. But we don't know what's suitable yet anyway, though there are enough men around here who'd know how to adapt it. Young Iain, for example. He was always messing around with the machinery when he was a lad. He's a fine engineer now. And he knows about textiles. It's a shame Philip wouldn't let him into the business as an equal partner, and Iain wouldn't take less.'

Jenny sighed. 'The trouble is, even if we can adapt the machinery, and get hold of the fibres, we need to find out if there's a market. It won't be any good presenting these ideas to my client if they're still only ideas. They have to be presented as a properly researched strategy.'

Kirsty didn't speak for a minute. 'Jenny, you referred to Mr Grant-Dempsey as your client. You're here because of him. Why are you so set on making the mill profitable? Shouldn't you just do what is best for your client?'

Jenny took a breath. 'Yes, I should. But before I was a virtual assistant – before I had clients – I worked for a dot.com company. Like so many of them, we went bust. But the people who set it all up left with money – quite a lot of money. I'm not at all sure how they did that, but we – the workers – were got rid of with no severance pay or anything. I had my suspicions that something was wrong with it before the crash happened, but when nearly every dot.com business went bust, no one questioned anything. It's why I wanted to work for myself, and it's why I'm on the side of the workers.' She paused to get her thoughts in order. 'I am not a disloyal person. I do have feelings of loyalty to my client. But I don't see why he can't make money without sacking everyone and developing the site, whatever.'

'Developing the site?' asked Kirsty, ignoring Jenny's tale of woe. 'Hm. Do you think that's what he intended to do?'

'Possibly. I don't know, he hasn't told me. But it's the sort of thing he's done before, as far as I can gather. Why?'

'I just wonder if Philip's taken the copies of the deeds because he has the same thing in mind.'

'Oh God. You mean you think *Philip's* thinking of developing the site?'

'Maybe, but I'm just wondering – if we got the deeds back from Philip –'

'Difficult, considering we don't know where he is –'

'If we drew up plans, got provisional planning permission or something, for some of the site – the offices, say – to be turned into flats or starter homes or whatever it is they're called these days, we might be able to convince Mr Fancy-Pants not to close us down, but to use the money he'll make over that for further investment. At least it would mean he wouldn't have to put his hand in his own pocket to keep us going.'

'But if Philip's got the same idea, we can hardly beat him to it. And I dare say he's got different plans for the money. And we haven't got the deeds. We couldn't sell anything without Philip anyway.'

'We could get copies of the deeds. We could get some plans drawn, and then scour the hills for Philip.'

Jenny nodded. 'It's a good idea, but in the meantime I think I'll work on a plan to make the mill viable, using all our mad ideas.'

Kirsty regarded her firmly. 'You'll be needing to get on with that.' She glanced at her watch as if expecting Jenny to have done it by lunchtime at the latest. 'I'll carry on clearing up.'

'You're a bit of a surprise, Kirsty,' said Jenny as she reached for a pad and pen.

'Oh?'

'When we first met, I would never have put you down as someone who'd respond to an idea as wild as this one.'

'We're not exactly spoilt for choice,' she said drily.

Jenny left Dalmain Mills a little later and went directly to Meggie's house. Meggie appeared happier today, less frustrated by her confinement.

'Hello there, what are you doing out of school at this time of day?' She struggled upright on her sofa. 'Have you jacked it all in, or just decided there's nothing to be done except call in the receivers?'

'No, I'm researching a completely mad idea. It's pretty much a last gasp, but I want to see if it's possible.'

'What is it?'

'It's such a shot in the dark and so unlikely to come off, I almost don't want to tell you.'

'Want to or not, you're telling me!'

'Well, don't laugh or anything.'

'Just spit it out, woman!'

'I want to see if it's possible to turn the mill into somewhere which produces quality stuff, like it did in Miss McIntyre's parents' time.'

'Yes?'

'You know about textiles – what are the chances of finding a market for really high-quality designer wear?'

'What sort of thing are you talking about?'

'About hand knits, probably, but also suitings which are so light you can hardly feel you're wearing them. Made out of unconventional fibres.'

'What sort of fibres?'

'Llama, alpaca, that sort of thing.'

Meggie considered. 'A friend of mine at college did go into that. She has a shop in London. I could get in touch, ask her how things are going.'

'And if there was a market, could you be the designer?'

Meggie shook her head. 'I love playing about with texture, as you can see.' She gestured to the curtains and throws that Jenny had noticed on her first visit. 'But I'm not really a shape person. No, the person you might want for that, strangely enough, is Felicity.'

'Felicity? I thought you had no time for her.'

'I haven't. I doubt she and I would ever get on, but she's got a good eye. Have you ever seen the embroidery she does? Designs it all herself. Lady D.

119

despises it, of course, but I have to admit, it's lovely. Most of it's old-fashioned, traditional. But she's done some modern pieces. Actually' – Meggie heaved herself upright – 'if you look on that chair, over there, under the pile of magazines, you might find the cushion she gave me and Iain last Christmas.'

Jenny burrowed in the seat of the chair and pulled out a cushion. It was stunning, clear, bright colours, embroidered in a chevron design that was modern and startling. 'Felicity did this?'

'Yup. You should have heard her mother. "Darling",' Meggie drawled, in a fine imitation of Lady Dalmain, '"is that not a little garish? I'm sure Margaret and Iain would have preferred something a little more subtle." That cheered up Christmas, I can tell you!'

Jenny shuddered. 'Do you have to have it at Dalmain House? I can't imagine anything worse.'

'We only go for the lunch, then we bugger off down to my folks and get roaring drunk. You need to after being there. She's the only one who ever calls me Margaret, and only because she knows I hate it.'

'Well, I think the cushion's great. I must ask Felicity to show me all her work. Honestly!' Jenny became indignant on Felicity's behalf all over again as she inspected the stitching. 'Hasn't Lady D. ever heard of Kaffe Fassett?'

Meggie laughed. 'You're joking! She'd probably think William Morris too modern for good taste. Anything post Jacobean, vulgar, my dear.'

Jenny got reluctantly to her feet. 'If neither Lady D. nor Felicity have succumbed to the vapours and are prostrate on the hall floor, I'll be up at The Haggis later.'

120

'You've still got time for it, with all this going on?'

'At the moment, yes. I'll let you know if things change. At the moment it's a good place to think.'

Lady Dalmain was suffering from nothing more dramatic than extreme disgruntlement and so Jenny went to The Homely Haggis as soon as she could.

It didn't look very homely when she arrived, however. There was a brisk wind, laced with rain, and it was blowing across the lay-by, flattening the grass and throwing up spurts of gravel. But by the time Jenny had got the door unlocked and herself inside, she managed to convince herself that the whole idea was not a complete waste of time. Getting out of Dalmain House was bound to help her thought processes, even if she had no customers. In fact, customers would be a nuisance. It would be far better if she could just make herself a hot drink and a sandwich and get some ideas down on paper. This, of course, was the cue for a trickle of hikers to come by for hot drinks and a couple of locals made a point of stopping to ask about Meggie. Eventually everyone had left and Jenny was halfway through her sandwich and a list of things she had to do that were impossible, when she became aware of someone approaching. It was him.

All the moisture in her mouth vanished and her muscles and sinews turned into overwashed elastic, but it was the feeling of being punched, so that her body sank in the middle, that was most difficult to cope with.

I must have willed him to come, she thought, guilt coursing through her as she struggled to get herself into a state to greet him normally, wishing she had time for a drink of water. Otherwise, why on earth is he here? It can't be coincidence. What have I done?

'Hello,' he said.

Jenny cleared her throat and was surprised to hear her voice sounding reassuringly like itself. 'Hello. What can I get you?' This was bound to invoke some sarcastic comment, but she couldn't think of anything snappier at such short notice.

'Nothing. I saw you arrive and I came down to say hello.'

A quick intake of oxygen and she managed another sentence. 'You saw me arrive? How did you do that? With binoculars?'

'Yes, actually. I was doing some bird-watching – I heard a rumour there was a hen harrier in the area – and I saw your car. I thought I should come and say hello and try to make up for being so –'

'So what?' Now he was here, and they were actually talking, Jenny didn't feel quite so fluttery. In fact her brain and her mouth seemed to be working quite well together. 'I could supply the word for you, but you might not like it.'

He scowled. Strangely, it didn't make him any less attractive. 'I came here to make peace –'

'But it's hard, being so totally out of character, so we could just carry on making snippy remarks to each other. Or I could make you a cup of coffee, or something?'

'But could you? That's always been in doubt.' There was a definite sparkle in his eye, not quite a smile, but going in that direction.

'Not for me. I've always known that I can make

coffee. But I don't feel obliged to prove it to you.'

'I would like a cup of hot chocolate.' He didn't say please, but there was a twitch at the corner of his mouth that meant he didn't have to.

'Oh, very well. I haven't got much else to do, after all.' Giving the appearance of being grudging would, Jenny hoped, disguise the fact that she was still not quite in control of her breathing.

It would have been better if he'd been a holidaymaker, then he would have gone away and, eventually, she would have forgotten him. But if he was training to join a mountain rescue team and for some reason made a habit of looking out for her arrival at The Homely Haggis, she was going to have to be careful.

Of course, being a strong-minded woman – and it was only Henry who thought she was vague and incompetent – she should be able to put him out of her mind whether she saw him or not. She sighed. Perhaps Henry was right. Perhaps she was a silly 'little sausage' who could no more control her mind than she could stop breathing.

There was a huge tin of instant hot chocolate, but Jenny chose to boil milk, add powder and to whisk it into froth. Even as she did it, she didn't know if it was because she wanted him to have an especially delicious drink, or because she wanted to stretch the process to keep him with her longer. Guilt swelled within her, matching the milk in the pan.

'Would you like squirty cream with that?'

'What?'

'You know.' She produced a can from the fridge. 'Cream in a can. Everyone knows it as squirty cream.'

'Everyone except me, apparently.'

'You don't count. You're far too elevated to talk the same language as ordinary mortals.'

He appeared taken aback. 'What did you say?'

'You heard what I said, you just didn't know what I meant.'

'Whatever –'

'I meant that you evidently don't mix with ordinary people on a day-to-day basis. This means you don't understand the catchwords. It probably means you don't watch *Who Wants to Be a Millionaire?* either.'

He was too weather-beaten to blush – either that, or he wasn't embarrassed by this dig. 'Should I?'

'No. It's just that everyone else does. Now, here's your hot choc. Would you like something to eat?'

He took the drink, not commenting on the beauty of the fudge-brown foam, the swirl of cream she'd added for artistic effect, or the fine sprinkling of chocolate crumbs, gleaned from the bottom of a box of Flakes.

'I really would like to take you out for a drink, some evening when you're not too busy.'

If the turmoil within her became external, the trees would have lost their remaining leaves, the van would have blown over, and reports of a hurricane would have reached Michael Fish. Up to now, she'd led a sheltered life in which nothing had happened to prepare her for this moment. What should she do? Should she cling on to the thought of Henry? Or should she leap into the Niagara Falls of lust? There was no choice, no decision to be made. Stay safe at all costs.

'Why would you want to do that,' said some other woman Jenny didn't know, 'when we obviously don't get on?'

'I get bored in the evenings sometimes, and all the local girls are taken, so I'm told.'

'Mm. They told me that about the boys.' Looking at him she realised that to describe him as a boy was a definite misnomer. She also realised that she wanted to go out with him very much. What was wrong with her?

'So? How about it? Will you risk having to sit in a cold pub all night, sipping lager and not having anything to say to each other?'

'You make it sound so attractive. Can I resist?' She hesitated. 'Yes, I think I can.' Phew! She'd refused him! For a moment there she'd thought she really might accept.

'Oh, come on! You must get bored sometimes too.'

'A nice spell of boredom would suit me just now – so yes, I will come for a drink with you.' Oh, mouth! Why did you have to let me down like that? Has the cable to my brain become disconnected, or has it melted as though struck by lightning?

She did slightly regret being so rude as he stared down at her, incredulous and not pleased. He wouldn't want to take her out now, and so she'd be safe. And seeing him glare made her feel she'd made the right decision. She wouldn't feel at all safe without The Homely Haggis counter between her and him. It was like taunting tigers in a zoo – all very well when there were bars between you and them – a little too exciting when there weren't.

'Women don't usually find me boring,' he said eventually, having revealed signs of controlling his outrage.

'How do you know? I mean, they're hardly likely to tell you they're bored, are they?'

He took a calming breath. 'You can usually tell if you're boring someone, or at least I can. I can't speak for you, of course.'

'Thank you for pointing that out.'

He made a sound that was a cross between a roar and a growl. 'I don't think you'd be so quick with the back chat if there wasn't a counter between you and me.'

Jenny agreed with him. 'But there is a counter between you and me. Or should that be I?'

He made that growling, roaring sound again. 'I dare you to come out of that van, to come out here and tell me you'll go out with me.'

Jenny's knees had been giving her trouble since she first saw him approach. Now it wasn't just lust that was affecting them, it was sheer terror. But a dare was a dare, and she hadn't played fairly – it wasn't fair to taunt the tigers and she should face up to the consequences.

She emerged, shaking slightly, on to the chippings. She looked up at him, apologetic, pleading and laughing, all at the same time. He took three strides to reach her. Then he put his hands on her shoulders, pulled her to him and kissed her, so hard his teeth pressed painfully against her lips. His hands left her shoulders and he wrapped his arms round her so tightly she couldn't breathe. When he released her they were both panting, and Jenny staggered.

'I'll ring you,' he said, before turning abruptly away and striding back towards his car.

Jenny leant against the van, trying to get her breath

back. She didn't feel assaulted, violated, or even plain insulted; she just thought plaintively: But how will you ring me, when you don't know my number?

After that, her brain wouldn't work, nor would her knees, and there was no point in staying much longer. It wasn't as if the lay-by was packed with punters, so with a clear conscience she could drive back to Dalmain House.

It was ridiculous to behave so foolishly when she had so much on her plate, and needed every brain cell, every ounce of emotional energy for getting Dalmain Mills sorted out. And not only did she feel disloyal to Henry, but to the project, to all the people who depended on her.

She went to look for Felicity. Not finding her anywhere else, Jenny knocked on her bedroom door. It opened a crack.

'Felicity – I was wondering how you'd like to become Dalmain Mills' designer –' she began. Then she stopped. 'Oh! What's the matter?'

Felicity flung herself at Jenny and burst into tears.

Chapter Nine

Felicity cried heartily for some moments. Jenny held her, patting her back, making soothing noises, and steered her backwards into her bedroom. The landing wasn't the place for that sort of thing. She gently propelled Felicity onto the bed and sat down next to her.

'Now, what's the matter? Shall I get the Rescue Remedy?'

Somehow she wasn't surprised when Felicity shook her head and hiccuped. 'There's a bottle of whisky under that table. You have one too.'

Jenny poured whisky into a glass for Felicity, but as she didn't yet know if she would be required to have her wits about her, or drive anywhere, she didn't have any herself.

'Now, what's the matter? Has anyone died?'

Felicity shook her head. 'Unless you count my chances of having a life.'

'Well, you tell me what's happened, and then we can see if your chance of life is completely moribund.'

Felicity wasn't listening. She drank the generous two fingers Jenny had poured and coughed. 'I usually have mine with water.'

'So, tell me!' Jenny was firm. She wanted to help Felicity, if she possibly could, but she had a feeling that if she showed too much sympathy, Felicity would just go on crying.

'I had a letter from Lachlan.'

'Oh – breaking it all off?'

Felicity shook her head. 'No! Inviting me to have lunch with him.'

'But that's good news, surely?'

'It would be if I could go. I didn't tell Lachlan I have agoraphobia. If I don't go, he'll think I don't love him. I could make excuses for a bit, I suppose, but eventually he'll just think there wasn't anything between us after all. Oh God!' Her face crumpled, and Jenny knew Niagara was going to fall again.

Before it could she said, 'How would it be if I took you? Where does Lachlan live?'

'Miles away. I couldn't ask you to take me. You're far too busy.' This was said more as a question than a statement.

'I am busy, but I should be able to find an afternoon free. What I'm concentrating on now is finding ways to make the mill profitable; I don't actually have to be at the mill to do it. In fact, a visit to Lachlan might count as valuable research. When does he want you to go?'

'The day after tomorrow.'

'Very short notice.'

Felicity started to cry again. 'Not really. The letter came the day after he came to supper. He delivered it by hand. Mama didn't give it to me. She said she forgot because of Philip.'

'Oh dear.'

'If Philip were here, he'd probably take me. But now he's gone, I'll have to look after Mama all on my own. I'll be stuck here for ever!' She sniffed loudly.

Jenny pulled off a bit of loo paper from a roll by Felicity's bed and handed it to her. 'But I've already said I'll take you. Now, will you phone him?'

Felicity nodded. 'On the mobile. There's a spot in the garden which gives you perfect reception – providing you're on the right network.'

'Do it now. While you're feeling – fortified.'

Felicity shook her head. 'I'd better get dinner on.'

The prospect of one of Felicity's dinners wasn't cheering. 'Tell you what, shall I help you with that? It'll be quicker if we do it together, and I need to use the oven to make some flapjack for The Haggis. I really want to talk to you about design. Meggie says you're really good.'

'Meggie did? But she hates me!'

'I'm sure she doesn't hate you! She showed me a cushion you'd embroidered for her, and it was lovely. She says you have a really good eye for colour.'

Felicity sniffed. 'Well, yes, I have. But I'm very surprised that Meggie said that.'

'So do you think, after you've phoned Lachlan if we did supper together, got it all on the go, we could look at your work? The mill really needs a designer. Wouldn't it be wonderful if it were you who saved the mill, or contributed? That would make your mother respect you.'

'Well no, it wouldn't.' Felicity laughed through her tears. 'She'd hate me to go out to work, hate me not to be at her beck and call.' She blew her nose. 'But I would love to show you what I do.'

While a tray of flapjack and an oven-baked rice dish were cooking, Jenny was led up a little flight of stairs to one of the turrets. It was a revelation.

To begin with, it was surprisingly bright.

'Natural daylight bulbs,' Felicity explained. 'They cost a fortune, but without them this room would be useless in winter. You need good light if you're dealing with colour.'

'You've certainly got plenty of that.'

There were baskets ranged against the curved wall. In the baskets were hanks of wool, a different colour in each, and, within that, a seemingly infinite number of shades.

'I don't know how to tell the difference between these.' Jenny put her hand in a basket of green.

'It's like having an ear for music, I suppose,' said Felicity. 'You can hear if it's wrong. Or in my case, see it.'

On the walls were hangings, some finished, some not, all with little swatches of wool and scraps of paper, showing ways of doing it differently, or future plans pinned to them. There was a neat pile of cushion covers on a small table, enough to supply a minor branch of John Lewis. A battered, but comfortable-looking armchair, with an Anglepoise lamp above it, was drawn up by a small, empty, fireplace. Beside that was an ancient worktable, its drawer open, revealing scissors, packets of needles, and more hanks of wool. Under the table, next to a packet of cigarettes, was a bottle of whisky. Felicity picked it up.

'Welcome to the sanctuary.' She found a glass and waved it. 'Want one?'

Jenny shook her head. 'I don't want to lose track of what's in the oven. This is amazing!'

131

'It's a bit cold, I'm afraid. I only light the fire in winter.'

Jenny looked about her, fascinated. That Felicity, who was obviously such a victim of her mother's cruelty, should have this secret refuge, full of light and colour, was a shock. And Meggie had been right about Felicity's design skills. Not that Jenny was an expert, but she knew quality when she saw it. The workmanship was detailed and exact, but the designs were original, eye-catching and beautiful. Fantastic birds swooped up and behind exotic flowers and foliage. Mythical beasts challenged each other across cloths of gold. Musical instruments hung from trees whose branches forked and curled, dripping with jewelled fruits. That all this richness should come out of down-trodden and despairing Felicity was astounding. 'And did you do all these hangings yourself?'

'Yes. Mama thinks they're a complete waste of time. She thinks I should dedicate myself to redoing all the dining room chairs, of which there are twelve, and then restoring the wall hangings in the hall.'

'But they're beautiful! Where did you get the wool? It would have cost a fortune to buy.'

'It did, and I still spend most of my money on wool. Daddy left me enough for a small monthly income, much to Mama's fury, and now I have a network of people who send me what's left over from the kits they buy. Sometimes they get me to finish them. That earns a bit of extra. I have thought of writing to one of the big firms who make up the kits, to see if they'd be interested in me finishing embroidery for people who've bought kits and then lost interest. But that would mean me working other people's designs, and I really want to create my own.'

Felicity sank down into the armchair and lit a cigarette. 'Are you sure you don't want a whisky?'

'Quite sure.' Jenny, perched on the arm of a chair that was piled with bulging plastic bags, shook her head. 'What are all these?'

'Those are ends of wools waiting to be sorted. I could spend all my spare time sorting wool, but I like to get on and do some embroidery as well.'

'I'm sure you do. Felicity, has it ever occurred to you that you could make money out of this?'

'I do make a little money. I supply some small shops with cushion covers. Unfortunately, they mostly want conventional designs – flowers, cats, that sort of thing. It's hard to sell anything really unusual in small towns.'

'You haven't tried to find outlets in bigger towns? Edinburgh? London, even?'

She shook her head. 'There's no point. I couldn't supply enough, and what with looking after Mama, and the house, I haven't got time. It's going to be even worse with Philip gone.' She sniffed, but to Jenny's relief, she didn't cry.

'So it will. Is your mother very distraught under all that rigid control?'

'Yes and no. She's sure he'll come back because she can't believe he can live without her and I think guilt will bring him back eventually, for a visit, but as for ever living here again, there's no chance.'

'You haven't any ideas about where Philip might be, have you?'

'Not really.' She lit another cigarette and sighed with satisfaction as the nicotine reached her lungs. 'Do you need him? I thought Kirsty could run the mill with one hand behind her back.'

'Only up to a point.' Jenny didn't refer to missing papers but gestured to the embroideries. 'Honestly, Felicity, you have real talent. Did you go to art school, or anything?'

Felicity shook her head. 'One term of an access course, and then I got ill.'

'It's amazing. I'm sure we can use your talent, use it to get Dalmain's in profit again. What would your mother have to say about that?'

Felicity laughed, genuinely amused. 'She'd be furious. She'd say, "I did not bring up my daughter to be a mill hand!"'

Jenny laughed too. Felicity's imitation of her mother was so accurate. 'You're right! That's exactly what she would say, but she might not say it for long if it meant she could keep her house and her standard of living.'

Anxiety brought Felicity forward in her seat. 'We're not really likely to lose the house, are we?'

Jenny shook her head, cursing her slip of the tongue. 'No, not *likely*, but it is just possible, if we can't turn things around.'

'And how are you planning to do that?' Now Felicity was beginning to panic.

Jenny took a moment to compose her thoughts. She thought she'd been doing the right thing, involving Felicity, exploiting her genuine talent, but if she was going to get hysterical at the mere thought of her miserable life not continuing as before, perhaps it would be better to leave her out of the plans, at least until they were more concrete, with some hope of success.

She slumped for a second. And if she couldn't sell her idea to Felicity, who had a vested interest in its success, she'd never convince her client and his chums to invest more money, or – as he would undoubtedly put it – throw good money after bad.

Banning all such negative thoughts with immense effort of will, she took a breath. 'I want you to design knitwear – hand-knitted, exciting, interesting things to wear – cat-walk stuff, nothing ordinary – using unusual fibres, bits of silk, feathers, ribbon, garments we can charge a small fortune for. I'm thinking about producing fabric as well, but I expect we'd sell that on.'

'I've never done anything like that. All my work is two dimensional.'

'At the moment,' said Jenny. 'But there's nothing to stop you having a go at clothes, is there?'

Felicity hesitated while Jenny forced herself to practise a relaxation technique. 'I suppose not,' Felicity said eventually. 'In fact, it sounds fun. But why are you asking me? There must be lots of other people around who could do it.'

Jenny abandoned relaxation and gritted her teeth. 'No there aren't! Talent like yours does not grow on trees. And you're here, it's your mill, or your family's, and it's in your interest to make it work. Besides, you'd do it for nothing, at least to begin with, wouldn't you?'

Felicity thought this highly amusing. 'I've hardly ever been paid for anything in all my life.'

'So, will you give it a go?'

'You want me to design cardigans?'

'Yes.' Now it suddenly seemed ridiculous, as if she'd asked Felicity to design a moon rocket.

'OK. I'll give it a go. You'll have to get me something

to draw on, some paper, pencils, pastel crayons, stuff like that. I don't get out much. But no, I'd like to try.'

Jenny went forward and hugged Felicity. She received the hug awkwardly, as if unaccustomed to the gesture, but then she relaxed, and hugged Jenny back. 'Thank you,' she whispered huskily.

'What for? I haven't done anything yet. Now, let's go and rescue the rice.'

'Oh! I almost forgot! There's a parcel for you! It's what prodded Mama into giving me my letter. I think it's from your mother.'

When they were back downstairs, Felicity handed Jenny a squashed, badly wrapped bundle. It was indeed from Jenny's mother. Seeing her handwriting on the 'Reuse Paper Save Trees' label almost made Jenny cry.

Felicity handed Jenny a letter opener from the hallstand and Jenny struggled with the sellotape. When she finally got inside, she read the card.

Darling, I thought as it's so cold with you, you might as well have this. It's my cashmere jumper which I washed wrong, and now is dress-length. It looks terrible but is wonderfully soft and warm. The thermal underwear will take a little longer to arrange.

I hope you're not trying to solve everyone's problems and fight everyone's battles. I know you're very capable, but it doesn't mean you can perform miracles, so don't beat yourself up if you can't.

Your loving Mum.

The jumper did indeed look like something you'd give your cat to sleep on, but when she slipped it over her head, Jenny was instantly aware of its warmth.

'Mm,' said Felicity. 'If that's the sort of thing you want me to design, I might have a few problems.'

'Silly cow,' said Jenny affectionately. 'But it is blissfully warm. Now, let's see what's going on in the kitchen.'

Two days later, Felicity and Jenny set off to visit Lachlan.

The thought of spending a day away from the mill, Dalmain House, and even, slightly against her conscience, The Homely Haggis, was bliss. At the mill she was surrounded by spreadsheets and figures and spent all day doing sums, and then redoing them, to try to get more favourable answers. At Dalmain House she had to fight the cold and field Lady Dalmain's enquiries about her son and what lengths Jenny had gone to to find him, as if finding him was somehow her responsibility.

And there was the added stress of wondering if she would ever see Ross again. She felt so torn. Part of her desperately wanted to see him, and part of her just as desperately didn't. Guilt, she decided, was addling her brain.

Both women felt they were playing truant. Jenny had told Lady Dalmain that she needed Felicity for something. Without actually lying, she managed to convey that their errand was to do with finding Philip, and she let them abandon her with a plate of sandwiches and relatively good grace.

'I should have left her something hot,' said Felicity as they drove away.

'Nonsense. She's not crippled or anything. She can make her own lunch if she wants more than a sandwich.' Jenny felt the sooner Felicity started standing up to her mother, and realising that the sky wouldn't fall in if she did, the better. 'Now, do we need a map, or can you direct me?'

'We need a map, but not yet.'

Scotland was at its most majestic. The purple heather, the granite of the mountains and dramatic light of a stormy sky were not kindly, but their drama was undeniable. Sheep were dotted about the lower slopes of the hills, their fleeces appearing very white. As Jenny swooped up and down the roads, which were pleasantly free of traffic, she wondered about the warehouse full of wool. Perhaps that could be used more imaginatively than just for spinning and knitting. Felt was a possibility. She seemed to remember seeing something about a very fine felt in a fashion magazine. Perhaps Lachlan would know, or, if not, know someone who did.

'You don't mind being away from home and in scenery like this?' Jenny asked Felicity, remembering her agoraphobia.

Felicity shook her head. 'It's bliss to be away from home, and scenery doesn't bother me. It's mostly crowds. Agoraphobia means "fear of the market-place", you know, not fear of open spaces. Mama's fixation with the classics taught me that, at least.'

'Well, let me know if you feel uncomfortable or anything and –'

'And what? What will you be able to do about it?'

Jenny laughed. 'Well, I don't know. What would you like me to do?'

'Allowing me to smoke in your car would help.'

Jenny opened a window, suppressing her objections with an effort. 'Will smoking prevent a panic attack, then?'

Felicity nodded, a cigarette between her lips. 'To be honest,' she said when she could speak, 'I'm so happy at the thought of seeing Lachlan, I don't think I could be ill if I tried.'

'So my car is going to smell of smoke for ever, when it didn't really need to?'

'No, not really. I need the fag as well.'

Jenny had to laugh, and Felicity joined in as if laughing was not something she was much used to doing.

They reached the point where they needed the map and, later, Felicity produced some written instructions. At first, they were easy to follow, but then suddenly the distances seemed all wrong.

'Now, it says go along as far as the crossroads, take the first left and then wind our way down the hill until we get to a junction. Left again, go for two miles, and there should be a sign,' said Felicity.

'Sounds simple enough,' said Jenny, knowing instructions were never simple enough and they were bound to get lost at least once.

'Does it say down, or up the hill?' asked Jenny, a few minutes later. 'Because this is definitely up.'

'Mm. It does say down. Perhaps we go down in a few minutes.'

The mountain refused to flatten out. 'Let's go back and start again,' said Jenny.

Eventually, when they had retraced their steps

several times, and Jenny secretly felt there was no chance of them ever finding it, Felicity said, 'Look – across the river – over there. Llamas!'

'Really? I didn't know he kept llamas! I thought he just clipped them.'

'Alpacas. He clips alpacas. He has a few of those, as well.'

Having seen their objective, it was relatively simple to drive to it. 'Thank goodness,' said Felicity, as they approached. 'I was starting to worry. Ruthven's Farm, that's it. It should be down this track.'

There were more llamas in the fields either side of the road. 'Do you think we can stroke them?' asked Jenny. 'Or are they terribly bad-tempered?'

'I'm sure they're not. Lachlan wouldn't like them so much if they were. Shall I open the gate?' Felicity jumped out of the car with girlish alacrity.

A farmhouse appeared as they rounded a bend. It was long, low and grey, with a stand of conifers behind it. The river flowed along one side of the property, and in front of it, across the plain, the mountains rose majestically.

'What a heavenly spot,' breathed Jenny.

'Mm. The house seems quite small.'

Felicity had flushed slightly and it was hard to tell if there was criticism in her comment.

'It's in a perfect position, though,' said Jenny. 'And there would be bound to be an outbuilding you could have for your work. Oh, sorry. My mouth's gone off on its own. Don't take any notice of me.'

'No, it's all right. I *was* wondering if perhaps I might live here one day. It's hard not to dream, isn't it?'

Jenny nodded, wishing she didn't understand as

140

well as she did. What was she doing, thinking about one man so much, when she was practically engaged to another?

'But I would have to find out if I could cope with it,' went on Felicity, unaware of Jenny's internal struggle. 'I couldn't be a burden to Lachlan.'

'I'm sure you wouldn't be. And it would be up to him. He may rather have you as a burden than not have you at all. Oh – there he is.'

'So why didn't you say at dinner the other night that you kept llamas?' asked Jenny, when they had got out of the car. 'Lady Dalmain would have been impressed, surely?'

'I have no wish to impress Lady Dalmain,' said Lachlan firmly.

Jenny glanced at Felicity and could understand her wistful expression. He may not have been Jenny's personal type (though she no longer knew if she had a type – possibly it was all down to pheromones) but he was strong and manly. And if ever there was a man to make Felicity stand up to her mother, and get a life for herself, it was Lachlan.

'Now,' Lachlan went on, 'shall we have lunch? Or would you like a tour of the policies – that is – property, first?'

'Will the lunch keep?' asked Jenny, when Felicity remained silent, possibly overwhelmed by being in Lachlan's presence.

'Oh yes. It's just soup and some salad, with some bread and cheese.'

'Then I'd love a guided tour. I've got hundreds of questions to ask you. Will you mind?'

'Oh no,' he said, in a way that made Felicity sigh again.

Llamas, it appeared, came in all shades, from bright white through every shade of silver, grey and cappuccino, to burnt sienna.

'I love their colours. They remind me of chocolate,' said Jenny. 'White, milk and plain and every variation in between.'

'And they'd all look brilliant together. Almost any combination would be wonderful,' said Felicity, beginning to emerge from her stupor of shyness.

Lachlan nodded, a little mystified. 'Well, yes.'

'We've got a plan,' said Jenny. 'to make Dalmain Mills pay. I need to ask you some questions. But first, can I stroke a llama? I've heard that they are terribly bad-tempered and spit.'

Lachlan was outraged in a restrained, Scottish way. 'Not at all. They would only be bad-tempered if kept under stressful conditions, like in a circus, or something like that. Come and meet some unstressed ones.'

The llamas were tall and stately and looked down at Jenny and Felicity from beneath the most substantial eyelashes Jenny had ever seen. They had dark, kindly eyes and wryly amused expressions.

'They're excellent sheep guards,' said Lachlan. 'With those long necks they can see for miles, and you see how their ears twitch? They catch every sound. Put a llama in a flock of sheep, and the foxes won't come near. Come along to this field. I've got some mothers and babies.'

If possible, the babies were even sweeter than their parents. Like a cross between lambs and deer, they gambolled about together, long legs straight, heads swinging around with curiosity.

'These are only a couple of weeks old,' said Lachlan. 'They can stand very soon after they're born. These are the offspring of my finest male. He can produce fibre of under twenty microns.' He regarded Jenny and Felicity patiently. 'That's very fine. It makes wonderful fabric.'

'Does it? Tell me, do you know all about textiles?'

'Certainly not. But I know a little about camelid fibres.'

'What about felt? I seem to remember reading something in a magazine about a special kind of very fine felt.'

'Nuno, possibly? I don't know much about it, except that it's made on a net base and that when it shrinks it pulls in. A bit like smocking, I suppose.' Bored with felt, he went on, 'Now, do you want to see the alpacas, or have lunch?'

The alpacas were as entrancing as the llamas, only not as big.

'So,' asked Jenny, 'if you have all these animals to care for, how do you have time to go all round the country clipping them?'

'The llamas take very little looking after. If I'm going to be away, there are several people locally who could keep an eye on them for me. Now, come and have lunch. I don't know about you, but I've been up since six, and I'm starving.'

Chapter Ten

Lachlan served them lentil soup with vegetables from a tureen on the Aga. Then he took a loaf of bread from a crock and set it on the table and produced cheese and butter from the fridge. The kitchen was simply furnished with a table and chairs, a grandfather clock, and a small settle. There were a few pots of geraniums on the windowsill, with a canister full of cooking utensils. After the clutter of the Dalmain House kitchen, it seemed very attractive, light, bright and, because of the Aga, comparatively warm.

'This is very good bread,' mumbled Jenny, as she crunched down into the crust.

'It should be, I made it,' said Lachlan.

Jenny regarded him with attention. Here was a man indeed. She looked around for a machine to do it with. No, he was not a gadget man. While he was nothing much to look at if you required machismo or saturnine glowering, he had a determination about him that was truly impressive. Felicity was obviously impressed too. Jenny hoped that she would not be put off by the fact that the kitchen was one half of the living space, and that upstairs there were probably only two small bedrooms and a bathroom. Could she cut loose from the artificial grandeur of Dalmain House and come and live with this man, who could offer her a simple, real life?

'So, tell me,' Jenny went on, unable to check that the plan she'd made for Felicity fitted in with her own dream, 'if we did manage to find a product that would sell, using unusual fibres and that felt you mentioned, do you think we could get big enough supplies for the fibres? You must know all the people who own exotic species, like llamas.'

'I don't think of llamas as exotic,' he reproved her gently. 'In South America they're just part of the landscape. They do everything. They're only seen as exotic here because they're not sheep.'

'OK – but you do know all the people in the area? In the country, perhaps? Including England and Wales,' she added hastily, in case he decided to be pedantic again.

He nodded. 'I should imagine I do.'

Jenny was beginning to take back all the kind things she'd thought about him. 'So do you think we could get enough of these – unusual fibres – to make garments to sell, at the very top end of the market?'

'I have no idea. How much fibre would you need?'

Jenny looked at Felicity, who looked back, equally blank. 'Kirsty's bound to know. But it would be a shame if we got this good idea, and it was to fail because we couldn't get enough raw material.'

'You could always import more,' said Lachlan. 'You'll have to import merino wool, anyway, if you're going to make felt.'

'We already have a huge supply of that,' said Jenny. 'But couldn't we use Scottish wool?'

Lachlan shook his head. 'It's not suitable for anything finer than tweed. But tweed is an excellent fabric.'

'It is,' said Jenny firmly, 'but there are other people

145

who do it. We need to find a gap in the market, which only we can fill.'

'Are you on the Internet?' asked Lachlan. 'I have the email address of a woman who might be useful to you. I'll give it to you later.'

When everyone had finished eating, and Lachlan had refused help with the washing up, Jenny, knowing that Felicity must be longing to be alone with Lachlan, and Lachlan was probably equally keen, said, 'I know it's an awful cheek, but I couldn't borrow your computer for a bit, could I? I really would like to email that person you suggested, and perhaps explore some websites? I know it must seem frightfully rude, but I am keen to get this underway.'

'Don't give it another thought,' said Lachlan in his soft accent. 'I'll show you where it is, and if you need to ask any questions, you'll find Felicity and me somewhere about the place.'

Felicity was maddeningly quiet on the way home. She assured Jenny that she was all right, wasn't feeling anxious and didn't need to stop, but she chain-smoked and didn't tell Jenny what had happened between her and Lachlan.

It's only because my own love life is so unsettling at the moment, Jenny thought, shivering in the icy blast that came in through the window. If I was really in love with Henry, say, or having a relationship, even with that dreadful man, I wouldn't be so fixated on Felicity and Lachlan.

Then she blinked and almost swerved. It was the first time she had acknowledged, out loud, as it were, that she did not love Henry. The realisation was a huge shock. She'd always assumed that one day she'd have the big wedding and the babies, and Henry was the most likely candidate to have them with. Now, the thought of being married to someone like Henry, with a Home Counties bridge-playing mother-in-law, was suffocating. But this change of feeling was also too much of a volte-face to think about all in one lump. She had to let herself get used to the idea, little by little. She'd start by expunging the thought of the big white wedding and the big white dress. She'd redesign Henry later.

Just before they got home Felicity said, 'Thank you for taking me. I had a really lovely time. I'm going to work on plucking up the courage to go there on my own, now. After all, you don't really want your car full of smoke, do you?'

They arrived home to find Lady Dalmain waiting for them. She had an air of reluctant excitement about her, as if she was pleased about something, but was pretending not to be.

'Iain telephoned,' she announced. 'He's taking his wife into hospital. The baby's on its way.'

'Oh, that's wonderful!' said Jenny. 'You must be so excited.'

'Yes, well,' said Lady Dalmain, following Felicity into the sitting room, ready to accept the celebratory glass of whisky. 'It's not as if it's the child of my first born, but it's still exciting.'

'So, if it was me having the baby and not Meggie, you'd be jumping up and down?' Felicity faced her mother and for once looked directly at her, instead of sideways.

Lady Dalmain did appear a little abashed. 'Of course, dear, I'd be thrilled, but let's face it, you are far too old to have a baby. Philip could father children for some years yet.'

Felicity sipped her drink, and for a moment Jenny wondered if there was going to be a showdown, and suddenly hoped there wasn't. She needed Felicity to be a designer. If she was all taken up with running off with Lachlan, she might not have the time.

'Well,' Jenny said brightly, stealing Felicity's slot, 'why don't I make us all an omelette, or something, and then I think I should pop up to The Homely Haggis. There are a few people who come late, and all the locals have been asking about Meggie's baby. I should put up some sort of banner.'

'The Homely Haggis?' repeated Lady Dalmain, horrified.

'Yes. I've been helping Meggie out with it, since she's been so pregnant.' Jenny found herself blushing. It was as if she were one of Lady Dalmain's children, caught out in an act of common behaviour. It took her all her willpower to remind herself that she was an independent woman, her own boss and a true professional. And when she'd done it, she wasn't convinced.

'I was under the impression that you were here to help Dalmain Mills and to find Philip, not to sell hot dogs to tourists!'

'I can do both, Lady Dalmain,' Jenny said with dignity. 'And we don't serve hot dogs. Now, who would like an omelette?'

She was peeling potatoes as if her life depended on it when Felicity joined her in the kitchen.

'She hates any mention of The Homely Haggis. She

148

tried to stop Meggie having it, saying it brought shame on the family.'

'Oh. I should have kept my mouth shut.'

'She's thought up to now that when you weren't with us you were slaving away over your computer, saving the family fortune.'

'I have done quite a lot of that! The Homely Haggis is a little much-needed relief! I do feel entitled to a bit of free time. Sort of.'

'Oh yes. You are. I'm just explaining how Mama feels about it,' said Felicity, placating her. 'Can I do anything to help?'

'You can slice the potatoes very thinly and then bring them to the boil. I'll sauté them. Have you got any decent oil?'

Felicity produced a dust-covered bottle. 'Will this do?'

'I should think so.' Jenny paused, her temper having receded. 'I've just had an awful thought. By cooking dinner for your mother, she'll think I'm just a domestic!'

Felicity laughed. 'Maybe, but she'll be glad of a decent meal. She just doesn't live in the real world.'

Jenny sighed. And here I am, busting a gut, thinking up new ideas so she can go on not living in it. 'When I get home,' she said to a rather startled Felicity, 'I may just get a job in a coffee bar, and give up everything else.'

Later, having left Felicity to do the washing up, Jenny went upstairs to make some notes. While she was on Lachlan's computer, she had found some interesting items about nuno felt. But while she knew that ideas

149

for the future of the mill were important, what it really needed was a large investment of cash. Philip running off with the building plans and copies of the deeds had given her and Kirsty a hint as to just what valuable assets the buildings themselves were, but without the copies of the deeds, at least, there was nothing they could do about it. Really, finding Philip, getting him to agree to the mill buildings being sold, and the money reinvested, was the first priority.

But even if they could find him, would he give up his chance to pay off the loan secured by Dalmain House?

She chewed these imponderables over later in The Homely Haggis while serving a couple of hardy walkers, trying not to scan the skyline for cars that might possibly belong to Ross Grant.

There was a pattern to people's behaviour. When they first arrived at the counter, they were polite, but unforthcoming, muttering their orders from between frozen lips. Then, as the hot drink penetrated their frozen stomachs and filtered out to their mouths, the rigidity of their expressions softened, they began to smile, and eventually became quite chatty.

When the couple had gone, the rain, which, while lurking in the clouds, had kept away all day, now came down in fine, icy, flurries. She thought of Meggie and Iain, giving birth to their first child, she thought of Felicity and her secret romance, of Kirsty, who had put so much of her life into Dalmain Mills, of Philip, who had abandoned his responsibilities. She didn't blame him for running off with the woman he loved – any man in his situation might be driven to do that – but she couldn't forgive him for taking away what might represent the future for the mill.

Just then she saw Felicity's car draw up. Jenny went out to greet her. 'Is the baby born? What kind is it? Everything OK?'

'No,' said Felicity, panting and excited. 'Iain forgot the bag with all Meggie's tapes and aromatherapy oils and massage stuff. She says she won't give birth without them and would you please take them to her in hospital?'

'Goodness me, surely the baby will be born long before I can get there!'

Felicity shook her head. 'Apparently she's not very far along at all. In fact, she wanted to come home only they wouldn't let her. Mama is absolutely furious. She says they should just induce the baby, and let Meggie go through the pain like every other woman, because when she had us, she didn't have tapes and lavender oil or any of that nonsense.' She giggled. 'It was just stirrups and chloroform, gin if you were lucky. You should have heard her go on. When she heard that Iain was actually going to be present at the birth, she nearly had a fit. "It's really quite unreasonable of her to expect Iain to witness all that unpleasantness. So selfish." '

'Honestly! Poor Meggie! I wouldn't want to go through childbirth without my best friend there.' She frowned suddenly. 'Presuming my partner was my best friend, of course.'

'Well, I don't know, and never will. Mama's right. I am too old to have a baby, and I haven't even got a husband.'

'Oh, Felicity! I think you and Lachlan may very well get it together. He's so nice.'

'Oh, he's nice, but he'd need something more than just me in a partner. I'm too pathetic for him. I could never do the farmer's wife things he'd need.'

Jenny was busy closing up the van. 'Rubbish! You run Dalmain House, don't you? If you can do that, Lachlan's dear little farm would be a doddle. And you'd soon get used to llamas having babies and stuff. It would be so sweet.' She pulled down the shutter with a rattle and emerged from the side door. 'And if you were really in love, he'd be tolerant.'

'Do you really think so?' Felicity sounded so wistful, Jenny put her hand on hers.

'Yes! And if you were the top designer for Dalmain Mills, who saved the whole business, well, he'd respect you so much.'

The thought of people respecting her turned Felicity silent.

'And you're sure I can get Meggie's stuff to the hospital before the baby comes?'

Felicity returned to the matter in hand. 'Oh yes, I think so. She's determined not to have it until she's got it, anyway.'

'I don't suppose she has much choice in the matter. I don't think you can say, "Oh no, not now," and put the whole thing on hold.'

'Iain seemed fairly sure there'd be time. They wanted to give her an injection to move things along a bit but Meggie refused. I gather she's being difficult.'

'Hell! The woman is giving birth! She's entitled to be difficult.' She frowned. 'How will I get into the house?'

Jenny found herself with plenty to think about as she drove along. Would she want Henry with her as she gave birth? The thought was so bizarre it made her laugh. He was so squeamish he hadn't been able to put a sticking plaster on for her once, when she'd cut her thumb. He'd never cope with yelling, obvious pain and mess. Hating herself, even as she did it, she wondered if she'd want Ross Grant there while she gave birth. Trying hard, but failing, to force the idea out of her mind, she found that actually, she would. For however many million other faults Ross Grant had, she was willing to bet that squeamishness was not one of them.

She dragged her thoughts back to Henry. Perhaps she could have Henry's baby without him there. Apart from the row they'd had before she'd come up here, they didn't often fight. And that was as it should be. They would have the big white wedding, the exotic honeymoon, and then live in a small converted rectory, until they could afford to live in a large one. Henry would expect her to cook his meals and iron his shirts and collect his dry-cleaning, and while she had no moral objection to these tasks, sitting opposite Henry after a long day of being a wife and mother did not seem sufficient reward. Particularly when his lovemaking was so dull.

No sooner was the thought formed than she gave herself a mental kick in the shins for being so unkind. It wasn't his fault she faked every orgasm. If she had ever plucked up the courage to talk about sex to him, she may not have had to. The trouble was, it was so much easier to do a bit of heavy breathing, and make a few mewing noises than it would be to explain what she wanted. It was her fault. She was sure he would spend hours looking for her G spot if only she'd ask him to – well, if not hours, a few minutes. But she preferred to fake it. It gave her something to do.

And yet Ross Grant, who had driven up out of the mist, had turned her into a jelly just by looking at her, and one kiss from him had been more exciting than Henry's entire repertoire of strokes and tweaks and little bites.

She'd have to break up with Henry, she decided. After her work was finished here, she'd have to explain she didn't think they were suited. Her mother might be a bit upset, of course, and Henry's mother would be devastated. Marjorie had practically picked Jenny out for him. She was the perfect little executive wife, pretty enough, a good cook – she even had a little job she could do from home before the 'smalls' went to prep school. Henry's father would be upset too, the old lecher. He'd have to find some other young thing to hug too often and make remarks that couldn't quite be described as being off colour, but that were somehow offensive.

Jenny felt relieved as she drove round the town, looking for signs to the hospital. It was a decision she should have taken a long time ago, but now she'd taken it, she felt almost light-hearted. She wasn't looking forward to telling Henry, of course, she hated the thought of hurting him. But how much, apart from his pride, would she hurt? She wasn't entirely convinced it was her he loved anyway. More likely he just saw her as a set of wifely qualities, wrapped in a beddable package.

It took a surprising amount of money to park the car in the hospital grounds. Fortunately, Jenny had brought the takings from The Homely Haggis and had plenty of change.

'I'm here for Mrs Dalmain,' said Jenny, through the intercom. 'I've got her things.'

'Have you? Thank God for that,' said the voice at the other end. 'Push the door when you hear the click.'

She met a nurse the other side. 'She's been driving us all mad,' said the nurse. 'She's bored as much as anything. Do you want to just give me that, and you can be off?'

Jenny suddenly felt hurt. She'd driven a long way, and the thought of not seeing Meggie after all that was disappointing.

'Oh no, don't go,' said Iain, appearing from a room dressed in green scrubs, a mask hanging round his neck. 'Can't she come in and see Meggie? She'd be so fed-up if Jenny made that long journey and just went home again.'

The nurse considered, obviously weighing up the pros and cons of having a non-family member in the labour ward when the mother concerned was being so difficult.

'Are they very close friends?' she asked.

'Not really,' said Jenny.

'Yes,' said Iain, more loudly.

'Then I'll find you a gown and a mask. You can help keep her ladyship entertained.'

Chapter Eleven

They called the baby Anna. The four of them, Meggie and Iain, Jenny and Anna, lay in a huddle on Meggie's bed.

'Isn't she the sweetest thing?' said Iain. 'She looks just like you, darling.'

'Bright red in the face, eyes half shut and fists clenched, I should hope she doesn't.' But Meggie's indignation didn't fool anyone, and indeed, Jenny thought the little bundle, wrapped in a green cloth, did look surprisingly like Meggie.

'If she ends up half as pretty as her mother, she'll be fine,' said Iain.

'She'll be fine anyway. She's got us for parents – what more could any child want?'

As Jenny left the little family she realised that she and Henry would never have what they had, that her decision to leave him was the right one. Seeing Iain support Meggie through her labour, knowing he was still there, through all the gory bits, long after she, Jenny, had abandoned them to flick through aged copies of the *People's Friend*, and pace about in the day room, she knew that nothing less was good enough for a relationship to survive. Her mother hadn't compromised when she had married her father and she shouldn't either. Staying with Henry was wrong, and the moment she was free to go down south to tell him, she would. And then she'd move back home until she could afford a place of her own.

'A girl,' said Lady Dalmain.

Jenny hadn't had to break the news. Iain had telephoned, and Jenny had hoped, as it was four in the morning, that no one would be up and she could just slip up to bed, but the moment she got through the front door and the sea of dogs, Jenny realised there was a reception committee.

Felicity came up behind her mother, holding a half-empty bottle of malt whisky. 'So Meggie didn't get a boy, either.'

Alcohol didn't suit Felicity, Jenny decided. It made her small-minded and self-pitying. Perhaps if she married Lachlan, she wouldn't feel the need to drink so much.

'Yes! A lovely little girl!' said Jenny, determined that if there was going to be a party at four in the morning it would be a cheerful one. 'Anna. Isn't it a pretty name? And such a sweet baby. I hope you're going to make a cushion or something for her, Fliss, with her name and dates on it.'

'My daughter's name is Felicity,' said Lady Dalmain, with slightly more sibilants than necessary, and Jenny realised that she too was the worse for drink. She'd seen her hostess consume vast amounts of whisky before, but never had she shown signs of it affecting her.

'Shall we go into the sitting room?' said Jenny, making ushering movements, rather as if she were herding unruly sheep back into their field. 'Where we can sit down?' She didn't want either Felicity or her mother collapsing onto the stone floor; she'd never get them up again. If they passed out in chairs, she could just leave them there.

'If she'd been a boy, she would have been called Arthur, after her father,' Lady Dalmain went on, her train of thought unbroken by the change of venue, and the chair under her.

Realising that Lady Dalmain wasn't referring to Anna, Jenny asked, 'So why didn't you call Philip Arthur, then, Lady Dalmain?' Jenny accepted the glass Felicity handed to her on the basis that their drunkenness would be more tolerable if she was drunk herself.

'Because he wasn't the first-born. It was a terrible disappointment to my husband.'

'Then why did he call me Felicity?' demanded her daughter, with an unusual display of Dutch courage. 'That means happiness.'

'I know what it means! And he pretended to be happy, but I knew I was a terrible disappointment to him!'

The thought of Lady Dalmain drunk was bad enough, to have her maudlin and weeping was too horrible. Jenny decided a little tough love was required.

'I don't suppose you disappointed him for a moment. After all, the sex of the child is determined by the man, and I dare say your husband was well aware of that fact.'

Lady Dalmain regarded her, aghast. Jenny couldn't decide if it was because she'd used the word 'sex' or because she'd told Lady Dalmain something she hadn't previously known.

'Is it?' Lady Dalmain demanded. 'Are you sure?'

'Quite sure.'

'How do you know?' Lady Dalmain was very persistent.

'We did it at school,' said Jenny firmly, not wanting to go into details she couldn't remember. 'The sex of the baby is determined by the father.'

'So it wasn't my fault?' The voice was getting quavery and pathetic. 'Not my fault that Felicity wasn't a boy?'

'No,' said Felicity, to whom this was also news, apparently. 'Jenny says it was Daddy's fault. And he called me Felicity, which meant he didn't mind. So perhaps now you can stop being such an ungrateful, miserable, neurotic old cow!'

In Jenny's opinion it was a shame that Lady Dalmain had fallen asleep before she could hear Felicity standing up for herself, but Felicity, who sobered up the moment she realised she'd called her mother a cow, seemed relieved.

'Oh my God! What did I say?'

'Nothing that didn't need to be said, in my opinion,' replied Jenny briskly.

'Poor Mama! We'd better get her up to bed. Can you help me? I'm not sure I can manage on my own. I've been drinking.'

'Surprise, surprise,' she muttered. Louder she asked, 'Since when?'

'Since we heard the news about Meggie's baby, just after midnight.'

No wonder they were both paralytic. 'Couldn't we just cover her with a rug and leave her here?'

'Good God no! She'll get all cold and stiff. She might

159

catch a chill or something. We must get her into bed. You get one side, I'll get the other.'

'You must love your mother very much,' said Jenny, heaving one of Lady Dalmain's arms over her shoulder.

'I know she's an old boot and she hates me, but she is the only mother I've got. And she does need me.'

'You know,' said Jenny, panting, as they hauled Lady Dalmain up the stairs, 'I think she'd respect you a lot more if you stood up to her. It's because you put up with the treatment that you go on getting it. Try being braver. And you mustn't let the fact that she needs you stop you getting on with your own life.' Jenny was still in 'tough love' mode.

'It's all very well,' Felicity opened the door of her mother's bedroom with her hip, 'being brave, when you've got the best part of a bottle of whisky inside you. You try it when you've got a hangover which would kill a bull.'

'Drink plenty of water before you go to bed. Or something sweet and fizzy, like lemonade.'

'Are you going to bed now, Jenny?'

'I certainly am,' she said firmly, knowing Felicity would have liked to spend the rest of the night talking. 'It's almost morning already and I've a lot to do today.'

'You don't want to stay up for a nightcap?'

'Felicity, you've had the whole damn négligé, gown, robe, slippers and all. You don't want a nightcap as well. I really think you should just go straight to bed now.'

'Oh, OK. I'll say good night then. Oh, and you won't forget to get me that paper, so I can begin doing some designs? Lachlan thinks it's a really good idea.'

'Jolly good. Now good night, and don't forget the water.'

Swaying, more from fatigue than alcohol, Jenny got herself to her room and into bed. She just had time to exchange one set of warm clothes for another, before she fell asleep.

In the days since the birth of baby Anna, Jenny had become more and more certain that the sooner she drove down south and told Henry how she felt, the better it would be. The trouble was now, with just a week before Mr Grant-Dempsey arrived at the mill, she couldn't possibly spare the time.

'There's no way we can put Mr Grant-Dempsey off coming, I don't suppose,' asked Kirsty. 'Or at least, coming just now? If we found Philip –'

'But do you think he'd go along with our plans? For the mill buildings, for the merino wool, for the workers? And would he be willing to use llama and alpaca fibre? Because if you think we're in with a chance there, we could hire a private detective and find him.'

Kirsty hesitated. 'He is very traditional and always did suffer from "not invented here" syndrome. But as for hiring a private detective, we'd have to go to Glasgow, probably. It would be easier to find him ourselves. And cheaper.'

'Well, that's true. I tell you what, I'll send my client an email, implying his visit isn't necessary, just on the off chance that he doesn't really want to come. Do you think I could tell him the weather's filthy?'

'I am not in a position to say what the tenor of your emails to him are,' said Kirsty drily. 'Do you usually give him meteorological reports?'

'There's no need to go all Jean Brodie on me. I won't mention the weather. How are you getting on with the business plan?'

'It looks very encouraging, if you ignore the fact that we can't develop the offices into starter homes and executive housing. Not without Philip and the deeds, anyway.'

'The fact that the plan is unworkable is a detail we can't do anything about. As long as it would probably work is all that's necessary.'

Kirsty made a querying gesture. 'How do we know what would work? You can't predict fashion. Our industry is dependent on the whim of designers who know nothing and care less about the people who produce their designs.'

Jenny concealed a sigh. She was tired and it would be easy to get depressed. What Kirsty said was probably true. 'Well, predict as much as we can, like how much it would all cost. I'll see if I can stave off the wicked mill owner.'

'Come now, dear; we don't know he's wicked.'

'Don't we? This visit is causing so much anxiety, he can't be good. Anyway, I'll compose my email.'

Eventually, after three cups of coffee, she showed Kirsty her final draft.

Plans for the mill progressing well. Managers have projections for the long, medium and short term. The prospects for its future success in the long term are promising. Unless you particularly want to, I don't think it necessary for you to visit. Though of course we would be glad to see you.

'What do you think?'

'I think it reads like a letter to a teacher telling them there's no point in marking a test, because all the answers are right.'

'You don't think it'll stop him coming?'

'No. On the other hand, I don't know what you could say that would. Send it, and see what happens.'

Jenny was nibbling a piece of Kirsty's home-made shortbread when she opened her client's reply.

> I am glad that the projections are so optimistic. I look forward to seeing them when I visit. I do hope you have borne in mind that we are not a charitable organisation.

'It could have been worse,' said Jenny to Kirsty, later.

'How?'

'I don't know! I just said that to make myself feel better. What we must persuade him is to let us fulfil the orders we've got up until Christmas, and only send the machines back afterwards. By that time we might have done quite a lot of the retraining.'

'It all depends on how this woman with the felt turns out. She sounded very fay on the telephone.' Kirsty was not a Scot who approved of 'fay'.

'I'm sure she'll be fine! At least her heart is in the right place.' Jenny was slightly worried about her herself, but as the 'cup half-full' part of the relationship, she felt obliged to sound positive.

'And how long will you be willing to stay? You won't want to be here until after Christmas, surely?'

'Well, I expect I'll go home for the actual event, but I

could come up afterwards. I've never known a genuine Scottish Hogmanay, after all.'

Just then Iain popped his head round the door with Alistair, the mill's oldest employee by several years, in tow. 'Why don't you go and see how they're getting on converting the new machinery?'

Jenny was surprised to see Iain there. 'Hello! I thought you'd be at home doting over Meggie and Anna.'

He shook his head. 'No, they're fine. Meggie's well able to cope so I thought I'd come see what these old codgers are up to.'

'Oh, laddie. I remember you when you were a pretty wee boy, not the great ugly brute you are now, and a father to boot. We can still teach you a thing or two.'

Iain accepted this compliment with grace. 'I'd have thought they'd have pensioned you off long since,' he said, his slight brogue becoming very broad. 'You were here before Methuselah retired.'

'It does your heart good to see the old machines in use again. I don't know why young Philip got rid of them in the first place.' Alistair was ecstatic to think the mill could be saved by reverting to old technology. *Sotto voce* (which, because he was deaf, was quite loud) he said, 'Iain always had the better idea of how to go about things. But the laird wanted Philip to take over. There was a bit of a falling-out between the lads, and Iain took to fixing cars.'

Glad to have this information, Jenny nodded, and was about to ask another question, when Iain put up a hand. 'Enough gossiping. I've a wife and child to support now. Let's see if these machines actually work.'

Later, back in the office, she was surprised to find Kirsty less enthusiastic.

'The trouble is,' said Kirsty, 'Alistair and his lot should have been retired years ago. There's enough young men going to lose their jobs; we shouldn't be keeping on old timers like them.'

Jenny sighed. 'On the other hand, the young men have got a much better chance of finding other work. Alistair and his like would just fade away.'

'We're not a charitable institution, as your client keeps reminding us.'

'We are until next week,' said Jenny. 'And if the plans for the building conversion ever go ahead, some of the younger men might get work doing that.'

'Not unless they happen to be skilled bricklayers, carpenters or electricians,' said Kirsty.

Jenny subsided into despair for a few moments. Being Pollyanna all the time was so tiring. 'I know!' she said, looking up, after putting her head in her hands for a minute or so. 'I'll tell himself he must pay for the young men to be retrained! I am sure there'd be grants for things like that.'

'A snowflake's chance in hell you've got of pulling that one off,' said Kirsty. 'Why do you think an organisation like Grant-Dempsey would bother with retraining workers to go and work for someone else?'

'To make themselves look good?'

'Away with ye, lassie!'

Subdued, Jenny 'awayed'.

It was four days later and Jenny went to see Meggie and Anna. She needed cheering up. The visit from her client was scheduled for the Monday morning, and she had another weekend at Dalmain House to look forward to. She planned to retreat to The Homely Haggis. There was nothing else she could do to prepare for the visit, anyway. And at The Homely Haggis there was a chance, albeit a faint one, of seeing Ross Grant. He hadn't reappeared since she'd turned down his drink invitation.

'Hello, Jenny! How lovely to see you!' Meggie was up and dressed, carrying Anna as if she'd been a mother for years, not days.

'Should you be up and about? Shouldn't you be *lying in*?'

Meggie pshawed dismissively. 'None of that nowadays. Could you do a cuppa?'

'Only if I make you one. Lying in might be out of date, but lying on the sofa with your feet up's all the rage. Ask any student.'

Meggie laughed. 'OK. You make the tea. I've got a wee favour to ask.'

'Well, I warn you, I'll say no. Doing you favours last time got me nothing but grief.'

Too late, Jenny realised that Meggie knew nothing of Ross Grant and his effect on her knees.

Meggie frowned. 'I thought you liked The Homely Haggis!'

'I do, but it got me started on cooking at Dalmain House, because of the flapjack and the gingerbread. And now I share the ordinary cooking too.'

Meggie laughed. 'That's just self-interest. Go and make the tea, and can I have a glass of water too? Then I'll tell you my plan.'

When Jenny came back with tea and water, and had produced a bag of flapjack from her bag, she grasped the nettle. 'So, what's this plan then? And how am I involved? I'm really pushed for time. We've got my client coming to the mill on Monday.'

'You've worked very hard for that place. You're seen as an angel down at the mill, Iain tells me.'

Jenny found herself blushing. 'I don't know about that.'

'Well, I'll think you're an angel too, if you agree to help me.'

'What? What can you possibly be hatching up now? I would have thought Anna would have kept you out of mischief, if not out of energy.'

'Come with Anna and me and do a Highland show tomorrow. It's a real miracle it's happening, as it's far too late in the season for them. This is a sort of extra one, a memorial for the person who ran it for ever. He told everyone he didn't want a service, just that this year's games would be held in his memory. Then he didn't die.'

'But I thought you said –'

'Sorry, I'm not making myself clear. He did die, but not in time for them to have the games at the ordinary time. When he realised he wasn't going by August, he said they were to try and fit it in this year, even if it was really late, because by next year he reckoned everyone would have forgotten about him. They wouldn't have, of course.'

'You're rambling, woman.'

'I know, it's because I'm so pleased I'm able to go. I've missed all the others – seeing the games, I mean. Of course, I couldn't do the Dalmain Games, what with Lady D. objecting to family members earning a decent living at it, but these games are always lovely.' She joggled Anna, who was now settled in the crook of her arm.

'Hang on! You're only just out of hospital! Having had a baby! You couldn't possibly spend all day behind the counter of The Homely Haggis!'

'I know, that's why I want you to help me. Come on, Jenny! It'll be extra Scottish and everything, because it's in Hamish's memory, full of pipers and tossing cabers, all that stuff. Everyone will come, so we'll be really busy, which is always fun. The head of one of the other clans will open it, and the speeches will go on for ever, but as it's not our clan, we can relax.'

Diverted for a moment from the enormity of Meggie's suggestion and the struggle to keep up with her explanations, Jenny said, 'What do you mean? Are you telling me that Lady Dalmain opens Highland games?'

'Oh yes. The Dalmain Games were earlier this year. Philip is the local chieftain, so he's really the big cheese, but Lady D. did the honours, presenting prizes, patronising everyone like mad. These games will be much nicer. You'll have to get Kirsty to make a double batch of shortbread.'

'Meggie, this is madness! What does Iain think about this crazy idea?'

'Haven't told him. But I reckon if you're there, Anna and I can go and rest in the car whenever we need to. I need to get back out into the world! I've been cut off from it too long. I've got a friend who'll tow the van there tonight. Oh come on, Jen! It'll stop me getting weepy! They say you can get terribly depressed when you've just had a baby.'

'Only one condition,' said Jenny, to whom the idea

of swapping a day at Dalmain House, with nothing much to do except listen to Lady Dalmain complain, for some short-order cheffing, was very attractive. 'That you clear it with Iain. In fact, I'll ask him myself. Where will you feed Anna?'

'Oh just behind the counter. Breast-feeding is dead easy, now I've got the hang of it.'

'That's not quite what I meant,' said Jenny, observing Anna having a snack. She sounded like a pig sucking on a melting ice lolly. Even Meggie noticed.

'She has no idea how to be discreet, that's her trouble.'

'Small wonder, considering who her role model is.'

Chapter Twelve

Even the most hard-hearted Sassenach would have been moved by the sight of the showground. Next to a peat-coloured river, which gurgled merrily over the rocks, surrounded by heather-covered hills, bathed in sunlight, it could have been a Medieval jousting ground. The sky was a deep blue, reminding everyone to enjoy this last, brief, spell of fine weather before winter swept in and drove the warmth away.

Jenny was enchanted. 'This is all so pretty!' she exclaimed to Meggie, as she accepted the various bags and baskets without which Anna couldn't travel.

'Aye. Hamish must have arranged for it to be this fine, and it's always a grand occasion, even though it's small. All the big throwers will be here, and we should hear some good piping too.' Meggie unbuckled Anna and swept her into her arms. 'Although you might not like that so much, being from England.'

'Actually, I love the sound of bagpipes,' admitted Jenny. 'Perhaps I've got Scots blood in me I'm not aware of.'

'Can you manage that bag as well? I think I can see the van over there. We should make our fortunes today.'

'You can only make your fortune if you can do it sitting down,' said Jenny, trying to keep up with

170

Meggie and Anna. 'Talking of which, do you think there might be a palm reader?'

'Now why would you want one of them? Looking for a handsome stranger? I thought your future was assured with a boyfriend at home.'

'I have; I'm just not sure he's the right one.'

'Well, if you've thought that out for yourself, you don't need a palm reader. But there might very well be one here.'

The van was in a circle of similar vehicles. There were stalls selling old-fashioned sweeties, tablet, cinder toffee, humbugs and Edinburgh rock. A horn carver offered horn-handled knives, spoons especially for boiled eggs, walking sticks, thumb sticks and shepherds' crooks.

Similar tents and stalls sold all sorts of Caledonalia, everything tartan covered, thistle embossed, Highland laddie-painted. From tea towels to tartan bed jackets, it was all available. There was a man selling fishing tackle, amazing waders, which looked as if you could cross the Atlantic in them, deer-stalker hats, tam-o'-shanters, berets, and bonnets.

'I might do my Christmas shopping while I'm here. I won't be able to get anything like this down south,' said Jenny, when she had finally forced Meggie to sit down with Anna and they were waiting for customers.

'I hope you're not being sarcastic,' said Meggie, then leapt up. 'Hello, what can I do for you?' she said to the woman who was carrying a baby, a few months older than Anna, who was crying loudly.

'A cup of tea, please. And would you have any way of heating up a bottle? They told us in the hospital it was all right to give it to them cold, but it doesn't seem right, does it?'

'It does seem a bit brutal,' said Meggie. 'I'll put it in a pan of boiling water. It'll take a wee while, but not too long, I hope.'

'Actually,' said Jenny, pushing Meggie back down into her seat. 'I'll do it. My friend,' she said, pouring milk, 'shouldn't be here. She's hardly out of hospital.'

Expecting support, she was disappointed when the woman snorted, 'Huh! I was in the hospital for six hours and then sent home to look after the other weans.'

'You see,' said Meggie.

'Shut up and sit down,' said Jenny.

There was a small rush of people, and Meggie served flapjack one handed, while Jenny dealt with boiling water and change. Then, when Anna finally went to sleep, and there was a lull, Meggie insisted that Jenny went for a wander round.

She did this with one eye constantly on The Homely Haggis so she could dash back, should a customer appear. She was slightly put out to discover a stall that sold, among other things, alpaca jumpers. The feel of them was wonderful, but, she decided, the designs were dull and they were all imported. There was such an enthusiasm for home-grown products, the Scots would surely accept local alpaca fibre with open arms. Provided it wasn't too expensive, of course. She bought a pair of walking boots, not quite knowing why. It wasn't as if she'd use them much in Surrey, after all.

Jenny had minded the sleeping Anna while Meggie went round herself, and they were all beginning to feel tired when Meggie, resting Anna's weight on the counter while she fed her, suddenly squeaked, causing Anna to do likewise.

'I don't believe it! Is that who I think it is? The Matriarch, and some man I've never seen before. They're coming this way! What on earth is she doing here? Oh fuck!'

Jenny followed Meggie's gaze. 'Oh my God! This is awful! What are we to do? Can I hide?'

'Why would *you* want to? You're not feeding your baby in front of your mother-in-law. Come on, Anna, we'll have to shift.'

Anna, still sucking hard, took no notice. 'I don't know if I should unplug her, or just move. What's bothering you? You're not frightened of the old bitch, are you?'

Jenny shook her head, still wondering if she could duck under the counter and stay there until Lady Dalmain and her companion went away. 'It's not her, it's the man with her. It's bloody Henry!'

'Who's Henry?'

Jenny didn't have time to explain before the pair were on them.

'Hello, Lady Dalmain,' said Jenny quickly, aware that Meggie was still tucking shawls about her loudly sucking child. 'And hello, Henry!'

She had to raise her voice, several entrants to the piping competition having begun practising behind the row of tents and stalls. 'What on earth are you doing here? There's nothing wrong at home, is there?' She started to panic – there must be something wrong with her mother. 'It can't just be a social call, can it?'

'I came to see you, sweetie.' Henry leant across the

counter and kissed her nose. 'Aren't you pleased to see me?'

Instead of relief, she felt extreme irritation. 'Of course, but it's such a surprise.'

'For me too. I didn't expect to find you serving behind the counter at a place like this.' His infinitesimal hesitation indicated precisely his opinion of The Homely Haggis. It was on a par with Lady Dalmain's.

'I expect you are surprised to see us,' said Lady Dalmain, staring horrified at Meggie. 'But when Henry arrived and asked for you, I naturally told him where you were. Then he very sweetly offered to drive me over. Such fun! I haven't been to a Highland games where I have no official duties for years. And, of course, dear Hamish was a pillar of the community. It's only right to pay one's respects. Margaret,' she addressed Meggie, 'I know it's none of my business, but should you be doing that here? It can't be hygienic.'

'Oh, it's fine. She doesn't get anything except me, I make sure of that.'

'I meant for the customers.'

Meggie's brow darkened.

'Can I get either of you a cup of tea?' asked Jenny, pushing Meggie back onto her chair. 'Now, what would you like? Henry?' she added sharply.

Henry, having taken in what Meggie was doing, was staring, half fascinated, half horrified.

'You know how you like my flapjack,' Jenny persisted. 'Or have you just eaten?'

'Henry took me out for lunch. It was quite good, wasn't it?' Lady Dalmain was looking at the plates of flapjack and shortbread. 'But we didn't have pudding.'

'I'm sure you'll find the tea and shortbread very superior.'

Henry raised a quizzical eyebrow. 'Darling, how can it be? This is a fast-food stand.'

Certain that any moment Meggie would put Anna down and deck both her mother-in-law and Henry, Jenny gabbled on, 'Because we only use the highest quality ingredients and everything is home-made. I make the flapjack myself.'

Lady Dalmain frowned. 'Do you? And where do you do that? You couldn't bake here, could you?' She peered behind the counter, causing Meggie to pick up a cloth and fling it over Anna's head.

'I do it at Dalmain House,' said Jenny. 'But only when the oven is on anyway. And I have put a portion of the profits aside to pay for gas. Not really,' she added to Meggie, who was still steaming, protected from committing murder only by her feeding baby.

'Good,' said Lady Dalmain. 'I wouldn't like to think of you taking advantage of my hospitality.'

'Oh, Jenny would never do that, Lady Dalmain,' said Henry. 'She's absolutely scrupulous.'

'Well, thank you,' said Jenny. 'Now, Henry, if you don't want anything to eat, and do want to see a caber being tossed, you should make your way over there. I think I see them starting up.'

'What? Oh, that thing that looks like a telegraph pole? Good Lord! I think I can do without that. I came to see you, Jenny. Any chance of you coming out from behind there?'

'No!' she said hastily, before Meggie could say yes. 'Where are you staying?'

'At the Achnabrech Arms.'

'My dear young man! It's frightful! You can't possibly stay there.'

Lady Dalmain had obviously taken a shine to Henry, and sensing what might be coming, Jenny broke in. 'I expect he needs to be there, for his work.'

'So what is it you do?' asked Lady Dalmain.

'I'm a property consultant.' He gave her the patient smile he gave everyone who needed further explanation and flicked back his soft, brown forelock. 'It's not quite the same as an estate agent – we don't sell houses as such. We work with the client, seek out suitable properties, which may not even be for sale until we meet the owners, and make a match.'

'Although you do negotiate the sale, then,' said Jenny, wiping furiously at the clean counter, feeling that Henry shouldn't be allowed to dissociate himself entirely from the sordid financial aspects of the job, however much he might like to appear to be above that sort of thing.

'Well naturally,' he agreed reprovingly, 'our client isn't going to want anyone else to do it by that time. We'll have worked up a good relationship by then.'

'So the hotel is probably well placed for you?' asked Jenny, crossing her fingers.

'Actually,' Henry smiled. Jenny realised she'd never noticed how oily he could be before, 'most of the properties are in the same neck of the woods as Dalmain House, but my secretary couldn't find anywhere decent for me to stay round there.'

'There isn't anywhere decent,' said Lady Dalmain, with satisfaction. 'Why don't you stay with us? We could do with some masculine company. I get terribly bored with female chatter.'

Now it was Jenny who was about to commit murder.

'I couldn't possibly impose on you like that,' said Henry, meaning that he could, only too well.

'Actually, Henry,' said Jenny, 'could I have a word?' She indicated with her head that they should meet outside the van. For both her own sake and Henry's, she felt obliged to warn Henry about the eccentricities of Dalmain House and its plumbing. He was a man who needed a bidet and a power shower to be comfortable. Having to manage with a miserly trickle of tepid water would make him very unhappy.

'Well, I could certainly do with a welcome kiss, sweetie. It doesn't feel like you're my little Jenny Henny behind that counter.'

Jenny and Meggie squeezed past each other so Jenny could get out of the van. Meggie seemed to be enjoying herself.

Henry's arms were round her and his lips on hers before she could draw breath. She felt suffocated and crushed and she could taste game pie. She tried to get into the kiss. This was Henry, with whom she lived, shared a bed, made love to. Had he always been such an awful kisser? If so, how did they get beyond the third date?

'God, I needed that!' he murmured. 'It's good the old lady has invited me to stay. I can't wait for a bit of – you know –'

'If you mean sex,' Jenny hissed back, 'you can forget it! We'll be staying under Lady Dalmain's roof! It would be terrible to abuse her hospitality like that!'

'Come on, Jen! You're not usually so prudish!'

'I know,' she patted his arm, 'and I'm sorry. But I've been under so much pressure lately, and what with

177

one thing and another the thought of creeping about in Dalmain House, which is absolutely bloody freezing by the way, is just not appealing now.' She didn't mention her client's visit on Monday – she couldn't bear to have to start explaining everything.

'You mean I've driven all this way, and you won't even –'

'I didn't ask you to drive to Scotland to see me! And, anyway, I thought you said you had business.'

'I have, very good business, in fact.' He laid his finger against his nose in a gesture that made Jenny want to hit him. 'One of the reasons I'm keen to see Dalmain House.'

It took Jenny a moment to take in the significance of this. 'You mean, you've got a client interested in Dalmain House?'

'No names, no pack drill.'

Jenny wanted to scream. 'Just tell me, has someone asked you to sell Dalmain House?'

Henry made a concession. 'No, I've just been asked to look at it, to see if it's suitable for a certain client, that's all.'

'Because as far as I know, it's not for sale.' Unless Philip had somehow managed to get the deeds to the house as well, and was doing something dirty behind everybody's back.

'Everything's for sale at a price, Jenny,' said Henry pompously.

'Not everything,' she snapped. Not me, for instance, she added silently. 'Now why don't you have a wander round? I don't suppose Lady Dalmain will want to stay long, and then she'll order you to drive her home.'

'Oh, don't worry about Lady D. I've got her taped. I happened to notice she had a Whittard when I very first arrived. She was so thrilled, now I can do no wrong. Look how she's invited me to stay!'

Jenny decided not to ask what the hell a Whittard was, and was about to reprove him for taking advantage of a poor old lady, when she remembered who the poor old lady was. 'Well, I hope you don't regret saying yes. The house is dreadfully uncomfortable.'

'But think how useful it will be for me to have actually stayed in a house I'm selling! Really valuable information to be had there!'

'I thought you said you weren't selling it!'

'I may be, I may be not. You know how confidential my work is, Jen. You should know better than to ask questions.'

'Oh, bloody hell, Henry! I'm staying there too! These people are becoming my friends! Well, not Lady Dalmain, of course, but her daughter. I feel you should tell me if you've been instructed to sell the place.'

'OK, OK, don't get your feathers ruffled, Jenny Wren. I've a client who might be interested in buying it. But no one has instructed me to sell it. Satisfied now?'

'Sort of.' She gave his arm a little rub. It was meant to be in affection, but in fact she found herself pushing him away. 'Now go and enjoy your first Highland games. It may be your last.'

'Not until I've had another kiss. I haven't given up hope of changing your mind about the other.'

Jenny submitted, wondering why she suddenly felt so repulsed by Henry. She opened her eyes, and then

179

shut them again. She must have conjured him up! It was Ross Grant! Staring at her! How long had he been there? Did he arrive during or after she was kissing Henry?

She broke free. 'Off you go, Henry. Lady Dalmain is looking very disapproving. Go and escort her to the caber tossing, or the piping competition, or whatever.'

Lady Dalmain was indeed looking disapproving, but it was at Meggie, not at Henry and Jenny. Ross Grant seemed to have disappeared, and Jenny wondered if she had imagined him. While Henry and Lady Dalmain were discussing what they wished to see, Jenny tried to decide if she wanted to have just imagined him, so he hadn't seen her kissing Henry, or wanted him to be real, so she might see him again. She had just decided it would be better if he had been a figment of her imagination when she saw him again. He was examining a thumb stick with deep concentration at a stall just across the way.

She was just about to tell Meggie that they'd been here quite long enough and that they should pack up and go home, when a young woman and someone who was obviously her mother appeared at the counter. They squealed delightedly when they saw Meggie.

It turned out that the young woman was Meggie's oldest friend, and that the mother had a VW camper van parked a little way away.

'Come across to us and have a wee rest,' urged the mother. She smiled at Jenny. 'I'm sure your friend can take care of things here for you. You could have a nice lie down in the camper.'

'Yes, of course I can manage! In fact, I'll manage a

darn sight better without you and Anna cluttering up the place! I feel so guilty agreeing to let you come.'

'Oh, she'd have come anyway,' said the mother. 'Always headstrong – has been from a lassie. It's good you were able to help her out.'

Jenny was watching Lady Dalmain and Henry. They were a little distance from her, perfectly visible, but unaware of her. Lady Dalmain had obviously met some old friends who were standing by an old Rolls Royce shooting brake, complete with half timbering at the back. They were all wearing tartan in some form. The older woman, quite a bit younger than Lady Dalmain, was wearing a tartan suit. Her daughters, who shared their mother's pale red hair and freckled skin, but not her desire for the all-over look, were wearing jeans, Gucci loafers and tartan jackets. They definitely looked as if they would have been more at home in Sloane Square than at such a country event. While Jenny assumed they were true Scotswomen, born and bred, they didn't quite fit in with the kilts and hand-knitted socks, which looked unbearably prickly, or with the local worthy ladies, who wore knee-length tartan skirts with no concession to fashion. They were clustered round Henry in a rather overenthusiastic way.

Jenny tried to feel jealous. There she was, watching Henry being charmed and flattered by three very young women, and she couldn't summon up even the smallest twinge.

She was just wondering how she'd feel if she saw Ross Grant in the same position, when he appeared. She nearly jumped out of her skin. All the moisture vanished from her mouth and her knees threatened to buckle.

'Oh God!' she said, short of breath. 'You gave me a fright! What do you mean, creeping up on me like that?'

'I didn't creep up on you! I arrived in a perfectly normal manner, as you would have seen if you hadn't been looking longingly at your boyfriend!' He seemed bigger than Jenny remembered him, and he'd seemed quite large before. He was wearing faded jeans and a navy sweater. On his feet were socks and walking boots. The jeans made it clear how flat his stomach was, how long and muscular his legs. Henry, whom she had previously considered to be a fine man, suddenly seemed effete and puny.

'What? Oh, you mean Henry! I wasn't looking longingly!'

'Oh?' He sounded sceptical. 'Don't you feel just the tiniest bit jealous? There he is, his saliva hardly dry on your lips, charming the pants off those young women.'

She shuddered. 'That is the most disgusting thing I have ever heard.'

'You should get out more. Talking of which, how about that drink? I know it was a while ago that we talked about it, but I've been away.'

Jenny stared at him in complete amazement. 'You don't really expect me to go out with you, now, when you've been so incredibly rude, do you?'

Amusement danced in the back of his eyes. He shrugged. 'Well, you certainly won't if I don't ask you.'

Terrifyingly, she found herself responding to his enjoyment. 'But why on earth would I go out with you? You've seen for yourself, I've got a boyfriend.'

He didn't answer immediately. He looked into her

eyes, apparently sizing her up. 'That didn't seem evident when I kissed you before. Then, you seemed completely – unencumbered.'

Small, incomprehensible sounds emerged from her throat as Jenny tried to get a grip. She should slap his face or something, and she might have done if there hadn't been two feet of stainless steel and several plates of home baking between them. 'You are – just – I can't believe you!'

'Of course, if you'd rather spend the evening at Dalmain House with – him –'

'His name is Henry.'

'It would be. If you'd rather spend the evening with Henry, I quite understand. But the choice is yours.'

'I know!'

He looked back towards where Henry and Lady Dalmain's friends were standing. 'I won't press you for an answer now, because *Henry* looks as if he's on his way back and you have some thinking to do, but I'll ring you later.'

Determinedly not looking at him, she rearranged the flapjack with the serving tongs, breaking off a large chunk of one bit, rendering it unsaleable, as she did so.

'How will you do that, when you haven't got the number?'

'Well, you could give it to me. Or I could just call round in person. Whichever you prefer.'

Her fingers were slippery as she burrowed in her pocket for a pen. 'I'll give you the number.' The thought of Ross Grant turning up at Dalmain House, having to explain him, was too dreadful. She grabbed a napkin and wrote the number on it. 'Here!'

'Thank you.' He gave her another penetrating glance

before leaving, just as Henry and Lady Dalmain arrived at the counter.

'What were you talking to that man about?' demanded Henry.

'I was just giving him directions,' she said calmly, wondering why she didn't feel guilty for lying.

'Oh. I thought you gave him something.'

'A paper napkin with directions on it. Now, are you going to eat something or just interrogate me? We'll be packing up soon.'

Later, Henry found her in the kitchen of Dalmain House, mashing potatoes. They hadn't set out to be mashed potatoes, but had taken that career move when they became so overboiled. It was, thought Jenny, going to be impossible for them not to taste watery. She added a large lump of butter, which, in self-defence, she'd started buying herself.

'Darling!' Henry was indignant that she didn't instantly throw down her masher. 'You might be a bit more pleased to see me! I have driven over seven hundred miles to see you!'

Jenny relinquished her weapon and allowed herself to be kissed. 'I thought you were up here on business.'

'I am,' said Henry, 'but I wanted to see you too. I wondered when you were coming home.'

'I'm not sure. There's a lot to get done.'

He gave her the mocking smile she had once thought so attractive and that now irritated her more than she could say. 'But, sweetie, you're always telling me how efficient you are! Surely you're not having trouble organising the closure of a tin-pot woollen mill!'

Jenny turned back to her potatoes to stop herself hitting him with the masher. 'I'm trying not to close it down; that's the point!' She opened the oven door. Several slices of smoked haddock lay in a Pyrex dish, flinching from the milk that lapped at their sides. 'Do you think there's time to turn all this into fish pie?'

Henry shrugged. 'You do make awfully good fish pie, sweetie, but, personally, I'm starving.'

She glanced at her watch. It was already nearly eight. Bloody Ross Grant! Why hadn't he rung her? She wasn't going to go out with him, but she wanted the chance to turn him down. 'Henry, why don't you go and change for dinner? I'll get on faster by myself.'

Felicity came in, but waited for Henry to leave before saying, 'Gosh, he's really nice, isn't he? He's been brilliant with Mama.'

'Are you going to help, Felicity? If not, I am rather busy.'

'Oh! No, I came to tell you that there's a man on the phone for you. God knows who. Take it in Mama's room. She's in the drawing room, having a drink.'

'Right!' Jenny flew up the stairs to take Ross's call. Boy, was she going to turn him down! She picked up the phone. 'Hello?'

'Sorry I didn't ring before. I had to rescue a sheep. I've only just got back. So, have you made up your mind?'

She sucked in a deep breath through her clenched teeth. 'I'll meet you at the bottom of the drive at nine,' she snapped, and slammed the phone down.

Chapter Thirteen

As Jenny stumbled down the drive in the dark, wearing an old coat she had pulled off the newel post, she wondered how she'd ever got this far.

At the speed of light, she had turned the haddock into fish pie, with the aid of a packet of cheese sauce (Felicity's favourite culinary aid) and some very sweaty orange cheddar. In spite of its shortcomings, this was consumed, and pudding eagerly awaited. Panicking mildly, Jenny threw some partially stewed apples (there wasn't time to finish cooking them) into a Pyrex dish and sprinkled them with flapjack crumbs. She put this on the table, hoping that Henry wouldn't comment on its similarity to the first course, and announced to the company that she had to go out. She'd worry about explanations later. They were probably all still sitting at the table, staring at the space she had left.

The Land Rover was parked a little way down the drive.

Ross Grant got out of it as he saw her approach. Without speaking, he opened the passenger door and helped her in. She sat down, and didn't speak.

For a second the thought flashed into her mind that she'd got into a car with a man she hardly knew. No one knew where she was or where she was going. *She* didn't know where she was going. She tried very hard to worry, but nothing seemed as bad as an evening watching Henry sucking up to Lady Dalmain, and vice versa.

'There's a little pub I know up in the hills. I'm going to take you there.'

'Fine.' From somewhere she found her voice, which she took to be an encouraging sign. It was only a drink in a pub, although at that moment not a single casual remark or light topic of conversation occurred to her. Perhaps he wouldn't mind if she just sat in silence.

'Wake up. We're here,' said Ross.

To her horror Jenny realised that not only had she fallen asleep, but that Ross had noticed. What would he think of her? Then she almost laughed. Why worry? At least if she was asleep she was unlikely to throw anything at him.

'Sorry,' she said, yawning. 'It's been a long day.'

'Here, let me help you.'

She found herself swung down off the high seat and supported when her knees buckled slightly as she landed. He took her arm and led her into the pub.

It was strange, she thought, as she felt his arm under hers, how often she had held Henry's arm, and how it had never felt like this. Now, she allowed herself to be manoeuvred into the lounge bar and seated next to a fire that glowed and crackled and gave out heat.

'What would you like?'

She dithered, only for a second, but he took control. 'I can recommend a particularly good single malt. Would you like to try it?'

She nodded, although she knew she should refuse.

She'd already had one of Felicity's monster drinks, and had had Henry muttering to her, 'You know I don't like to see you drink spirits.'

Ross, she noticed, when he came to join her at the table, glasses in hand, was drinking ginger ale. The thought that he might be trying to get her drunk so he could have his evil way with her flickered into her mind and out again. The fact that he wasn't drinking actually made her feel even safer. Henry sometimes drank a little more than she would have liked, when he was driving. And he would never let her drive his car, insisting it was too powerful for her.

He raised his glass. 'I hope you like that. It is quite smoky.'

She sipped, and felt several hundred years of peat bog slide down her throat. 'It's lovely. But I'd better not have too much. I've been drinking already today.' A shuddering sigh escaped her and she tried to turn it into a smile.

'You're tired. Well, please don't feel obliged to sit there and make polite conversation, although the novelty of that would be entertaining. If you're bushed, just drink your whisky and enjoy the fire.'

Jenny was a well-brought-up girl from the Home Counties. She was not in the habit of going out and just 'enjoying the fire'. In her antiquated book of rules, if you were on a date, especially a first date, you asked your escort about himself, and his opinion of the latest world crisis.

'No, I'm fine really. And if I'm tired, I just think how my friend Meggie must be feeling! She's hardly out of hospital after her baby, and she can't even guarantee getting much sleep tonight.'

'True, but I imagine going to the Highland games was her idea?'

'Well, yes, but if I'd said no . . .' She sighed deeply and suddenly. 'So, do you go to all the Highland games in the area, or was it just coincidence that you were at that one?'

He shook his head. 'Not really. I'd heard about Hamish, of course, and the games in his memory, but I wanted to see you.'

'Oh?' She suddenly stopped feeling safe and sleepy. Remembered dislike and desire welled up and confused her.

'It's all right; I'm not a stalker. There was just something I wanted to talk to you about.'

'Which is why you asked me for a drink?'

He nodded. 'Partly. The other part is that you are a very attractive woman, for all your assertiveness.'

Jenny giggled. 'No one has ever described me as that before.'

He shrugged. 'But I'm sure you fight for things that matter to you.'

'Oh yes! Absolutely – to the death! But in a controlled, considered kind of way.'

He laughed. 'Now that I *would* like to see.'

'What?'

'You being controlled and considered.'

Jenny tried very hard not to laugh back. 'I think I threw that cup of coffee in a very controlled way. It got you just where I intended it to get you.'

'Did it?'

Jenny shut her eyes and turned away. What was it about his voice that seemed to stroke every erogenous zone? She opened her eyes and turned towards him.

'Yes,' she said briskly. 'Now, what was it you wanted to talk to me about?'

For the first time he seemed slightly uneasy. 'First, tell me a little about your work. You're not full time at The Homely Haggis.'

This seemed a safe enough subject. She would give him the usual sound bite, he would look blank, she would explain again, and he would say, 'Ah yes, I think I understand,' while not understanding at all, just bored with the subject.

'I'm what is known as a virtual assistant. Which means –'

He broke in. 'Actually, I am familiar with the concept. I work with computers myself.'

'Oh. Well, there's nothing much more to say.'

'Yes, there is. VAs usually work from the comfort of their own homes, don't they?'

'Well, yes, but at the moment I'm being a bit more hands-on than I am usually.'

'And you're working at Dalmain Mills.'

There seemed no point in denying it. His sources of information were obviously excellent. 'How do you know that? Do you spend all day gossiping?'

'Not quite.'

Then she remembered. 'Oh no, you rescue sheep as well, don't you? What was wrong with it?'

'It had got over on to its back, but I didn't bring you here to talk about sheep.'

'Pity. I have an interest in wool at the moment. Although, apparently, you can't use Scottish wool for very fine fabrics. But, of course, it's excellent for tweed.'

He seemed surprised by this snippet. 'Do you know all about wool, then?'

She shook her head. 'Not really, in fact, hardly anything. But I have been learning about it since working at the mill. It's fascinating, when you get into it. Apparently the wool is affected by what the sheep eat.'

He frowned. 'Surely you don't need to learn about wool to –'

'To what?'

'Be a virtual assistant.'

'Well no, but as I'm working at a mill at the moment, I do think it's important to get all the background information you can, particularly –'

'Particularly if the mill's in trouble?'

She shrugged. 'I suppose it's common knowledge.'

'So why the interest? Why don't you just look at the figures, and if they don't add up, just let commercial forces take over?'

'Listen! You must have some good instincts! You rescued a sheep, after all. Do you really think it's morally acceptable just to close down a mill, a working community, just because the numbers don't add up? Without even *trying* to see if anything can be done about it? Well, I don't! Of course, it may have to close, but not until I've done absolutely everything in my power to keep it going.'

'I said you were a fighter.'

'Well, perhaps I am –'

'I also said you were a very attractive woman.'

Jenny swallowed. Then she took a calming, sensible breath. 'And you said you wanted to talk to me about something.'

'Now doesn't seem a good moment. Can I get you another drink?'

Before she could say no, he had got up, taking her empty glass. She closed her eyes, the warmth of the fire warming her bones.

Seconds later, he woke her up again. 'So, in your work as a VA, have you rescued any other failing companies?'

'Oh no. But most of my work is done at long distance.'

'So why don't you have a normal job, where you could work with people more often?'

'My mother tells me that my besetting sin is trying to sort everybody out all of the time, which I suppose may be what I'm trying to do now.'

'You haven't answered my question.'

'About why I'm a VA?' Jenny took another sip of whisky, aware that the Dalmain House whisky she consumed so much of was very poor stuff compared to this soft, straw-coloured drink. 'The firm I worked for went bust. The workers, me included, were all dumped, with nothing, not even our last month's pay cheque. The bosses all walked away with a small fortune and started up another business. I decided I wanted to be in control of my own destiny from then on.'

'And will you mind going back to working on your own, after you've been working here with other people?'

It was a worryingly pertinent question. Life had been extremely difficult and high pressure since she'd been in Scotland, and while she couldn't really say she'd loved every minute, she had felt totally alive. The thought of the Home Counties, Henry, and all that entailed, did seem very flat and pointless.

'I don't know. I don't have much choice in the matter.'

'You could be proactive about it. You could demand to be made manager of the mills.'

She frowned. 'I don't think so. That job should go to Kirsty – she's brilliant, but has never been allowed responsibility – if there is such a job, and the whole place doesn't go belly up.'

'Why did it get into such a state, do you think?'

'The mill? Well, I don't really know, but I don't think Philip, the owner, ever really had much interest in it. His answer was to just borrow money and get through the next few months. He wouldn't ever look at what the basic problem was.'

'And what was that?'

'Well, it's only my opinion, and I haven't been there five minutes, but I think he should have stopped trying to produce what everyone else produced, only less profitably, and look for other, more unusual markets. Diversify, in other words.'

'Mm. It's an interesting concept.'

'Only if you're interested in mills, which I don't expect you are.' One of her other Home Counties rules was that you took it in turns to do the talking, at least, if you were a woman. In Jenny's experience, men usually felt this meant the woman saying, 'Yes, Henry,' every so often. 'So, what brought you to the area?'

'It's a long story. If I tell it, you'll probably go to sleep again.'

'Try me – but don't take offence if I do. I've had far too much to drink.'

He laughed. 'Well, there isn't a lot. I work from

home, which is why I'm free to live where I like, and I love this area. It's where my mother's family come from. And I've always wanted to become a member of a mountain rescue team.'

'But I thought you told me you were on holiday? That first time?'

'I'd taken the day off.'

Jenny frowned. 'So you came up here just so you could join a mountain rescue team. Why are you so keen?'

'That story will definitely send you to sleep.'

'Go on,' she prompted softly. 'I don't feel nearly so sleepy now. Unless you'd rather not tell me about it.'

He frowned. 'Strangely, I don't think I would mind telling you, although I never usually talk about it at all.'

'Go on.'

'I was about fourteen. A friend and I decided we'd go up Snowdon. We made all the preparations. He'd been up before, said it was easy. A train runs up there, for God's sake, but at the last moment, he couldn't come. Can't remember why now, but I decided to go on my own. Pure bravado, I expect. I'd told the people I was staying with – they were keen hill-walkers – that I was going to climb Snowdon, and I didn't want people to think I'd been scared or anything.'

He paused. Jenny said nothing. The secret to being a good listener was to listen, not to talk.

'It was fine to begin with. You could see where the trail went. I wasn't ill-equipped. I had proper walking boots, a good anorak, some sandwiches. But I missed the path, and the weather began to deteriorate. I got to a place where I couldn't go down, only up, and eventually I couldn't do that any more. I found a ledge and sort of leant against it, clinging on for dear life. I shouted for help, it seemed the only thing I could do, but you can't actually do that for very long, it takes too much energy.'

He paused. 'Would you like another drink?'

Jenny shook her head. 'What happened then?'

'I kept on calling, whenever I could gather the strength. I knew I mustn't go to sleep, but I was starting to lose my grip. I thought I was going to die.' He frowned. 'Strangely, I didn't feel frightened of death, exactly, more of what would happen if I didn't die.'

'Did you think about your family? Your mother? Did she know you were out there? In danger?'

He shook his head. 'My mother died when I was seven. There was only my dad. He was staying with friends abroad and he didn't know where I was.'

'But what about the friends you were staying with? Wouldn't they have raised the alarm?'

'They had no reason to. I'd gone there by train, and I was due to go back by train, but not until much later.'

'God!'

Ross smiled. 'Well yes, that thought did occur to me too.'

'That there was one, or there wasn't?'

He shrugged. 'That he was there, but that it didn't matter to the world if I lived or died.'

Jenny found her stomach tying itself in knots. Ross, on the other hand, seemed more relaxed. 'Eventually, after a spell of calling, I thought I heard someone call back. I won't go into the details, but four hours later, after a fairly hairy time, I was back down the mountain. But if it hadn't been for a lot of people risking their lives for me, I wouldn't have been. It was their skill and training that saved my life, but it could have been at the expense of their own. They told me afterwards that I was in an exceptionally difficult situation – hard to get me from the bottom, harder to get me from the top.'

'So, what happened?'

'It's all a bit of a blur. I was starting to suffer from hypothermia by that time. I spent the night in hospital, under observation, and in the morning I went back to the friends I was staying with. They had been told what had happened, and were pretty shocked. They rang my father, thinking he'd want to fly home and pick me up, but he didn't.'

'Why not?'

He shook his head slightly and turned his glass round. 'I don't know. I was out of danger by then. Perhaps he felt there was no point in putting a stop to his holiday when I was OK.'

Jenny didn't respond. Her own father had been dead for four years now, but she knew that while he was alive, there would be no journey he wouldn't undertake for her, no holiday plans he wouldn't break.

Ross sighed. 'Now, I've talked far too much. Let me get you another of those.' He picked up her glass and went with it to the bar.

Ross's story clung to Jenny, as if she had been stuck on that mountain herself. The thought of the boy, alone on a peak, holding onto that ledge with his hands, steadily growing colder and weaker, wouldn't leave her.

Ross came back with her whisky and a cup of coffee

for himself. Jenny blinked and tried to look bright and attentive. He smiled, as if touched by her effort but not convinced.

'So, what happened then?' She was determined to keep awake. 'You obviously didn't forswear mountains for ever. I would have done.'

'I did for a bit, but no, I learnt to climb properly, and did it as a hobby for years. Although hill-walking is what I like best.'

'Then?'

'Then, when I was in a position to, like now, I wanted to give something back. I think I was embarrassed that my father didn't do anything for the people who rescued me at the time. He seemed to think that it was their job, that they did it for the glory or something. So that's why I tried to persuade the local team to take me on here.'

'And have they?'

'They will do. But I have to live here for a year before they'll let me join.'

'Do you have to do much training? Prove you're fit?'

He shook his head. 'They kind of assume that if hill-walking is your hobby, you are fit. But there are training exercises. I was given a very thorough interview by the team leader who finally said I could join if I commit myself to the area by living here.'

'I would have thought they'd have been grateful for anyone willing and able to do it.'

'For some teams, I'm sure that's the case. But round here there's a bit of competition for places.'

'So why here? Why not in Snowdon?'

'As I said, my mother's family came from these parts.' He stopped, as if there was more to tell.

Jenny didn't press him, she just looked at him. She wanted nothing more than to take him in her arms. The irony of it didn't escape her. She had wasted a lot of energy disliking this man.

He looked back at her. He seemed calm, relaxed. She, thinking of the fourteen-year-old boy whose father stayed on holiday with friends when his son had nearly died on a mountain, didn't know if it was the boy she wanted to hug, or the man.

'Do you see much of your father now?' she asked.

He picked up the spoon lying in his saucer and traced a pattern on the table. 'No. He lives abroad, and although I did travel a lot at one time, I only visit him about once a year.' He regarded her, anticipating her reaction. 'It doesn't do to be too sentimental, Jenny. Life is tough, full of difficult decisions. It doesn't help you make them if your mind is clogged up with emotion.'

She nodded, as if agreeing, but how, she wanted to ask, do you get rid of emotion? The feelings that well up, influencing your decisions? Sending you down paths you know you shouldn't follow?

He didn't answer her unspoken question. 'I think I should get you back now. You look three-quarters asleep. I shouldn't have kept you here talking.'

She looked at her watch. It took a little while for her to make sense of the hands, but she realised that although it felt like one or two in the morning, it was actually only eleven. 'I don't know why I'm so tired.'

He laughed. 'I expect you've had a long day insulting customers, throwing coffee on them and boiling tomatoes. It takes it out of you.'

She wanted to snap back with some witty response,

but could only smile inanely. She countered the smile with a frown. 'You know, I think I *should* go home now. While I still remember the way up to my bedroom.' Then she put her elbows on the table and put her head in her hands and groaned. 'Oh God!'

'What?' He sounded concerned, and put his hand on her shoulder.

'I've just realised I walked out on everyone halfway through dinner. They're probably all waiting up, just so they can shout at me. I wish there was a back way in.'

He left his hand on her shoulder. 'Do you want me to come in with you and create a diversion, so you can slip away unnoticed?'

This made her smile. 'Would you do that?'

'Of course.'

She shook her head. 'It's all right. I'll cope. It's my problem, after all.' She winced. 'Although I do feel guilty! In fact, I don't know why I agreed to come out with you in the first place! I abandoned Henry on his first night here and he'll never forgive me. Oh hell!'

He stopped her putting her head back down on the table. 'Come on. Let me get you back. If anyone looks like talking to you, I'll divert their attention. Start a small fire, or something.'

He took her elbow, led her out of the pub, and helped her into the passenger seat of the Land Rover. She knew she was drunk, but she felt strangely safe with this man whom she hardly knew.

The drive back to Dalmain House was blissful and short. He stopped the Land Rover at the bottom of the drive.

'I'll sneak along and find out if people are still up. If

they are, we can walk to the house, and get you in quietly.'

'There are dogs . . .'

'That's all right. You go in – you've got a key?' She nodded. 'And if the dogs come, I'll shut the door and then knock on it, pretend I'm asking the way, or something.'

She sighed. 'That's so kind.'

'Wait here, and I'll see if all that nonsense is necessary.'

It seemed like only moments before he was back.

'They're all still in the drawing room, at the front.'

'Plan A then.'

'Yup – just one thing first.'

He helped her down and pushed the heavy door to. Then he put his arms around her and hugged her until she could almost hear her ribs crack. His lips fused to hers in a kiss that made their first kiss seem like a peck on the cheek. She seemed almost to lose consciousness as whisky, desire and passion combined and sent her senses spinning off into the dark night. It went on for ever and was over in a moment.

He supported her as he set her down, and she realised her feet had actually been off the ground. She couldn't think of what to say, how to send words from her brain to her mouth.

'I'll see you on Monday,' he breathed into her hair.

'Right.' She couldn't, just then, remember if they'd made an arrangement, but Monday seemed fine to her, if it couldn't be Sunday, or even the rest of Saturday night. It was a lowering thought, but she knew that if he had laid his waxed jacket on to the cold, stony drive and suggested she laid with him on it, she wouldn't have hesitated. She burrowed in her bag for her key. As she found it, he took it from her.

She had just got through the door when the dogs started. Jenny fled up the stairs, hearing Ross shut the door and then bang on it, loudly. God, he was a nice man. She dumped her handbag on the hall table and hauled herself upstairs.

Just before she fell asleep, she realised he still hadn't told her what he'd wanted to see her for. Not caring, a lunatic smile on her lips, she drifted off to sleep.

Chapter Fourteen

Jenny planned to get up early and get out of the house before anyone could see her. With her client arriving on Monday morning she wanted to spend a day at the mill making sure everything was absolutely as it should be. They hadn't arranged it, but she was fairly sure Kirsty would be there too. It was but a faint chance, but they both secretly hoped that Mr M. R. Grant-Dempsey was the sort of man to be dazzled by beautiful presentation, glossy folders and elaborate graphs. Jenny was a whiz at that sort of thing.

She knew it had been a mistake to want breakfast when Henry appeared in the kitchen the moment she got there.

'Jenny! What time did you get back last night? And where did you disappear off to?'

'I'm not sure really. I'd never been there before.' And as she probably couldn't get there again on her own, this vagueness was partly justified.

'Jenny! You just disappear off, before the pudding, for God's sake, and now you won't tell me who you were with! We are an item, you know. Or are supposed to be!'

'You didn't ask who I was with, Henry. I can tell you that! It's a man I met at The Homely Haggis who needed some advice about something. Of course, if you'd had the courtesy to tell me you were coming I would have arranged to see him at another time.'

'You shouldn't be seeing him anyway. You're my girlfriend.'

She plugged in the spare kettle she had borrowed from the mill and brought it downstairs with her. She could have mentioned the amount of flirting he had been doing at the Highland games, but as her conscience was far from clear, she didn't. 'It wasn't like that,' she lied. 'And why are you up so early?'

'Damned lumpy bed!'

Jenny nodded sympathetically. 'I did try to warn you about accepting Lady D.'s invitation to stay. This house is desperately cold and uncomfortable. You'd be much better off in a hotel.'

'I thought perhaps I might share your bed.'

'Mine's not only just as lumpy, but it's single, too. And I did explain yesterday that we can't sleep together in Lady Dalmain's house. Which, I'm sure you've found out by now, is far too cold to creep around in, anyway.'

'So where are you going now?'

'To the mill. My client is coming tomorrow. I've got to make sure everything is absolutely in order.'

'But it's Sunday!'

'I know. But I still have to work.'

'Well, what am I supposed to do with myself all day? I came to see you!'

'I suggest you try and find somewhere to stay that has constant hot water and a decent mattress. You'll be miserable here.'

Henry yawned. 'Oh, I don't mind roughing it a bit, and Lady D. knows everyone who is anyone in the area, and she really is a character. Quite fascinating on her own subject. She can introduce me to all sorts of useful contacts.'

'That's true. But will you have time to take advantage of them?' This was said with a hint of irony, given his fast work the previous day, but it was lost on Henry.

'Oh yes. I expect to be here at least a couple of weeks. Didn't I tell you?'

Jenny felt suddenly weak. 'Why so long?'

'Aren't you pleased? I thought you'd be happy that I've managed to wangle this job up here so I could be near you!'

'Happy?' she repeated feebly. 'Well, of course, I'm pleased to see you, but I'm frantically busy.' She looked at her watch. It was ten to eight. 'I've got to be off now. Why don't you use my kettle, make a cup of tea and go back to bed for a while?'

'Jenny, I've never seen you like this before! It's all that whisky you drank last night with Felicity. I've told you, you shouldn't drink spirits, especially neat.'

As he didn't know about half the whisky she'd drunk last night, and she did feel slightly light-headed, she nodded, lips pursed. 'You may have a point there, Henry, but I must go to work now. Felicity will be up soon, I'm sure, to do Lady Dalmain's tray. She'll see you get some breakfast. Now, goodbye.' She walked out of the room for a couple of paces and then turned back. 'Oh, by the way, don't worry about the dogs. They won't hurt you once they've had a good sniff.'

'I met the dogs last night –'

'Oh it takes them *days* to get used to you. Just stay in here until Felicity appears.'

Jenny saw a light on in the offices as soon as she drove into the car park. It was Kirsty. She had made coffee and a big tin of shortbread.

'How did you know I was coming?' Jenny asked.

'I knew. Have your breakfast, and we'll get started.'

'It's bloody Philip,' Jenny said half an hour later. 'If he hadn't separated the offices from the rest of the mill, we'd have had enough money to finance this whole thing, without asking for another penny from His Nibs.'

'It might have been better if he hadn't mortgaged his mother's house, as well as borrowing against the value of the offices,' added Kirsty.

'Yup.'

At half-past three, Jenny went home. She crept into the house, hoping to avoid everyone, knowing she couldn't for long. She managed to be in the kitchen, making scones with some sour milk before anyone discovered she was back. She didn't go into the sitting room to see Lady Dalmain, until she had the scones, hot out of the oven, ready to serve, along with a pot of tea.

Kirsty and Jenny met again the following morning just before eight. The good weather of the weekend had gone, leaving lowering clouds, a bitter wind, and rain that promised more to come. The mountains appeared stark and threatening, looming over the town like glowering giants. There were waves on the surface of the river, defying anyone to see it as tranquil. Jenny felt anxious and uneasy, her spirits not helped by the weather. Bloody Scotland! she thought. Why does it have to do this? We need good omens, rainbows, sunshine, not squalls and icy wind.

'So, how did it go last night, with Henry – is it?' asked Kirsty, when the two of them were settled in the office.

'Don't ask. It was boring at the time, and it hasn't got any more interesting.' It had been downhill all the way after the scones. Jenny dismissed an evening slightly less enjoyable than watching paint dry while having one's fingernails torn out with a wave of her hand. 'What time is he expected?'

Kirsty didn't ask whom she meant. 'Half-past eight. Effie's on hand to usher him up.'

'That's inhumanly early! It's also in about ten minutes!'

Kirsty gave a small shrug. 'We might as well get it over with. Executions are always carried out at dawn.'

Jenny sighed and went to look out of the window, down at the mill building. It appeared very dark and Satanic – appropriate for the day, she thought. A Land Rover pulled up. Automatically, her heart lurched. She batted it back down severely. 'Get a grip, woman,' she muttered.

A tall man in a suit got out. He seemed a little familiar, but from that angle, she couldn't see him very clearly. She looked more intently. 'God! I think I know him! But it can't be –'

The man disappeared into the building.

'Can't be what? Or who?'

Then she realised it could be, indeed it was. 'Oh fuck!' she breathed. 'Fuck, fuck, fuck.'

'Jenny!'

The door opened, and Effie ushered Ross Grant into

the office. Jenny felt faint. She put her hands behind her on the desk to stop her knees giving way completely. She was sweating. Emotions swirled around her head like party lights, dizzying, confusing, nauseating. When Ross Grant looked at her, her overriding feeling was of betrayal.

He took one look and turned his attention to Kirsty. 'Hi. Ross Grant-Dempsey. You must be Kirsty McIntyre.'

Kirsty took the outstretched hand and winced as it crushed hers.

Jenny took a few calming breaths. When he turned his attention to her she could at least speak. 'And I am your VA, Genevieve Porter. But you knew that, didn't you?' She wanted to kill him, slowly, with her bare hands. But professionalism, not just pride, forced her to keep her dignity, even if it was only the pretence of dignity.

'Yes, I did. I did try to tell you.'

'Did you? Not very hard.'

He closed his eyes briefly. 'I know. I'm sorry. Now, shall we get down to work?'

'I'll get some coffee,' said Jenny, and left the room before anyone could stop her.

Unable to make sense of it, Jenny stared at the coffee making equipment. It shouldn't be difficult, she'd made coffee possibly a million times. Like riding a bicycle, it must surely come back to her. She spent a few moments pondering on when the last time had been. It seemed easier than actually making any now.

How much had she told Ross about the mill? Had he actually got all the information he needed to close it down? A few malt whiskies and he was set to make a fortune. And the kisses – both of them. Were they a necessary part of his plan? Probably. He probably ensured she'd be interested enough to go out with him, interested enough to let him make her drunk, and tell him all he needed to know. Oh, what an idiot she'd been! How naïve! How gullible!

Instant coffee was good enough, she decided. She put quite a large teaspoon of it into a mug – not one of Kirsty's good mugs, but one of the old ones, with rude slogans and chips around the edge. She was about to pour on the water when she thought of Kirsty. Poor Kirsty. She was going to lose a job she loved, a mill she'd worked all her life for. She shouldn't have to add shame to the list.

Five minutes later, having made a cafetiere full of Kirsty's favourite coffee, Jenny picked up the tray, now set with cups and saucers and a jug of milk, and claimed shame all to her self.

Had she been as wanton as she felt? Could he have told how much she wanted him from that last kiss? Did he assume, from her behaviour, that she would sleep with him at the same time as she dismantled the mill for him, allowing him to strip the assets in the same easy way he had stripped her inhibitions from her? She kicked the door with the toe of her shoe, only partly so someone would open it.

She didn't look at Ross as she set the tray down on the desk, nor did she pour the coffee. Her hands were slippery and shaking, she didn't want to spill coffee on Ross's beautiful suit. She sat down on a chair a little away from the others, intending to keep quiet, and pick up from what the others were saying what had gone on.

It was too much. 'So, you're going to shut down the mill, are you?' she demanded, aware she was on the verge of tears. 'Or will you take a token look at our plans for it? Which would make it successful, if that's what you want. But it isn't, is it? You just want to asset-strip. You're probably longing to live in Dalmain House.'

'Jenny!' Anguished, Kirsty got up to deal with the coffee.

Her mention of Dalmain House added to Jenny's own distress. Henry's appearance might not just be an irritation for her, but an indication of Philip's plans. If you wanted to sell a property, and not let anyone know what you were up to, hiring Henry or his ilk was the way to go about it.

'Shall we just stick to what we've got in front of us?' said Ross. 'I haven't had a chance to look at your proposals yet. Though at a quick glance they do seem very speculative. You don't seem to have done much research into the possibilities of these new products.'

'We've hardly had time to write the damn report, let alone research obscure fibres and uses for merino wool.'

'Jenny?' Kirsty's agony was increasing, and Jenny felt a stab of guilt.

'I think I should explain, Miss McIntyre,' said Ross, 'that Jenny and I have met under different, not to say difficult, circumstances. She didn't know who I was.'

'But, surely, you're her bo– client.' Kirsty corrected herself quickly.

'I know, but we've never met, up until now.'

Ross looked across at Jenny, and this time she faced his gaze. He seemed stern, unyielding, the man she had first met at The Homely Haggis. It was a relief.

He took them through the report, page by page, asking difficult, niggling questions they often didn't have the answers to.

'Can you make nuno felt on a large scale?'

'I don't know. I have tracked down someone who does it locally, but there hasn't been time to do in-depth research.' You bastard, Jenny added silently.

'You'd obviously need new machinery if you're going to make fabric out of llama and alpaca fibres. You haven't costed it in.'

'Actually,' said Kirsty, possibly gaining courage from Jenny's abrupt manner, 'there's a shed full of machinery. We have a very skilled and experienced workforce. The intention is that the old machinery should be adapted, and thus incur no cost.'

'What about a designer? Is one of your workforce also very skilled and experienced at that and prepared to do it for nothing?'

'Felicity Dalmain is going to do that,' said Jenny. 'She's enormously skilled, and, as it's her family's mill she'll be helping to save, she's willing to do it for nothing initially.' If this wasn't already true, Jenny was prepared to use some pretty brutal methods to make it true.

Jenny and Kirsty were both exhausted; Jenny was longing to go to the loo and had a headache that made her skull feel like it was going to split open, all over the plans that were now spread on the table like cheap margarine on stale bread. Kirsty's lipstick was all eaten off and her silk blouse was beginning to look a bit limp. This was the moment Ross chose to really twist the knife.

'And where's Philip Dalmain? Why isn't he here?'

Jenny's attempts at politeness hadn't gone terribly well so far, but now they disappeared completely. 'Why the fuck didn't you ask that before? You must have noticed his absence?'

Ross's manners had been doing better than Jenny's, until that moment. 'And why the fuck didn't you tell me he was missing? You work for me! It was your duty to tell me what was going on! To keep me informed! Why the fuck did you think I sent you here if not to keep me up to speed?'

'I think you sent me here to report back. And then you'd get me to stay and do your dirty work for you. You knew I'd find the company in such a bad state I'd say it would have to be closed so you'd ask me to arrange it. That way you wouldn't be on the coal face, you wouldn't be spotted, laying off workers, selling off equipment cheap – no, you'd wait until I'd done all that, and then swan in, do what you like, and still be loved by the locals, with your mountain rescue team and heaving sheep out of the ditch! Well you got the wrong woman when you chose me, because I'm on the side of the people who produce the wealth, not on the side of those who spend it! Now if you'll both excuse me, I have to go to the ladies.'

She had splashed her face with cold water and was drying it on the roller towel, when she heard the wash-room door open behind her. 'I'm so sorry, Kirsty. I have so fu– messed this up! I couldn't have done more to get this mill closed down if I'd set fire to it. I am so, so sorry.'

Kirsty's hands on her shoulders felt surprisingly strong. It was only when she had turned round and her

211

nose was buried in a very fine lawn shirt that she realised that the arms around her were not Kirsty's. It was too late to pull away – she tried, but her efforts had no effect on the iron bands that held her. She stopped fighting, she resisted the temptation to kick his shins; there was no point. The battle was lost.

She let herself stay there for a few moments, to allow his strength to seep into her, pretending he was the man she'd thought he was. The moment she raised her head from his chest and looked up at him, the spell would be over, she would be back with reality and her crushing failure.

She had failed the mill. If only she had come clean about Philip. M. R. Grant-Dempsey would never forgive that, which would mean he wouldn't give their carefully thought out plans a second glance. He would just foreclose and move into Dalmain House, throwing Lady Dalmain and Felicity out into the snow. Perhaps Henry would help her find them somewhere else to go.

I've been a fool before, she thought, her last ill-starred job in mind, but never such a big one as this. She wiped her nose on his shirt and stepped back. His arms fell away, setting her free.

'You'll probably want me out of here right away,' she said, her voice croaky. 'And, of course, I'll leave – today. But I would just like to tell you –'

His finger came firmly down on her lips. 'I don't want you to tell me what you think of me. I know that already. And I don't want you to leave. I just want you to stay and clear up the bloody mess. And if your half-cocked ideas have any chance of working, you'd better get your arse into gear and do something.'

She removed his hand and shook her hair out of her

eyes and stared up at him. 'I hope you don't expect me to say thank you.'

'I'd die of shock if you did –'

'And I expect you want us to turn the whole mill round in about a fortnight.'

His eyes glittered. He was more angry than she'd quite realised. 'I was thinking a month. Let's split the difference and say three weeks.'

'Bastard!'

'I've got to be out of the country for that long. You'd better have something concrete for me to see when I come back. And I shall be finding myself a new virtual assistant.'

'And I shall be charging you for every second of overtime I do, and if you don't pay me, I shall make sure there isn't a virtual assistant in Europe who'll work for you. You haven't heard the –'

'Oh shut the fuck up.' To make sure she did, he kissed her, long, hard and intently, concentrating on every square millimetre of her mouth, using his lips and tongue and teeth.

By the time her brain was working again, she was staring at the door he'd slammed behind him.

Jenny didn't go back into the office. She needed time to get herself together, to face Kirsty, to make a plan. She went down into the car park to walk along the river. If it hadn't been so cold and so shallow she might have considered throwing herself into it. Visualising her body splatting onto the rocks restored her sense of humour sufficiently to give her the courage to go back to find out just how much harm she'd done. The feeling of betrayal would never leave her, but she wouldn't let anyone see. Her anger would boost her pride and keep her head, if not high, at least level. She watched his Land Rover drive away and felt as if her heart was driving away with it.

'That man is such a bastard!' she announced, as she swept into Kirsty's office, a good healthy anger keeping her tears at bay.

Kirsty raised her eyebrows. 'I thought he was quite reasonable, in the circumstances. He's told me exactly what we have to do, which I admit, is going to be difficult. But knowing what is required is helpful.'

'So, what do we have to do?'

'Find markets for all our new ideas, the felt, the fabric, in fact, everything. If we don't have named customers, projected figures, he'll pull the plug.'

'He can't expect us to do all that in three weeks!'

'We've to do our best. Oh, and we do have to find Philip, though,' she added.

'And how the fu– hell does he expect us to do that? I'm not a private detective!'

Kirsty shrugged. 'Don't shoot the messenger.'

Jenny sighed deeply, rubbed her forehead and bit her lip. 'Look, do you mind if I go back to Dalmain House? I've got the most God-awful headache and something might come to me on the journey. I'd better see Felicity too. As I've more or less told that vile man that she's the best designer since Stella McCartney, I'd better find out what she can do. If you never hear from me, or see me again, you know she's only up for doing antimacassars.'

Dalmain House seemed blissfully empty. Henry's car wasn't parked in front of it, and the dogs were all quiet and happy.

Jenny met Felicity in the kitchen. She was making a cup of tea.

'Hi!' she said cheerfully. 'Want one?'

This offer was both welcome and surprising. Felicity usually offered whisky whatever time of day it was. 'Yes, please. Where is everyone?'

'Henry's taken Mama off for the day. He's so good with her. He can talk about her miniatures, and antiquarian books. Just like Philip used to do.'

Felicity hummed softly as she inspected mugs for cleanliness, rejecting one or two as she did so.

'So why are you so cheerful? Lachlan?'

Felicity gave the kind of ecstatic sigh Jenny would once have given if she had heard from Ross. 'I rang him and he was so lovely . . .'

'He is lovely,' said Jenny briskly, so jealous of Lachlan's wonderful straightforwardness it was a physical pain. 'I should think that tea is about ready to pour now.'

'Oh, is it? I like it quite strong.'

'But you don't like it stewed. Or at least, I don't. You haven't got an aspirin or something tucked away anywhere? Or shall I pop upstairs?'

'I've got some ibuprofen. Headache?'

'Mm.'

'Well, take a couple of those and you'll be fine by the time Henry comes home. He is nice, isn't he?'

It took Jenny a few moments to remember what Henry was like. Her memory had been blasted clean by someone so much more powerful. It was like trying to remember a small hillock when you've just climbed Everest. 'Yes, yes he is nice.'

Felicity handed Jenny a mug. 'You don't sound – I mean, are you and he not . . .?'

'Confidentially, Felicity, I'm not in love with him any more, but I haven't got time to tell him, just now. I was going to go home and do it, then he turned up here.' Jenny sipped her tea, taking time to wonder at the contrast between the kitchen mugs, thick, chipped and grimy, and the drawing-room china, absurdly delicate and antique.

'It seems a shame. He seems so nice. Good-looking, good family . . .'

And what was Ross like, apart from the biggest rat of the century? Good-looking? Probably not – far too rugged, in spite of the beautiful suit he had been wearing. Good family? Practically no family. Rich? Probably, but that was against him. How had he got rich? Off the backs of innocent workers. This was no good. She'd have to get him out of her mind. 'There's really nothing wrong with him, Felicity; it's just the chemistry's not right any more. And you know how important that is, with Lachlan.'

'Mm.'

Felicity's expression bordered on the ecstatic. Although happy for her, Jenny couldn't bear to let her indulge in such happiness just at the moment. 'Felicity, one of the reasons I'm home early is that there's been a meeting at the mill. I really need you as a designer. Could you bear to show me what you've done?' Then, because she felt so mean, she added, 'And I'll give you a lift to Lachlan's soon, I promise.'

'Will you? That would be wonderful.' She sighed deeply, and then, to Jenny's relief, pulled herself together. 'Well, if you'd do that for me, I'll do some

216

designs for you. Let's take our tea upstairs to my workroom.'

The designs were impressive. Felicity had used a huge range of lovely colours – in fact, all the colours in the box of pastels Jenny had had sent after her first visit to the turret workroom. The shapes were flattering and interesting too.

'They are fab, Fliss. What I don't know is how well they'll translate to the sort of production we'll be doing.'

'Meggie will be able to help you there. And although they look complicated, all the garments are made up of simple shapes.'

'They certainly look lovely. I haven't met the felt woman yet, but I'm hoping nuno is as versatile as it looked on the website.' Jenny took a sip of tea. 'Well done, Felicity. You've done a brilliant job. Now I really must go and catch up on some emails. We'll talk later.'

'And you'll give me a hand with supper? Cooking is so much more fun when you're not doing it on your own.'

'Of course.' I can do that, thought Jenny, fighting bitterness, jealousy and resentment, emotions she was not accustomed to. I've only got to be a private detective, find markets for previously unknown products, and create a catwalk collection out of mashed up wool and llama hair. Knocking up a meal for four will be easy.

Chapter Fifteen

'So, did you all have a good day?' Jenny, caught in the hall as Henry and Lady Dalmain got home, made a pre-emptive strike.

'Lovely!' said Lady Dalmain. 'Henry's been so kind! He drove me to Lochnavan to see the Malcolms. Do you remember? They were at the Highland games. We called in for drinks and it was really quite pleasant. They were very pleased to see Henry again, but I suppose with all those daughters, they must be very keen to get them off their hands. You modern young women have no idea how to keep a man. If you don't pay him a bit more attention, my dear, you'll find him snatched from under your nose.'

'I have been busy –'

'Oh yes. At the mill.' Lady Dalmain dismissed her source of income as too boring to talk about. 'Jock lent me a charming little book about Scottish standing stones. Only a third edition, of course, but I might see if I can get a better one to add to my collection. I haven't had a chance to show you my books yet, Henry, have I?'

'No, Lady Dalmain, but I do hope there'll be an opportunity.'

'Why not now? Come into my study. I'm sure Felicity will bring us some tea. Or perhaps Jenny.'

Jenny received the kind of smile Lady Dalmain might have given to a servant she was faintly fond of. Jenny smiled back, and said behind her teeth, 'Why don't you ring a bell and summon the domestic?'

Henry, who heard her, gave her a horrified glance, and Jenny retreated to the kitchen, not because she was anxious to do Lady Dalmain's bidding, but because she'd suddenly had an idea. Philip had given his mother a book that first evening. She remembered a bookmark with the name of the shop sticking out of the top. If she could find the bookmark, she could ring the shop. It was a very long shot, but if Philip collected books too, he might have ordered something. And if he had, they would know his address.

While she found cups and saucers and made tea, Jenny wondered if she should tell Lady Dalmain of her idea. She decided, when she finally got the tray together, that she would play it by ear. It wasn't so much that she cared how Lady Dalmain felt, but that if it went wrong there would be so much wailing and gnashing of teeth, and she didn't have time for it.

She set the tray down where Lady Dalmain indicated, knowing that she longed either to ask Jenny to pour the tea, or to dismiss her, as she would have Felicity. But Jenny crossed the room determinedly, having spotted the book Philip had bought in a pile on a table.

'I just want to have a look at something,' she said, looking, before Lady Dalmain could protest. 'Thanks, that's fine.'

Then she left them to it and went straight up to Lady Dalmain's bedroom to use the telephone. As she entered the room she realised that a day or two ago, she wouldn't have dreamt of just barging into someone's private space. But since this morning, she had changed.

Her first call was to Directory Enquiries. She could, of course, have taken the bookmark, but that would have involved a lot of explanation, and the name of the shop, Toshak and Fiske, was memorable enough.

Before she dialled the number Directory Enquiries had given her, she made sure the door was firmly closed. Then she took a deep breath, and put on an accent heavily based on Miss Jean Brodie. She was sure it wouldn't have fooled anyone.

'Halloo? Is that Toshak and Fiske? Guid afternoon. I was wondering if you cuid help me.' Aware her accent was wandering from Morningside to Morayshire and back, she tamed it. 'I'm phoning on behalf of my boss, Mr Philip Dalmain?'

'Ah yes, Mr Dalmain.' The voice sounded reassuringly unfazed by her music-hall brogue.

'Well, he asked me if I would ring and check you have the correct address for him. He's not residing at Dalmain House at present.'

'Er no –'

'I think you have a book on order for him, and he wanted me to check it would go to the right place. Can you tell me the address you have for him?'

'I'll just look in the book.' There was a nail-biting pause while Jenny listened to pages being turned over. 'Ah yes. Glenreekie.'

This was a start. 'Could you just read me back the address please? Mr Philip wasn't sure he'd given you the correct postcode.'

'We've got 17 High Town, here, and the postcode . . .'

220

'Thank you so much,' said Jenny, still as Miss Brodie, having written it all down. 'He'll be so relieved he didn't make an error.'

She was sweating slightly as she left the room. Being brash and ignoring all the rules of good behaviour, not to mention lying to innocent shop assistants, would take getting used to.

'Have you any idea where Glenreekie is?' Jenny asked Felicity, as they made macaroni cheese together.

'It's miles away. Way further than where Lachlan lives. Why do you ask?'

'I've got an address for Philip there.'

'Oh my God! That's amazing! Does Mama know?'

'No, and I don't want to tell her, not until we're sure he's there.'

'So how will you find out?'

Jenny, risking her knuckles with a very ancient lump of cheese and a grater almost as old, shrugged. 'Go there and see, I suppose. I can't go tomorrow, but, when I do, would Lachlan's be on the way?'

Felicity nodded. 'It is – right on the way. Why can't you go tomorrow?'

Before he turned out to be such a rat, Jenny had felt like that about Ross. Now, the pain of his betrayal was a physical ache. 'I've got the felt woman coming. I managed to arrange that before I left the building, screaming.'

'Jenny! What's wrong?' Felicity was shocked.

Jenny realised that she was a person who must always be happy and positive. It was not her role to be desperate, or miserable, or, indeed, anything but sunny. It was the role reversal that was worrying Felicity most.

'Oh, trouble at t'mill,' she said. 'The man I work for

came today. We've got about three weeks to get every-thing up and running. Well, not running exactly – even he wouldn't expect that – but with markets in place, the machinery sorted out. Stuff like that.'

'I see. Well, anything I can do to help . . .'

Seeing genuine concern, Jenny patted Felicity's shoulder. 'You have helped, by doing those fabulous designs. And we'll go the day after tomorrow. OK? Now, shall we put breadcrumbs on top of this? It'll make it go further.'

'Only if you don't mind a little blood in among them. That grater's lethal.'

'Don't worry. I'll tear the bread up with my hands.' And pretend it's Ross Grant-Dempsey, she added, under her breath.

Jenny's 'felt woman' came wearing her product. Both she and it were extremely beautiful but not, Jenny gathered, quite of this world. The fabric was soft, almost transparent, and fell beautifully. Rowan, its creator, had the same transparent quality about her; very pale skin, red-gold hair and grey eyes. She was wearing a necklace of semi-precious stones on gold wires that looked as if she might have made it herself. A harp would have complemented her outfit nicely.

'What I would really like,' said Jenny, after some time was wasted in finding a suitable hot drink that didn't contain caffeine, discussion of the state of the planet and whether shearing sheep was exploitative, 'would be for you to come here and teach the women how to make Nuno felt so they can create textiles for a commercial market.' She knew she'd said the wrong thing the moment the words were out of her mouth.

'Commercial market?' repeated Rowan, whose name was pronounced the Scottish way, to rhyme with 'how'. 'But what I do isn't commercial. Each piece is individually made, with the wearer in mind.'

'No, I know,' said Jenny carefully, aware that Rowan might not be willing to share her skills in order that Dalmain Mills could create cheaper versions of what she probably charged the earth for. 'But we couldn't have those high standards. We would be creating something far less special than anything you do. We wouldn't be poaching on your territory, or anything.'

'Poaching on my territory? I don't understand.'

'I mean, what you produce is wonderful, individual stuff. I would quite understand if you didn't want anyone commercial, like us, to imitate you. But we won't want to imitate what you do.' Jenny wasn't quite sure she was telling the truth here, but she was desperate. 'If you would just teach our women the techniques . . .'

'I couldn't do that. I can only teach one person at a time. Every piece has a soul of its own. It wouldn't translate to the mass market.'

Jenny persevered for a bit longer, then excused herself. 'I'm sorry, can I leave you here, drinking your camomile and ginseng, while I just make a quick phone call?'

'Meggie?' she said dramatically, when she answered the phone. 'I need you!'

Meggie didn't flinch. 'What?'

'I'm at the mill and I've got this mad woman here! She won't teach the women to do her special felt thing, she'll only teach individuals. That's you! Then you can teach the women.'

Meggie gulped.

'I know you've got Anna – and I'll promise I'll look after her so you can do this.'

'But I've never taught anyone anything, and how do you know I'll be able to learn it myself?'

'Because you did textiles at college! Now don't be difficult!'

Meggie laughed. 'I'll do my best, but you can't blame the poor woman for not wanting her techniques reaching the High Street.'

'They won't reach the High Street! At the moment we'd be lucky if they reached the front door of the mill!'

'You're awful crabby this morning, Jenny.'

Jenny took a deep breath. 'I know. I'm sorry. It's just – never mind, no time for that. I've got a woman whose soul is caught up with her work. It's very tiring!'

'I dare say everything with her is deeply felt,' said Meggie.

Jenny slammed the phone down.

Rowan was perfectly happy to teach Meggie, it turned out, when Jenny put the idea to her. And she wasn't worried about the basic technique being commercially produced. She just didn't want to teach a roomful of women how to do it. Especially women, she confided, who might damage her spirituality.

'I'm not good with crowds,' she said. 'They suffocate my aura.'

'Of course we won't be producing anything nearly as beautiful or as individual as you do,' repeated Jenny, as she showed Rowan out.

'I know,' said Rowan. 'Everything I produce has a little bit of my soul in it.'

Just then, Jenny felt that everything the factory would ever produce would have a big bit – several pints, in fact – of her blood in it.

'Well done,' said Kirsty, as Jenny poured herself a cup of strong coffee. 'One hurdle over.'

Jenny nodded. 'And I think I've got a lead for Philip. Would you mind if I didn't come in tomorrow and looked for him? He's at Glenreekie. Felicity says it's miles away.'

Glenreekie, it seemed, was a small fishing town on the coast, about fifty miles away. Felicity was in good spirits as they set off the following morning and although it was raining, icy rain, Jenny was grateful for an excuse to be away from the mill. Not, she realised grimly, that she would think about it and Ross Grant any the less because she was absent, but because once she'd dropped Felicity off, even if it did degenerate into a miserable wild-goose chase, no one would talk to her.

Jenny declined Lachlan's offer of coffee, kissed Felicity's cheek, and wished her luck. 'Have a really lovely day. I'll ring when I'm likely to pick you up.'

She gave Lachlan a cheery wave then turned the car round, drove back up the lane, and headed for Glenreekie.

Rather than spend hours driving round the narrow streets in the ever-worsening rain, Jenny decided to park, put up her umbrella, and look for Philip's address on foot. Having done this, she called in at a newsagent's to ask for directions, regretting the umbrella, which now flapped wetly by her leg.

'Oh,' said the man helpfully. 'It's not very far. Just up this road, then take the first left . . .'

Jenny was glad it was 'not very far', because it felt very far indeed, in the sleeting rain. She no longer hoped to make Philip see sense, or feel philanthropic or anything. She just hoped that (a) Philip still lived there, (b) he was home, and (c) that he would offer her a cup of tea or coffee. Anything else was a bonus.

At last she found the narrow doorway, wedged in between an estate agent's and a computer-games shop. She lowered her umbrella and banged on the door with it, having searched in vain for a bell.

Don't be surprised if there's no reply, she told herself, deciding the umbrella was still necessary. He probably doesn't live here, and if he does, and he opens the door, what on earth are you going to say to him?

Eventually, the door was dragged open. A tall, skinny youth in a ripped black T-shirt and combats draped with chains stood there. He had a bandanna round his head and bad spots. On his feet were trainers the size of small sofas.

'Hi,' said Jenny. 'I don't suppose I've got the right address for Philip Dalmain?'

'Philip?' The accent was very strong. 'Aye, he's here.' The youth shouted over his shoulder. 'Hey, Philip. There's a woman for you.'

Jenny put on as unthreatening an expression as she could. She didn't want to put him on the defensive; she wanted him to trust her. She just needed the right, gentle, opening line. She was just thinking it would be like trying to reassure a frightened animal and wondering if she should try to breathe up his nose, when he appeared. She had no opening line ready.

She took a breath. 'It's a pig of a day, Philip. Can I come in?'

He gave her a shadow of his usual charming smile. 'I suppose you might as well. Gloria's out. How did you find my address?'

'I was a bit underhand, I'm afraid. Shall I put my umbrella here?' She propped it in the corner by the door, knowing she'd never see it again.

Philip showed her through the narrow passage and up the stairs. 'We're above the estate agent's,' he said with a wry smile. 'Slightly better than the shop.'

Jenny became very aware of his anxiety, his prickliness, his embarrassment. He opened a door. 'Come in. This is the sitting room.'

A large black, plastic-covered divan took up most of the space. It faced a television that was playing a computer game. Another youth, similar to the one who had opened the door, lounged with the first one. Neither of them reacted to her presence.

'Do you want to sit down?' asked Philip.

Given the choice of squashing in between the lads and their games machines or perching on an upright chair in the corner, Jenny found that she didn't. 'I'd love a cup of coffee.'

'I'll make you one.'

Jenny followed him into a tiny kitchen.

'It's a bit of a change from Dalmain House,' he said. 'Did my mother send you?'

Jenny shook her head. 'Ross Grant-Dempsey – the man the mill owes all the money to? He's going to foreclose in three weeks unless we've got new plans in place, and you're there. But your mother does miss you very much. Do you miss her?'

He shook his head, uncertain. 'In a way. I miss the mother I love, but not the control freak.'

'I can understand that.'

He looked up as if surprised. 'Can you?'

'Oh yes. So much was expected of you. You were never allowed to be less than the perfect son.'

'Really? You could see that?'

'It wasn't hard, Philip. I should think most people could have seen it if they'd been there at the time.'

'I don't think Fliss understands.'

'She has her own problems. Although, she's getting better. I left her at Lachlan's on my way here. And she's done some lovely designs . . . But you probably don't want to hear about the mill.'

'Is there anything left of it to hear about?'

'What do you mean?'

'I would have thought it was all closed down by now. Workers laid off, buildings repossessed.'

'Including Dalmain House? I don't think I'd have been talking about whether or not your mother missed you if she'd been thrown out of the house she loves!' Jenny was trying very hard to be non-judgemental, but that had come out unexpurgated.

Philip looked down at the mugs. 'No. I suppose not. It seemed like all I could do at the time was to borrow more money, and use the house as security. So it hasn't gone yet?' He picked up an electric kettle and filled it. 'I didn't think it would take you long to see how parlous things had become.'

'No, it didn't. But I decided that closing down the mill wasn't the only option. I'd just made a few plans when Ross Grant-Dempsey came to see us in person.' She paused. 'He was furious with me for not telling him you'd gone.'

'Why didn't you?'

'Because I thought he'd just sweep in and close everything down. Which is more or less what happened. Philip, I don't think I like your mother very much, but I really don't want to see her thrown out of Dalmain House.'

He shrugged and turned away.

'Is that why you left? Because you didn't want to see it either, even though it was you who would have made it happen?'

He sighed, and Jenny decided there was no point in going on about it. She looked around her, trying not to show her frustration. The tiny kitchen was dominated by a fifties food cupboard, painted yellow, with a pull down work surface, cupboards fronted with beaded glass. She nodded towards it. 'Nice.'

Philip glanced at her as if she was mad. 'Don't you think I'm a complete shit?'

That did pretty much sum up how Jenny felt about him, but she didn't want to make him feel worse about himself than he did already. 'I think you're a bit of a coward, Philip. But now is the time to prove you're not. Come back to the mill and see that there are other ways of making money apart from producing cheap sweaters that don't wash very well.'

'You sound like Kirsty McIntyre.'

'Kirsty and I have been spending a lot of time together. She's a pearl beyond price, Philip. Without her the mill probably would have gone down years ago. It still might, of course. But Kirsty and I, and the entire workforce, are determined not to go without a fight. Iain is proving really good at adapting the old machinery.'

'So, what's happening?' He poured boiling water into the mugs. Then he opened the fridge and took out a carton of milk, sniffed it, and put it back. 'Is black all right for you?'

'If you've got some sugar. Why don't you come back and see?'

'I'm with Gloria now. I don't want to leave her.'

'Would you have to leave her? Couldn't you bring her with you?'

'She's got two sons. You've seen them.'

'So? They're welded to the sofa, are they?'

Philip laughed. 'I think they are, actually. But how could I come back?'

This wasn't a rhetorical question, so she answered it. 'You could rent a flat near the mill. Are the boys in education? Would moving disrupt that?'

He shook his head. 'Gloria's got a job, but she doesn't like it.'

'Where did you two meet?' Jenny leant back against the food cabinet and sipped her coffee. It was surprisingly heartening.

'In a pub. It's what she does, she's a barmaid.' Another wry smile. 'A cliché, isn't it? The laird's son running off with a barmaid.'

'Except that you're the laird, Philip. Your father's dead.'

He sighed. 'I know. But no matter what I do, I'll never fill his shoes.'

'I don't want to offend you, but I don't think he ran the mill all that well. I'm sure you could do better if you tried. Or you could get Iain involved in the management.'

He shrugged again.

'And if Gloria is a barmaid, she could surely get another job?'

'I suppose.'

'You don't have to come back for ever. But you should see your mother, Philip. I know she's a very domineering woman, but she loves you and you love her. If she should die and you hadn't seen her, you'd never forgive yourself.' She hesitated. 'I'm so sorry if that sounds like emotional blackmail. It wasn't meant to, but I think what I said is true.'

'Mm.'

'The plans we've got for the mill are very exciting. We're going to use all that merino wool in the warehouse and make a special sort of felt out of it, which can be made into wonderful clothes. We're going to use unusual fibres, like llama and alpaca – probably spin them and knit them into designer sweaters.'

She stopped, aware that one major money-making scheme was dependent on Philip.

'Come back and be part of it, Philip. Why don't you?'

'I can't believe you found Philip!' squealed an already excited Felicity as they joined the main road. 'Is he coming home?'

Jenny adjusted the windscreen wipers, glad that the rain was beginning to ease off. 'He's coming for a visit, on his own. He's not making any promises. He's not sure about the mill either.' She didn't add that she shared this uncertainty. What did Ross Grant-Dempsey plan to do to him? While psychologically, for the workers, having Philip back might be very positive, from her and Kirsty's point of view, he might be just another obstruction. And they had enough of those to make Jenny very wary of letting him through the door. She would have to discuss it with Kirsty tomorrow.

'But that's marvellous! Mama will be so pleased!'

'I take it you had a nice time, Fliss.'

'Blissful. He is such a nice man.'

Jenny wanted a bit more than a long silence. 'Did he kiss you, then?'

Felicity nodded.

'Anything else?'

'Not telling.'

'I'll take that as a yes, then.'

Felicity closed her eyes. 'As you wish. But I do think it's good that Philip's coming. It'll make Mama so much more amenable to my marrying Lachlan.'

'Oh? It got that far, did it?'

Felicity shook her head. 'Not yet. But I'm fairly sure it's going that way.' She sat up and looked at Jenny. 'And I'm sure you'll think I'm awfully shallow and that I should just go and live with him, but I really want a proper wedding. White dress and all. Be married from Dalmain House.'

'I think that's a lovely idea,' said Jenny, as enthusiastically as she could. 'Just as long as you don't want me to organise it.'

'Oh no. It won't be until the spring at the earliest. He hasn't actually asked me yet, after all.'

Having decided not to be mysterious about her day, Felicity spent the rest of the journey talking about Lachlan, his property and his plans. She had also picked up quite a lot about llamas. When she got on to the subject of her wedding dress, Jenny broke in,

'Well, I think for the sake of family loyalty, your dress should be made of nuno felt. It would be so unusual, and could look sensational. You should see the pictures the felt woman brought with her. Some of the clothes were lovely.'

'It's a thought, I suppose. Oh! Did I tell you? I was playing around on the Internet while Lachlan was doing something, and I came across the name of a girl I was at school with. She's got a little shop in Covent Garden.'

'Oh.' Jenny was tired, and was beginning to wish Felicity would stop talking.

'Yes. It sells designer knitwear and special hand-made clothes. I thought if I designed it, she could make my wedding dress.'

'Or,' said Jenny, swerving slightly as she took her mind off her driving, 'she could be an outlet for Dalmain Mills! We might have to go down and pay her a visit. Was she a good friend?'

'Very. The only one who wasn't a complete bitch.'

'Would your agoraphobia let you go as far as London, with me, on a train?'

Felicity nodded. 'Might do. Having Lachlan, even if I don't see him much, does make a difference.' She lit another cigarette. 'Sorry, Lachlan doesn't like me smoking, so I'm a bit low on nicotine.'

'I'll try and organise the London trip right away.' If she could tell bloody Ross Grant she had a designer shop in Covent Garden willing to take their stuff, that would bloody well teach him!

'No hurry,' said Felicity. 'After all, he hasn't proposed yet.'

Chapter Sixteen

When Jenny saw Ross's Land Rover parked outside the house, her heart lurched, sank, and ended up spinning, like a coin, undecided which way it should fall. Her brain was equally affected. What was he doing there? He was supposed to be away.

By the time she'd parked the car she had rejected the idea of dropping Felicity off, and driving off to visit Meggie. She ought to know why he was there. He could be threatening Lady Dalmain, measuring up the windows for new curtains (which, God knew, they could do with). Information was power, and if she ran away, she would only get it second hand.

'Are you all right?' Felicity asked, as Jenny slammed the car door. 'Does that Land Rover belong to someone you don't want to see?'

'Pretty much,' she said. 'But don't worry, I won't be rude, or anything.'

Felicity giggled. 'I can't imagine you ever being rude, Jenny.'

Oh, can't you? Well, let's hope I don't threaten your imagination too much, she thought, wisely allowing Felicity to go in front of her, so she would get the first shower of dog hairs.

As Jenny looked through the open door of the drawing room she saw Lady Dalmain seated, a glass in her hand, a man on either side of her. She looked happier and more handsome than Jenny had ever seen her. And she's going to be even happier than this when I give her my news, she thought. Only then did she allow herself to glance at Ross. He was wearing a kilt.

'You're back at last!' called Lady Dalmain. 'Come and have a drink.'

'I must just go to the loo,' said Jenny to Felicity, unwilling to see Ross without a few minutes to prepare herself. 'I'll join you in a sec.'

What is he doing here, and why is he wearing a kilt? Is it a good or a bad sign? Her reflection in the speckled mirror gave her no answers, it just revealed mascara under her bottom lids, and a distinct need for lipstick. She didn't want to look as if she'd made an effort, but on the other hand, lipstick did make one braver. They didn't call it 'The Red Band of Courage' during the war for nothing. She fished about in her handbag and smeared some on.

Felicity was already established with a drink in her hand when Jenny arrived in the drawing room.

'There you are at last,' said Lady Dalmain. 'Ross, this is Jenny, Jenny Porter. Ross Grant-Dempsey.'

Ignoring Ross's outstretched hand, Jenny said, 'But we've met. Ross Grant is the man Dalmain Mills owes all the money to. Surely he told you that?'

'Jenny –' Henry was shocked and horrified by her directness – 'there's no need to be rude!'

'Yes, really, child,' Lady Dalmain snapped. 'Mr Grant-Dempsey has made it perfectly plain who he is. There's nothing underhand going on. I consider it only good manners that he has come here to introduce himself.'

'Oh, good.' Unrepentant, Jenny glanced at Ross out of the corner of her eye, better not to look at him directly. She would either cry, throw something, or worse, kick his shins, and Henry would never forgive her. And it wouldn't do a lot for the mill, either.

'Felicity, get Jenny a drink, will you?' went on Lady Dalmain, 'and remember Jenny likes her whisky neat.'

'Oh, I'll get it,' said Henry, horrified all over again. 'I don't think it's a good idea for Jenny to drink whisky without water.' He was, she noticed, wearing a very nice suit. He was a handsome man, but somehow, next to Ross in his kilt, his handsomeness seemed somehow soft, unmanly, almost. 'After all, you don't drink it at all at home.'

Jenny, who could have really done with one of Felicity's mammoth drinks, concealed a sigh. 'Thank you, Henry,' she said, taking the glass.

Without looking at him, she could sense Ross despising Henry. How dare he? So far, Henry had not spectacularly betrayed her, although if he was secretly negotiating to sell Dalmain House, he might, but he hadn't yet behaved as badly as Ross Grant. She allowed herself another quick look at him. It proved a mistake; whatever her brain thought about him, her body still thought he was the most attractive man on earth.

She crossed the room to an empty chair and sat on it, wishing she had a proper drink – either whisky or water, or a cup of tea, but not this pale, luke-warm fluid.

'So, what have you girls been up to today?' asked Lady Dalmain.

'This and that,' said Jenny, hastily, wishing she'd

thought to warn Felicity against mentioning Philip. Jenny didn't want anyone to know she'd found him until she'd had a chance to think how best to break the news. 'You've been busy entertaining.' She directed a smile at Lady Dalmain, her face muscles resisting the effort. 'How nice on such a horrid day. And I thought Mr Grant-Dempsey was going away.'

'Jenny's got some good news,' volunteered Felicity, seeing her mother about to pounce on Jenny again.

'Oh?' Lady Dalmain regarded her, head on one side.

'I'll tell you all about it later. It's a bit boring for general consumption. I think it would be much more interesting to hear Mr Grant-Dempsey's plans.'

'I came to introduce myself. I find it a good idea to discover the most interesting person in the district and then try and make a friend of them.'

Lady Dalmain was quite as charmed as Ross intended she should be. Jenny seethed.

'But you told us at the mill that you were going away.'

'I am, tomorrow.'

It was no surprise to her, but somehow the news felt like a blow. However much she hated him, she wanted him near, possibly to hate him better.

Henry was standing behind Lady Dalmain's chair. Jenny watched him, aware that never, even when she first met him and was delighted by his charm and his good looks, did she want him in the way she wanted Ross Grant. But was it sensible to give up Henry, whom she knew and understood and had once loved, just because he didn't affect her like a man she knew to be so thoroughly bad? Just because the man turned her whole body into one fluttering, pulsating, erogenous zone? No, definitely not. But she was going to do it anyway. Ross may not be the man for her, but Henry wasn't either. Better to be alone.

She glanced at Ross, and he caught her glance. He didn't smile.

'Well,' he said, draining his glass. 'I must go. It has been so nice to meet you all.'

'Well, you must come again,' said Lady Dalmain. 'For dinner. Jenny's a very good cook.'

'I can vouch for that,' said Henry.

'But he's going away,' said Jenny.

'But I am coming back. We have a meeting, if you remember.'

'We'll arrange it for when you come back, then,' said Lady Dalmain. 'We'll have a dinner party. Write your telephone number down somewhere, and I'll be in touch.'

'That would be very kind, Lady Dalmain,' said Ross, 'but I wouldn't want to put anyone to any trouble.'

'Oh, doing a dinner party is no trouble to Jenny,' said Henry. 'We have them all the time at home, don't we, sweetie-pie?'

Jenny forced a smile, trying to be non-committal.

'In which case, I would be delighted to come.'

'I am extremely committed at the mill,' said Jenny, 'as you know, Mr Grant-Dempsey.'

'Don't fuss, pork chop. I'll lend a hand. And I'm sure Felicity would too.'

'Yes, of course,' agreed Felicity. 'Can I invite Lachlan? Oh, and Philip.'

Every eye in the room turned on Felicity. Only Jenny was shaking her head mouthing, No, no!

'What did you say?' demanded Lady Dalmain.

'Was I not supposed to tell anyone, Jenny? Jenny's found Philip.'

Now every eye was turned on Jenny and she felt her colour rise in response.

Lady Dalmain sank into her chair. 'What! Oh, how marvellous! When is he coming home?'

'I don't think he's actually going to come home just yet,' said Jenny. 'But he would like to come and see his mother.' She didn't look at Ross.

'So I should imagine!' said the mother in question. 'But why won't he come home?'

'He has – dependants,' said Jenny, thinking of the black-clad, long-legged, much pierced youths and their computer game. It would be a moot point which would find the other stranger; Lady Dalmain probably hadn't set eyes on a teenager since Iain had been one, and it was unlikely the lads had ever come across anyone like Lady Dalmain outside a video nasty. 'I didn't meet his – his woman-friend.'

'You've seen him? Oh, the darling boy. Is he all right?'

'He seemed fine.' Jenny wasn't quite sure this was true – in fact, she had felt that Philip was perhaps finding living in a tiny flat above a shop with two huge teenagers harder than he'd imagined – but it was possible that true love was making it easily bearable.

'This is such good news. How did you find him? Can I telephone him?'

'I haven't actually got a number for him,' said Jenny carefully, feeling a call from Lady Dalmain might not be welcome. 'I did ask him to call you and he said he would.'

'Well, if Philip is going to be there,' said Ross, 'wild

horses wouldn't keep me away from your dinner party, Lady Dalmain. It would be so good for management relations, don't you think, Miss Porter?'

Miss Porter sent him a look which should have felled him, or at least created a half-decent lightning bolt. It was disappointing that he was still standing, and looking perfectly healthy. But he would find out that while she would do anything for anyone, she would not be bullied.

As Lady Dalmain was still in a state of ecstasy, it was left to Felicity and Henry to usher Ross off the premises. Jenny had no intention of being alone with him, even for a few minutes.

'Pour me another drink, please, dear,' said Lady Dalmain. 'This is such good news. How did you track him down?'

'It took a bit of detective work, and a call to Directory Enquiries.'

'So you have got a number for him!'

'Oh no. That call was to the bookshop. Now, if you'll excuse me, someone's got to do something about supper.'

'Do you want me to peel the spuds or anything?' asked Henry, coming back into the room.

'No, thank you, Henry,' said Jenny, not because she wasn't impressed by this offer, or didn't want the potatoes peeled, but because if Henry was in the kitchen, she couldn't help herself to the large whisky she felt she both needed and deserved.

Over the chops and mashed potatoes, Lady Dalmain told Henry about Philip. 'I'm sure you two will get on. He's a very cultured man, you know. He's inherited all his father's interest in books and my fascination with history. You do know I'm writing a book, don't you, Henry?'

'I do indeed, Lady Dalmain. I hope to have the pleasure of reading it sometime. Jenny, do you fancy a walk after supper? There are one or two things I want to discuss with you.'

Jenny glanced at her watch, knowing she hadn't an excuse to say no, although being alone with him was the last thing she wanted. He had rapidly picked up the piece-by-piece washing-up routine of the antique china. He, Jenny and Felicity could get through it really quite quickly.

'That would be lovely. After all, it's still quite light.'

'That's something I always notice when I go to England,' said Lady Dalmain. 'How dark it is in the evenings. Not in high summer, obviously, but generally, the summer days are longer up here.'

'And the winter ones are shorter,' said Felicity. 'I think we all suffer from Seasonal Affective Disorder. Do you mind if I clear now?'

The Homely Haggis looked stark and lonely, crouched at the bottom of the great hill that eventually became a mountain. Jenny realised that, since she'd been at Dalmain House, winter had firmly pushed the autumn aside and taken its place. The men at the mill were all muttering about winter coming early. Jenny hoped it was just the meteorological kind, and not the loss of everyone's jobs they were predicting.

'You know, I can't help noticing, Jenny Wren, that although you're obviously being frightfully clever, you're not the same Jenny I fell in love with,' said

Henry, as the two of them walked up the path towards the brightly painted little van, its colours braver for the starkness of its surroundings. 'Since you've been here you've become harder, somehow. You only think about business.'

'That's not true!' Jenny thought about Ross Grant, almost continually. 'But I have been under enormous pressure. If you knew what trouble the mill is in – it's a miracle I ever come home at all. I should just camp out there.'

'Ross Grant-Dempsey seemed decent enough.'

'Did he? Well, he isn't. He's a swine, pure and simple. He's made impossible demands on me, Kirsty at the mill and everyone.

'He's a businessman. So am I.'

'I'm glad you've brought that up, Henry. Who is your client? You've told me that it's Dalmain House he – or they – is interested in.'

'Sweetie! You should know better than to ask me who my client is. It's all highly confidential. But I'll tell you one thing, I'm hoping to wrap up the Dalmain House sale fairly quickly.'

Jenny felt sweat break out along her hairline. Her first thought was that Philip had somehow arranged to sell Dalmain House separately, but then she realised he couldn't. Dalmain House was definitely part of the surety for the loan. 'You can't do it unless someone is in a position to sell it. Now if you just told me –' she tried.

'I *can't*.'

'But –' She hesitated. Should she tell Henry it wasn't up to Lady Dalmain? She had her own rules of confidentiality to consider. 'I'm not sure – I mean, it is just possible that the house doesn't belong to Lady

Dalmain. I'd hate you to go to all the trouble of convincing her that it would be a good idea to sell Dalmain House if she couldn't.'

'That might not be a problem. After all, your boss isn't going to want Dalmain House, is he? If he could sell it off separately, he could get more for it, and get his money back quicker.'

This conversation was making Jenny very depressed. 'I just don't like the idea of you trying to sell Dalmain House behind Lady Dalmain's back! And you are a guest in her house.'

'So are you, but I bet she doesn't know everything you get up to.'

Jenny swallowed. 'No, but it's all for her good, directly or indirectly.' This at least was true, even though she doubted if Lady Dalmain would thank Jenny for everything she did, like encouraging Felicity to be more independent, and possibly run off with Lachlan.

'That's just your opinion. In my opinion, it might be much better for Lady D. to have a smaller place, easier to heat and run. All those sort of practical things you never seem to think about.'

Jenny suddenly felt very tired. 'Oh, do let's stop arguing. It's so exhausting. Here! I've got an idea! Let's open up The Haggis and have something. It would be fun!'

'So, what do you sell? Salmonella sausages? BSE burgers? CJD on rye?' Henry asked, when Jenny had opened up and got herself behind the counter. It felt familiar and safe. If running The Homely Haggis was her full-time job, she would be so happy.

She didn't react to his jibe. 'Mostly home-made stuff,

actually, but I'm not sure what's here. I haven't been for a while, and I don't expect Meggie has. What's in this tin? Oh, flapjack.' She gave the tin a sniff. 'It doesn't smell stale. Would you like a bit?'

He nodded. Was he developing a little paunch? Or was it just that his stomach didn't have the hard flatness that frequent, arduous exercise produced? She was about to suggest that Henry went to the gym, and then realised how hurtful it would be. It was the sort of thing that he would say to her. She sighed.

'What's the matter, pork chop? Feeling blue because you haven't been getting your affection ration? Why don't you come over here and have a cuddle?'

She followed his suggestion and found comfort in the feel of his arms around her but not enough to assuage the guilt. It was another man's arms she longed for, another man's hand she wanted to stroke her hair. She should tell Henry that she no longer wanted to be with him, and that he should go home and find another woman. He kissed her and she kissed him back, and tears formed in the corners of her eyes. Perhaps she should stay with Henry, who was at least here, available to her, rather than hanker after a rat who obviously cared nothing for her.

'Better now? That's my girl. That's my little pork chop.'

'I wish you wouldn't call me that.'

'You never used to mind. I tell you, you've definitely changed.'

'I don't think I've changed, Henry. I think I've always been like this, always ready – perhaps too ready – to fight for the underdog. But I'll tell you what, apart from the huge stress, and the pressure that your

244

friend Ross Grant-Dempsey has put us all under, I have almost enjoyed the challenge. There's something about having your back against the wall, and fighting your way out.'

Henry nodded. 'I'm thinking of setting up in business on my own. I've made loads of really good contacts up here. You could be my secretary. Stop working for all those other people. That would be a challenge.'

Typing Henry's reports wasn't quite the sort of challenge she had in mind. Should she take this opportunity to tell Henry that it was all over between them? She took a breath, about to do it.

'By the way, I meant to tell you earlier. My parents are renting a place up here for Christmas. Should be fun, all of us together.'

Jenny started to walk, her resolve gone. If she and Felicity got a good outlet, when all the samples were made, if the mill wasn't closed, then she'd tell him.

'Hold my hand, Henry,' she said, hiding her bleakness under a smile. 'Let's run up to that rock and then go home again.'

As they walked down the hill, still holding hands, Jenny spotted a Land Rover, far away, on the opposite hillside. Her thoughts flew back to Ross Grant, as if he was the only owner of a Land Rover in the world.

A few days later, Jenny spent a very happy afternoon watching Anna sleep in her Moses basket, while Meggie learned from Rowan how to make nuno felt. Before Rowan went home, Jenny arranged to visit her so she could buy something as a sample. It would mean there was one item fewer for the mill to produce.

One of the mill workers' mothers, who had worked at the mill all her life, had hand spun a quantity of both alpaca and llama fibre. One of her male contemporaries (it was a delight to see them teasing and joshing like they must have done in the old days) had adjusted a loom. A friend of Effie's, Nettie, wove the spun fibre into cloth. Everyone was pleased with the samples, but they weren't large enough to make a garment. Meggie, Kirsty and Jenny felt that one of Felicity's designs should be produced – a potentially beautiful cross between a pashmina and a cape. This required more fabric, therefore more hand spinning.

'The longest journey starts with a single step,' said Kirsty, eyeing the metre of material, reluctant to admit its beauty, softness and drape.

'Oh, Kirsty! It's fabulous! You know it is!' said Jenny. 'Now I've got to go back to the house, and if Philip hasn't phoned his mother yet, I'll go and drag him home myself.' She frowned. 'But do we want him back at the mill?'

Kirsty pursed her lips. 'It would be good if we could make him give us back the buildings, so we can raise some cash. But I'm not sure how he'll regard all this.' She gestured to the length of cloth. 'He always was very set in his ways.'

'So we'll be fighting Philip as well as Ross Grant-Dempsey.'

'I don't think it's quite like that.'

'Yes, it is. He's been totally unfair, asking us to get everything in place in such a short time. It would be better to work for Philip.'

'At least Mr Grant-Dempsey seems to care about the mill.'

Jenny forgot her own bad temper. 'But, Kirsty, you

love Philip – you've been so loyal to him over the years.'

'More fool me. Philip walked out on the mill, keeping a nice little chunk of property for himself.'

'Perhaps he was in love, and it seemed the only way.'

'Fiddlesticks! The man is spineless, and I just haven't let myself see it before now. I think we should get as much done and dusted before he's likely to set foot in the place. He's still the managing director. He could pull the plug on the place himself, never mind your client.'

'I should never have gone looking for him, should I? Or, at least, I should have waited until we were further on with all this.' The fabric, which lay across the desk, a shawl of cream, coffee, and chocolate colours, all natural, made Jenny want to wrap herself up in its gentle, edible warmth.

'Nonsense, child! You were asked to find him. And when he turns up, we've got to persuade him to give up his right to the buildings. And the Dear knows how we're going to do that.'

When she saw the smile on Lady Dalmain's face, the moment she got past the dogs and through the door, Jenny knew Philip had phoned.

'Darling boy! We talked for nearly an hour. He's coming for supper next week. We must make sure we've got something nice. We'll have a joint. Felicity will go and get one from the farm up the glen. Their beef is superb.'

Felicity was nursing a glass of whisky, sitting glumly by the fire. 'Yes. They do a very nice line in fatted calf.'

'Darling, do get Jenny a drink,' went on Lady Dalmain, ignoring this dig. 'I wonder where Henry's got to?'

'It's awfully kind of you to have Henry to stay like this,' said Jenny, taking what might be an opportunity to encourage Lady Dalmain to send him home.

'Oh, that's all right, dear. His firm are paying for his keep. He's negotiating something over the other side of the river. Another European businessman buying a Scottish estate, I expect.' She sighed. 'It's such a shame the old families can't afford to keep them any more. When I think of Dalmain when I first came here as a bride. Thousands of acres – all sold off, bit by bit.'

'So, was Philip well?' Felicity asked, giving Jenny a glass of whisky, and preventing her mother from dissolving into sentimentality.

'I think so. I feel that he may be coming to his senses about that woman. After all, any man might want to sleep with a barmaid, but living with one is quite another matter. They can have nothing in common.'

'Surely,' went on Felicity, 'if he only wanted to sleep with her, he would never have left home. He could have just had her whenever he wanted her.'

Lady Dalmain frowned. 'Don't be vulgar, dear.' It was obviously one thing for her to talk frankly about sex, but another for her daughter. 'No, I think with him it was a protest. He's been under such a lot of pressure with the business lately. It's perfectly natural for him to wish to turn his back on everything for a while. Now Ross Grant-Dempsey is in charge, I'm sure things will be a lot easier.'

Jenny sighed. If only that were true.

Chapter Seventeen

By the time Henry finally put Felicity and Jenny onto the sleeper at Fort William, bound for London, they had five days before Ross Grant-Dempsey was due to return to the mill. It was also freezing cold.

They had with them a case full of samples of fine suiting, a dress bag with Rowan's most beautiful example of a dress made of nuno felt, their own clothes, and a shawl, designed by Felicity, that only extreme strong mindedness prevented Jenny from wearing. They also had a list of useful addresses. Some of the addresses Jenny had researched through the Internet; one was of Felicity's old school friend, and one, a very upmarket tailor in Savile Row, had been provided by Meggie, on a rare visit to her mother-in-law.

They had withdrawn to Jenny's bedroom so Meggie could feed the baby. Jenny had followed her to make sure she had everything she needed, and Felicity had gone with them because she hadn't wanted to stay and hear her mother and Henry discussing the pedigree of some ancient family he was working on to sell their estate, even though Meggie had told her she definitely couldn't smoke near the baby.

'We met at college when we were both doing textiles,' Meggie had explained, fussing with Anna in an uncharacteristic way. 'If he says he doesn't remember me,' she glanced up and then down again, 'tell him that we slept together behind the sofa at Heggie Johnstone's twenty-first. But if he does remember me,' she went on hurriedly, 'don't say anything about that. Bit of an old flame,' she added, in case they hadn't got this point.

When Meggie had gone home, and she and Jenny were washing up the tea cups, Felicity had said, 'Well, I suppose if you're going to sleep around at college, it might as well be with someone useful.'

'Or, even if you only sleep with one person,' said Jenny, 'it's good if it's someone useful.'

The two women regarded each other. Felicity and Meggie might respect each other, like each other, but they'd always have their differences.

Felicity had had quite a lot of contact with her old school friend and they were assured of lunch, if nothing else, from her.

'She sounds just the same,' said Felicity. 'I can't wait to see her. She went to a school reunion recently, and she's going to tell me all about it.'

'As long as you impress on her what a good idea it would be for her to use our exclusive products,' said Jenny, wondering if there was a moral difference between sleeping with the right people at college, or having the right friends at school. None of her own old flames or friends had yet turned out to be remotely useful.

They were going to spend two nights with Jenny's mother. Jenny had been looking forward to it like a child looks forward to Christmas.

*

'Now you do know which cup and saucer she likes for morning tea, and which ones for afternoon tea?' said Felicity to Henry, as he stowed the luggage on the train.

'Large in the morning, small in the afternoon, though she knows I'm not always in at teatime. Now, have you girls got everything?'

'It's too late now if we haven't,' said Jenny, ignoring his patronising tone.

'I'll get off then,' said Henry. 'It's a long drive back.'

'We do appreciate you bringing us, really we do,' said Felicity. 'I don't know how we'd have got here without you.'

'To be fair, Iain did offer,' said Jenny.

'Even if you want to travel all this way in the back of a van, I don't,' said Felicity firmly. 'Thank you, Henry.'

As Henry kissed both women goodbye, it occurred to Jenny, although she admitted it might be wishful thinking, that he kissed Felicity just as warmly as he kissed her. Perhaps there was another reason for his continued presence in the Highlands.

Once settled in their sleeper, the women lay on their bunks and Felicity passed Jenny, on top, a small pewter cup of brandy from the flask pressed on her by Lady Dalmain.

'I prefer whisky myself,' she said, 'but Mama always travels with a flask. Not that she does travel very often.'

Remembering that Felicity didn't either, Jenny said, 'I'm so proud of you, Fliss. It can't be easy for you to contemplate such a long journey, in such a confined

251

space. It's going to be really difficult to smoke too,' she added, making it clear that no way was she going to do it in their sleeping compartment.

Felicity didn't answer immediately, and although Jenny couldn't see her doing it, she knew that now she was inspecting the small Victorian ring that had recently come to grace the fourth finger of her left hand; she'd done it every ten seconds since Lachlan had put it on, in spite of Lady Dalmain's sniffy remarks about garnets being only semi-precious. 'Knowing Lachlan loves me makes everything possible.' Then she added, 'Besides, I've got to get my wedding dress sorted out. And I've got nicotine patches on. And some chewing gum.'

Jenny sank back as the brandy began to take effect. Yes, being in love with someone who was also in love with you would help, instead of a complete –. She stopped the thought. It would only bring her sorrow and frustration.

As a distraction, she turned her thoughts to Philip. Would being in love make him willing to give up the buildings if it would save the mill? Or didn't he care? Would feeling he wasn't totally responsible, that other people were helping him, make him behave responsibly? Morally?

'Do you think Philip will bring Gloria to that dinner party?'

'I should think so. If I were him, I'd introduce her to the family when there were as many people as possible around, so Mama can't interrogate her.'

'But her boys? I mean, I've seen them. I'm sure they're nice lads and all that' – Jenny wasn't sure, actually, but said it anyway – 'but how are they going to cope with a formal dinner party? They may have never eaten at a table in their lives.'

'We'll just have to help them out with the knife and fork thing,' said Felicity, not much interested. 'It was nice of Mama to say it could be like an engagement party, for Lachlan and me, wasn't it?'

'It certainly was. Unprecedented, even.'

There was a pause. 'The trouble is, I know she'll turn it into an engagement party for Philip and Gloria, when the time comes.'

'Unless she hates Gloria, that is.'

Felicity sighed. 'She won't dare hate Gloria, because she knows if she does, she'll lose Philip again. I bet we find she says she's "got character" or something.'

'To be fair, she was fine when you told her about being engaged to Lachlan.'

'I expect now she accepts I'm never going to marry into the aristocracy, and might as well settle for an artisan. She may kick up a fuss when she realises I really am going to leave home, which will mean there's no one to tend to her every need.' Felicity suddenly giggled. 'I've just had a thought. Do you think she'll expect Philip and Gloria to move into Dalmain House so they can look after her for the rest of her life?'

Jenny shuddered. 'Poor Gloria! I haven't met her, but I'm sure she doesn't deserve that.'

'No. But I've had it for years and years, and I didn't deserve it either.'

'True.'

'If only I hadn't been ill, and could have stood up for myself. Lachlan and I would have had ages together by now, children, possibly.'

Jenny never felt there was much point in looking

back at what might have been. 'You might have got bored with each other and be divorced by now.'

Felicity was shocked. 'It's not like you to be cynical, Jenny.'

'Isn't it?'

As the train got into Euston early, they decided to go straight to Jenny's mother, rather than drag all their possessions round London with them. 'We've still got all the samples,' said Jenny as they piled onto the train to Guildford, having crossed London by taxi. 'That's quite enough luggage in my opinion. How are you doing?'

'Surprisingly well,' said Felicity, who looked crumpled from her night in the train, but happy. 'Talking to Lachlan helped.' She rubbed the ear that apparently had gone numb from being pressed against a mobile phone for so long.

Jenny was beginning to think that her pre-conceived notions about Highlanders being taciturn and of few words were quite wrong. Felicity's phone had rung the moment they got off the train, and they had been talking more or less ever since. It was a relief when they finally lost the signal.

'We'll take a taxi from the station to my mother's house. Then we'll both have baths, and then breakfast. It'll be bliss. I've missed my mother so much.'

It was Felicity's turn to feel wistful. 'I suppose if I'd ever been away from her, I might have had a chance to miss mine.'

'Darling!' Jenny and her mother hugged each other so hard their ribs were at risk. 'It's so lovely to see you! You look – you look – a bit tired.'

'Do I? It's probably just train-lag. I'm all right really. Mum, this is Felicity.'

Felicity was also hugged. 'It's lovely to meet you,' said Jenny's mother. 'I've heard such a lot about you, about your lovely designs. You've got one with you? Lovely! And you're coming down to sort out your wedding dress? You must show me what you're having the minute you've had a bath and something to eat. You go in my bathroom, Jenny, as it's a bit of a mess. But I've cleaned the family one just for you, Felicity.'

'It's terribly kind of you, Mrs – Porter.'

'Goodness, you must call me Fay. Now come along, let me show you the bath oil I've put out for you. I do like to have something nice to have in my bath, don't you? Especially as you've been on a train all night . . .'

Felicity's friend's shop in Covent Garden was tiny, but Jenny wanted to put on everything in it, immediately. Gelda, owner and creator of it all, embraced Felicity enthusiastically. It occurred to Jenny that Felicity had probably been hugged more in the last few hours than in all the years since her father had died. Lady Dalmain reserved her physical affection for men.

'You must meet Jenny.' Felicity drew her forward. 'It's because of her I'm here. I'm agoraphobic and I could never have got here on my own.'

While Jenny shook the outstretched hand, she studied the small, eccentrically dressed woman before her. She wasn't, and probably never had been pretty, but she had such style and energy, she was hugely attractive.

'I love everything you've got in here,' said Jenny. 'I hope it's a good omen.'

'An omen for what?' asked Gelda.

Jenny glanced at Felicity, who shrugged slightly. Jenny had been under the impression that Felicity had told Gelda about Dalmain Mills and their hopes for Gelda's contribution to its survival. Obviously she had been wrong. Possibly she'd felt shy about showing something she'd designed to her old school friend.

Jenny took a breath, hoping the right words would come to her. They didn't.

'Listen,' said Gelda. 'Why don't you two come into the back and I'll put the kettle on? You can fill me in on the last thirty years, Fliss. And you can show me what you've got in that dress bag.'

'There's something in the case you should see too,' said Jenny, but Gelda was out of earshot.

Felicity and Jenny sat drinking 'Women's Tea', a black, peppery brew which they both enjoyed more than they'd expected to. Gelda was in the shop, laughing and talking animatedly to someone. Felicity, overcome by curiosity, tiptoed to the door and peered out.

'Oh my God!' she whispered. 'It's – you know – that model. The one who –'

Jenny joined her at the crack in the door. 'God! Yes! So it is! Wow!'

They were both sitting down demurely when Gelda came back in.

'Was that really – you know?' Felicity searched for a name.

'Daffy? Yeah. She often comes in. She's a mate. She says she'll model for me if ever I do a catwalk show.'

'Would you do that ever, do you think?' asked Jenny.

Gelda shrugged. 'To be honest I've got enough work without any of that stuff. I'm just not big enough at the moment. So, what's in the bag? And why have you come to see me?'

'To talk about my wedding dress,' said Felicity quickly.

'And to see if you'd be interested in being an outlet for Dalmain's Designer Fabrics,' said Jenny, hearing the name of the product for the first time as she made it up. 'This is one of them, or it will be. What do you think?' She pulled off the garment bag and gave the dress a shake, hoping it had survived its night on a train.

Fortunately, it had. Gelda didn't comment immediately. She looked sideways at it, fingered the fabric, and took hold of her lip with her teeth. 'Mm. Not sure about the design. There's quite a lot of that sort of stuff about. But I love the fabric. What is it?'

'Nuno felt,' said Jenny and went into her well-rehearsed spiel about how it was made, what it was made from, and what other uses it had.

Gelda nodded. 'Olive oil soap? That explains why it smells so nice, and I'm always on the lookout for something new. And your mill can produce this in quantity?'

'Not yet. But it will be able to,' said Jenny, hoping the gods weren't about the strike her down for over-confidence. 'Would you be interested in it? I mean, we could use Felicity's designs and get the clothes made up ourselves, and get you to be our outlet –'

Gelda shook her head. 'Sorry, I don't sell anything I haven't designed myself.'

'Before you say that,' Jenny persisted, 'can I show you something Felicity designed? I know she'll kill me for showing you, but I think you really ought to see. It shows what you can do with other fibres, like alpaca and llama.'

Felicity got up and went through to the shop. Jenny could fully understand her nerves about having her work exposed to a professional eye. But Jenny was confident it was good enough. Even Henry, the fashion fascist, had genuinely admired it.

Gelda looked and fingered and scrunched for what seemed an agonisingly long time. 'It's lovely. Good old Fliss. She always was arty at school, but her parents didn't want her to go to art college. I remember the art teacher being really indignant about it.'

'Would you be able to sell this? Or things like it? Or would you rather you just had the fabric and did your own design?'

'I don't usually work with weaving like this. I feel this probably works so well because it's been designed round the fabric, rather than the other way round. If Fliss could do more like these, I would put them in the shop. I always felt she got a raw deal.'

'She did –' but before Jenny could explain further, Felicity came back in.

'It's all right, Gelda. I don't mind if you don't want to sell it. Just tell me it's not complete rubbish, and I'll be happy.'

'It's not complete rubbish, and I'd be happy to sell it in my shop, provided you can produce as many as I need. It's quite unlike anything I do, but I think there might well be a market.'

Felicity sat down quickly. 'What did you say?'

Gelda laughed. 'You heard right the first time. I'll sell these if you can keep me supplied. I'd like six to start with, to see how they go. Mind you, if they don't go, I'll send them back to you.'

'You are so kind!' said Felicity.

Gelda shook her head. 'I may be kind as a person, but, as a businesswoman, I'm a walking balance sheet. I haven't the space to clutter my shop up with stuff that hangs around.'

After Felicity had been talked down off her cloud enough for Jenny to feel safe to change the subject, she shook out the dress again.

'How would you feel about using nuno felt for your own designs?' They needed Gelda to do more than just take Felicity's stuff, if she was going to be of real use to them.

Gelda nodded. 'I might be interested. I'd need to look into it a bit more. But it does fall beautifully. And you can incorporate different colours into it, you say?'

Jenny nodded. 'Would you like to see our other samples? Fabric made of alpaca and llama fibre? They can be spun or woven. I've got both here.'

By the time Gelda finally shut up the shop and carried them off to lunch at a restaurant where Gelda seemed to be a friend of the family, Jenny's spirits were rising. No promises had been made beyond taking Felicity's shawls, but Gelda was definitely interested in the nuno felt, although not the suitings. Almost interested enough, she felt, for Jenny to say with some confidence that they had a market for the felt. But could she get Gelda to put anything in writing? Jenny decided that lunch somewhere really nice was a legitimate business expense. She just hoped the business would exist long enough to pay her back.

Grateful that they had no more appointments for that day, Jenny looked forward to falling onto a train and going home. But Felicity, her confidence hugely boosted, wanted to go shopping. As she hadn't been for several years, it seemed unfair for Jenny to discourage her. No one, she discovered, liked shopping better than an agoraphobic in remission.

'I can't believe I'm in Selfridges and not having a panic attack!' Felicity kept saying. 'Shall we take a cab to Harvey Nicks? I haven't been there for years.'

'We don't want to look like we're something out of *Absolutely Fabulous*,' said Jenny plaintively, but Felicity hadn't heard her and was waving down a black cab like an old retail-therapy hand.

The next day, in spite of having made an appointment, Jenny had to go through several layers of assistants before she reached the person whose name was on Meggie's bit of paper. The man in question looked busy and authoritative, some years older than Meggie. Jenny hoped she didn't have to mention Heggie Johnstone's twenty-first birthday party.

'Hi.' She stretched out her hand. 'Jenny Porter. You don't know me, but your name has been given to me by Meggie – Meggie – oh God, I have no idea of her maiden name.' After all her careful preparations, how could she have made such a silly mistake? She gave Alan Frazier her most charming smile. 'You were at college together. Can I make a quick phone call?' Why hadn't she brought Felicity with her, instead of leaving her to sleep the sleep of the dead in her mother's house? She fumbled for her mobile phone, the personification of incompetence.

Alan Frazier perched on the edge of the desk. 'Wait a minute, what does she look like?'

'Smallish, reddish hair, curls. Very vivacious.'

He nodded. 'I know Meggie. A very pretty girl.' He had just enough of the Scots in his accent to make his voice very attractive.

So far, so good. 'Well, she suggested I get in touch with you. She said you were the best tailor in London.'

'And she would know, of course, having buried herself in the Highlands with Iain Dalmain?'

Oh God, don't say he was jealous of Iain, and wouldn't help anything with Dalmain in the title. Jenny shrugged. 'She's probably quite wrong, of course.'

Alan Frazier laughed. 'She's not as far out as she is far away. Is she happily married?'

Jenny nodded. 'She's just had her first baby. A girl. Called Anna.'

'Would you like some coffee? Tea? Meggie didn't say anything about Heggie Johnstone's twenty-first, did she?'

Jenny blushed. 'Do you mind if I take off my jacket? It's awfully hot down here, after Scotland.'

'Be my guest. Now, what have you got to show me?'

Jenny got out her case. 'You could either buy the fabric from us, and produce your own garments using it. Or you could market it under your own name.'

'Very kind of you – Jenny – did you say your name was?'

She nodded, blushing again. 'I'm so sorry. I came

down on the sleeper yesterday and I think I left all my tact under the pillow. It was rather hard.'

He laughed. 'Let's see what you've got . . .'

She met Felicity for lunch, and by the time they finally got back to Fay Porter's house, Jenny was too tired to talk. She just sat in an armchair by the fire and listened to her mother and Felicity chatting. They were surrounded by magazines and were talking wedding dresses, the meringue versus the sleek silk suit.

'Of course, if you have a wedding in the evening,' said Fay, 'which is getting very popular, I gather, you can wear a more eveningy dress. What do you think, Jen? Personally I feel white net has rather had its day.'

Belatedly, Jenny realised her mother was trying to talk Felicity out of a meringue, and needed support, but she didn't have the energy to form either an opinion or an argument. She didn't know if she'd brought anything off or not. Both Gelda and Alan Frazier were interested, but they hadn't confirmed their interest sufficiently for Jenny to feel jubilant.

'Whatever Felicity feels happiest in,' she said.

Her mother frowned. 'I think it's time you went to bed. Would you like some hot chocolate?'

'Oh, Mum! That would be bliss!'

Chapter Eighteen

When Jenny and Felicity arrived back at Dalmain House, no one seemed very much interested in how they'd got on in London. The dinner party was all Lady Dalmain and Henry could talk about.

Jenny couldn't decide if she had genuinely forgotten about it, or had just blanked it out, but she and Felicity were cursorily greeted and then drawn into the conversation as if they'd never been away. Although it was lunchtime, no one was eating, and Jenny was glad that she, Felicity and Henry, who'd met their train, had called in at a pub for a snack on the way home.

'We couldn't wait for you girls to come back from your jaunt,' said Lady Dalmain, in high spirits. 'So we set a date. It's tomorrow! All the guests are invited, and I've ordered the beef, so it should be plain sailing for you, Jenny.'

Jenny clutched at the glass of whisky Felicity had put into her hand rather desperately. 'Have I missed something? What's this to do with me?'

'Well – you agreed to cook for me,' said Lady Dalmain.

'Did I? Are you sure? It's terribly short notice. I've only just got back, and I've got to write a –'

'Really, sweetie! You can't think of letting Lady

Dalmain down.' Henry was at his most disapproving.

'I wouldn't dream of it,' Jenny persisted. 'But when I agreed, if I did, I didn't think it would be the day after I got back from London. These things take time to organise.'

'But you know how good you are at pulling things out of a hat! You should see her at home, Ismene. The kitchen's in chaos, and I can't believe anyone's ever going to get anything to eat, and then she produces a fabulous meal. It's like living with Delia Smith.'

'Not quite,' hissed Jenny through clenched teeth, wondering how long Henry had been on first-name terms with Lady Dalmain.

'Nigella Lawson, then, but don't you worry,' he smiled reassuringly at Lady Dalmain. 'I know Jenny will do you proud.'

Jenny, disturbed at being likened to two such celebrated cooks and confused why she should be obliged to emulate them, was just about to ask, when she caught Felicity looking pathetically like a child who has been told it can't go to the zoo after all. She sighed and realised she would have to do it, for Felicity's sake. The others could go hang, she decided, but Felicity deserved a treat. Seeing Lachlan in a kilt was a small reward for all she, Felicity, had done, but Jenny would make it possible.

'I've invited Philip's new . . . the sons of his – friend too. Philip tried to put me off, saying they were totally uncivilised, but if they're part of the family, they had better get used to our ways.'

Jenny disguised her chuckle with a choking fit. Perhaps there was a god, and Lady Dalmain might yet get her comeuppance. 'They are rather – streetwise.'

'And what does that mean, exactly?' asked Lady Dalmain.

'It's hard to give it an exact meaning,' said Henry. 'I expect Jenny means they are boys who'd be more at home in a pub or a club, or on a street corner, than in a civilised drawing room.'

Lady Dalmain frowned. 'Well, I've told Philip they're to come now. If they're too bad, they can eat their dinner in the kitchen.'

This time Jenny nearly did choke. 'You can't!'

Fortunately Felicity and Henry joined in. 'Really, Mama!' 'I don't think, Lady – Ismene . . .'

'Oh very well, but we must make sure they don't get the very best china.'

'So, how many people have you invited?' said Jenny, who felt she'd better take some interest, given she was supposed to be cooking. 'Will it just be Philip's new family, and Meggie and Iain?'

Lady Dalmain regarded Felicity sternly. 'Principally, this is a dinner party for Ross Grant-Dempsey, for him to meet some of the local families –'

'But, Mama!' broke in Felicity, not quite the cowed woman she had been before she left Scotland. 'You definitely said it could be an engagement party for me and Lachlan!'

'Did I, dear? Well, it could be a joint engagement for Philip and' – only the tiniest pause – 'Gloria.'

'Why, are they getting married?' demanded Felicity.

'Well, no. I gather there's a little problem with her divorce,' said Lady Dalmain. 'Gloria most wisely didn't want Philip involved in it, so they're waiting until her first husband – or is it her third? – has been gone the requisite time.'

'So they're not really getting engaged at all?' persisted Felicity.

'Darling, I don't know quite why you're so keen on having an engagement party. I mean, you're not a spring chicken any more, are you?'

'Mama,' said Felicity, quiet but firm, 'I have been known as the Spinster of the North by everyone who is anyone in this area, more or less since I came back from school. I would quite like it to be known that even if I am no longer a "spring chicken", as you call it, I'm not too old to get a husband.'

'Oh. Very well. Though I would have thought you'd want to be more – well, anyway, I've invited the Malcolms. Fiona Malcolm will do for Ross Grant-Dempsey.'

Jenny found herself squeaking and turned it into a word. 'Oh?'

'Henry's met the family, haven't you? And she's charming, really quite attractive. All that expensive orthodontia finally paid off. She's hardly goofy at all, now.'

'The younger girls are complete bitches, if I remember rightly,' said Felicity.

'Nonsense! Of course they're not. It's only you being neurotic, as usual.'

Suddenly, Jenny could bear it no longer. She was very tired, extremely anxious and everyone around her seemed to be living in an alternative universe.

'Actually,' she said, 'I feel I should just point out that Ross Grant-Dempsey is not just a new eligible male who's arrived in the area, up for grabs by any female under fifty, he is the man who holds the fate of Dalmain Mills in the palm of his hand. I have to have

266

written a viable plan for their continuation, having provided markets and outlets, and he wants it on Monday. I really have got more important things to do than to cook dinner parties for him!'

'This is exactly my point!' declared Lady Dalmain triumphantly. 'If Ross Grant-Dempsey is so important to the mill, it is imperative that we entertain him decently. It's events like these that oil the wheels of industry. You young things just don't acknowledge the importance of old-fashioned hospitality.'

'Quite right!' agreed Henry. 'Anyway, I don't know why you're being so difficult. You've cooked for business contacts of mine often enough.'

'I give up! I obviously can't make you understand. Perhaps I am overtired, perhaps later I will be able to explain how difficult it will be for me socialising with a man who may or may not put dozens of people out of work, practically the evening before he does it. But I must unpack first. Now, if you'll excuse me!'

Her attempt to leave the room was halted by Felicity, who said, 'Jenny!' in a wobbly voice.

Certain that if Felicity cried now, she would come out in sympathy, Jenny raised a reassuring hand. 'It's all right, Felicity; I'm not refusing to help. I just need a bit of time to get my head round it.'

'I expect you girls have been doing a spot of retail therapy,' said Henry indulgently, making Jenny clench her teeth.

'Oh no, Felicity never shops,' said her mother. 'She has agoraphobia, you know'

'Actually, I did,' said Felicity, pleased to contradict her mother. 'I found I was all right if it wasn't too crowded.'

'Oh.' Lady Dalmain wasn't as pleased as she might have been. 'Don't tell me you've been spending money like water!'

'No, I wasn't extravagant. But I also got quite a lot of Christmas shopping done.'

'Christmas! Ghastly commercial event,' said Lady Dalmain. 'It's only designed so shopkeepers can make money. And it's not for ages yet.'

'According to Oxford Street, Christmas is just round the corner,' Felicity persisted. 'And I think most people are fed up with getting hand-stitched cushions from me.'

'Oh, I bet they're not,' murmured Jenny, desperate to leave the room.

'Well, I refuse to think about Christmas until I have to,' said Lady Dalmain, striking an unexpected chord with Jenny. 'Let's get this dinner party out of the way first.'

'So I'll just go and sort myself out,' said Jenny firmly.

'Oh, very well, but I would like to discuss the food with you. We might have to make it a fork supper.'

'Fine,' said Jenny, 'as long as there is a caterer in the neighbourhood, and you've booked them.'

'Jenny!' The howl that greeted this was from everyone.

'Oh, it's all right. I'll cook for your – dinner party.' She would have sworn only she knew Henry would have lectured her about it, and cooking for any number of people would be preferable to that.

After she'd made herself feel more human, Jenny slipped out of the house to go and visit Meggie. The discussion about the party was still going at full throttle. She hoped Henry wouldn't spot her passing through the hall.

Meggie was satisfyingly agog for news. 'Well?' she demanded, opening the door, Anna in her arms, 'Tell me all. Did he remember me? It's all right; Iain's out.'

'You might offer me a cup of tea, or something. We got back to Dalmain House and all anyone can talk about is Lady D.'s wretched dinner party.'

'Oh yes. We've been invited. I told her we'd have to bring Anna. She didn't seem to understand that you couldn't just leave a baby with someone for hours when you're breast-feeding. Now, come with me into the kitchen. You can hold your goddaughter while I make tea.'

'My goddaughter?' Jenny took the sleeping bundle.

'Yes. Didn't I say? I mean, ask you? You were so much part of her birth. We'd love to have you.'

Jenny hooked a chair out from under the table with her foot. 'The trouble is, it'll be hard for us to keep in touch when I go back down south.'

Meggie dismissed this notion. 'Rubbish! It'll be a good excuse for you to keep on visiting dear Dalmain.'

Jenny laughed.

'Now,' said Meggie, when she had presented Jenny with a mug of hot water with a tea bag in it, a spoon, and a bottle of milk, 'did Alan Frazier remember me?'

Jenny squashed the teabag with the spoon for a while, causing Meggie to whimper with frustration. 'Oh, all right; yes, he did.'

Meggie blushed. 'Here, let me take Anna, then you can drink your tea. Now, tell me everything.'

'Well, I felt a complete fool because I'd forgotten to ask what your maiden name was.'

'Oh God! I can't believe I was so stupid not to tell you! What did you do?'

Jenny explained what had happened.

'So you didn't have to mention Heggie Johnstone's twenty-first?'

'No, but he did.'

'What!' Meggie's exclamation caused Anna to stir in her sleep. 'Oh, I'd better put her down.'

'Seems a shame, such a pretty baby, nothing much wrong with her,' murmured Jenny.

Meggie went into the sitting room and came back a moment later. 'I can't believe Alan remembered me! He was older than the rest of us, and all the girls fancied him like mad.'

'Well, he remembered you, and Iain. Seemed put out that you lived so far away.'

'Ooh!' squeaked Meggie. 'It's not as if I don't love Iain and Anna more than life itself, but it's nice to know that the – the one-night stand – wasn't just that, really. Because whatever Felicity and her mother may say about me, I'm not, nor ever was, a slut.'

'They wouldn't say that with me in the room,' said Jenny. 'Anyway, if ever you go down to London, I'm sure he'll be very pleased to catch up with you.'

Meggie shivered with remembered pleasure. 'It's silly, I know, but since I've had Anna, I've felt dreadfully blobby and unglamorous. I've felt terribly motherly, and that's what I am now, but it's nice to remember when you could still pull.'

Jenny laughed, more merrily than she felt. 'Anyway, he seemed quite impressed with the samples. Obviously, unless a client chooses to use it, he won't order any.'

'We must get a client to order it!' declared Meggie. 'Who do we know that's rich?'

'Well, I don't know anyone, and although Lady Dalmain obviously does, anyone who is anyone, that is, I don't suppose even she could dispatch them down to London to order a suit from a tailor he probably hasn't heard of.'

'I'll have a think.'

'Don't tell me there's someone else you slept with who might come in useful?'

Meggie threw her used teabag at her friend. 'So, tell me, what are you going to wear?'

'God knows! I haven't had a chance to think about it. My navy-blue suit, I expect. What about you?'

'I'm going to wear long, because I hardly ever have a chance to dress up and I've a skirt I can leave undone at the top.'

Jenny's teeth caught at her lip. 'Oh dear. I haven't got anything long, and I don't suppose there are any handy little dress shops round here likely to sell me anything, are there?'

Meggie shook her head. 'Not unless you're after something in tartan, no.'

'And all the other women will be dressed up too? What will her ladyship wear?'

'Going on past form, something black, with diamonds. You'll have noticed, she has terrible dress sense, but fabulous jewellery.'

'Diamonds eh? So I can't go in my Marks and Spencer navy suit, then?'

'Well, you could, I expect. But I thought you told me your boyfriend was the style police. He won't like it.'

Jenny was just about to declare she didn't give a

damn what Henry felt, when she remembered that however much she didn't want it to be the case, Ross Grant-Dempsey was going to be there. 'And the other women will dress up too?'

'Absolutely. We all appreciate a chance to put on something skimpy.'

'I hope they stoke up the fires, then. Don't want anyone catching a chill.'

Meggie gave her a pitying look. 'We all wear thermal underwear, sweetie. But I expect they will have good fires going, because her ladyship's dress is low at the back. In-filled with black net. It's a period piece, really. The men will all wear kilts. Iain looks heavenly in a kilt.'

As Jenny remembered, Ross did too. 'Oh God! I've got enough to do without having to worry about what to wear. Couldn't I just put on a black skirt and a white blouse and pretend I'm the hired help?'

'No! Of course not! The Matriarch would order you about as if you really were! And who would Henry have as a partner?'

'It's a dinner party – surely partners aren't really necessary?'

'Jenny, you're not dressing up as a maid, even if it is Henry's secret fantasy. Why don't you come upstairs and have a rummage through the bit of broom handle stuck on two poles I laughingly call my wardrobe. Before the baby, I was about your size.'

After saying goodbye to Meggie and Anna, clutching a polythene bag on a hanger and a pair of shoes, Jenny went back to Dalmain House. She wanted to tell Kirsty about the trip to London and, too weary to drive over to the mill, telephoned her instead.

Kirsty was cautious in her optimism, as was Jenny, but they both concluded that the trip had been a success of sorts.

'The trouble is, with this bloody dinner party –'

'Language, Jenny.'

'Bloody was the expurgated version,' said Jenny. 'I'm not going to have time to write up a half-decent report.'

'Well, you've told me most of it. I'll write the report, and you can come in early and we can alter anything I've said wrong.'

'You're a star, Kirsty. Now, all we need is someone to order a suit to be made from one of our fabrics, and we'll be made. They are so lovely. Alan Frazier was impressed; I could tell.'

'I've been thinking about that. Would a magazine article about our fabrics, the unusual fibres used, and such like, be of any use at all, do you think?'

'Well, yes! Are you saying that's a possibility?'

'I have a niece. I might be able to ask her to do a piece. A very nice girl. A pity she moved to London.'

'Actually, not a pity at all, if she could get an article published about Dalmain's Designer Fabrics. Is she – I mean – I don't want to appear rude – but is she – has she had articles published before?'

'Oh yes. Her mother told me there was one in *Vogue*, just the other month.'

Jenny closed her eyes, glad Kirsty couldn't see her. 'If you could set that in motion, it would be wonderful. Why didn't you mention this niece before?'

'It didn't occur to me she might be useful,' said Kirsty huffily.

'Sorry. I don't suppose it would have occurred to me

either.' Jenny sighed. 'I'd better go, or Lady Dalmain will expect Dalmain Mills to pay her entire phone bill, and as she's asking half of Scotland to a dinner party, it's going to be a high one.'

After that, Jenny slid into bed, wearing all her clothes, and fell asleep.

When she got downstairs again, she found Henry and Lady Dalmain still discussing the dinner party.

'We've decided that if we put both leaves in the table, we can all sit down together. I hate wandering round trying to juggle a plate and a glass, and I don't want food ground into my carpet.'

'So, how many will we be?' asked Jenny.

'About sixteen. We should be able to fit that many round, don't you think, Henry?'

'What about chairs?' asked Jenny. 'I mean, you can always fit the knives and forks in, but have you got narrow enough chairs?'

'Oh, we've got plenty!'

'You don't think that trying to serve roast beef to sixteen people without staff might mean we all end up with it cold? Especially as you don't like your plates warmed first.'

'Then we'll have it cold!' Lady Dalmain was gleeful. 'Cold roast beef and salad. Nothing nicer.'

'In summer,' said Jenny. 'Not in winter.' She could have added, 'In an unheated dining room that would take days to defrost even if it was allowed to have heating in it.' But didn't.

'Jenny,' said Henry sternly, 'I don't think you should take it upon yourself to comment on Lady Dalmain's menu.'

'If I'm expected to be in charge of the cooking,' she said firmly, 'I expect to have some input into what we're having. Is there someone local we could get in to help serve?'

'Of course,' said Lady Dalmain stiffly. 'Mrs Sandison has already agreed to come in and wait at table.'

'Who?' asked Henry. 'Oh, the cleaning lady.'

The dogs were barking and covering the first dinner-party guests with hairs before Jenny reached her room. She stood with her back against the door for a moment, appreciating the coolness for the first time. She was still in her jeans.

'This is the moment to climb out the window,' she muttered, 'and run to the hills. Then I won't have to get changed, make myself presentable, and face all those people who've had plenty of time to get dressed.'

She moved to the mirror to size up the task before her and closed her eyes. In that quick glance she had observed her scarlet face and neck, her hair clinging to her forehead, in dire need of washing, and either this morning's mascara, or terminal fatigue, smudging her eyes. It must have been tiredness – she surely hadn't had time to put on make-up, had she? She opened her eyes and sighed. The morning was such a long time ago, how could she remember what she'd had time to do?

The whole day she had been preparing vegetables, making trifle, cleaning, arranging flowers and place settings, finding dishes, hiding cracks, matching china, resetting the table over and over again, and by now she no longer cared if the beef was the texture of boot-leather, if the potatoes squished rather than crunched, or if the gravy had lumps the size of peat hags in it. It hadn't had lumps in it when she'd left it but, knowing her luck, they would have waited for her to stop whisking and go away before developing.

At least now the smoked salmon was being served with pre-dinner drinks, and was unlikely to spoil.

'And now you have to get dressed and go downstairs, Jenny,' she told herself firmly.

Henry, knocking at her door, reaffirmed this. 'Come on, Jenny! People are here already! You can't spend all night dolling yourself up.'

'Why not? You've had a good half hour.'

'Don't be childish. Lady Dalmain needs you.'

'You go down. I'll be as quick as I can.'

She growled loudly in frustration and deliberately stood in the middle of the room, doing nothing. Henry had been out today, and had made no contribution to the dinner-party arrangements apart from impractical suggestions and tweaking the flowers. Felicity, although supportive, hadn't done a lot either, wandering round the house all day with mud on her face and her hair in curlers, painting and repainting her nails. It was an important occasion for her, Jenny realised, but she couldn't help wishing that Felicity didn't need quite so long to make herself presentable.

Lady Dalmain had changed her mind so often about which guest should have which plate or glass or knife and fork, Jenny found herself saying, 'It kind of makes you wish that instead of all these beautiful antiques you just had a bog-standard set of china, Paris goblets and stainless-steel cutlery, doesn't it? Shall I ring the hotel and see what they can lend us?'

Sometimes you have to be cruel to be kind, she thought, as Lady Dalmain, nearly fainting from the horror of this suggestion, took herself off to her bathroom.

Now, Jenny forced herself to confront the eternal question: should she wash her hair or not? It certainly needed washing; there was no doubt about that. Sweat, steam, anxiety and capillary contrariness ensured that, but could she get it dry and into some sort of style in less than an hour?

She brushed it. It had got long since she'd been away from home and she gathered it from the back of her neck. If I put it up, she thought, it won't show so much that it's dirty. I can raid Felicity's room for hairpins and clips and be ready in fifteen minutes, max. After all, she went on, convincing herself this was the best course, who have I got to impress? I've done the bloody cooking, what more does anybody want?

Before she'd even become aware of what she was doing, Jenny had filled her electric kettle and switched it on. She may yet be proved to be an abject failure with the mill, Ross Grant-Dempsey no longer trusted her, and she'd been a drudge all day. But she was not going to face the most attractive man on the planet with dirty hair, not for Henry, or for Lady Dalmain, or anyone else, even if she did hate him. They could just wait dinner for her. In fact, they'd have to, because unless Felicity did them, the vegetables still needed cooking. Mrs Sandison, Lady Dalmain's 'treasure', was only hired to wait at table, not to cook.

Jenny hovered at the top of the stairs thirty-five minutes later. Her hair, still wet, was pinned up, her make up was on, and so was Meggie's equivalent of a little black dress. It was little, but it wasn't black.

Putting it on now, Jenny wondered if this had been the dress Meggie had been wearing when she had seduced Alan Frazier behind the sofa at Heggie Someone's twenty-first. It was not a dress you wore to a polite Scottish dinner party. It was a sexy dress and being on the small side for Jenny did not make it less sexy. In fact, Henry would say it made it indecent and Jenny wasn't at all sure he wouldn't be right. Very low cut, front and back, it was nominally long, as requested. But the slit up the front made the skirt an irrelevance; the moment she took a step, the sides fell back, revealing a lot of leg. Her one sensible decision, Jenny decided, had been to provide herself with some good tights. She put on two pairs, but she still felt like a showgirl. She wondered if Felicity had some feathers she could put in her hair, to complete the effect.

Still pursuing warmth and decency, Jenny had put a black cardigan on over the top of her dress. This at least covered her back and meant she could wear a bra, but there was still a lot of her on display at the front. She tried doing the cardigan up, to hide a bit of bosom, but it didn't do up high enough to cover much, and the corset effect it created drew more attention to her cleavage than ever. Besides, why should she hide all her charms?

She had some long, jet earrings, but round her neck, not wanting, besides being unable, to compete with Lady Dalmain's stunning jewellery, Jenny put a length of black ribbon. She definitely looked like something out of the Moulin Rouge now, but who cared? No one was going to notice her with the beautiful Malcolm sisters and Gloria to distract male attention.

Somehow she got down the stairs on Meggie's high heels without twisting her ankle.

Chapter Nineteen

✦

Her plans to slip into the drawing room unnoticed were thwarted by a lull in the conversation. She found herself in the doorway, with everyone's eyes upon her.

'Good Lord,' she heard an upright, but elderly man mutter.

Lady Dalmain audibly hissed, and Henry moved forward quickly. 'Let me get you a drink, darling,' he said loudly, then whispered, 'For God's sake! What do you look like? This is a dinner party, not a tarts and vicars! Where did you get that dress from?'

'It's a very good label . . .'

'And you didn't need to wear your Wonderbra! Can't you do up the cardigan?'

'It looks worse, and I'm not wearing a Wonderbra. This is all me and Meggie's dress.'

'You look – completely inappropriate.'

'Don't I look sexy, Henry?'

He shook his head. 'I can't possibly say; you look so out of place.'

'Thank you for that little boost to my confidence,' she murmured, and looked around the room, hoping to see someone more outrageously attired.

Meggie, she noticed, was wearing a long, floating number in emerald green. She had a multicoloured shawl and Anna, both lovely accessories. Now, she looked across at Jenny with an approving smile, and Jenny had the uncomfortable feeling she'd been set up for something, but didn't know what. She took a piece of smoked salmon on brown bread which Mrs Sandison was offering to her. At least Mrs Sandison, who had seen Jenny hard at work all day, smiled kindly.

There was a woman in a high-necked jersey dress in royal blue, talking anxiously to Philip. She had blonde hair in a very tight French pleat, and was slightly red in the face. That must be Gloria. Jenny noticed that the room was, for once, very warm, and hoped she wasn't tempted to remove her cardigan.

Philip, who she hadn't seen since she'd discovered him in his flat, caught her eye and smiled. Jenny smiled back, but as everything was still so uncertain, it was rather strained.

Behind Gloria and Philip, definitely trying to hide, were two youths in black jeans and dark shirts, their hair gelled, their spots scrubbed and glowing, their eyes wild. Gloria had done well to get them to come, thought Jenny; it would be the most dreadful ordeal for them.

Felicity and Lachlan stood by Philip and Gloria. Felicity was talking to them both, her expression tense. While Jenny was watching, she saw Lachlan put his arm round Felicity and give her a little squeeze. Felicity looked up at him and smiled. What a nice man, thought Jenny. Felicity is so lucky – but at least she knows it.

Over by the fireplace were the Malcolm girls, with their parents, as beautiful as described. She would have identified them by their porcelain skins and disdainful expressions, even if she hadn't seen them at the Highland games. Even from that distance Jenny could tell that it was shyness and self-consciousness that made the younger two look so haughty. She caught one of them sliding a glance across at Gloria's sons but couldn't see her reaction. It could have been horror, or longing.

Under a gale of laughter caused by Iain and Philip, who had gravitated together, Henry said, 'Are you sure you can't do anything about your bosom?' He pushed a glass of sherry into her hand and looked down at the offending object.

Jenny ignored the look and glanced at the glass. 'Is this dry?'

Henry was still furious. 'I don't know. I do wish you hadn't chosen to draw attention to yourself like that. Hadn't you got anything else to put on?'

'No. I didn't pack dinner party clothes so I had to borrow this from Meggie. But it's perfectly all right. If you don't draw attention to me, no one will think I'm wearing anything out of the ordinary.'

Henry pursed his lips and looked across at Meggie, ready to disapprove of her, but not only was she looking the picture of pure young motherhood, she was talking to the older man Jenny assumed was Duncan Ritchie, Lady Dalmain's beau. Lady Dalmain was at his side, and, judging from her expression, Meggie was being far too entertaining.

Jenny scanned the room on her own behalf. It was both full of people and strangely empty; Ross Grant-Dempsey wasn't there.

The evening would be far simpler for her if he didn't come. Perhaps he had had some pang of conscience that meant he had decided to stay way. But on the other hand, the thought of him not being there was worse. She had mentally prepared herself for his presence and, however illogical, she knew she would be bitterly disappointed if he didn't appear.

She glanced at her watch and found it missing. She must have left it on the washbasin. 'I've left my watch upstairs; I'd better get it.'

'No!' snapped Henry. 'You're late enough already!'

'But I won't be able to cook without knowing the time,' she snapped back. She took a sip of sherry. It was very sweet. She handed the glass to Henry. 'I'll just pop up and fetch it. You don't know if anyone's phoned to say they can't come, do you?'

'Ask Fliss,' he suggested, taking the glass with bad grace. 'I thought everyone was here.'

Jenny pretended to count. 'No, one missing. When I come back, I'll ask Lady Dalmain if I should rearrange the table.'

Inside her heart was breaking. All day, while peeling and washing, and digging antique platters out of the backs of cupboards, she had thought of him. Of his eyes, which could snap with irritation or be so kind and sexy they made her insides melt. She thought of the feel of his strong hands on her as he helped her into his Land Rover; she thought of his mouth on hers. She remembered the comforting safeness of being with him that night in the pub, beside the fire. It was completely insane, when he held the wealth and happiness of so many people in the palm of his hand, but she felt there was nothing she wouldn't do to be with him.

Having negotiated the stairs both ways successfully

for the second time, she was alone in the hall, doing up her watch, when she heard his knock. She knew it was him, and she knew that she had to open the door. The dogs had been shut away and no one else would have heard such a subdued sound; the volume of a roomful of people who'd been drinking for over an hour was rapidly rising.

He stood there in the dark and hesitated a moment before coming in. She moved out of the way and he entered.

She heard his quick intake of breath, saw his hand reach out for her, and took a step back. Her body wanted to throw itself into his arms and be held by him until it couldn't breathe. Her brain feared his power. Both parts of her knew it would be fatal to allow physical contact between them.

'Hello,' she said, hearing the tremble in her voice and praying he didn't. 'Come in.'

'I'm sorry I'm late.' He shrugged off his overcoat. Unlike the other men, except Henry, he wasn't wearing a kilt, but a dark suit. As he handed Jenny his coat her hand brushed against his arm and she shivered.

'It's all right. You're not really late. I've only just come downstairs myself. I'll get rid of this for you. Why don't you go on through and have a drink? But don't touch the sherry; it's disgustingly sweet. Mind you, they'll probably offer you whisky, as you're a man.'

He didn't move while she hung his coat on a hanger. It seemed unbearably heavy, her arms didn't seem to work properly. Why didn't he go away and give her a chance to pull herself together? Or if he must hover, why didn't he say something?

Free of the coat at last, she felt that she should make some bright remark, something that would break the tension and prove to him that everything was fine, she wasn't terrified of what he was about to do to the mill, or that if he touched her, even accidentally, the place wouldn't burst into flames. No bright remarks came to her. In fact, not even the most unbright, mundane pleasantry about the rain came to her.

'Shall we go through?' he said.

Jenny wobbled on her heels. He put his hand on her waist to steady her and she nearly twisted her ankle. She made a decision. 'I think I've got to change my shoes,' she whispered. 'I'll break something if I stay in these.'

She hadn't meant to whisper, she realised, running upstairs, her shoes in her hand – it was that only a whisper had come out. In her room, pushing her feet into her loafers, she cleared her throat a few times. 'You've got to be able to talk to him normally,' she said out loud, practising speaking properly, 'or he'll think you're stupid, and then he'll reject all your plans and ideas out of hand.' Then, silently, so she could pretend she hadn't admitted it, she added: And he won't want anything to do with you, even if you are wrapped up for him like an early Christmas present.

By the time she got down into the drawing room again, Ross had been absorbed into the bevy of Malcolm beauty. Lady Dalmain was there, making introductions. The Malcolm parents were looking on approvingly. Fiona Malcolm, who had been invited specially for Ross, was smiling enticingly up at him.

Henry was on the edge of the group, smiling

pleasantly, drawing out the younger Malcolm girls. I'm supposed to be his partner, thought Jenny. I'll go and stand by Henry. She was just about to move, having thought up something faintly amusing and appropriate to say, when Lady Dalmain caught her eye.

Jenny went towards her instead, feeling impossibly tired.

'I think we'll eat as soon as you say it's ready,' said Lady Dalmain. 'Could you go and see how things are getting on in the kitchen and come and tell me?' Jenny nodded. 'By the way,' went on Lady Dalmain, 'if you didn't have anything suitable to wear in your wardrobe, you could have just asked me. I could have found you something.'

'That would have been kind, but I didn't think we were the same size.'

Lady Dalmain squeezed her lips in an imitation of a smile. 'I have dresses from years ago. I was much slimmer than you are when I was a girl, you know.'

Jenny returned the expression with a smile just as insincere. 'Then they wouldn't have fitted either.'

'But then, neither does what you have on, dear.'

Jenny went into the kitchen, defeated, but reluctantly admiring.

'Right, Mrs Sandison,' Jenny said, having put on an apron and heaved a series of sizzling dishes out of the oven, 'give me five minutes to get back in there, and then come and announce dinner, would you? Are you sure that silver dish isn't too heavy for you with the joint on it? I could send Philip in to collect it.'

'Now, I'll be fine, lassie. I don't mind serving at

table, I've always done it. It's just the cooking I'm not fond of.'

'Philip's going to carve. I sharpened the knives and they're by his place.' She cast a critical eye over the potatoes, the Yorkshire puddings, the vegetables. 'The gravy's all ready to put in the boats, which are warm, but please don't fill them until you've brought in the meat. With cold plates, I don't want it congealing before it hits them. I don't want it congealing at all, really.'

Mrs Sandison ignored her ramblings, and possibly her instructions. 'Your hair's falling down at the back, dear,' she said.

'Don't even think about what's falling down at the front. Perhaps I'll keep the apron on.'

'Away with you – foolish girl.'

Back in the drawing room, apron removed, cleavage adjusted and her hair pinned up again, Jenny stood by Lady Dalmain. 'Mrs Sandison will announce it in a minute.'

'I do hope the beef's not overdone,' said Lady Dalmain. 'When one has spent so much money on a piece of meat, it is a shame if it's not at its best.'

'Perhaps you should have cooked it yourself, Lady Dalmain,' said Jenny. 'Then you could have been sure of it being perfect.'

'But Henry assured me you were a very good cook, and it's hard to be a hostess and cook at the same time. Especially when one is a widow. Now, where is Duncan? I haven't had a word with him all evening.'

As she had spent a large part of her day rearranging the *placement* under Lady Dalmain's critical and vacillating eye, Jenny knew exactly where everyone was sitting. The only thing she didn't know was which of Gloria's sons was which, and which of the younger Malcolms she should have sat them next to.

Ross would be sitting next to Fiona Malcolm, and she would be next to Henry. But although it had been dreadfully difficult to accommodate Lady Dalmain's requirements, she had managed to seat herself opposite Ross. It was unlikely that Lady Dalmain or Henry would allow conversation across the table, but she could at least look at him, while he imbibed Fiona Malcolm's loveliness, and listened to her soft, Celtic voice.

Mrs Sandison came into the drawing room, looking completely the part in her white blouse, black skirt and white apron. When Jenny had last seen her, she had been wearing a capacious overall.

'Dinner is served,' she announced, not loudly, but somehow audibly. Possibly hunger had alerted everyone's antennae to the summons.

Jenny sensed Ross behind her, felt his tall presence and longed to either turn around, or lean back against him. 'Can I take you into dinner?' he murmured.

'You take Fiona, Ross,' commanded Lady Dalmain, answering his question. 'Henry, you take Jenny, and you might like to go in first, so Jenny can check everything's in order.'

'I knew I should have just donned the pinny and helped Mrs Sandison serve,' she muttered to Henry as they led the way into the dining room. 'It would have been so much easier.'

'You're being very ungracious,' said Henry. 'Lady Dalmain has arranged this delightful dinner party and you seem to begrudge helping.'

Jenny didn't bother to reply.

Everyone was seated when Philip stood up again. 'Ladies and gentlemen. I know my mother is not expecting this, but I thought as this is by way of a celebration, champagne is in order.'

For the first time, Jenny noticed one end of the sideboard covered in glasses, flanked by bottles of champagne. 'Oh dear,' she muttered to Henry. 'Now everyone's going to get drunk.' She sighed. At least they'd devoured quite a lot of smoked salmon. That might absorb some of the alcohol.

Jenny decided to limit herself to one glass of champagne and nothing else except tap water. Others could get drunk and raucous, but she had to keep the meal going. Besides, if she lost control, she might do something really embarrassing, like fling herself over the table at Ross – or take the carving knife to him.

'I'm going to propose several toasts,' said Philip, once the champagne had been distributed, mopped up and peered at suspiciously by Gloria's two lads. 'First, my dear sister, Felicity, who has asked me to announce her engagement to Lachlan. They deserve every happiness.'

Jenny sipped. It was very good champagne. It was a shame she'd resolved to drink so little of it.

'Secondly, Gloria and I have an announcement of our own. We too are going to get married, sometime next year.'

More cheers and congratulations, and one of Gloria's boys deciding the Moët wasn't too bad after all. Philip and Iain topped up glasses.

'The toast is my mother, for arranging this lovely evening for us all.'

Jenny didn't join in the toast, and not only because she was anxious. Everything was getting cold, and already the younger members of the party were showing signs that the champagne was going to their heads.

'Next, Jenny, who did all the cooking.'

Cheers, hoots and cries of 'Speech' turned Jenny from pink to scarlet.

'And finally,' Philip was obviously enjoying himself. 'Dalmain Mills. We've been through some tough times, but now I think we're back on track, and should be going from strength to strength.'

Jenny stared at him, as if this would somehow help her work out what he meant. Was he saying that he intended to give back the office buildings, so there'd be some capital to work with? Or what? Or was he just trying to impress Ross Grant-Dempsey, instructed to do so by his mother? She glanced across at Ross. He was looking maddeningly enigmatic. No amount of lavish entertainment and sucking up would affect his decisions. Jenny blushed in embarrassment on behalf of the Dalmains.

She picked up her water glass and took a sip, she felt obliged to do something to occupy herself. It was a mistake. She choked. Henry patted her on the back so hard it hurt.

'Well done, Philip,' said Iain. 'Now, Mama, can we eat?'

'Yes, Philip.' Lady Dalmain's toast was too long ago for her to be the centre of attention. 'Do carve. And, Iain, perhaps you'd see to everyone's glasses?'

Jenny, weeping from her recent choking fit, tried another sip of water. As she put her glass back on the table, she saw Ross's hand reach across to it. Their fingers brushed together and she felt it like a bolt of electricity. She raised her eyes and met his. He smiled, sympathetic, ironic and knowing. She looked away quickly. God, he was such a dangerous combination, she thought. She didn't smile back.

'Pass your plate down, Jenny,' said Henry, sounding cross. 'Philip's waiting to serve you.'

Jenny passed her plate and looked at Henry to see if he'd noticed her and Ross. He was looking at Fiona Malcolm, who was displaying quite a lot of bosom herself.

I bet he wouldn't tell her she was exposing herself, she thought.

'These look like really delicious Yorkshire puddings,' said Ross, from across the table. 'Did you make them?'

'No, they're out of a packet,' she replied, in the yawning silence of people waiting for the signal to eat.

Jenny found herself alone with Philip when they were moving furniture out of the sitting room so that Lady Dalmain and Duncan Ritchie could demonstrate to the assembled company how to waltz. It might have been alcohol and company, or the social context, but he seemed to have lost his angry edge. She wondered if tonight she might find an opportunity to ask him about the mill, or if this would put him back on the defensive again.

'I would never have believed your mother would be encouraging people to dance,' she said, pushing an armchair into the window embrasure.

'Oh yes; in the right mood, Mama can be very

sociable and jolly. Also, she knows Duncan likes dancing. The trouble is, after the perfect waltz, he'll try and involve us all in obscure Scottish dances which no one knows, and then tell us off for getting it wrong.' He put the Staffordshire figurine of Flora Macdonald close enough to one of Bonnie Prince Charlie to make her look very coy, with a Lion Slayer as chaperone, to make room for an arrangement of stuffed birds. 'Like anything obscure and Scottish, Mama adores it.'

'Oh my goodness! I may have to start the washing-up! But at least the sweet young things will be spared that. Where have they sloped off to?'

'Sweet young things?' He chuckled. 'My old room. It's quite big and has a hi-fi. I suggested they all go up there. Ewan and Gavin have brought some CDs with them. And several dozen cans of lager.'

'Have you heard how they are getting on with – Sophie and Marissa, is it? They look so snooty! I know they're desperately shy, but are Ewan and Gavin going to know that's all it is?'

'Actually, those girls aren't shy at all; they are just snooty. Fortunately Ewan and Gavin appeal to their sense of danger, "having a bit of rough". My sister used to go out with all sorts of terribly unsuitable types when she was their age.'

'You couldn't describe Lachlan as unsuitable.'

'He was the last in a long line of terrifying youths, as my father called them. He had the sense not to criticise, but Mama just couldn't keep her mouth shut and sent him away. Fliss got ill around that time. Just take this end, will you? We can put it in the hall.' Together they carried out the elegant sofa table and set it against a spare bit of wall.

They went back into the drawing room together. 'I heard one of the girls say she wasn't going to spend all night being stepped on by idiots who didn't know an eightsome from the Gay Gordons,' Philip went on. 'A couple of fit young blokes and garage music must seem a better option.'

He pronounced it 'garridge' and Jenny was impressed. 'Learning the language, Philip?'

'Och aye. I'm learning.' Philip looked round the room that seemed much larger and much more attractive, now that half the furniture had gone. 'Mama really should get rid of some of this stuff permanently. Do you think there's enough space now?'

'Well, without dragging anything out onto the drive, this is probably the best we can do.'

Philip nodded. 'I'll go and tell Mama.'

This might be the moment, thought Jenny, putting her hand on his sleeve. 'Philip, while I've got you on your own, about the mill . . . ?'

He didn't jump or run away, which was encouraging. He looked down at her. 'Yes?'

'Have you made any decisions? Did Kirsty talk to you?'

'Yes, Kirsty talked to me, and I'll come to this meeting with Grant-Dempsey.'

'But . . .' She gritted her teeth and asked the question. 'But are you going to sign the buildings back over to the business?'

'Why should I, Jenny? I've got a family to support.'

'But, Philip –' Tiredness pushed Jenny close to despair. Without the buildings to provide capital, all her hard work, Kirsty's and even Felicity's, was for nothing. And Dalmain House would probably be sold.

'Your mother's house – you can't let that go instead.'

'I can, actually. It's my inheritance, after all. But I haven't said I won't sign the buildings back over. I just want to hear what Grant-Dempsey has to say before I decide. I'm not making any promises.'

Jenny felt dangerously close to tears. You're just tired, she told herself. You've spent all day fighting with Lady Dalmain, trying to make her do things for her own good, and you can't do it any more.

Philip looked at her and then said, with relief, 'Oh, here come Meggie and Felicity.'

'What are you two doing alone in here?' asked Meggie.

'Creating a ballroom for my mother,' said Philip. 'Will you be dancing, ladies?'

'I'd be delighted to look after Anna for you, Meggie,' offered Jenny quickly. 'Apart from being dead on my feet, I'm one of the idiots who don't know an eightsome from a Gay Gordons.'

Felicity seemed a little shocked. 'Really? They're quite different, you know.'

Meggie was less critical. 'Well, if you're sure. Although I expect Duncan would relish the opportunity to show you a Dashing White Sergeant. It is a contact sport, you know.'

'Mama would hate that,' said Felicity, shuddering. 'She's terribly jealous.'

'And I'd much rather find a quiet corner with Anna,' said Jenny, longing for an excuse for some quiet time alone, and horrified at the thought of making Lady Dalmain jealous with the charming but ancient Duncan Ritchie.

'Anna would probably like that too, really,' Meggie

breezed on. 'I can't imagine why she's not asleep, I've been feeding her all evening.'

There was a moment's pause while Felicity took in the significance of this. 'Meggie! You didn't breast feed . . .'

'Oh, don't go getting all het up. No one noticed what me and Anna were getting up to under the shawl. You go off and get Lachlan. He's a nice man.'

Appeased, Felicity went, and Meggie handed her bundle, complete with shawl, to Jenny. 'She'll go off any minute now. She's full as an egg.'

But Anna decided she liked parties, and especially liked watching too many people dancing in too small a space. She liked the music, operated by Duncan Ritchie, master of ceremonies, and she liked the shouts and halloos of the men as they swirled the ladies round, the curses as people got stepped on, and the sighs of frustration as people got it wrong yet again.

Eventually, exhausted herself, even if her charge wasn't, Jenny took her back to the dining room. The table, which had taken her most of the day to arrange, looked like the remnants of a drunken orgy. An inordinate number of bottles were scattered about, some of them on neither cloth nor coaster. At least three glasses were lying on their sides, and cheese rind, grape stalks and clementine peel were scattered freely over the table. Cigarette and cigar butts lurked perilously near the butter dishes, and oatcake crumbs and broken biscuits seemed ground into the cloth. The best part of a whole Stilton was missing.

Jenny looked, bewildered. She knew the party had got a bit rowdy, and bottle after bottle had appeared on the table, but surely no one had been this careless and no one would filch a cheese, would they? Then she realised what had happened. The dogs had got in, probably while she and Philip were moving furniture, and had pinched the Stilton. It was a miracle nothing had got broken. But if the dogs were sick, Jenny decided, righting the glasses, it was not her job to clear it up.

For a fraction of a second, she debated clearing the table one-armed, but instead arranged some large cushions cosily on the floor. She turned off the lights and arranged the candles to make the room seem smaller and cosier. Then she sank into the cushions and gently rocked her goddaughter.

'Here you are,' said Ross softly, a few minutes later.

Chapter Twenty

When she'd last seen him a few minutes ago, he'd been whirling Fiona Malcolm round strongly enough to catapult her into next week if he let go.

'Yes,' said Jenny, not knowing what else to say. Anna had at last relinquished her hold on wakefulness and Jenny had been enjoying the oasis of quiet she had created among the noise of people enjoying themselves.

'I didn't see you slip away.' He pulled a chair out from the table and sat opposite her. 'You must be tired, after arranging all this.'

'A bit, yes.' Actually, she felt she could have slept for ever, if her thoughts and anxieties would let her, and as he encapsulated both, she couldn't decide if she wanted him there or not.

'And you've only just got back from London.'

Was this a question or a statement? 'Yes.'

'I can tell I'm making you nervous. Would it help if I promised not to talk about the mill?'

'I don't know. It rather depends on what you're not going to say.'

He sighed. 'I'm trying to make a difficult situation easier.'

'I'm sure you are, but I don't think that's possible.'

He took a breath, holding in his irritation with

visible effort. 'It's perfectly possible. We just carry on as if –'

'As if you're not preparing to disregard all the effort me, and all the people at the mill, have put into saving it?'

'Please don't pre-empt me. Unless you know you've got nothing positive to report, of course.'

'No! I never said that!'

'Well, don't be so defensive. Look, you're upsetting the baby.' He took Anna from her, adeptly putting one hand under her head, the other under her bottom.

'Her name is Anna,' she told him grumpily.

'Anna,' he murmured gently.

Jenny felt a pang that was worryingly like jealousy, caused, she realised, by the knowledge that if he whispered her name in that same tone she would turn to jelly. Just as well he didn't, she told herself crisply; it would make a hideous mess on the carpet.

'You look very at home holding her,' she said, somewhat grudgingly.

'Do I? It's the first time I've held a baby, to my knowledge.'

'Really? You are good at it!'

'I'm glad there's something I can do which will earn me credit in your eyes.'

She hauled herself to her feet. 'Would you like a glass of port, or something? I think there's some on the table, in among all the cigarette ends and orange peel.'

'No, thanks. I'm driving later. I recommend that you have some, though. It will do you good.'

She turned back to look at him, almost smiling. 'You mean it might make me less bad tempered?'

He raised his eyebrows. 'That's a very unfair question. Whatever I answer will be wrong.'

'I know. I'm sorry I'm being so difficult. I'm sure I don't need to explain why.'

'No.'

She found a clean wine glass and filled it with port. She felt suddenly reckless, as if she was too tired to pretend anything any more. It was a bit frightening. What if she told Ross that she thought he was a complete bastard and then ravished him on the Persian rug? She took a small sip of her drink and decided to regard it as a tranquilliser, to let the rich nuttiness of it calm her, and take away both her anger and her desire.

She went and sat down on the floor, opposite Ross and watched him nurse Anna. She's a fairly good contraceptive, she thought. With her there I won't do anything outrageous.

She felt overwhelmingly weary. Her head jerked a couple of times as she nodded off; the next thing she knew, she was enfolded in Ross's arms, her head against his chest, waking after what felt like a fairly long nap.

She opened her eyes and took in how she came to be leaning against Ross, asleep. Anna was lying on her back, a small pool of baby-vomit beside her on the threadbare, antique cushion. Ross had both his arms round her, holding her from behind, his hands clasped in front of them both.

This is so embarrassing, she thought. Falling asleep. It's worse than ravishing him would have been. At least that would have been a proactive gesture. Falling asleep is like passing out, totally passive. She felt his breath in her hair. Most of the pins had fallen out so it was more down than up. She tried to pull herself upright and his hold tightened.

'No, don't move. It's comfortable.'

'It can't be. I must be cutting off your circulation.'

'That's my choice.'

It would be undignified to struggle so she stayed where he was, letting his body melt into hers. They were both fully dressed – or at least he was, her dress was pretty much a token gesture – but she felt closer, more intimate with Ross than she had ever felt with Henry.

'So, Henry is your fiancé?'

'Oh no! We're not engaged. And he's only up here temporarily.'

'I'm sure it's only a matter of time.'

It was a relief to go back to hating Ross. 'Why should you assume that's what I want? Not every woman dreams of floating down the aisle in white net, you know.'

'Well, I think you should tell him. He could hardly keep his eyes off you all through dinner.'

She was about to tell him that Henry's frequent glances hadn't been from love, or admiration, but from anxiety that she might fall out of her dress, do or say the wrong thing in some other way. For some reason Henry had been agitated. Jenny knew this, but didn't know why.

'I don't think he can be all that enamoured of me. We've been here long enough for me to have a nap.' In spite of everything, a giggle erupted. 'Technically, I've slept with another man.'

'I don't think it counts as infidelity if you're not conscious at the time.'

'That's all right then.' Jenny wriggled and Ross loosened his grip. 'I think Anna might be getting cold. I should find something to put over her.'

'Your cardigan, perhaps?'

'Then I'd be cold – not to mention indecent.'

'My jacket, then.' He stood up, took it off and laid it gently over the sleeping baby. 'There we are, little one. That should keep you nice and warm.'

'What about you?'

'I have an idea that might just work.' He sat down again, sliding behind Jenny and holding her tightly from behind. 'Yup. I'm not cold at all now.'

His jacket had been very soft and warm to lie against. His body through his shirt was much firmer, but even warmer. His shirt was made from very fine lawn. He does wear lovely fabrics, she thought, as she fought every instinct to turn her face into his chest, or just to stay in his arms. Somehow she pulled herself away.

'Supposing someone comes in? They're bound to, in a minute.'

'I'll just say you're protecting me from hypothermia. Anyway, what's the big deal, if you're not committed to Henry? We have kissed, you know. And we went out for a drink.'

'I haven't got Alzheimer's; I remember perfectly well.'

'Could we go out again? Or do you need to dispose of Henry first?'

She turned round to face him, finding herself pressed against his shirt. The warmth from his body and the faint aura of his cologne were more intoxicating than any amount of alcohol could have been, but her head fought her heart and body, and won.

'I think you're forgetting that you're the man who has a project which is very close to my heart in the palm of his hand. I don't think "going out" would be appropriate!'

'It might be very appropriate. It might help me decide, one way or the other.'

She didn't really think for a moment his decision would be affected by anything she did or didn't do. 'I don't think it would,' she said, wishing she wasn't so honest. 'I actually don't think me swinging from the chandeliers without my cardigan would affect any of your decisions about the mill.'

He sighed. 'You're right. It wouldn't, although my blood pressure would be very affected indeed. You're an extremely attractive woman, Genevieve Porter. I just wish –'

Before Jenny could find out what Ross wished, whether it was that she was free from all attachments, or that her plans might save the mill, Meggie came in.

'There you are! Ross, I think Fiona's looking for you, and everyone's after you, Jenny. Where's Anna?'

Felicity came in behind Meggie. She was pink in the face and out of breath. Her hair was hanging in tendrils round her face. She looked remarkably pretty.

'Oh my God! Mama will go ballistic! That cushion is genuine Jacobean needlework! And Anna's puked on it!'

Jenny took back all the nice things she'd thought about Felicity.

Ross said, 'If it's that old, baby puke is probably the least of its troubles. It's probably had blood, and urine

302

and all sorts of unpleasant substances on it. Besides' – he took a handkerchief from his pocket and rubbed the place by Anna's open mouth – 'it's gone now.'

'Now it's on your handkerchief. Disgusting!'

'So you and Lachlan aren't planning to start a family then?' asked Meggie, holding Anna protectively.

'Good God no! Why would I want to do that?'

'I think I should get up now,' said Jenny. 'I'm getting stiff.'

Ross helped her up and Felicity suddenly took in Ross and Jenny's proximity. She frowned.

Before she could speak, Henry came in. 'There you are, Jenny! I've been looking everywhere for you. Lady Dalmain thinks you should make more coffee.'

The washing-up took all morning. Jenny, unable to sleep, got up early and organised it. She wanted to do it on her own, not out of a sense of martyrdom, but because she didn't want to hash over the evening. Her feelings were in such turmoil, she needed to give them time to settle before making decisions, or coming to conclusions. The huge, practical task ahead of her would be soothing and satisfying.

The evening had gone well, on the whole. Lady Dalmain had been quite gracious towards Felicity and Lachlan, possibly because Duncan Ritchie had been. Gloria and her boys had behaved in a perfectly acceptable manner – on the surface at least. When Jenny went into Philip's old room, to where the young things had retreated, to fetch glasses, she found roaches in among the dozens of glasses, overflowing ashtrays, and crumpled lager cans. Although Philip's prospective stepsons would be the first suspects if it came to enquiring who had brought drugs into Dalmain House, Jenny wouldn't have been totally surprised if the dope hadn't been supplied by the younger Malcolm girls.

There appeared to be no breakages, and although washing each dish separately took a long time, and she was constantly having to reboil the kettles to provide hot water, there was no hurry, and she enjoyed seeing each dish appear from the water, shining and clean.

Lady Dalmain was the first of the rest of the household to appear. In a dressing gown, with her hair in a plait down her back, she seemed less formidable, almost cosy.

'My dear! You're not doing all this on your own! Mrs Sandison will be here soon. And Felicity should be up to help you.'

'Actually, I'm quite enjoying myself. I love handling fine china and porcelain.'

'Do you, my dear? I'm so glad. Henry obviously has very good taste in ceramics, and it's nice to have an interest you both share.'

To get off the subject of Henry, Jenny said, 'I've laid the clean things out on the dining table, in case you want to rearrange the cupboards. It might be a good opportunity, when everything's out of them.'

'That is a good idea. In fact, I do need to sort things a little. With Philip getting married, he'll need plates and dishes, things to set up home. I might ask Henry to help me catalogue it all. There are some quite ugly pieces Gloria might like.' Unaware of what she'd said, she picked up a bundle of forks and inspected them. 'Were these cleaned before they were used, last night?'

'Oh yes,' said Jenny, and they had been, in a cursory

way. Neither Jenny nor Mrs Sandison had had time really to get between the tines.

'I'll go and see if there's anything I don't want,' said Lady Dalmain.

Well, don't give anything away you actually like, thought Jenny, wishing she had the courage to say it out loud, envisaging Gloria's two boys eating frozen pizza and chips off Lady Dalmain's cast-off Minton, mutton pies and mashed neaps off Coalport.

Before Lady Dalmain left the room, Jenny did say, 'Of course, Felicity will need things too. And she and Lachlan might appreciate antique china a bit better than – than Gloria and her two big sons.'

Lady Dalmain took the point. 'There is that. On the other hand, I could sell what I no longer want, and then Philip could buy something more suitable.'

'They probably would prefer something dish-washer-safe. But Felicity would really love to have things that have been yours.' Jenny hoped that Felicity would appreciate this attempt on her behalf to get her fairly treated and not hate having her mother's castoffs.

Lady Dalmain regarded Jenny, slightly bewildered by the notion that she might show more affection to Philip than to Felicity. 'I'll make sure I treat them both completely equally, of course. I'll just go and see what's there.'

As she didn't appear again, Jenny carried on doing the washing-up on her own.

Henry came into the kitchen, deeply hung over. 'Want a hand, Jen?' he asked, one eye shut, the other only partly open. His shirt buttons were done up wrong and his jumper was all twisted round. For someone who cared so much about his appearance, he was a mess.

'No, it's all right. I'd be worrying about you dropping things all the time. You can put the furniture back later.'

'Good do, though. Well done. I thought you did the food really well.'

'Thank you. I thought I did the other things well too, like setting the table, arranging where everyone was to sit, clearing out the drawing room for dancing.'

'I suppose you're grumpy because you've got a hangover. God knows, I have.'

Jenny sighed. 'No, that's not the reason.'

'Is there anything I could take, do you think?'

'Lots of water, vitamin C and carbohydrates,' she murmured, as she always murmured when he asked this question. 'Oh, and bicarbonate of soda wouldn't hurt.'

'I meant something in a packet,' he grumbled. 'Something they advertise on television and works instantly.'

She had to smile. 'Nothing works instantly with a hangover, love,' she said. 'You know that.' Then she cleared her throat, preparing to say what had been on her mind for so long.

'Have we got any orange juice?'

'No. There are apples. You could eat a couple of them. Oh, and someone brought a chocolate orange. You never know, it might have some distant relative to a vitamin in it. Have some water.'

'I want coffee.'

'Water first, while the water's boiling. Henry, there's something I want to say to you.'

306

'Oh, not now, Jen! Not when I feel so bloody awful.'

'But what I'm going to say might make you feel better. And I don't know when I'm going to get another opportunity.'

'Oh, go on then.' He pulled out a chair and sat at the table, his elbows in among a pile of clean saucepans. His hair flopped over his forehead and his eyes still weren't focusing properly.

'I'll probably be going home soon.'

One eye opened a fraction. 'What! What on earth for?'

'Because, after the big meeting tomorrow, I don't think I'll be needed.'

Henry's other eye opened enough to peer at Jenny in horror. 'Why do you think that?'

'Because I've no great hopes for the mill. Oh, I have worked hard, Kirsty and I have made plans, I've found markets, all that he asked us to do, but I still think he's going to close it down.'

'Did he say anything yesterday?'

'Not about that, no.'

'But, sweetie, what about me?'

'What about you? Your work here must be just about done too, isn't it?'

'No! And, anyway, I don't want to go back yet. I'm still planning to persuade Lady D. that this place is too big for her.'

Jenny sighed sharply. 'Well, I don't think much of your chances. She was loving having all those people dancing in her drawing room last night.'

'She could have all that somewhere else.' His headache was making him petulant and sulky. 'Where's the coffee, for God's sake?'

She produced a jar she'd hidden last night, so there wouldn't be a coffee-crisis in the morning. 'So could your client, whoever he is. Tell him to look elsewhere for a stately home.'

'Actually, my first client has pulled out. But I've got another, and the Office is keen for me to stay up here a bit longer. They're talking of setting up an office in Inverness, putting me in charge.'

'Oh.'

'Not that that should make you feel obliged to stay up here for ever,' he went on, spooning instant coffee into a mug as if it was a delicate task requiring a lot of concentration.

'Oh?' Jenny didn't feel so obliged, but Henry had a subtext and she wanted to discover it.

'No, I mean – I've been meaning to talk to you about us for a little while now.'

Oh my God, thought Jenny, please don't say he's going to propose now, still half drunk, covered in stubble, with breath like a dragon's after a beef vindaloo.

'I know I haven't been very attentive lately . . .'

Jenny hadn't noticed. She hadn't been very attentive herself. 'We've both been busy –'

'That wasn't why, though. The thing is, sweetie –'

Felicity chose this moment to appear. Her hair was falling down her back and she was still wearing last night's make-up. It was her slightly inane smile that told Jenny she'd smuggled Lachlan up to her bedroom.

'Hi, Felicity,' she said. 'Henry and I are just having a bit of a chat. We'll go away and have it somewhere else. Let you get your tea.'

'Fine,' said Felicity. 'We can catch up later.'

Jenny drew Henry out of the kitchen, along the hallway and out of the front door. 'Now, Henry, are you going to propose, or are you going to dump me? I should say that I'd prefer you to dump me, as I'm certainly not going to agree to marry you.'

'Oh,' said Henry. 'Well, I wouldn't have said I was going to dump you, but there is someone else, yes.'

'You weren't going to keep me on, as a fall-back position?' Jenny's voice was serious, but inside she was beginning to see the funny side.

'No, of course not.' He paused. 'I was going to ask you to pretend we're still together, so I could go on staying here. Bit pathetic, I know.'

'Because it's convenient for visiting Fiona Malcolm?'

Henry nodded. 'God, I am a cad!'

Jenny laughed. 'What a lovely old-fashioned word! And you're not one, really you're not. But I can't stay here unless I'm needed at the mill. Surely you can see that?'

'You don't want to go, do you?'

She sighed. 'In some ways, I suppose not. Now I've got used to the cold, and I have learnt to love the mountains. They have a sort of stern beauty that's grown on me in a way I didn't quite expect.' How much of this was tied up with her feelings for Ross Grant-Dempsey she couldn't untangle. 'Oh look! The snowline's much lower now.'

'Apparently it's going to be a really hard winter. All the locals say that once in five years the snow gets really deep.' He hesitated. 'You love snow. Stay here and enjoy it. I know that Lady D. really likes having you here. She won't know if you're needed at the mill

309

or not. We've had so many happy times together. I would hate to fall out with you, Jen.'

'I won't fall out with you, Henry.'

'So you'll stay? At least until the New Year?'

'I really don't think I can if I'm not needed. But I won't rush off before I've tied up all the loose ends. Will that do you?'

He kissed the top of her head. 'You're a real poppet.'

As she went back into the house she wondered how it was that when you were parting from people, they often became far more endearing than they had been for ages.

She did have her own reasons for staying – at least until the New Year: Ross's last words, said to her among the bustle and noise of everyone's leave-taking, had been, 'See you at Hogmanay.'

This was mystifying. She'd see him the next day – in possibly very difficult circumstances. He couldn't have forgotten. Or was he hoping to carry on a relationship with her, after the mill was closed? Could she have anything to do with a man who had put dozens of people out of work, who had obviously planned to move into Dalmain House, (she realised now that he must have been Henry's original client) and had probably only stopped wanting to evict Lady Dalmain when he saw the ghastliness of her domain?

It wasn't hard to answer. It was no.

A small voice suggested to Jenny that perhaps she'd better wait until he'd actually done all those things before she made up her mind. Another wondered how his potential villainy squared with his wonderful tenderness with Anna.

Ignoring them both, Jenny went back to the kitchen where she found Felicity and Lachlan, debating whether or not to announce his presence to Lady Dalmain or keep quiet about it. Lachlan was all for being open, but Felicity was in a froth. Jenny added her two penn'orth to Lachlan's side, saying that Lady D. didn't have to know where Lachlan slept – he could easily have used Philip's old bedroom – besides, Felicity was over forty and was entitled to a sex life. Then she retreated. She had a report to write. Besides, there was a lot of furniture still to move and a huge pool of dog sick outside the pantry.

When she looked up from her laptop, seemingly hours later, freezing cold and stiff, she saw it had been snowing. The world was bathed in purple shadows, with patches of gold where lights from the house shone on to the falling snow. 'Oh wow!' she said, and ran downstairs, wondering if anyone had a sledge.

Jenny shouldn't have been surprised that the Dalmains didn't share her Sassenach enthusiasm for snow, but she thought they might have been a bit happier about it. From the hall, Jenny could see Lachlan, sitting awkwardly on a chair with a Royal Worcester cup and saucer on his knee. Lady Dalmain was delivering a lecture on the decline of civilisation as demonstrated by their reluctance to do Scottish dancing.

'Lots of young people enjoy reeling,' Lachlan replied, eyeing Jenny, but not betraying her. 'It's just the Malcolm girls had possibly had a bit much of it, their parents being such enthusiasts.'

'I still feel it was bad manners for them to leave the party like that and disappear upstairs. I expect Philip's room smelt like a public house after they'd been there, didn't it?'

Jenny hovered, not wanting to have to join them in the drawing room, yet eager to hear Lachlan's reply. It was worth waiting for.

'I didn't sleep in Philip's room,' he said. 'I slept with Felicity.'

Chapter Twenty-one

When Jenny awoke the next morning she was aware of the light being different. She staggered across to the window, pulling on clothes at random. The snow now lay in drifts.

Usually she loved snow – no child with a new sledge wanted thick snow more than Jenny, normally. But today she had to go to the mill and face Ross Grant-Dempsey, and discover everyone's fate. And a lifetime in the Home Counties had not taught her to drive in snowy conditions.

She went downstairs to see what it looked like close to. The dogs scampered about in it, burying their noses in it, sneezing, biting it, and attacking little hillocks with an abandon Jenny wished she could share. But although it seemed fairly deep, the road wasn't completely covered. There may be no reason at all why she shouldn't just drive to the mill in the normal way.

Her car, half buried under a snowdrift, was going to take some time to clear. The meeting was scheduled for ten o'clock. It was now only seven. No need to worry; there was plenty of time.

Felicity came into the kitchen while Jenny was boiling kettles to defrost her car. There had been an almighty row between her and her mother, which, much to her surprise, Felicity had won. Lachlan was still at Dalmain House.

'Hi!' said Felicity. 'What do you want all that hot water for? The pipes aren't frozen, are they?'

'They may well be, but I need this for my car. I have to go to the mill today, remember?'

'No chance! You'll never get down the hill, not in a car, anyway. Lachlan's just rung a neighbour and asked him to do the llamas for another day. They won't have gritted the main road yet, and no one can get anywhere until they do that.'

'This isn't a matter of choice, Felicity. There's a very important meeting, I have to be there!'

She shrugged. 'When there's this much snow, we just have to stay put. Easier for those of us with agoraphobia, I agree.' Felicity smiled. It was possibly the first time she had ever been able to make a joke about her condition. 'Just as well there are plenty of leftovers. Perhaps you could make soup.'

'There's nothing I'd like more than to make soup, after I've built a snowman, of course, but I have to go to work!'

'You'd better ring Iain, then. He might be able to help.'

Iain sucked his teeth, tutted and, although Jenny couldn't see him, she knew he was shaking his head.

'It's vital I get there, Iain. I'm not just being over-conscientious. The whole future of the mill is at stake!'

'I know that, hen. Could you get down here to us, do you think?'

'Oh yes. I'll walk, slide, no trouble. Then what?'

'I know the guy who drives the gritting lorry. He might give you a lift as far as the main road. I've a pal along there who's got the right sort of vehicle to take you the rest of the way. But before you set off –'

'What?' She tried not to sound abrupt, but was sure she had.

'Just a thought, but will anybody else be able to get there? You don't want to have a meeting on your own.'

'Well, Kirsty lives really near. I'm not sure about Ross Grant-Dempsey, and he's got a Land Rover.'

'And it may not be so deep over that side of the glen.'

A snowflake-sized hope that possibly the world had come to a halt melted. 'I'll start putting on clothes then.'

'Aye, and don't forget to lag your legs.'

Jenny laughed politely and hung up.

She had already warned Kirsty that she would be late, and fended off suggestions that she shouldn't risk her life to come in – it was only a meeting. Because, in spite of her robust protestations to the contrary, she knew that Kirsty wanted her there, even if the Demon King himself didn't turn up.

It took her three hours to get there, and, having checked that no Land Rover in the car park did indeed mean no Ross Grant-Dempsey as yet, another half hour to turn herself from an extra in a movie about the North Pole into a quasi-management consultant. Not for a moment would Ross confuse her with the under-dressed, light-hearted girl he had sat with the night before last.

Kirsty had walked, or rather dug, her way into work and had used the hours she'd been there on her own to create a set of the most beautiful reports possible. They were laminated, bound, interleaved with glossy

315

photographs (taken by Iain with his digital camera) and, although only three of them were expected to be present, there was a small pile of the brochures.

Jenny and Kirsty wandered round the office, straightening the reports, changing the arrangement of chairs round the table, watching people fighting their way through the snow, and children playing. Kirsty, who was looking out of the window, suddenly said, 'My goodness. It's Philip! He must have followed the gritting lorry. I didn't know he was coming, did you?'

'Oh, yes! Now I come to think about it, he did say he'd come, at the party. I'd completely forgotten. Is this good or bad?'

Kirsty shook her head. 'I have no idea. It could make it look as if we're a team.'

'But are we? He's got the buildings and we need them.'

'Perhaps he's had a change of heart,' suggested Kirsty unconvincingly. 'Perhaps he's come here to tell us, to be a knight in shining armour.'

'Doesn't sound like the Philip I know, and there was no suggestion of that the other night.'

Kirsty made more coffee. 'Want some?'

Jenny shook her head. 'I'm edgy enough as it is. Philip! How nice to see you,' she added a moment later.

'Hello, Philip,' said Kirsty, a little restrained. 'Will you take a cup of coffee and a piece of shortbread?' She handed him a cup and saucer and wafted a hand towards a plate. 'Goodness knows when Mr Grant-Dempsey will get here. If he does at all.'

'Oh, he'll get here. People always do, where money is concerned,' said Philip.

Jenny felt instantly defensive on Ross's behalf. 'Is that why you're here, Philip?'

He shrugged as he bit into a finger of shortbread, dropping crumbs all over the table. 'I suppose it must seem like that.'

'Then what is it like?' demanded Jenny. 'I mean . . .' she tried to soften her tone. 'I mean –'

'What Jenny means,' said Kirsty, 'is, are you going to sign the offices – these offices – back to the mill?'

Perfectly sure that wasn't why he'd come, Jenny pressed too. 'Yes, are you? It would make all the difference. With the buildings, our plan is almost totally viable.'

He brushed more crumbs off his waistcoat with the back of his hand. 'I'm sure it is. But why should I give back what I consider to be rightfully mine?'

'But they're part of the mill! They're not yours more than any other bits are!' said Jenny.

'Exactly. I've only taken a small section.'

'I didn't mean that!' Jenny was beginning to feel really despondent. All morning she had kept herself going with the thought that if she could only get to the mill all would be well. Now she was there, she realised that it probably wouldn't. She might as well have stayed at Dalmain House and made a snowman.

'What do you want the money for, Philip?' asked Kirsty.

'All the usual things. To keep my family, pay bills, eat. Gloria's expecting, by the way.'

'Oh! How marvellous!' So much for Lady D.'s assumption that Gloria was too old. Jenny didn't feel there was another way to respond to news like that,

317

although how they could persuade him to give up the offices now, God alone knew.

'So, what will you do?' persisted Kirsty. 'Invest the money and live off the interest?'

'No!' Philip was indignant. 'I shall buy a bookshop.'

'A bookshop! What a good idea! Your mother will be so pleased,' said Jenny.

'Because selling books is a slightly more gentlemanly occupation than running a woollen mill, you mean?'

'Well, of course, with your mother, those things are always a consideration. But I meant that books are her passion.'

'Oh yes. I got my interest in them from her, I suppose.'

'It's just a pity she'll have to live in the apartment above the shop. It might be rather squashed with five of you, and the baby,' said Jenny. She hadn't meant to be bitchy; she really had meant to be positive and supportive in the hope that sweetness would get them further than bitterness, but she was tired, and it had just come out.

'Look,' said Philip, responding to her anger, 'there is absolutely no need for my mother to leave Dalmain House if she doesn't want to!'

'But it's been signed over, as security for the loan,' said Jenny.

'I know. But she's got plenty of money of her own. If she wants the house, she can buy it, probably at a cut price, because no one else will want it.'

'That's true,' said Jenny. 'So, are you telling us that Lady Dalmain has a private fortune?'

'Absolutely. And not just in stocks and shares. There

318

are antiques and jewellery in that house which would buy this place several times.'

'My goodness, all that wealth and no central heating. Are you sure about the antiques? I know there's a lot of furniture, but is it actually valuable?'

'Certainly. Mind you, she'd never consider selling anything. She likes owning things too much.'

'She would if the alternative was being homeless,' said Jenny. 'No point in being surrounded by Chippendale on the street.'

'I don't think any of it is actually Chippendale,' said Philip seriously, 'but lots by his students, of course.'

Jenny was about to suggest he smuggled a few smaller items out of the house and sold them – no one would ever notice they were missing – when Ross Grant-Dempsey came in.

He caught them all off guard. Jenny jumped as if someone had threatened to mug her, and Kirsty looked positively flustered, flapping crumbs onto the floor, grabbing the coffee pot.

'Sorry I'm late,' he said. 'Had a spot of bother coming in.'

'It's hardly surprising,' said Kirsty. 'This snow!'

'It wasn't that. I found some people who needed digging out of their car.'

Jenny took a breath to ask for more details but realised they would not be forthcoming. Kerbside Angel one minute, Boardroom Devil the next, that was her client.

'Coffee, Mr Grant-Dempsey?' Kirsty handed him a cup, having already put shortbread on the saucer.

'Thank you. Now, I'm sure you'd all like to get on.'

319

'There's a copy of our report, Mr Grant-Dempsey,' said Kirsty. 'And one for you, Philip.'

Jenny and Kirsty already knew what was in it, the slightly massaged figures, optimistic market trend predictions (llama cloth is going to be big in the autumn collections), and flagrant name-dropping. (Jenny was only grateful they managed to leave Heggie Johnstone's twenty-first birthday party out of it.) So, while the men were reading they went through torture. When she wasn't wondering how Ross would tell everyone they were out of work, just two days before Christmas, Jenny wondered how she'd get back to Dalmain House. When she wasn't mourning the fact that nuno felt might never become a major fashion statement, she was wondering which bits of furniture she would encourage Philip to sell; the drawing room would be quite handsome without all that junk in it.

At last, after what seemed like hours, but was probably only fifteen minutes, Ross cleared his throat.

'Well, you seem to have done a good job. There is just one problem –'

'It's all right,' said Philip. 'I give in. I'll sign back the offices so you can have the capital you need.'

'But what about the bookshop?' Jenny asked, suddenly feeling guilty, as if she'd put undue pressure on him.

'I'll ask my mother. You're right, Jenny; she will think it sufficiently gentlemanly, especially when I tell her it's Toshak and Fiske I'm planning to buy. They're a well-respected name.'

Even if their customer confidentiality isn't up to much, thought Jenny.

'That actually wasn't the problem,' said Ross.

'Then what the hell is?' Tension and too much coffee finally got to Jenny. 'We've worked so bloody hard, thought of everything, found markets, talked people into giving us catwalk shows – Christ! Kirsty's niece is writing a piece for *Vogue* – possibly the *Sunday Times* too. What the hell can be wrong with that report? This mill could run like a sewing machine given half a chance. Just have a little vision! Just look at something other than the bottom line for once in your life!'

Aware that everyone was looking at her as if she'd completely lost it, she blushed scarlet, suddenly far too hot in her extra layers. 'Sorry,' she murmured. 'I think I'll go to the loo.'

She washed her face, which was a mistake, because the water made her skin feel unbearably tight. She put hand cream on her face, which was a mistake, because it stung like the devil, then she found she'd wiped off all her eye make-up, which was definitely a mistake. After doing the best she could with paper towels, horribly ashamed of leaving Kirsty on her own, with two hostile men, she fled back into the boardroom feeling slightly less attractive than a newborn piglet, and not half so cute.

Everyone looked at her as she came in. As no one else seemed willing to speak, she thought she'd better. 'Well, is Kirsty going to type out the redundancy notices, or do we need a lawyer?'

Kirsty frowned and shook her head. Philip gave her an old-fashioned look. Ross just regarded her as if she was barking.

'You don't understand,' said Kirsty. 'It's going to be all right.'

'Is it?' Jenny had spent so much energy bracing

herself for failure, she couldn't possibly believe in anything else.

'If everything goes to this very optimistic plan,' said Ross. 'Do you want a lift home, Jenny? I didn't see your car in the car park.'

Jenny blinked at him, still trying to take in the news. She shook her head to clear it. 'No, thank you. I'm fine.'

'So, how will you get back? Presumably someone gave you a lift here.'

'Three someones, actually, counting Iain.'

'So how will you get there?'

She would walk back, if the journey took her days, weeks even, rather than accept a lift from him. She felt such a fool and she almost hated him for letting her misjudge him.

'Philip – Philip will take me. Won't you? He wants to speak to his mother.'

Philip seemed somewhat disconcerted at the prospect of driving along snowy roads with a madwoman in his car, but he coped like the gentleman his mother thought he was. 'Er, yes, fine. Of course. No trouble.'

'Good.' Ross scooped up the papers in front of him and swept them into his briefcase. 'I'll be off then. Let me have those other figures, Kirsty. Bye.'

A moment later they were in the vacuum of a large presence now absent. It was like the moment after an explosion, before the birds start singing again, and life begins to deal with itself.

'Phew.' Jenny shivered. 'Thank God that's over. Don't worry, Philip; you don't really have to drive me home. I'll ring for a taxi or something.'

'It'll be something, at this rate. It looks like there'll be more snow before long.' Kirsty shook her head, trying not to appear smug for living so close to her work. 'You could always spend the night with me.'

'No,' said Philip. 'I think driving you home now would be a good idea. I'll ring Gloria and tell her everything's going to be all right, but that I might stay at my mother's.'

'But *is* it going to be all right?' asked Jenny a little later, when, both well wrapped up, armed with a flask of coffee and the rest of the shortbread, in case they got caught in a snow drift, they set off for Dalmain House in Philip's sensible Volvo. He obviously had to trade in his sportscar.

'It will be for the mill. I'm not so certain about the bookshop.'

'I'll do everything I can to help. I'll tell your mother it was all Ross's fault and you deserve the money for saving the mill.'

'You don't need to tell lies for me, Jenny, although moral support might be useful.'

'It would only be a white lie. After all –'

'Actually, it would be diametrically opposed to the truth. It was because of my mismanagement that the mill got into trouble in the first place. It was me who looked for an angel investor and found Grant-Dempsey. I didn't know they'd – he'd – want quite such a large slice, although I know now it's standard.'

'So how much money will you need for the bookshop?'

'Not more than a couple of Jacobean tables and a Landseer,' he chuckled.

'You are joking, aren't you?'

He shook his head. 'There's one in the attic. All I

have to do is persuade Mama to sell it. I thought perhaps Henry might help.'

'Doing what? Selling it? Or persuading your mother?'

'Well, both. The house is grossly overfurnished.'

'You can say that again.'

'The house is grossly overfurnished.'

It wasn't really funny, but they both laughed and laughed.

Jenny wiped her eyes, feeling much better. 'I'm so looking forward to going home for Christmas. I can't believe it's only the day after tomorrow. I must organise a train ticket, or something. Or I could fly from Inverness, couldn't I?'

'You could, at any other time of the year,' said Philip, correcting a skid with the ease of one brought up to drive in snow. 'But every seat on every train and plane will be booked. And you're not going to be able to get your car out for a while.'

Jenny wanted to cry. She'd been so strong, so full of fight and courage, suddenly the thought of not spending Christmas with her mother turned her into a little girl again. It was utterly pathetic. 'Oh. I don't like to think of my mother spending it alone.'

'I'm sure that won't happen. People will queue up to invite her.'

They already had. Fay Porter had accepted a last-minute invitation to spend Christmas on a luxury cruise, someone having broken their leg. 'You'll be all right up there, won't you?' she asked, when she'd finished telling Jenny all the details.

'Me? Oh yes, I'll be fine. It'll be brilliant to have a white Christmas. I can't remember the last one.'

'And you'll have Henry with you.'

'Yes. Actually, Ma, sorry to cut you short, but I must go.'

'So should I; I've still got packing to do. It'll be such fun, dressing for dinner every night. Still, I won't keep you. Bye, love. I'll give you a ring tomorrow, before I go. Will you be at Dalmain House?'

'For the foreseeable future,' she muttered. 'No, only joking! Yes, I'll be here.'

Jenny sneezed loudly. She felt supremely sorry for herself, wanted to howl and bite the pillow. But Philip was still with his mother, and she wanted to be available in case he needed her support, so she went downstairs, after the briefest sob and not even a nip at the lumpen mass she rested her head on every night.

She found Henry and Felicity in the sitting room. Henry was reading and Felicity was finishing a cushion. The atmosphere was that of a dentist's waiting room.

'Philip's with Mama in her study,' said Felicity. 'I know she'll give him the money he needs, and I know that, if it were me, she wouldn't let me have a penny.'

'Where's Lachlan?'

'He dug out his Land Rover and went home. He did want to get back to his llamas, but I think he also found the atmosphere here a bit stultifying.'

'I expect we all feel a bit flat after the party,' said Jenny, remembering it only because the furniture wasn't all back, and the room looked bigger. 'I know, why don't we decorate the house? For Christmas?'

'We never do,' said Felicity.

'Jenny's addicted to fairy lights,' said Henry, indulgently. 'She has to buy a new set every year, and find somewhere else to put them.'

'I don't think we've got any fairy lights, or any decorations. If we have, I've no idea where.' Felicity made it clear she was not about to go rummaging in attics to find ancient treasures to decorate a tree.

'Well, we could pick greenery, boughs of holly, that sort of thing. Goodness me, the place is surrounded by conifers. Let's go and cut some and bring them in!'

'I'm not sure Mama would like it,' said Felicity. 'She doesn't really approve of Christmas. Hogmanay is more her thing. She only sends cards to very old friends.'

Now she looked, Jenny noticed that there were surprisingly few Christmas cards tucked around the dead birds and animals. 'Well, what about you?'

'I don't get many.'

'Do you send many?'

'No, none at all.'

'Why on earth not?'

'Well – because I've been ill.' Felicity seemed affronted at the suggestion that she might indulge in an activity most of the rest of the world did as a matter of course.

'It is a lot of work, but it's nice to keep in touch. I usually send loads.' The thought of all her unopened cards at her mother's house and her own made her feel guiltier than ever for not having got round to sending any this year. Somehow, away from home, she'd lost sight of the approach of Christmas, had assumed she'd be home before now, and so had missed the boat. 'I expect I'll be struck off everybody's list.'

326

'You do always go over the top a bit at Christmas,' said Henry.

'Maybe. But I'm going to try and find a bit of holly, or something.'

By the time Philip and his mother emerged from her study, both appearing tired and emotional, Philip clutching an empty whisky bottle, Jenny had found enough greenery to satisfy her. Felicity, taking pity on her, produced some ribbon, and while the decorations weren't exactly opulent, they had a sort of *Country Living* rusticity.

'Philip and I are going to run a bookshop,' announced Lady Dalmain. 'Such fun. He's going to man the shop, and I'm going to deal with the antiquarian books, over the Internet.'

If Jenny had been prone to fainting, she'd have done it then.

Chapter Twenty-two

Jenny woke on Christmas morning knowing she was going to hate every minute of the day. She didn't usually condemn a whole day the moment she opened her eyes, but for this one, she felt she was justified in feeling despondent.

There would be family presents at eleven, and then everyone would process, in as many cars as necessary, to the Malcolms', for drinks. They would come back here for a snack lunch (smoked salmon and whisky) and after a long period of sleeping or being intensely bored, they would go to the lodge Henry's parents had rented, for Christmas dinner. Henry's mother was delighted at the prospect of a real title at her dinner table.

'Do you not want to see your first grandchild on Christmas Day?' Jenny had asked, feeling that a quick visit to Meggie and Iain would be a little much-needed relief.

'No. They're going to spend the day with her parents.' The 'her' had just enough emphasis to make their social standing clear. 'We're having them up here for Boxing Day, remember? And Philip and Gloria, of course. And her sons.'

Jenny pulled the duvet up round her head. Shall I pretend I'm ill? Lie here all day and wallow in my misery? No, that would be a foolishness too far. She retrieved her mother's cashmere sweater from the side of the bed, put it on, and got up.

More snow had fallen in the night, but now the clouds had cleared and the sun shone. It was nine o'clock. There were no stockings to open, no last-minute presents to wrap, no presents bought, even, beyond the things she had managed to get at a village shop, after Philip had broken it to her that she wouldn't get home for Christmas. Boxes of chocolates, a scarf pin for Lady Dalmain, tartan socks for Henry, some soap and a very pretty scarf made from llama fibre (a sample) for Felicity, didn't take much tartan wrapping paper. Her efforts at decorating the house had been regarded as a strange flight of fancy.

Usually, on Christmas day, when she was still living at home, she'd make tea, and take it into her mother. Then she would get into her mother's bed, as if she were still a child, and they would open their stockings together, both having done one for the other. Then, when they'd put on all the wearable items, eaten several of the edible ones, and made themselves feel slightly sick, they got up and ate croissants and cherry jam before going for a walk.

Deprived of two of these homely rituals, and even of Henry's less-enthusiastic, 'Oh, happy Christmas' Jenny felt entitled to have the third; she would go for a walk in the snow.

Before she went downstairs to make tea, she logged on to see if her mother had managed to send her a message from her cruise ship. She had. Trying not to let her self-pity show in her reply, she went on about the beauty of the snow, ending,

I'm going to make a snowman later, no matter how much they laugh.

She wasn't really expecting one, but there was a time when her client Ross Grant-Dempsey might have emailed her a Christmas message. For a ghastly moment she wondered if her laptop, which had been the means of communication between them for so long, before she knew who he was, of course, would always remind her of him. If they weren't so expensive, she'd consider getting a new one. From somewhere came the thought of Lady Dalmain becoming computer literate, a silver surfer, selling books from the Internet. In spite of feeling so low, she smiled. Philip certainly knew how to manipulate his mother if he persuaded her she wanted to do that!

No one was about downstairs. Lachlan had trekked back over the previous night and driven Lady Dalmain to see a neighbour. Henry wouldn't wake for hours. Jenny let the dogs out and watched them scamper over the snow. Like the rest of Scotland, which had not welcomed her at first, she was now used to their hairy exuberance. She didn't intend to take them with her for her walk, though.

When she opened the front door a little later, she was dressed as appropriately as she could be. She had put on thick socks and her newly acquired walking boots. Underneath she had on thick tights, her tartan trews, and many other layers of clothing, including the dress-length cashmere jumper. She slung a small bag over her shoulder into which she put a bottle of water, a bar of chocolate she had intended to put in someone's stocking, before she realised that no one did stockings in Dalmain House, a couple of clementines, and a packet of bought shortbread she had had to keep hidden from Kirsty.

She had left a note, giving her time of departure and expected arrival home too. It seemed rather dramatic, given she was only going to flounder through the snow for a few hundred yards, but with Ross's harrowing story about being rescued from Snowdon, she was determined to do everything right. She would probably be back before the others were up anyway.

She was tempted to just walk straight up the hill behind Dalmain House, but knew the snow would be too thick for easy walking, and that it would be better if she found the path she knew to be a little way to the left. Even just getting to the path made her hot, and wish she'd put on slightly fewer layers.

The way to the top of the hill was marked by stones splashed with paint, now two feet under the snow, but Jenny was fairly confident of finding her way. There were no hidden gullies that she knew of, it was early in the day, and the walk only took an hour, or so Philip had told her as they'd driven back together the other day. She had been complaining that she still hadn't had an opportunity to climb the local mountain.

'All those walkers telling me about it at The Homely Haggis, me living so close, and no time to climb it myself.'

'I'm not sure it qualifies as a mountain, but it's a nice walk on a good day. You can see the whole next mountain range from the top. Now they really are spectacular. They are for real climbers, not just hill scramblers.'

Conveniently forgetting his rider that it would be

best to wait until the snow had thawed a bit before she tried it, Jenny set off with confidence. She should be at the summit and back before the rest of the household even stirred from their beds. And if she didn't make the summit, at least she'd have a good walk, and feel better for it.

She seemed to make very slow progress. Of course, walking through snow is slow, but however far she walked, every time she looked up or back, she seemed to be in the same place.

At half-past eleven she wondered if she should go back. All those social engagements she would be missing. Still, she'd missed going to the Malcolms' now, anyway. And they weren't really her social engagements, she was only invited because she was part of the household and so had to be.

Eventually, she reached what would pass for a summit. She sat on a rock that was only lightly dusted with snow, and looked at how far she'd come. Her path was clear, disappearing from time to time, revealing when she had come to a summit, only to find another one ahead of her.

She was tired now, and realised that she should have set herself a shorter target, knowing that she was totally unfit. But it was Christmas, and this walk, this time alone, was her present to herself. She ate the bar of chocolate, hoping it would give her the energy for the homeward trudge.

'It should be much quicker going down,' she said out loud.

Now, the prospect of Christmas with Henry's parents, going through the pretence of she and Henry still being a couple, seemed a lot more attractive.

Henry's mother was a good cook, and although she would expect Jenny to help, helping was a lot easier than running the show.

The sun had gone, its absence reminding Jenny that there were very few hours of daylight left. But still, she reckoned, it should only take her just over an hour to get down. She'd be back, lighting the fire, if no one had already, by four. She thought hungrily of the mince pies she'd made. She didn't really like mince pies, but now a mince pie and a cup of tea sounded like heaven. A few sips of water quenched her thirst, but didn't satisfy her like a cup of tea would have done.

All went well until she put her foot into a snowdrift disguised as a section of path. Her foot went down and down, and, unable to stop the rest of her body from following, she tumbled, head first, into about three feet of snow, descending several yards as she did so.

Winded, she allowed herself to stay still for a few moments before struggling upright. She had just got her body and legs into a sitting position when she screamed.

A figure, dark and menacing, had suddenly appeared before her.

'Don't panic. It's only me.'

Jenny closed her eyes and did her panicking silently. It was Ross. He seemed quite real, but had she just conjured him up, out of the snow, because he'd been so much part of her thoughts? Was she suffering from mountain sickness, or some special delirium that made you hear voices and see figures when none really existed? The trouble was, the Ross in her thoughts and dreams was different from the flesh and blood one, who she was still fighting with.

He was still there when she opened her eyes. She felt incredibly foolish; not only was she sitting in a snowdrift halfway up a mountain, hardly a dignified position, but the last time she had seen him she'd behaved like a madwoman. Perhaps she should try to pretend there had been nothing untoward between them.

'Happy Christmas,' she said. It was the first time she had spoken that day, and it came out very croakily.

'Happy Christmas yourself. What are you doing here?'

It was no good. She couldn't pretend he was just someone she vaguely knew. She had loved him and hated him with such fervency, she couldn't behave normally. She couldn't help snapping, 'If it isn't obvious, I'm not going to explain! I just came for a Christmas walk. What's your excuse?'

'Came after you. I saw you from the road.'

'How could you possibly have known it was me?' The thought that he had made her feel suddenly paranoid.

'I didn't know for sure, but I didn't think anyone else would be so foolish as to come up this high in these conditions.'

'I have not been foolish! All I've done is go for a walk! It is allowed, isn't it?'

'Not without a woolly hat, it's not.'

'I hate woolly hats. They prickle my head.'

'You still shouldn't go climbing mountains without one. Here.' He pulled off his own hat, and she put it on. It was warm, and because it was fleece, didn't prickle at all.

'Now you're climbing mountains without a hat.'

He shook his head and put a hand into the pocket of his coat. 'I have a spare.'

The snow was beginning to penetrate Jenny's clothes. She wanted to get upright, preferably without assistance, but wasn't sure she'd make it. Sensing her predicament, he put out an imperious hand, and she took it.

'Thank you,' she said briskly, grudgingly, brushing herself down. 'Now I'll go home.'

'No you won't.'

'Yes I will. They'll be expecting me. I said I'd be back by now.' He might almost be a member of a mountain rescue team, but she was not going to be told by him what to do.

'Look at the weather.'

Jenny looked. What had been a bright, clear day had turned suddenly grey. Snow-filled clouds blocked out the sun and the wind had begun to freshen. 'Well, it's not as nice as it was earlier, but it won't take me long to get back, I'll probably slide half the way.'

He shook his head. 'I'm afraid going back isn't an option now.'

'What do you mean? It's not as if staying here's an option!'

He was maddeningly patient. 'We won't be able to get back safely now. We'll have to move on.'

'But why would moving on be safer than going back? It doesn't make sense!'

'Yes it does. I know a safe route upwards, to somewhere where we can get some shelter. If we went down, we'd risk falling into a hidden gully. You were extremely lucky to get this far safely.' His brows drew together.

But Jenny wasn't going to give him an opportunity

335

to lecture her. 'Not lucky, well-organised. I knew where I was going, and I've got the right clothes on. And I left a note.'

'I know. I rang Dalmain House.'

'Oh?'

'I spoke to Henry. I must say, he didn't seem very concerned considering you and he are practically engaged.'

'Not any more.'

'Even so. People die on the mountains every year.'

'I can do without the propaganda, thank you. Anyway, I thought that when you saw me from the road, you didn't know it was me?'

'I said, no one local would be so foolish.'

'I suppose you expect me to be grateful for you coming up here to rescue me.' Because she felt guilty, gratitude was beyond her.

'Not at all, and please don't be. Such a dramatic change in character would be very unsettling.'

She took a shuddering breath. 'You are such a bastard.'

'I know. If you haven't actually told me in so many words, you've made it quite clear how you feel.'

Jenny regarded him. When she hadn't been hating him, she'd been yearning for this man for weeks. Now he was here, in front of her. She did something very foolish. She picked up a handful of snow, formed it into a ball, and lobbed it. At such close quarters, she couldn't miss.

When she realised it had landed on the few inches of his skin unprotected by clothes, she ran away, or rather tried to. Not even in nightmares is running so slow as it was then. She saw him take time to take off his pack and put it somewhere safe before he came after her. He still caught up with her in seconds, and she fell, with him on top of her. Together they rolled down the mountain, over and over, until eventually they stopped, buried in snow.

Jenny was panting. Nothing hurt, so she knew she wasn't injured, but she was totally winded, and she was being squashed by the weight of an apparently very angry Ross.

'Now listen!' he said, his breath hot on her face. 'This is not the local park where you can throw snowballs all morning and then go home at lunchtime! This is serious stuff! I've already told you that people die on mountains, and the reason they die, mostly, is because they've been silly. Now either you behave yourself or –' He paused.

Lying underneath him she could see where his breathing had formed condensation on the collar of his coat. She could see the pores of his skin, which was flushed by cold and exertion. She saw flecks of gold in his eyes, which were a sort of olive green colour, where his eyelashes were slightly paler at the ends. She could see where his beard was just beginning to make an appearance.

His body was crushing hers and she should have felt suffocated. Her instinct should have been to push him off, to get out from under the weight that was pressing her into the snow. She glanced at his mouth and then looked away, but she didn't move. 'Or what?' It was hardly even a breath.

He caught his bottom lip between his teeth as his gaze flicked over her face and away. 'Oh Christ, I really didn't mean this to happen now.'

He felt cold at first, and then hot as he kissed her with intense concentration, paying attention to every corner of her mouth with his tongue, his teeth, with everything.

She lay beneath him with her eyes closed, almost swooning with desire. When he lifted his head she decided if dying was the penalty for kissing in the snow, it would still have been worth it. Nothing Henry had ever done to her had made her feel like that, she realised, not even in the early days. Ross had not done it, she knew, because he particularly wanted to, but to shut her up. It was, literally, a punishing kiss, so why was it so sensational? It wasn't even the first time they'd kissed.

He got to his feet, angry, almost. 'This is bloody stupid. Now come on.' He dragged her upright, turned her round and then took hold of her wrist and more or less dragged her after him.

She stumbled and fell. He stopped and turned round. 'What have you got on your feet?'

'High-heeled stilettos, what do you expect?' She felt so hurt by his attitude: kissing her as though there was nothing more on earth he wanted to do, or cared about doing, one minute, biting her head off the next.

He picked up a booted foot and looked at it critically. 'They're not evenly laced. Too tight in some places and too loose in others. And are they broken in, or is this the first time you've worn them?'

She declined to answer, but sat sullenly while he re-laced both boots, but when he pulled them tight, tied them, and hauled her to her feet, she fell over.

'You're cutting off my circulation! I won't be able to walk a step.'

He ignored her, tucked in the loose ends, and then hauled her upright again. Then he pulled the collar of her jacket up, found the hood concealed in it, and put it on, securing it tightly. 'That's better. If you're ever tempted to leave the safety of the Home Counties again, make sure you're properly equipped.'

'Oh, for God's sake! I didn't set off to climb the Matterhorn! I was only going for a walk!'

'In Scotland, in winter, particularly when you're high up and there's snow on the ground, you are never "only going for a walk". Now come on!'

He took hold of her hand and pulled her along until they got to his pack. When he had put this back on he set off, expecting her to follow.

She hated him with every step she took. At first the tightness of her boots felt so strange, she wondered how she got her feet to work, but she didn't dare not do it. The pace he set seemed impossibly fast, but eventually she became used to it, and she had to acknowledge that her ankles now felt very secure. Lashed up like that they can't bend, poor things, she thought, angrier because he was right.

She was not going to let him see she was struggling, that it took all her breath and energy to keep up. But she did it. The sky was darkening all the time. The wind was getting stronger. The storm Ross had spoken of, which had seemed so unlikely, was on its way.

He stopped after about half an hour. She was panting, but felt warm and exhilarated. And still angry.

'Here, have something to eat.'

'No, thank you.'

'I'm not asking you, I'm telling you.'

'And I said no! I'm not hungry! I had a bar of chocolate not long ago.'

'Have a cereal bar now. Too much sugar can let you down later, and it's better to eat before you get really hungry. Otherwise it's difficult to regain your energy.' He sighed as she stood, refusing to take the bar he offered. 'I could make you eat it.'

He wasn't exactly menacing, but she was suddenly aware of his physical superiority, or how, if it came to a fight, he could so easily defeat her. She snatched it from him, ripped off the wrapper and crunched into it, as viciously as if it were a part of him she was biting.

'We've got a way to go,' he said more gently. 'And it's important we get there before the storm comes.'

Stuffing the wrapper into her pocket, she looked around her and was aware that she had no idea where she was. The tops of the mountains were hidden by thick cloud, and beneath the cloud were hillocks and valleys, which swooped and merged, giving no clear direction.

Not wishing to give him the impression that she had become any more biddable, she said, 'I still think we should have tried to get back.'

'It would have been impossible even from where I met you. And they won't be worried. I told them not to expect us back until tomorrow.'

'Tomorrow! But where are we going to spend the night?'

'Don't sound so horrified. You must have realised we're committed to sitting out the storm.'

'But where? Is there a hut, or something?'

'Or something. Now come on. We mustn't waste our energy chatting.'

'Chatting! Huh!'

She stomped off after him, but in spite of her rebellious manner, for the first time, Jenny began to feel frightened. It was some small satisfaction that Ross was probably suffering as much as she was, although in a different way. It must be very irritating to have to drag a woman he obviously thought several sandwiches short of a picnic up a mountain. A thought struck her.

'I won't have to do any climbing, will I? I've never done any.' She hadn't done much walking lately, either.

'I'll be able to haul you up where necessary. I've got a rope.'

'Oh. Fine.' She had a vision of herself trussed up like a Christmas turkey, being bumped up a cliff face.

He stopped and turned round. 'Don't worry. I'll look after you.'

'That's what I'm worried about!'

Chapter Twenty-three

The moment after she'd said it, she wished she hadn't. However she felt about him, he had rescued her, and while she might doubt it was necessary out loud, in her heart, she knew she trusted his judgement, about the mountains, at least.

'Sorry,' she added. 'I'm a bit tetchy. It's an odd way to spend Christmas Day.'

He nodded, accepting her reluctant apology. 'Two o'clock – people all over the country are pushing back their chairs after eating their turkey and Brussels sprouts.'

Jenny shook her head. 'Not at two o'clock. Most people won't have started yet. Very few people get it all together to start before two or three. Unless, of course, they got up at dawn. The gravy always takes much longer than you think.'

Ross shrugged. 'Are you ready to move on?'

Jenny nodded. 'Of course. I didn't stop, you did.'

Conversation soon became impossible, even if Jenny could have thought of anything to say that was not in some way contentious. She didn't mean to do it, but whenever she spoke, she became sharp, bitter almost.

He stopped again, and whenever he turned round, she tried not to pant. She didn't want him to know how unfit she was.

She had a feeling he wasn't remotely fooled when he said, 'So what jollifications has this excursion made you miss?'

'Nothing much.' She took her water bottle out of her pocket and found it had cracked and was empty. Without saying anything, he retrieved another one. Not only had he had the forethought to take off his pack before he went rolling down the mountain, but his water was in an aluminium bottle. She took a few sips. 'I can't remember. Oh yes, drinks with the Malcolms.' A vision of him whirling Fiona Malcolm off her feet flashed into her mind. So determined not to feel jealous, or worse, sound it, she gabbled on. 'Dalmain House don't do the fun things about Christmas, like Christmas trees and fairy lights, only the hard-work things, like meals. They don't even give each other stockings.'

'Do you and Henry? Did you and Henry?'

'I always did him one, but he didn't do one for me. It's harder for him to go shopping, and I like doing them. I always do one for my mother, and, of course, she gives me one.' Oh God! What am I talking about? He can't be remotely interested.

With the light behind him, she couldn't read his expression as he looked down at her. Suddenly she felt frightened and foolish and wished herself a million miles away. Or in Surrey. Even without her mother, or Henry, at least she wouldn't feel frightened, in physical danger.

'Don't worry,' Ross said quietly. 'I won't let any harm come to you. You'll come out of this completely safe.'

'Will I?' Suddenly she felt safe no longer just meant

alive, free from frostbite, not suffering from hypothermia. Safe meant not spending the rest of her life mourning her lost love, a love so hopelessly misdirected it would never find its way home. Which was worse, she pondered, being God knew where, up a mountain, in the snow, or falling for a man she couldn't exchange half a dozen civil words with, and who probably thought she was the silliest woman alive?

'You have my promise.'

Tears pricked her eyes, but as they were already watering from the cold and wind, he wouldn't notice. But she felt so vulnerable, entirely dependent on a man who cared no more for her than he would have done for any sheep on its back, or party of people who needed digging out of a car.

They stopped often. Each time he made her drink water, or eat a sweet, of take a few bites of a cereal bar. Jenny stopped trying to make polite conversation beyond, 'Thank you' and 'Here you are.' She was aching everywhere it was possible to ache. Her heart was definitely the worst; that wouldn't get better no matter how much sleep she had, how many hot baths.

'Here we are,' he said eventually.

Jenny looked. Above them, the mountain loomed blackly, too steep and windswept for the snow to cling. Beneath, was a gently curved hillock. 'Where?'

He indicated a small hillock, then heaved his rucksack off his back and opened it. From it he produced a folding aluminium spade. He made a few tentative prods and then started scraping away at the side of the hillock.

'You don't expect me to sleep here?' demanded Jenny.

'That's up to you, but this is where we're going to spend the night. Sleeping is optional.'

'But there's nothing here! We're on top of a mountain, with no shelter, and you talk about spending the night!'

'You'd be in worse trouble if I said we had to go for another hour. You're done for, I'm bloody tired, and this is where we can spend the night in some degree of comfort. Now shut up!'

Jenny bit her lip to stop herself going on at him. No woman likes to whine, and Jenny was aware that, however justified her anxieties, any further mention of them would be perceived as whining. Anxiously she watched as Ross scraped away at the soft snow. A shape emerged. It looked to Jenny like an igloo, but she wasn't going to say that and be mocked. Presently he straightened up.

'There. Wait here.' He wriggled into the snowy mass and, a few moments later, wriggled back out again. 'More of a palace, than a snow hole,' he said, panting slightly. 'Come in.'

Tentatively she dropped to her knees and crawled in through the narrow gap. It felt horribly as if she were surrendering to the snow she'd been fighting all day. But once inside the snow hole, she knew what he meant.

It was like a cave, only the roof had been smoothed over. Two platforms, like beds were raised either side of the entrance tunnel. Another, wider ledge, extended right to the back wall.

'Shove up,' said Ross, and shuffled in after her,

dragging his rucksack behind him. He sat on one of the platforms and opened it, pulling things out, hunting for others. 'Here,' he said at last. 'Take these. There's probably somewhere to put them already.'

She took the three candles and stuck them into the niches she spotted round the walls. 'Matches?'

He handed her a box. Lit, the candles turned the cave into a fairy grotto. Jenny was entranced by the beauty of it and looked around, amazed and delighted. 'It is awfully *Dr Zhivago*,' she said, demoting it several degrees. 'But what's to stop us freezing to death?'

'Sleeping bags.' He pulled out a folded bundle, then another.

'You knew we'd have to be out all night, then?'

'It's always a good idea to take precautions, but I did have a good idea that we would, yes.' He sighed, reading her mind. 'I know you don't believe we couldn't have got home from where I met you, but you have to take it on trust.' He hesitated. 'It's not all bad. I brought food, as well. And whisky.'

'But I thought alcohol brought on hypothermia. They always say that. All those huge dogs, little barrels of death round their necks.'

Ross laughed. 'It would do if we didn't have enough food or bedding. As it is, we'll be fine. It is Christmas, after all. Here, spread these out.'

Two plastic foam sleeping mats sprang into life the moment Jenny undid their ties. She laid the sleeping bags on top of them, one each side of the entrance tunnel.

Ross had produced a camping stove and set it up, ready to light. 'I'm going to get some snow, so we can have water. You make yourself comfortable.'

Jenny arranged herself on top of one of the sleeping bags. It would have been warmer to get in it, but that would have meant taking her boots off, and she knew that when Ross came back she'd have to go out herself. The snow hole might well have been a palace, and an awful lot better than spending the night on the side of a mountain, but it wasn't en suite.

The stove was alight and Ross was boiling snow when she came back. 'Why don't you get into bed and keep warm?' he suggested. 'You don't want to lose all that body heat you've spent all day building up.'

'OK. I must say, I would really hate to die of cold now. It would be such a pathetic end, it being Christmas Day and all.'

He laughed again as if her little witticisms were actually funny. 'They say it's very pleasant, but how they know, they don't say. Not that you're going to die of cold.' His look in the flickering, eerie light of the candles was very intense. 'I'm going to do everything in my power to prevent it.'

His reassurance made her more anxious. 'But it's not at all likely, is it? I was just being flippant.'

'Not with me here, no. Now, get your boots off and snuggle down.'

She fiddled fruitlessly with her laces for a while. 'I can't,' she said eventually. 'My fingers won't work.'

'Here, let me.' His strong fingers released her ankles from the grip of the boots, and as he eased each one off her foot, she felt blissful relief. Her foot lay in his hands. 'That feel better?'

'Mm.' It was wonderful to be free of the boot, but her foot, small and slightly damp in its scarlet sock, felt very sensitive to his touch. His thumb brushed her instep, so briefly she didn't know if it was deliberate. Then he started on the other boot.

When both feet were free, he said, 'Don't let them get cold. I'm going to make stew. Here,' he passed her his rucksack. 'Find the whisky.'

Jenny began to feel a sort of wary contentment. She knew it was temporary, but for the moment she and Ross weren't fighting, the rehydrated stew had a flavour all its own, but it was filling and warming. Ross had brought two huge wholemeal rolls to go with it, and the whisky took away any lingering anxiety. Just enjoy this moment, Jenny thought. It might be the happiest of your life.

Ross, tucked into his sleeping bag across from her, made her feel very safe. He was so near. She could reach out an arm and almost touch him. She sighed. He was still too far away. She closed her eyes and imagined not hating him, imagined him nearer, much nearer, without several kilos of down and nylon between them. It was a blissful fantasy. Even if he didn't think she was the most irritating woman in the universe, there was probably some ethical objection to making love to someone you've rescued, even if you wanted to. And he probably didn't much want to. He had kissed her a couple of times, but both times it had been to keep her quiet. And it had worked, damn it! Bloody men, bloody, bloody men. She sighed deeply, and without realising quite how it was happening, she fell asleep.

She awoke later. The candles had gone out, but the snow hole was full of strange, white light. She was very cold and very wide awake. She couldn't read her watch, but she sensed that it was still the middle of the night. She had gone to sleep very early. She had probably had her full quota of sleep and yet it was still dark, and still nighttime.

There was no sound from Ross. He slept very silently. In fact, if she hadn't seen his shape, dark and solid, she might have worried that he'd abandoned her. She wouldn't have entirely blamed him. She had been extremely difficult. He hadn't been perfect, of course, but she had acted completely out of character. She'd been petulant, difficult, downright rude. But then, he brought out the worst in her. Well, not any more. From now on she would be the Jenny Porter she knew and loved, who was polite, obeyed conventions and played by the rules. She turned onto her back, wondering how she was to pass the long, cold hours ahead.

'Are you cold?' he asked.

'A bit. Did I wake you?'

'Not really. I heard you stirring, but I wouldn't have done if I'd really been asleep.'

'What time is it?'

She heard him withdrawing his arm from his sleeping bag. 'About two.'

'We've got all the night ahead of us.'

'You sound as if that was a bad thing.'

'Well, isn't it?'

'Not when there's such a fabulous moon.'

'You can't see the moon.'

'I can see its light, and so can you. Come on. Let's go for a walk.'

'In the middle of the night?'

'It was you who were complaining about having all the night ahead of us! Now let's go out and play in the snow.'

'I never thought I'd hear a rough, tough, mountain rescue man use a word like "play" in connection with snow,' her good resolutions about being polite forgotten.

'It's not all grim reality, you know. We have fun as well.'

Extracting herself from her sleeping bag, finding her boots and putting them on, all seemed to take time, but at last she was ready.

'You go on out,' Ross said. 'I've got a couple of things to do.'

She scrambled out into the snow and as she stood upright, she saw the snow-hole glow. Ross had lit a candle.

The storm had been over long enough for the fresh snow to firm up a little. Although it was deep, it was satisfying to walk through. She felt stiff but as she loosened up, she began to feel light-hearted, a little childlike.

'I love the creaking and squeaking you get with each tread,' she said, almost skipping.

'Mm. I love snow altogether.' He took her hand, and suddenly, conversation no longer seemed either necessary, or particularly desirable.

The moon cast long, mauve shadows on the snow. The mountain above them no longer seemed lowering, but watchful, benign. They walked across the way, where the snow was thinner, crisper, and what before had seemed hard, difficult work, now seemed easy.

When they'd been out for about half an hour, Ross stopped. 'Look.'

Jenny turned, and seeing where he was pointing, saw their snow hole, glowing in the moonlight, like

350

something the fairies had built. 'It looks like it landed from outer space,' she said, keeping her fairy analogy to herself.

'I think it looks magical,' he said. 'Come on. We'd better go back, we don't want to give it time to get cold, and you'll probably be able to go back to sleep, now.'

They went back in silence. Jenny wished the walk could last for ever. She felt fit and fleet as if she could go on for miles and not feel tired. They reached the snow hole too soon.

'You go in first,' he said. 'I want to make sure the entrance doesn't get too blocked up by snow.'

'But it's not going to snow again now! It's a brilliantly clear night.'

'Didn't you feel that little flurry of wind? Could mean more snow before morning.'

Once inside, she noticed that Ross had moved the sleeping bags. They were now rolled up in a bundle on the ledge at the back of the cave.

As he crawled in he explained. 'I wanted to keep them together so they didn't lose their warmth. They should be warm to get back into. Here, let me help you with your boots.'

'It's all right. I can manage.' She suddenly didn't want him touching her feet, not if he wasn't going to touch the rest of her too.

She took her time over getting them off, embarrassed by her churlishness, not wanting to go back to the loneliness of her single sleeping bag. She heard Ross rustling, zipping noises behind her, and, slightly irritated, wondered what he was doing. When at last she turned round, she saw that he was lying on the ledge at the back.

'I've zipped the two bags together. It's much more efficient heat-wise, if we sleep in the same one. I hope you don't mind.'

Part of Jenny laughed. The irony of it! The object of all her dreams and fantasies asking her if she minded sharing a double sleeping bag! If she hadn't behaved like a spoilt brat on a picnic, this could have been an invitation to heaven. Apart from the fact that between them they were both wearing more clothes than the entire Hawkshead catalogue.

'I'm sure it'll be fine. Nice and warm.' She got in next to him. It was warm, and rather cramped, given that she was trying to keep a gap between them.

'I think you'll be more comfortable if you just relax against me.'

'Oh. OK.' She took a deep breath, let it out slowly, and relaxed. It was bliss, lying so close to him, but it wasn't conducive to sleep. And when his arm came round her waist it was more blissful still. Her breathing became faster and she struggled to control it.

'What's the matter?'

She couldn't tell him, so she made something up. 'I – I'm just lying on the wrong side, that's all. But I'll get used to it in a minute, I'm sure.'

'No need to. Just turn over.'

'Easier said than done.'

They both shifted about, both tight against the sleeping bag.

'Perhaps we should undo it,' she said.

'It's OK. I'll just get my arm free.' Then somehow, she didn't know how it happened, but she found herself lying underneath him. 'How's this?' he said, and kissed her.

This time there was no element of punishment. It was all sensuality. Her head spun and stars exploded inside it and she felt so near to fainting, if she'd been upright, she knew she would have fallen.

'God! I've been waiting a long time to do that!' he said raggedly, several minutes after their lips had first touched.

'You did it yesterday. Or was it today?'

'That was different.'

'Mm,' she agreed, putting her arms round his neck and pulling his mouth down to hers again.

'God! Jenny . . .' he breathed, and then he was pulling at her clothes, as she pulled at his. One of them unzipped the sleeping bag, but it was still a tussle as they fought off the layers. Eventually they stopped undressing each other and pulled the rest of their clothes off themselves.

Jenny had never felt such desire, such passion, such an intense level of sensation. His hands, his lips, his chest, made her both weak with longing and on fire with lust.

At one point, when they were both naked, both sweating and panting, he said, 'We'd better stop. I've got nothing with me.'

Realising what he meant, and what it signified, but unable to stop the torrent they had started, she said, 'I'm sure it'll be all right.'

He said, 'We'll just have to get married if it isn't.'

But he didn't move and she had to take matters into her own hands.

Afterwards she felt overcome with emotion. She wept, silently, trying to keep still, so he wouldn't notice. She was appalled at her reaction and was certain he would be too. She wasn't a virgin; she'd been living with Henry. She'd wanted what had happened quite as much as he had, and yet here she was, crying like an unwilling bride on her wedding night.

She was certain she hadn't been shaking, certain not a sob had got past her bitten-together lips, and yet he knew. He settled her head onto his shoulder, wrapping his arms around her.

'It hasn't been like that for me before either,' he whispered. 'Although I thought it would be pretty spectacular with you, I never guessed quite how spectacular.'

She let the last tear fall down her cheek onto his chest and sniffed. It was so lovely to be held, to hear the thump of his heart under her ear.

'Sweet Genevieve,' he murmured into her hair. 'I love you so.'

She sighed. 'I love you too.' She was so happy she felt there was a real risk of dying from it. It was such a perfect moment. She knew it was just a moment, and that the rest of life was hard and long and fraught with difficulties and disappointment. But this moment was perfect.

'We'd better get dressed, or we'll get dreadfully cold later,' he whispered. 'Let me get you your clothes.'

Later, she fell asleep in his arms, not knowing or caring which side she was lying on.

He woke her with a kiss, like a warm butterfly landing on her lips. 'We'd better get up. We've got to get home and it sounds as if the wind is back with a vengeance.'

He was right. When they emerged into the outside

world, the wind was almost visible, blowing the fallen snow around, and bringing more. It was as if that still, moonlit night had never existed.

'Oh, my goodness! Whiteout!'

Ross smiled, but didn't contradict her. 'Come on. Are your boots tight enough? Then come here and let me tie this rope round your waist. You might as well help me carry it.'

'The snow is making me feel dizzy,' said Jenny, a bit later, wishing they hadn't so far to go.

'One foot in front of the other will do it,' said Ross. 'It always does. Come on.'

Chapter Twenty-four

It took Jenny a while to realise that she really was feverish, and it wasn't just her surroundings that were making her head feel peculiar. She found walking through snow strange at the best of times, now she really was guessing and hoping each time she picked her foot up that when it came down it would eventually stop, but she couldn't calculate when.

Ross asked her if she was all right when they first stopped. She just nodded and said she was. Unless he could produce a sledge to lie her on, hot honey and lemon and several tons of goosedown to cover her, there was no point in telling him that her limbs were aching, she was hot and cold in turn and that her head felt like she was on some powerful but unpleasant psychedelic drug.

The second time they stopped he put his hand on her forehead. 'You feel as if you're on fire. Are you ill?'

Jenny's teeth were chattering so hard she could hardly speak. 'There's been flu going round the mill. I think I may have got it.'

He muttered an expletive. 'How bad do you feel?'

She couldn't think how to measure or describe the awfulness so she just flapped her hands.

After a moment of them both standing in the snow,

gazing at each other, nonplussed, he pulled off his rucksack and produced what was left of the whisky. 'I won't let you get hypothermia, promise.'

When she'd disposed of it, she felt so drunk she no longer cared about the aches in her bones, and it seemed quite right and proper for the landscape to swirl and move about.

It was very dark when they finally got back to Dalmain House. Jenny was looking at life from the wrong end of a very long telescope and found herself being half carried up the stairs, laid on the bed, and her boots being undone. When she realised it was Ross who was doing it, she felt terribly, terribly pleased, and terribly sad all at the same time. There was something about Ross that made her feel sad, but she couldn't remember what it was.

Hot-water bottles, a thermometer, and a surprisingly capable Felicity featured in the next half-hour of her life. She was given pills to take, a hot drink, which made her sweat, and extra pillows.

She heard fragments of conversation: 'Call the doctor', 'No point, he'll only say paracetamol, plenty of fluids, keep an eye on her.'

'I'll keep an eye on her.' Ross's voice came from a long way away. 'Just until she goes to sleep.'

Jenny didn't want to go to sleep. She liked lying in bed with Ross sitting in the chair next to her. But while it wasn't quite like sleep, she did lapse into a dream world of snow, and the mill and Ross, in which time passed quickly. When she came to, she was alone. She looked at her bedside clock but couldn't make sense of it. She took a sip of water and passed out again.

*

Time passed in a blur. Every now and then Felicity would appear with pills and insist she take them. Henry turned up with jugs of lemon barley water. And once, embarrassingly, Lady Dalmain came to see how she was getting on. Her eyes feeling like half-sucked boiled sweets, and her mouth and throat feeling as if they had just received a good rub down with coarse sand paper, Jenny said she felt fine, thanks. She didn't ask if Ross had phoned to see how she was. She didn't want to know if he hadn't.

On the fourth day after she had first been put to bed she awoke feeling better – very weak but no longer feeling drunk. She also felt for the first time as if she'd really been asleep, and not just on some long, convoluted journey in her head. A tentative trip to the bathroom was encouraging. She felt pathetic having to hold on all the way, but at least the ground didn't keep coming up to meet her.

She had just come back and was just looking round the room for her kettle, when Henry came in.

'Hi, there,' he said, more quietly than usual. 'How are you today?'

'Better, I think. I've stopped aching and I can only see one of you, and you're keeping still. I would really love a cup of tea, though. I've just been to the loo and I feel shattered.'

'No wonder. You've been really quite ill. I'll get you the tea. Everyone's been so worried about you.'

'Why? It was only flu, the same as everyone at the mill has had.'

'You're not usually this ill. Lady D. says it's because you spent all that time out in the cold. What happened, by the way? On Christmas night?'

It took a few moments to work out what Henry was talking about. It not only seemed a very long time ago, but it also seemed to have happened in an alternate universe.

'Oh,' she said, when she'd sorted out some of the relevant facts, and filed away others. 'We had to spend the night in a snow hole. Ross knew where one was. It was quite comfortable in a strange way. Cold, though.'

Now she wondered if everything she remembered had actually happened, or if it was just something her delirious mind had invented.

'It was just as well Ross found you. You could have died.'

'Mm. I do feel dreadfully guilty when I think about it. I never knew a simple walk in the snow could be so dangerous. I feel such a fool.' But it wasn't Ross rescuing her that made her feel guilty, that was so dangerous, or that made her a fool, but rather what had gone on in the snow hole. 'I don't suppose there's enough hot water for a bath? If I boiled a few kettles?'

'Lady D. said you're to use her bathroom.' Henry grinned sheepishly, reminding Jenny that he could be rather sweet. 'It was only when you weren't here cooking and organising everything that we all realised how much you did. And we all hope you're going to be well enough to come with us to the Malcolms', for New Year's Eve.'

'When is New Year's Eve? I've lost all track.'

'Tomorrow. Of course, if you're not well enough to come, someone will stay behind with you.'

That will be a popular assignment, she thought, somewhat acidly. 'Let's see how I feel after my bath, shall we?'

As she staggered along the passage, clutching her towel and her washing things, she knew that somehow she would make sure she was well enough for Hogmanay, and not only so no one would feel obliged to miss out on it with her. Ross would be there, and she wanted to thank him for rescuing her.

Only when anaesthetised by the blissfully hot water did she give herself a reality check, and force herself to acknowledge that she and Ross had had unprotected sex, and it had been her fault. She sighed so deeply she almost rose above the level of the water. But what sex! She closed her eyes as she admitted that she'd do it all again, given the opportunity. There was no hope for her. She'd turned from being a nicely brought up, sensible girl, to an idiot, driven by her hormones, in less than overnight.

'That man has stolen my critical faculties and my sense of self-preservation. He's dangerous. I should keep well away from him.' She spoke quietly, but firmly, trying to rustle up a bit of enthusiasm for her lecture. Then she sighed deeply again and submerged her head so she couldn't hear herself, and washed her hair.

The Dalmain House party, which included Meggie and Iain, were to have dinner before setting out in convoy for the Malcolms' ball.

Jenny, knowing she was still fragile and that she only had so much energy, asked if she could skip dinner and have a sandwich in her room while she got ready.

'It's going to take quite a bit of paint to make myself look less ghoul-like,' she said to Felicity, who was protesting. 'And I need to conserve my energy. I don't suppose it'll be the sort of party where I can just hang around in the kitchen.'

Felicity gasped in horror at the thought of Jenny being allowed near the kitchens at the Malcolms'. 'Jenny! Honestly! It's not that sort of house!'

'It's all right, Felicity. Even if I could find the kitchen, I probably wouldn't be able to walk that far.'

Meggie came and lay on Jenny's bed, feeding Anna. 'So, will Ross be there?'

'I've no idea. Do you think I've overdone the blusher?'

'A bit. I'll do it for you, if you like.'

'No, it's all right. You feed Anna, and it'll be time for you to go down and eat soon.'

'I can make an excuse to look after you, if you like. You know dinner with Felicity and the Matriarch isn't really my thing.'

'I thought you were all getting on much better lately.'

'Well, Felicity is certainly much happier, now she's got Lachlan, but she still makes snide remarks about my feeding herself here.'

'You wait. She might be doing it herself, a year from now.'

'Jenny! She's ancient!'

'Nonsense, plenty of child-bearing years left. Now if Anna's had her dinner, you'd better go and have yours and leave me to make myself look' – she peered into the mirror – 'like a hag.'

Meggie chuckled and picked up her baby. 'See you later, then, Morticia.'

'Huh! I wish!'

*

361

Relieved to be free of either anxious, or intrusive, questioning, Jenny took her time to get ready. She had lost weight. Meggie's red dress looked almost respectable, far less sexy and revealing than it had before. But her face did look a little drawn, and as too much make-up could make her look a whole lot worse, she took the whole lot off and started again. It would take discretion and skill to disguise the shadows. Morticia Addams was one thing, Barbara Cartland another.

Eventually, feeling she'd done the best she could, she went downstairs and joined the others in the drawing room, telling herself that the weakness in her knees was just pre-party nerves.

'You look great!' said Meggie gleefully. 'I think you'd better keep that dress. I'll never fit into it again.'

'You might if you stopped breast feeding,' said Felicity.

'Which I'm not going to do while Anna needs me,' snapped Meggie.

'It certainly looks a lot better than it did before,' said Lady Dalmain. 'Of course, some girls positively want to look like tarts on their night off, but not you, Jenny.'

'Either way, that dress works for me,' muttered Iain.

'I'd better have it back then,' said Meggie.

'I think you look – very nice,' said Henry, although the frown that fluttered between his eyebrows made Jenny wonder if he actually meant 'bloody awful'.

While outwardly smiling rather desperately, inwardly she worried. She didn't want to see Ross for the first time since they'd made love so uninhibitedly looking like a superannuated streetwalker.

They all packed themselves into Henry's car, as he and Lachlan had drawn straws, and he had got the short one. Meggie and Iain were bringing Anna, separately. Jenny had offered to drive, as she didn't feel alcohol was a good idea for her at the moment, but Henry and Lady Dalmain, who'd both seen her wobble as she came down the stairs, rejected her offer simultaneously – Lady Dalmain on the grounds that she wasn't fit to drive yet, and Henry, because they wouldn't all fit into her car, and he certainly wouldn't let her drive his, even if she hadn't just had flu.

So Jenny, Felicity and Lachlan got into the back of Henry's Rover and they set off for the Malcolms'.

Jenny dozed in the back, trying not to think of seeing Ross. He'd said he'd be there, but she was trying not to set her heart on it, and part of her didn't know what to say to him, anyway. Had they shared a wonderful experience? Or had they had a sordid one-night stand? The horror of this thought made her clear her throat so she could ask Henry to turn round and take her home, but before she could speak, Felicity asked her to sort out the back of her hair for her. By the time she'd done that they had gone too far to make turning back a reasonable request.

The party was already in full swing. The Malcolms lived in a small castle and for a moment, Jenny wondered how much of Fiona's attraction for Henry was bound up in her magnificent setting. Should she point out that the house probably didn't go with the job, even if he did get to marry the eldest daughter?

Inside, the ladies were swept upstairs to a bedroom to take off their outer clothing. Lady Dalmain, made handsome by excitement and anticipated pleasure, checked her hair and lipstick just like Jenny and Felicity.

'What about a touch of blusher?' Felicity asked Jenny. 'You look a bit peaky.'

Jenny, who'd washed all her blusher off, shook her head. 'I'll be red as a beetroot soon enough.'

'Will you be up to reeling?' asked Lady Dalmain, showing unusual concern.

Jenny wanted to say she'd been reeling for the past four days, every time she got out of bed, but just smiled. 'I probably won't dance much. I don't know what to do, anyway.'

'You'll be fine. As long as most of the couples know what they're doing, the odd one who doesn't can be steered round the course. You look lovely, dear,' she added, unexpectedly to Felicity. 'In fact, you both do. Now, let's go down.'

Jenny had time to wonder what had got into Lady Dalmain to make her so nice, all of a sudden. Perhaps she was looking forward to telling everyone she was going to run an antiquarian bookshop by email.

The ballroom was big enough to allow several sets of eightsome reels to be danced at the same time. Seeing the whirling kilts and dresses made Jenny's still-wobbly head spin. She wouldn't be able to see if Ross was there until they stopped. She couldn't see Meggie or Iain either, and presumed they'd stopped off at home to attend to Anna.

'Have you had a drink?' Duncan Ritchie appeared and summoned a young man holding a tray full of tumblers of whisky.

'I'd better not,' said Jenny. 'I've had a touch of flu.'

'A dram is just what you need. Henry's driving, isn't he? Thought so. Mind you, he didn't turn down a drink. He's over there. With Fiona. Ismene' – having furnished all three women with drinks, Duncan took Lady Dalmain's arm – 'there's something that might interest you in the dining room.'

'Well, he didn't waste any time,' said Felicity to Lachlan, who had just appeared. 'Do you think he fancies her?'

Lachlan shrugged gallantly. 'I dare say he does. She's a handsome woman. Now, are you dancing, Felicity? What about you, Jenny? Has Henry deserted you?'

'I'm not up to much, thank you, Lachlan. I'll just sit and watch.'

Jenny found a chair and sipped the drink she'd decided not to touch, realising that she didn't feel very well. The thought of watching everyone whirling and whooping, getting drunker and drunker as midnight approached, was making her feel slightly sick. She had been worried about seeing Ross again, didn't know what on earth you said to a man you'd recently made love to in a very uninhibited way, but hadn't spoken to since. Now the thought of not seeing him was enough to make her want to take several painkillers and sleep until next year.

Henry appeared, Fiona at his side. 'Come on, Jen. Come and have a dance. The exercise will make you feel better. Fiona's dancing with Fergus.'

It seemed less effort to agree than to argue, so Jenny obediently went to the other end of the ballroom and joined the set Fiona was making up. Her parents were part of it and Jenny realised that Henry and Fiona had asked her to dance on their instigation.

'It's very simple, you'll soon get the hang of it,' said

Mrs Malcolm, looking lovely in green satin with emeralds to match.

Jenny smiled politely, knowing those words meant she'd be more confused when they'd finished than when they'd started. She smiled at Henry, who was standing anxiously across from her and was glad that she'd learned to pas de basque at school, what felt like many, many years ago.

Henry was better at it than she was, and managed to steer, shove, or drag her into position and only stepped on her once. Jenny began to see, if one had not got up from one's sick bed slightly too early, or was not suffering from something which could be defined as post-orgasmic-stress disorder, Scottish dancing might be very good fun indeed. She was about to give an expurgated version of her thoughts to Mrs Malcolm, when someone tapped her shoulder. It was Ross.

'Come along, Genevieve. I want you to dance with me.'

'Is that a real name, or a pet name?' asked Mrs Malcolm delightedly. 'So pretty!'

'It's my real name,' Jenny said, as Ross pulled her along.

She frowned slightly as they stood opposite each other, waiting for the other couples to take their places. Was it significant that he'd called her that?

She curtsied to him as the dance required. He was looking very tall and serious, a little pale. He seemed uneasy.

'Did you get the flu, too?' she asked, as he led her down the set to the end.

'No.'

She pas de basqued to a nice boy in a red tartan kilt

with cheeks to match. He was sweating profusely, and her fingers slipped as he turned her round and delivered her into Ross's waiting hands.

A thought occurred to her, a thought so dreadful she tried to push it out of her mind. But it wouldn't go. Ross was embarrassed to see her because of what had happened. For him it had just been a one-night stand, a sort of Highland fling, but he knew for her it was more than that. Now he was preparing himself to let her down gently.

She found herself floundering in the dance. Firm hands positioned her, and she was opposite Ross again. Her lips were dry.

'Is there something you want to tell me?' she asked. But before he could answer, someone took her hand, turned her, and set her opposite the young man in the kilt. She was hot now too, and feeling dizzy, but she wanted an answer to her question.

'Well?' she demanded, when again they were able to talk.

'Well, what?'

He was being deliberately obtuse, she could see. It might have been because of the difficulty of trying to have a serious discussion while performing complicated dance steps. Or it might have been because he didn't know how to tell her.

Just in time, she remembered to set to the man opposite, take his hand and land with the man in the kilt who was now sweating onto the floor. Another hazard.

'I do need to know how I stand,' she said at the next opportunity. 'Whatever you're going to say, it's all right. But I need to know.'

'What are you talking about?' He seemed genuinely confused. Perhaps she'd got it all wrong. Perhaps her judgement was at fault.

A grand chain, when men and women moved in opposite directions taking hands with each other, separated them for several moments.

'We can't talk here,' said Ross, firmly.

Of course he was right, but Jenny wasn't satisfied. She wasn't prepared to shut up and carry on dancing as if nothing momentous had happened between them. She was about to duck out of the dance altogether when she was clasped round the waist by the sweating young man. He was so enthusiastic he lifted her off the floor. When she landed she staggered slightly and Ross caught her.

'Don't touch me, you rat!' she hissed.

'Jenny, what is the matter?'

'I've had flu. I need to know how I stand with you. For all I know, I might be pregnant!'

A couple of people turned to look at her and she realised she'd spoken more loudly than she'd intended. The dance was coming to an end. In a moment she could run away, find somewhere to cry, and then later, find someone to take her home. If only she could keep it together for a few more minutes.

Some part of the dance she didn't remember doing before meant she found herself being swung round again, only this time, by Ross. She was dizzy already from whisky and flu; she didn't need to have her equilibrium further disturbed. When he put her down, she slapped his face. While everyone else was bowing or curtsying to their partner, she walked off the floor, found her way to the door and, a moment later, to a downstairs cloakroom.

Someone came barging in after her. It was Meggie. 'Are you OK? I saw what happened. Why did you hit him?'

'I didn't hit him; I slapped him!'

'It comes to the same thing. Violence is never the answer.'

'Oh, shut up! Oh, I'm sorry, Meggie. I don't know what's got into me. I feel awful.'

She still had her head in her hands when she heard someone else open the door. 'God, why did I have to choose the loo to hide in?'

'Oh, hello,' she heard Meggie say.

'Can you leave us alone for a few moments?'

It was Ross.

'Is that all right?' Meggie asked.

'Of course it's all right!' said Ross irritably, and manhandled Meggie out of the door. 'She doesn't need a bloody chaperone!'

Jenny stood up. 'Don't I?'

'Look,' said Ross, his effort to control his temper obvious. 'What's got into you? I'm sorry about what happened – at least, I'm not sorry, but I never meant it to turn out that way.'

'Meant what to turn out that way?' Jenny was incandescent – with rage, confusion, or some virus, she was in no state to decide.

'For God's sake! Are you deliberately trying to misunderstand me? When I dragged you halfway up a mountain and kept you there for the night, I didn't intend to – to make love to you!'

'So what did you intend?' Jenny could see the marks

of her fingers on his cheek. They reproached her horribly.

'For God's sake! I was rescuing you! Stopping you getting lost, or freezing to death! You were in real danger. And seducing you was the last thing on my mind. We hardly know each other.'

She wanted to die. She felt abashed. She had been so wanton, so uninhibited. He was probably horrified at her being so willing. Willing enough, indeed, to have unprotected sex – with a man she hardly knew.

'I'm sorry.' She didn't know what to say, what to do, how to get through the next few moments. Her knees were dodgy and she knew if she wasn't careful she would cry.

His anger evaporated in a deep sigh. 'You don't need to be sorry! Look, I really hope you're not pregnant if you don't want to be, but if you are –'

'What?'

'If you want to, we'll get married. You can have your dress made out of nuno felt.'

'No, thank you.'

There was a bang on the door. 'Is anyone in there? I'm dying for a pee!'

'Oh God! Can't you hang on? Or go outside! We're trying to have a conversation here!'

'We can't monopolise the loo!' protested Jenny. 'And what if a woman wanted to come in?'

'Come on then.' He took hold of her wrist and pulled her up. He opened the door. 'There you are; it's all yours.'

Pulling her behind him like a train, he marched along the passage, opening doors and shutting them again. At last he found a small study and switched on the light. It was crammed with extraneous tables and chairs, which had obviously been dumped there because of the ball.

'This'll do.' He dragged her past the furniture to a small, leather sofa at the back of the room. 'What do you mean, "no, thank you"?'

'I mean, no, thank you. If I'm pregnant, I don't want to marry you. And I'm not sure about the dress either.'

'Jenny!' He was furious. 'What do you mean, saying you don't want to marry me? For fuck's sake! We made love. I know we fight all the time, and we don't know each other all that well, but I thought we loved each other! I distinctly remember you telling me you loved me in the snow hole. Or are you the sort of girl who always says that after sex?'

Jenny's head was swimming. 'Look, I'm not trying to be difficult, really I'm not. I'm just saying that you don't need to feel obliged to marry me if I turn out to be pregnant. You should be pleased.'

'But I want to marry you, you idiotic woman! God knows why, but I do! And I don't take kindly to being rejected when I haven't even had an opportunity to ask you properly.'

'I'm sorry, Ross. I've only just got up after having quite a high temperature. I think I'm confused. Could you run that by me again, slowly?'

He scowled down at her, and then lowered himself onto the sofa beside her. He took her hand in his. 'You do feel awfully hot. I think I should get you back to bed.'

'What do you mean by that?'

'Exactly what you want it to mean, my darling.'

371

He didn't move. He just sat and held her hand, looking at her.

'Ross, are you saying, did you say, or have I got it completely wrong, something about not wanting to be turned down before you've asked me properly?'

'Something like that.'

'But what were you going to ask me?'

He bit his lip, he sighed, he tipped back his head and laughed. 'Sweet Genevieve, sweet, sweet Genevieve, you are such a plonker. I want to ask you to marry me. I want you to marry me, whether you're pregnant or not. My only conditions are that you love me. Now can you take that in?'

She looked up at him. The single bulb that hung from the ceiling was dim and high; it did nothing but cast his face into shadow, concealing his expression. She had thought that he was going to let her down gently, tell her she was a really nice person, a lovely girl, but what had happened between them had been a one-off. Now he seemed to be asking her to marry him. She rubbed her forehead, trying to clear it. She usually considered herself to be quite intelligent. Flu seemed to have killed off most of her brain cells.

'Dear God, Jenny,' he breathed, and took her into his arms. 'Will you please put me out of my misery? Will you marry me?'

'Mm. Yes, I think so. If you're really asking.'

'I am! I really am!' He fumbled about in his pocket and produced a little box. 'I've been so worried about this. I'm sure it's a really old-fashioned thing to do, but I've got you a ring. If you hate it, you must tell me.'

She began to smile, just a little at first, but then it

spread so every part of her seemed to be smiling. 'Are you telling me that you were looking so shifty on the dance floor because you'd bought me a ring you thought I might not like?'

'You still might not like it. Here, let me show you.'

A boiled sweet on a curtain ring would have been perfectly acceptable to her, in the circumstances. So a gold band set with five perfect diamonds was more than satisfactory.

'It's fabulous,' she said, waggling her finger to see the diamonds sparkle. 'You're fabulous. Are you sure you want to marry me? I'm such a moody cow.'

'I'm strange that way. It's the moody kind I like best.'

'Just as well.' She gazed at her ring, thinking. 'Ross?'

'What?' He took hold of her hand and started caressing her wrist, but she held his fingers.

'I know I'm all through-other –'

'What?'

Her brain struggled to find another word to sum up how she felt, but this family expression was all she could think of. 'You know – in a state?'

'Yes.'

'But I do have to know a few things, the answers to a few questions. The answers don't matter. I love you just as you are. Your faults are just as much a part of you as your virtues.'

'Well, thank you.'

'Why did you send me up here? Was it to close down Dalmain Mills?'

He took hold of her hands and examined them for a few seconds before answering. 'In a way, yes.' He looked up at her. 'You see, I didn't see a way out for

373

them. I haven't the imagination to think of llama wool and nuno felt and all those cockamamie schemes you and Kirsty cooked up . . .'

'So?'

'So, I sent you up here to come to the same conclusions as I did, then, when you told me there was no hope for the mill, I was planning to ask you to begin closing things down.'

She frowned. 'But why? I'm only a glorified secretary, for goodness sake. Why get me to do something like that?'

'You'd already proved to me that you were far more than a glorified secretary, but I did feel it would be less painful to have your factory wound up by a pretty, sympathetic woman, than by a team of men in suits.'

'You couldn't possibly know what I looked like. That's ridiculous!'

'And then, when I came up to live here, and set up some small business, I'd be seen as a creator of jobs, not the destroyer of an industry.' He paused. 'I'm not remotely proud of how I acted, which is why I'm prepared to go on throwing money at Dalmain Mills for as long as it takes . . .' He hesitated again.

She helped him out. 'For our cockamamie schemes to work, you mean?'

'Uh huh. Now, is there anything else you need to know? I'm getting anxious about you, and think it's high time I got you back to Dalmain House.'

'About Dalmain House. Did you send Henry to get Lady Dalmain to sell it to you?'

He shook his head. 'I got Henry – or rather his firm – I would never have brought Henry into it if I'd known he had anything to do with you. That was the most hideous coincidence. When I saw him kiss you, it was like being stabbed in the gut. I have never felt like that before.'

Gratified, but not distracted, she squeezed his fingers. 'Never mind about Henry, what about Dalmain House?'

'I wanted to know how attached Lady Dalmain was to the place. If she was open to offers, I could then present myself as the buyer, and the saviour of her fortunes.' He cleared his throat. 'It was before I knew what the house looked like, of course. I just knew it was part of the Dalmain Estate.' He became a little sheepish. 'It could have been lovely – stop laughing, it's not funny.'

She was hardly able to breathe, she was laughing so much. 'Yes, it is. Imagine, the hot shot Angel Investor, forced to live in that dreadful building, with its draughts and its blood-coloured spiky bits.'

'Spiky bits or not, it's where you're going now, where I'll either give you a hot toddy and a couple of aspirin – or . . .'

'Or what?' She was still giggling faintly and knew it was partly excitement about what was to come.

'You know what, you wanton woman. Now come on.'

Expecting him to take her hand, she was rather surprised when instead he picked her up in his arms and carried her out of the room and through the house. Hugely embarrassed, she buried her head in his shoulder and kept it there, ignoring the cheers and catcalls that followed them until they reached his car. 'It's just like that film,' she heard Meggie say.

'Now don't lay a finger on me until I get you home,'

375

Ross said sternly. 'It's too cold for that sort of thing in the car.'

'It's no warmer at Dalmain House.'

Ross grinned at her. 'Warmer than a mountaintop, surely?'

She laughed back at him. 'But what about Henry? He'll be back eventually.'

'Bother Henry! Let's go.'